STACY M. JONES

Diamond King

First edition

ISBN: 979-8-218-35814-3

This book was professionally typeset on Reedsy.
Find out more at reedsy.com

For Jake
I know you love a good heist

Acknowledgement

Thank you to the detectives, special agents, and forensics teams I've had the pleasure of working with through the years and the knowledge and expertise shared with me. Your support when writing this story and all of those in my FBI Agent Walsh Thriller Series has been why these stories are so beloved by my readers. Anything I get wrong is my fault. You never fail to answer my calls and texts and some of you have even become readers. It's been a wonderful journey. Thank you!

Special thanks to 17 Studio Book Design for bringing my stories to life with amazing covers. Thank you to Dj Hendrickson for your insightful editing and Liza Wood for proofreading and revisions. Thank you to my early readers for their feedback and my loyal and new readers who have truly made this series a success. I'm so happy we are going on Kate's journey together.

CHAPTER 1

A hush fell over the Senate chamber as Senator Stephen Willis from Texas cleared his throat and called the meeting back to order. FBI Agent Kate Walsh's heart thumped in her ears, waiting for his first question. The speculation that he'd be the toughest among them had left Kate with three straight nights of insomnia. She had hoped after their last case in Edinburgh, Scotland, there wouldn't be further inquiries into how they had conducted the investigation. To call it unorthodox would have been an understatement.

They didn't get so lucky. After word spread about the case, a few senators decided they'd make an example of the FBI. They were gunning for the FBI for other reasons, and Kate and her partner, Agent Declan James, were low-hanging fruit. Even so, neither expected a full-blown congressional investigation. Martin Spade, their supervisor and head of their specialized unit, had tried to temper the growing partisan outrage, but even he couldn't quell the growing rumble of mistrust against the agency. Worse still, the senators had taken their case to the court of public opinion and had shown up on several news programs spouting about how they were going to bring the FBI down – starting with the specialized unit that had been Kate's home since the start of her career.

Even Spade had been called to testify. He went first and Declan was called the following day. Their counterparts in Scotland and England had sent statements. Kate knew the hearing was more performative than evidentiary. There had been no wrongdoing on anyone's part. She had nearly given up her life for the case.

The questions asked of Spade, Declan, and her ranged from speculative to downright uninformed. That's what worried Kate the most. Facts she could handle. Wild accusations that could forever tarnish her career weren't something she was used to as a government employee. Now, she'd face Senator Willis who was gunning for her specifically. All the questions posed to Spade and Declan by him were about Kate. She knew he wanted her job, if not her head on a silver platter. Of course, he was still questioning why the FBI allowed women agents.

Senator Willis drew out the tension as he coughed once and then paused to take a sip of water. He peered down at Kate from his perch. She had her lawyer to her right. There was no way she was coming in alone. The man was not one issued by the FBI but one she had hired. They were told legal representation wasn't needed. Kate wasn't going to risk everything she had worked for on the words of a group of men she considered partisan hacks.

Senator Willis didn't waste any time with fancy footwork or light jabs. His first throw aimed to be a knockout punch. He said it with a smirk for the cameras. "Isn't it true, Agent Walsh, that while investigating the Close Killer case in Scotland you developed a sexual relationship with the man known as the Phantom, which is why you let him go?"

Kate bit the inside of her cheek so hard she drew blood. She locked her gaze on him and didn't waver. Her voice wasn't meek but strong and clear, almost too loud. "No. That's not an accurate statement. There was no relationship developed between the Phantom and me. I used him as a source of information. He ultimately saved my life."

"You had sex with him though," he said with a wink and sly smile. His whole job was to discredit Kate personally. No other senators had gone down this line of questioning. It wasn't even appropriate.

Kate wanted to knock the smile off his face. She steadied herself. "I did not. There was never any physical relationship or otherwise. After I discovered him in Scotland and was not able to apprehend him, our team decided to use him as a source of information. It proved to be critical to solving the case."

The one thing they would not do is give up the name of the Phantom. As far as the senators knew, Kate and Declan didn't know it. They knew him by a range of aliases. Kate still wasn't sure if the name he had given her, Leo Lamiere, was real or not. But it wasn't one they were going public with now or maybe ever.

Senator Willis wasn't going to let go. "You expect us to believe an attractive woman like yourself didn't fall for this bad boy, not even a little. You're only a woman, after all, Agent Walsh. None of us could fault you." He looked across the bench at his colleagues who were all smiling in amusement and nodding their heads. The goal was to humiliate her.

Kate wasn't going to give them the satisfaction. "I'm sorry, Senator Willis, you might have a hard time keeping your hands off your young interns, but I have no trouble being appropriate working with men." She said it so smoothly and evenly that it took the man a second to process it, even though two of his colleagues gasped.

Once he realized what she had said, Senator Willis slammed his fist down on the table. "There has never been an accusation of anything like that during my entire career."

"There's never been an accusation leveled at me that has been so unfounded and without merit, Senator Willis. We can all say things and throw around lascivious accusations. It doesn't mean there's an ounce of truth to any of them. I did not have an inappropriate relationship with the Phantom. I have never in the history of my career nor would I ever entertain a relationship with anyone deemed a suspect, person of interest, or witness for that matter." She paused long enough to slow her breathing. "Do you have any questions that have any relevance?"

Red flamed up his neck and into his cheeks. She had set him back. "I'm in charge here," he said, slamming his fist on the table again, akin to a toddler throwing a tantrum.

"Then ask your question." Kate sat back, emboldened now. She crossed her arms over her chest. Kate didn't even bother looking at her lawyer. If she was going to get fired, she was going out swinging.

"If it wasn't a personal relationship, then why didn't you arrest the Phantom? He's wanted by every law enforcement agency across the globe. This would have been a major win for the FBI and the United States to be the one to bring him in. There must have been a reason why you chose not to." He had his eyebrows raised like it was a gotcha question. In truth, the other senators had already asked Kate this question three times over during her testimony.

Kate only had one answer. "As I have said, several times today, I was not able to apprehend him initially. Shortly thereafter, it became apparent to all of us that he'd be a valuable asset in this case. He was a suspect for a brief time and then cleared. He told me he was after the same killer and that he believed the killer was setting him up. We believed that if we let him go and didn't bring him in, he'd lead us to the killer. We reasoned the women's lives that had been lost and the ongoing threat from the serial killer trumped art theft at that point."

"You made a judgment call," Senator Willis said with a frustrated sigh.

"That's ninety percent of investigations. We are making judgment calls in every investigation and my education, ongoing training with the FBI, and more than a decade of experience guide those decisions." Kate was tired of answering questions coming from a bunch of men whose closest encounter to a criminal investigation was a television show.

Senator Willis looked at the sheet of paper in front of him. "Would you have any problem going after the Phantom now to arrest him?"

"If there was an investigation and I was able to apprehend him, I would." Kate said the words but there was a part of her deep down in a place she was barely able to admit that hoped she'd never have to.

Kate had to admit to herself that the senators' questions weren't too far off base. She was compromised and had come to believe Leo Lamiere was not what people believed. Even her feelings had changed about the man who had kidnapped her and held her hostage in France and then saved her life in Scotland. Kate had been wrestling with her complicated feelings for months and it wasn't sitting well with her.

Kate liked her emotions cut and dry. With Leo, it was a complicated mess she hadn't even begun to sort though. *Why had she really let him go?* She wasn't sure she could truthfully answer that for herself, let alone here in a congressional hearing under oath.

Senator Willis resumed. "Is there anyone who lives in your house with you?"

Kate sat in stunned silence. It took her a moment to process. "My partner, Declan James, lives in the house in a separate bedroom."

"Does he pay you rent?"

Kate wondered what this had to do with anything. She turned to her lawyer who shook his head. "That's not anything I need to answer here, Senator Willis."

He arched an eyebrow. "I'll take that as a no. Have you slept with him too?"

Kate's lawyer lurched forward in her defense but she put a hand on his arm to stop him. "I'll state again for the record that there was no sexual relationship between the Phantom and me. There is no sexual relationship between Declan and me either." It was the first time Kate lied outright in the hearing and she hoped her expression wasn't giving her away. Kate had no idea where he was going with this line of questioning or how he had come by this information.

Declan hadn't been asked any questions like this.

Kate's stomach roiled and she didn't know how much more of this she could take.

Senator Willis looked on the verge of striking again but was interrupted by a young male staffer who handed him a slip of paper. He unfolded it, read whatever was written on it, and jerked his head upright to look at Kate. "It looks like you might be able to redeem yourself, Agent Walsh."

Kate wondered what had happened. In the dramatic fashion Senator Willis had perfected, he glanced at his colleagues and shook the piece of paper before addressing Kate again.

"It seems *someone* just robbed the National Gallery of Art," he said stressing the word, his implication clear. "There was a break-in last night and *Lady in the Field* by Henri Chevalier was stolen. Do you have any idea how much this painting is worth?"

"I don't," Kate admitted, wondering if he was being serious about the theft or merely testing her. She wouldn't put it past him to have created this little façade to see her reaction. He stared at her without saying anything. Kate finally added, "Art theft is not my specialty. We were only brought in to work on the Curators case initially because the French police called us in. There had also been a murder to solve with the case."

"There's been a murder with this one," he said with disgust. "Two guards were shot dead and one of the restoration experts was also found murdered in his studio on the gallery's grounds. These men's lives are on your head for not bringing in the Phantom when you had the chance."

"Is someone suggesting this was the Phantom's doing?" Kate asked, not sure how he was making the leap.

"I'm suggesting it," he barked without any evidence to back it up.

"Was the painting being restored?" Kate asked, not taking the bait. She was trying to make sense of why a restoration expert got mixed into an art theft.

"I don't know the details but the case is yours."

For as much power as Senator Willis thought he had, he couldn't assign her a case. It's not how any of this worked.

None of this made sense to Kate. "Do you have evidence that this is connected to the Phantom?"

"Who else could it be?" Senator Willis threw the piece of paper down on the table. "There's been three murders so there you have it. Living proof that your poor judgment cost the lives of three Americans." He leaned over the table and pointed a finger at Kate. "You've got one chance. Find him and bring him in or consider yourself out of a job." He and the other senators got up and left so quickly that Kate didn't have a chance to respond.

Could it be? Would Leo be so brazen as to strike on U.S. soil so soon after Scotland?

Kate knew nothing about the origins of the painting. The one thing she knew for sure was that Leo's crew, known globally as the Curators, had never killed anyone during a heist. Leo had told her as much and the story behind why he was an art thief. Kate had so many questions swirling around in her head. The walls of the chamber seemed to be closing in on her.

She had to get out of there and get a breath of fresh air.

Kate thanked her lawyer and headed for the door. She was practically in a sprint as she tugged open the heavy wooden door and exited. She was so focused on getting out of the building, she walked right into Declan.

He steadied her with his hands and she stepped back out of his touch, remembering what Senator Willis had asked her about their relationship. "Outside," she said stiffly. "Wait until we are outside to ask me anything."

Declan raked a hand through his wavy brown hair that never was in place and followed her out. His long legs took one step for her every two. They reached the front door of the Capitol and Declan pulled it open for her.

Kate raced out and ran partway down the Capitol steps and stopped. She squinted her eyes from the mid-day Spring sun and took a deep breath. She could smell the light sweet fragrance of the cherry blossoms – the only good thing about their trip to Washington D.C. They had made it for the brief bloom. It was a reminder to Kate there were still good things in the world.

"Are you okay?" Declan asked when he caught up to her.

Kate turned her face up to look at him. "I'm not okay. All Senator Willis wanted to know was if I had sex with Leo."

"What?" Declan asked, his anger rising on her behalf. "He had no right to ask you that. Did the others ask you that?"

Kate shook her head. "They were all focused on why I didn't make an arrest. Senator Willis took it to another level. I think they were leaving him to last for that reason. The goal was to humiliate me and suggest I was a whore who slept with the suspect."

"What did you say?"

"I suggested he was inappropriate with his interns."

"Katie, no," Declan said, his words long and drawn out. He was trying to hide a laugh. "You didn't. Tell me you didn't."

"I did and that's when he wanted to know if we were living in the same house and if we were sleeping together." She watched as his eyes grew wide in a question. They had already talked about the plan should anyone ever ask. They had to lie. It was the only way to keep their partnership. "I lied under oath, Declan. It's the first time I ever did that."

"You didn't have a choice. He had no right to ask you that."

Kate knew she had a choice. Life was all about choices and consequences, but this side of their relationship was new. They were still in uncharted territory.

Declan gave her a look of sympathy knowing the tough situation she was in. "What else did he ask?"

"He didn't have a chance to ask anything else. A painting was stolen from the National Gallery of Art last night and three people were murdered. They suggested it was the Phantom and Senator Willis assigned me to the case. Catch him and I keep my job. We need to see Spade right now."

CHAPTER 2

They walked the few blocks between the Capitol and FBI Headquarters in relative silence. Kate didn't feel like talking and Declan didn't push her. She'd only have to tell the story over again when they met with Spade and some things didn't bear repeating twice.

To get to Spade's office they had to walk the labyrinth of hallways and pass through six security checkpoints. Spade was something of an enigma at the FBI. He had a background in military intelligence and his hand in several government agencies. He often acted as a bridge between the FBI, CIA, and NSA – even when, on paper, the agencies weren't working together.

Spade had a way of bridging gaps and opening doors that needed opening.

As soon as they arrived at his office, his administrative assistant walked them back to his inner sanctum. "He's been waiting for you," she said as she guided them down one more hall and used her keycard to open the door.

It had been a long time since Declan and Kate had been to D.C. They spent their time traveling from case to case. In down times between cases, sometimes Declan worked out of the Boston FBI field office and Kate worked from her brownstone in Boston's Back Bay.

They found Spade on the phone shouting a blue streak at someone on the other end of the line. He raised his eyes and waved them in. He shouted a few more things then slammed the phone into the receiver. "I heard the inappropriate questions Senator Willis asked you and I'm already in the process of taking care of that. He went public after the hearing."

Kate didn't know what to say. The news had traveled fast. "I'm okay, sir," she assured him as they sat. "No one seemed to care about the truth."

"It wasn't about the truth. It was about humiliating you and trying to discredit the FBI. Let me handle it." Spade appraised them both. He'd never looked like he aged. The first time Kate met him she would have guessed he was close to sixty and a decade later he looked the same. He had a weathered ruddy look about his face, a head full of white hair, and stood about five-foot-eleven. His body had not softened with age. Kate assumed he lifted his fair share of weights besides probably running daily.

Kate wasn't sure why else they had been called to his office. She offered up, "Senator Willis said the National Gallery of Art was robbed and three people are dead. Have you heard anything about that?"

"I heard about an hour ago." Spade arched a dark eyebrow in a question. "Do you think it's the Curators?"

Kate didn't know what to think. "It doesn't matter what I believe. I don't have enough evidence to know either way. The problem is Senator Willis believes it is and has assigned me the case." She held her hand up to stop Spade from telling her Senator Willis could do no such thing. "I know, Spade. I'm only telling you what he told me. He said my future with the FBI depended on me bringing the Phantom in."

"He has no control over who is hired and fired." Even as Spade said it, there was doubt in his voice.

Kate sat back in the chair and crossed her legs, resolved to her fate.

"That may be the case. The fact remains that our continued work hangs in the balance." She glanced over at Declan who had remained quiet this whole time. His jaw was clenched and she was sure he was thinking of several ways to dispose of Senator Willis should he ever get the chance. She waited to see if he was going to say anything and when he didn't, she turned her attention back to Spade. "If this is the Curators, then I want to be the one to bring them in. I need to show I've not lost objectivity. I also think there are extenuating circumstances other agents might not be sensitive to."

Spade caught her meaning. "You believed Leo when he told you he was only focused on Nazi-looted art?"

Leo had admitted to her in Scotland that all his art thefts had one purpose – to steal back what the Nazis had stolen and return the art to the rightful owners. This would be a major twist in his crimes if it were true. Kate had not had access to all the case files for his crimes and still hadn't had the time to go through them. Not just the time but the clearance. She was walking a fine line and hadn't dared arouse any suspicion after letting Leo go in Scotland.

That wasn't what Kate meant though. "I don't want to see him shot. Other agents might go after him as a prized lion. The Curators, in particular the Phantom, are larger-than-life figures. An agent might see their shot at fame in killing him. I'd like to avoid that, if possible." The more Kate talked about it, the angrier she started to feel. If this was Leo after everything they had gone through in Scotland, she might be tempted to shoot him herself. While she knew he was a criminal, this felt like a deeper betrayal.

Spade watched as she processed the emotion. He didn't say anything else to her though. He turned his attention to Declan. "Do you believe it could be the Curators?"

"I don't know, sir," Declan said with a calm that Kate wasn't feeling. "The Curators have never so much as injured a security guard. I don't see why they'd turn to murder now. I want to see the scene and reserve judgment until we get more evidence."

In response, Spade picked up the phone, punched in a few numbers, and spoke directly to the supervisory agent in charge of the unit who would have been assigned to the case. It didn't take much convincing for the case to be turned over to Spade's team. He was done with the call not even two minutes later.

"An agent who was assigned is bringing down the case file. They went to the scene already. You'll be briefed and then can head over there yourselves." Spade shifted his eyes between them. "I know you're staying in a hotel. Is that fine or do you want me to find you other accommodations?"

"The hotel is fine for me," Kate said and looked over at Declan who agreed. "We are walking distance to everything here in D.C. and if we have to take the Metro we are right near a stop."

"I'll have a driver available if you need it," Spade assured them.

They had taken the train down from Boston with the expectation of only spending a few nights. Kate thanked him and they left his office.

Once outside, Declan asked, "How are you feeling about the hearing after talking to Spade?" He had a concerned expression on his face.

"I can't say I'm fine but I'll be fine." Kate had honestly forgotten all about the hearing. She was focused on the betrayal and anger she felt for Leo if he had come to D.C. and committed an art heist right under her nose. He had told her in Scotland that the Curators hadn't been active because he had been so focused on stopping the killer in Europe who was framing him for murder. "I'm more angry about…" Kate glanced up, knowing they were being watched by someone somewhere deep in the bowels of the FBI. There were cameras everywhere in the building. "We can talk about it but not here." She cast her eyes up toward the ceiling and Declan got the message.

They didn't see the agent they were supposed to meet in the lobby so they headed outside. Once on the street, Kate paced back and forth. "I can't believe he'd do something like this."

"You don't know it's him, Kate. For all we know, it might not have anything to do with the Curators at all."

Kate turned and looked at him, anger written all over her face. "Why are you defending him?"

Declan held his hands up in defense. "I'm not defending anything. I'm saying don't get all riled up until you know some facts. You wouldn't have even thought about the Curators had Senator Willis not mentioned it first. We'd probably be on our way back to Boston by now." When she didn't say anything, Declan softened his tone. "I get it. It would be a terrible thing if he did this. It's a slap in the face after everything you went through together. He's a criminal though, Kate. What did you expect? He was never going to commit another art heist?"

Kate knew Declan was right. She had formed a bond with someone under extreme circumstances. It didn't mean she knew him or that he owed her anything. If this was Leo though, this time she'd bring him in – no matter what it took.

Declan hitched his thumb over his shoulder. "I think that agent we need to meet is here."

They walked back into the main lobby and greeted Agent Tom Coburn. He extended his hand. "I was told to brief you about the National Gallery of Art heist as well as all the information we have gathered on the Phantom."

"Lead the way," Declan said and they followed him back to the conference room on the third floor of the building not far from Tom's office.

The table had fifteen large file boxes stacked in a long line and piled three deep on top. "This is everything we have gathered over the last ten years. We have been working with our international counterparts on this case for a long time. Kate, I understand you've had some interaction with him. There aren't many people who have even seen his face."

"He took me hostage on a case in Paris and then in Edinburgh, he helped us solve a serial homicide case. He saved my life there." Kate told Tom about the case in Edinburgh and everything Leo had told her about saving her life by taking her hostage in Paris and then saving her again. "He's saved my life twice. The first time a long-time member of the Curators said I was getting too close and so he wanted to kill me. The Phantom took me hostage to protect me, which makes sense I guess. We had no idea who he was. He showed his face to me to protect me. In Edinburgh, he was instrumental in helping us solve the case."

Kate couldn't take her eyes off the boxes of evidence. It was far more information than she knew had existed. When they had been called to Paris to help the French, no one told her that the FBI had been collecting information on the Curators. She had assumed that if the FBI had information they would have shared it with them. Kate was so focused on the evidence she didn't hear Tom's next question.

She broke herself out of her trance. "I'm sorry. What did you say?"

Tom was looking at her as she was assessing the boxes. "I asked what he was like. You're the only one who ever interacted with him."

"He's not what I expected," Kate said softly, remembering the way the light had caught his eyes and the softness of his voice when he shared with her his painful childhood. She knew now that she had been foolish to believe him. "He's either a master manipulator or he's not what everyone expects. The jury is still out."

"Do we know how many times he's struck here in the United States?" Declan asked as he moved toward the boxes and flipped the lid off one. It was stacked to the top with papers and photographs.

"We only know of two art heists committed here by the Curators.

One at The Metropolitan Museum of Art in New York City and one at the Museum of Fine Arts in Boston. They left their calling card at both."

Kate remembered the Boston heist nearly ten years ago, but she couldn't recall the one in New York. She was familiar with their calling card. It was a simple white business card embossed with *The Curators* spelled out in gold lettering. There was nothing else on the card. They left it behind at every scene. Had they not left it, there was a chance no one would have ever heard of them.

Kate needed to know the truth about Leo, no matter how much it might shatter the image she had been holding of him. She pulled out a chair, knowing this was going to be a long briefing. "Tell me everything you know about the Phantom."

CHAPTER 3

It turned out Tom Coburn's information on the Phantom wasn't as good as Kate hoped. He provided them with an overview of the art heists connected to the Curators by the calling card. He also confirmed what Kate knew – the Curators had never once been accused of harming anyone. Guards were left tied up but unharmed. In most instances, art was removed from private homes and galleries without anyone being the wiser until long after the fact. It was like they slipped in undetected and out the same way.

In the New York theft, the painting was taken during a fancy political fundraiser and no one among the three hundred people in attendance or the staff had been aware. It wasn't until the end of the night, long after the last guest left, that a guard on his final walkthrough noticed the missing painting. In its place was the Curators' calling card.

No one in any law enforcement agency in any country was even close to knowing the identity of the Phantom and the Curators. That is, until now, with Kate. She wasn't even sure that Leo was his real name though and not another alias.

Kate had explained she believed he was Bulgarian by birth but had grown up in France and had gone to boarding school. At some point later, he had turned to a life of crime. Tom speculated the Phantom probably lived in some wildly flashy villa in the Mediterranean and hatched his evil plans from there.

Kate couldn't see the man she had met living in a flashy villa. She could see the Mediterranean but his dwelling would be understated and homey. She had shaken her head when the thought of Leo lounging at home on a Sunday afternoon with a glass of whiskey entered her mind. Kate had to keep reminding herself she didn't truly know him. It was a disconnect she was having trouble reconciling.

Kate asked Tom if he could compile a list for her of every known painting stolen by the Curators. He said they had a list and he could provide that to her when she returned to the office.

Kate had inquired whether he knew the provenance of all the art stolen. The job of a museum curator was to know the history of a piece of art from creation to how it ended up in their hands. Some museums did this better than others. Private collectors should have the same information from whatever art dealer they worked with to acquire the art. It didn't mean they did.

"We have it. Why do you need it?" he asked, confused by the request for provenance information.

"It might factor into the investigation," she had said not even glancing at Declan as she said it. Kate was holding back information from Tom. She hadn't told him Leo's name or what he had said about the Nazi-looted art. She wasn't sure when she'd share it. Spade knew and that was enough for now until she was able to confirm it herself. "I'd like access to everything you have. I never know what bit of information can lead to something bigger."

Tom understood that and assured Kate it was all in the boxes with each art theft. After finishing with Tom, Kate and Declan walked the few blocks to the National Gallery of Art. They stopped briefly on the sidewalk to take in the massive structure.

They were headed to the older West Building rather than the newer more modern East Building. The original structure was created in a neoclassical style that mirrored the National Archives and the Thomas

Jefferson Memorial. The building was made of Tennessee pink marble and had skylights that covered the entire three-acre roof to illuminate and unite the galleries. President Franklin D. Roosevelt gave the dedication of the National Gallery of Art on March 17, 1941. The East Building was added for a museum expansion in the 1970s. A sculpture garden sat on the other side of the West Building.

Like all things in D.C., history was ever-present. "Have you ever been inside?" Kate asked as they crossed the street.

"Outside of a brief stay in D.C. before heading to Quantico for the academy, I was only here once for a long weekend. I didn't see a fraction of what I wanted to see on that trip."

That's how it always felt for Kate. No matter how many times she visited D.C., there was always something new to explore. "Are you ready?"

"Something is bothering me."

"The fact that I held back information from Tom?"

Declan shook his head. "I understood why you did that. It's all speculation. I want to know why they gave up the case so easily. If they have been tracking the Curators for this long, why were they willing to give it up so quickly?"

Kate had been wondering the same thing. It wasn't like law enforcement of any kind to simply hand over a case and all of their evidence. "Maybe they are tired of chasing a ghost. Based on those evidence boxes, they have been at this for more than a decade. Everyone knows I had contact with him and built some rapport. It's possible they just want him caught and are willing to step aside to let us do it." Kate hoped that was the reason. "Then again, maybe they want to see us fail, me fired, and have our unit unfunded."

Declan chuckled. "Dark, Katie. You have to get your head right before you go in there. It's just like any other case we've had."

Kate knew it wasn't *just a case*. There was a lot more than that at stake – her career depended on it. She threw her shoulders back and marched toward the National Gallery of Art. The FBI had forced them to shut down the West Building for the day, given the vast crime scene that went from the front lobby to the second floor where another guard was killed and then to the back staff area where the art restorer had been killed.

Lady in the Field had been stolen from the main floor in the most western part of the gallery, which was home to 17th to 18th Century Spanish, Italian, and French works of art. It had been a long time since Kate had been in the gallery and she was glad Tom had provided them with a map. It was nearing eleven in the morning and the murders and stolen painting had been detected at six. Tom mentioned that the bodies had been removed and the crime scene techs had started work, but otherwise, the scene was untouched.

Kate and Declan flashed their badges to the D.C. Metro cops camped out in front of the building, keeping the media at bay. There were only a handful of other onlookers, probably mostly tourists who were either curious or hadn't heard about what had happened and had planned to spend the day at the National Gallery of Art.

One of the D.C. cops opened the door for them. "Where's Agent Coburn?"

Kate introduced herself and Declan. "We are taking over the investigation with support from the FBI art theft unit. Please don't let anyone else in without our authorization. Do you know where I can find Dr. Marcy Reinhold, the gallery's director?"

"Go through these doors and head down the hall to the right. Her office is through a set of double doors. You'll see two of our officers there. They can direct you."

Kate figured it was best to meet with Dr. Reinhold first. Then they could get the lay of the land before exploring more. The one piece of evidence Kate was not given was the Curators' calling card. Tom said one hadn't been found yet, which Kate thought was odd. They normally left it in place of the stolen painting. They didn't play hide and seek with it.

Kate and Declan found Dr. Reinhold's office and knocked on the closed door. The officers outside assured them she was there. After a moment, when they didn't hear anything, Kate turned the handle and pushed it open. Dr. Reinhold was sitting at her desk with headphones on staring at her laptop screen. She had a blunt bob of black hair and a thin face. She looked to be in her late fifties and the emerald and diamond necklace around her neck told Kate that she was well off financially.

Kate didn't want to startle her but didn't know of another way to get her attention. "Dr. Reinhold," she said again then stepped right in front of the woman's desk.

Instead of being startled, Dr. Reinhold snapped her head to attention and took off her headphones. "I didn't hear you come in." She did not explain what she was working on or apologize for not seeing them right away the way some people might have. Dr. Reinhold stood from the chair and was about Kate's five-foot-eight height. "Agent Coburn called me and said they were sending over two more FBI agents. I'm not sure why there was a change."

Kate introduced herself. "My partner, Declan James, and I are part of a specialized unit with the FBI. We have had contact with the man known as the Phantom and his art theft ring who call themselves the Curators. We were brought in to assess if this case was connected to them."

"It is," she said sharply and pulled a small blue business card from her desk. She handed it to Declan who wouldn't take it. "I found this on the floor near where the painting was taken."

Declan appeared as confused as Kate. "We were told no card was found." He directed her to put the card back on the desk. He reached for gloves in his back pocket and put them on before taking the card.

"Did you show this to Agent Coburn?" Kate asked, peering over at the card. As with previous cards, *The Curators* was embossed in the middle of the card but in white not gold lettering as it was in the original card. The card itself was blue this time, not like the original white. The words *The Phantom* were also added under *The Curators*. It was a significant change from the style of card the Curators had left at other thefts.

Dr. Reinhold pursed her lips. "I didn't show him the card."

Withholding evidence wasn't a great place to start. "Is there a reason you withheld it?"

Dr. Reinhold must have realized what she had done. "To be honest with you, I picked it up off the floor and put it in my pocket without thinking. I forgot to give it to him and have had it here on my desk since then. You're the first ones who mentioned the Curators."

It wasn't a great explanation but Kate could understand how she might be overwhelmed. "Dr. Reinhold, it would be helpful if you could give us the play-by-play of this morning when you entered the gallery. We understand you're the one who was first on the scene. Had you been alerted that anything was wrong?"

"No," she said, sitting down. "Please call me Marcy while we are working together."

Kate didn't return the offer of familiarity. As far as she was concerned, everyone was suspect. "What time did you get in this morning?"

"A little before six, my usual time. I'm normally the first person here. The night guards are still on. They started at midnight and were not relieved until eight. I came in the back staff entrance, so I didn't even know right away what had happened. I dropped my things off here and headed for the front of the building. That's when I saw the guard slumped over the desk. I touched him, not knowing what was wrong. I initially thought a medical emergency, but when I pushed him back I saw the chest wound and the blood. I caught a glimpse on the security monitors and saw that another guard was lying down on the main floor and raced to check on him. He was dead too. That's when I called 911."

Declan sat down next to Kate and raised his eyes. "Were you concerned for your safety at that point?"

"Oddly, no," Marcy said seemingly trying to make sense of it herself. "I should have been afraid. I assumed something had happened overnight. While I was on the phone with 911, I went through the gallery areas closest to me and that's when I saw *Lady in the Field* was missing. The card was on the floor and I picked it up and put it in my pocket. My only focus was continuing my search to see what else was missing. I didn't even look at the card until I got back to my office. It wasn't until the FBI arrived that we realized Gabriel Baptiste had been murdered in the studio in the basement."

Marcy paused as she said the man's name and her hand went to her chest. She sucked in a breath. "Gabriel was the most amazing man and restorer. I don't understand why anyone would kill him. It doesn't even make any sense. I was with Agent Coburn when we found him."

"You stopped searching for missing artwork at some point?"

"When I heard the sirens I went back to the front lobby to let the cops in. I didn't find anything else missing."

Declan was far more of an eagle-eye than Kate and he was itching to get to the scene. "Let's do a walkthrough of your route this morning and then we can head to the basement."

Kate agreed with him. "Have there been any threats against the gallery in recent weeks or months?"

"Nothing," Marcy said as she took a breath. She had a swell of emotion for the first time since they arrived. "We have never had anything like this happen here. I don't even know what to say."

Kate knew finding the bodies and the missing painting must have been hard for her. She had thought Marcy to be cold and unfeeling at first. Kate was warming up to her. "You might still be in shock." Kate wondered if it was something more, but she'd reserve judgment for now.

CHAPTER 4

Kate and Declan walked with Marcy to the front of the building to the security desk they had passed on the way in. The large U-shaped desk came up to Kate's chest. Behind it were several television monitors, two phones, and walkie-talkies. There was also room enough for two chairs. Guards could sit behind the desk and monitor the front door and the television screens with the video feed of everything happening across West Building.

Declan lagged looking for evidence, security cameras, and everything else he noticed that often escaped Kate's attention. It was why they paired so well.

While Declan was focused on the evidence, Kate focused on getting to know Marcy better. "Did you know the security guards that were here last night?"

"Stephen Beck and Jamie Taylor. They started around the same time four years ago. They have been excellent guards."

"Is it typical to have only two guards on at night?"

"Here in the West Building. We have other guards in the East Building. They were questioned this morning by Agent Coburn. My understanding is that they didn't hear or see a thing."

That was interesting to Kate. "Are they all connected to the same frequency on their earbuds and walkies?" When they had the case a few years ago at the Louve, Kate and Declan had a fast education about the kinds of security at galleries and museums such as this. It was extensive, which is why theft was so rare. Also, they should have all been on the same frequency and should have heard the shots, unless of course a suppressor was used. That wasn't out of the question.

"Agent Coburn would know more about that." Marcy turned her attention to the security desk. "Stephen Beck was shot here at the front desk. He and his wife had a baby about a year ago. I can't believe someone killed him."

The crime scene techs had already been there but dried blood spatter was still present on the desk and the floor around the chair. "Is the front door locked at night?"

"All of the doors are locked at five when we close. Security and other staff walkthrough shortly after to make sure everyone has left and, if not, escort them out." Marcy smiled then. "People lose track of time in here. I can't fault them for that. We have some magnificent pieces that you can lose yourself in. But we usher them out and the doors are locked for the night. By then, the afternoon guards are on shift and there is another shift change at midnight. That's when Stephen and Jamie started. As Agent Coburn said, we are looking at roughly a six-hour window when this could have occurred, probably shorter given I think they were dead for some time when I arrived."

Kate knew exactly what time the crimes had occurred. Tom had told her the security cameras were shut off remotely at two that morning. He was guessing that some kind of electric interference was used to disable the cameras because they hadn't been manually shut down and no wires had been cut. His theory was that someone had snuck into the electric room yesterday and hacked the system so they could control it from the outside. He had explained the tech behind it and it was a little over Kate's head. She trusted he was right because it made sense given the scene.

There were no broken doors or windows and it appeared that there had been an override of the system that unlocked doors and cut the security cameras. They turned the system back on after they left. Tom said there was no camera activity during a ninety-minute window from two to three-thirty that morning. She didn't share this information with Marcy.

Kate moved out of the way while Declan assessed the area. "Do you think they came in the front door?"

Declan held up a finger and asked her to wait while he walked out the front door. While he was gone, Kate explained his process to Marcy. "I let him do his thing. He'll tell us what he's seeing eventually. I've learned not to rush the process. In the meantime, you said earlier that there have been no big threats but what about security concerns – even minor ones matter."

Marcy craned her neck to look out the front door to see what Declan was doing. Kate couldn't see him from her vantage point, so she assumed Marcy wouldn't either. She turned her attention back to Kate. "There are always minor concerns – people getting too close to the artwork, parents not watching their children closely enough, people trying to touch the artwork or taking photos when they shouldn't. These are minor concerns each day which are addressed at the time by security and staff. We haven't had anything major the whole time I've been here. It would be an understatement to say this is shocking. I know other museums have been hit, but I can honestly say I never thought it would happen here."

Declan came back a few minutes later. "I don't think they came through the front door. There are street security cameras out there. We'll have to check, but my guess is they figured they'd be too exposed. The guard was behind the desk and facing the opening, not the door. He was still seated. If someone had come in the front way, he surely would have been on his feet and around the front of the desk. It looks to me like he was surprised. He hadn't even had time to draw his weapon." Declan looked around the area and spotted a door across the lobby cattycorner from the desk. It was marked as a staff-only entrance. "Where does that door go to?"

"There is a hallway with a few offices and also a door to the basement."

"Is there access into the building from that direction?"

Marcy shook her head but then reconsidered. "There is one door in the basement that you can access the outside, but they would have had to walk across the full length of the basement to get to that door."

Kate didn't think it was out of the question. "Gabriel was shot in the basement. It's possible they surprised him and he was shot first."

Declan agreed with that assessment. He walked over to the staff door and assessed the line of sight and angle from that door to the guard desk. He held his hand up like a gun and aimed. "Perfect line of sight."

"Let's move on then," Kate said as she let Marcy guide her to the main floor where the second guard was killed near the *Lady in the Field* painting. They reached the level and passed by the bronze six-foot sculpture *Mercury* in the rotunda. Kate stopped for a moment and looked at the statue of the naked muscular man with wings on his ankles. He balanced on the toes of one foot as the other leg and one arm were raised up. His scepter, tucked near his side with his other hand, is two entwined snakes with wings on the top. Mercury was an Ancient Roman Olympian god and was portrayed here with wings on his cap and heels to signify his swiftness. Kate's mind played over her professor's description of the statue she heard in her art history class at Harvard.

Declan passed by with barely even a glance and kept on going toward the Lobby Court. Kate wondered if he ever appreciated art. It wasn't something the two of them discussed much over the years.

"This statue is our mascot here at the National Gallery," Marcy said as she passed it.

Kate caught up with them as Marcy pointed to the area that had been roped off with yellow crime scene tape. "Jamie must have been on his rounds when he was killed," she said and sniffled. "He was so young too, just recently married."

Declan recalled what Tom had told them. "He had his gun at his side still in his hand. The assumption is he heard something but didn't get a chance to get off a shot. It appeared to Tom he was facing the way we just came in. I assume the killer took the same path we did."

Jamie had been shot once in the chest. There was still significant blood on the floor where the man had bled out. Kate stared at it then looked to her right. "Is it down that hall to reach where the painting was located?"

"The section starts right here as we entered this gallery space, but that particular painting was farther away, almost reaching the section of 15th and 16th Century Netherlandish and German paintings and sculptures. It's tucked away in the back."

"How big is the painting?" Kate asked as they walked to the location.

"Not large at all. It was roughly two feet in height and one foot across and had a heavy gold frame. Not heavy enough that it couldn't easily be carried though. The painting was Impressionist and similar to Vincent van Gogh's Wheat Field series if you're familiar with that."

Kate was familiar with nearly all of Van Gogh's works. He was a favorite artist of hers and Leo knew that. It was something they had discussed in Scotland. "Was there anything important for us to know about the artist, Henri Chevalier?"

"Only three of his paintings survive. This was the first in a series and there are two others. *Man in the Field*, which when side by side creates a mirror image of *Lady in the Field*. The final in the series is called *Summer Sunday* and it's of the two figures meeting near a haybale in the same field. It signified strangers to friends or so they say. Chevalier famously never discussed the meaning of his work. He left it for the interpretation of the viewer."

After inspecting the area where the painting had once been hung on the wall, Declan walked over to the two of them. He stood with his hands on his hips. "When you say only three of his paintings survive, what do you mean?"

"Only three survived," Marcy said like the meaning was obvious. "Chevalier lived in the south of France. He, like many artists of his time, was suffering from unknown mental health issues. Today, he'd probably have a bipolar diagnosis. He was often manic and then would fall into deep bouts of depression. No one knows the true story, but some say he was murdered and others say it was suicide. Either way, his barn with all of his art was burned to the ground with the paintings still inside – except these three. They were the last he ever painted and he had given them to a neighbor before his death. Since then, rumors swirled that there are images on the back that point to his killer. I have no idea if the neighbors he gave the paintings to ever knew. The legend says that Chevalier knew he was being targeted and he painted these last three to indicate his killer."

"He never told the neighbor who was threatening him?" Kate asked, wondering why he'd be so cryptic with the message.

"I guess not." Marcy shrugged and sighed. "There's a lot unknown but there were images on the back of the painting that didn't make sense. I've never seen the backs of the other two."

Kate had many questions and wasn't sure where to start. "Do you know if this might have been a piece stolen by the Nazis in World War II?"

"It was not. I can't tell you the provenance off the top of my head but the records were clean. I know that much. The records are downstairs and I can show them to you. Is there a reason you asked?"

Kate wanted to hold that information close to the vest for now. "It's come up in other cases. We need to know what we are working with going into the investigation. What was the value?"

"Eight million dollars. It was shared with us from the Andrew W. Mellon Collection, which as you might know is the founding collection here at the National Gallery of Art," Marcy explained and then continued, giving them a history lesson. "Andrew Mellon offered to give his art collection to establish a national gallery. He sent a letter to President Franklin D. Roosevelt proposing endowment funds and plans for a museum building that he would erect. He named the new museum the National Gallery of Art and did not want it named after himself. This painting was among his collection long before World War II."

Kate stared back at the section where the missing painting had been. "Were the two others in the series in the collection as well?"

"No. Andrew Mellon only had this one. *Man in the Field* is currently in the hands of a private individual here in D.C. and *Summer Sunday* is at the Metropolitan Museum of Art." Marcy paused for a moment and furrowed her brow. "Each painting alone is worth about eight million but together they'd fetch close to fifty million, mostly because of the speculation that the holder of all three might be able to solve the circumstances of Henri Chevalier's death. The three have never been shown together. The art world has been pushing and speculating for years about it. It's one of those theories that float around the art world."

"There's a chance that since someone stole this one, the other two are at risk." Kate said the words and considered the implication.

Marcy's eyes grew wide. "I'd say there's more than a chance."

Kate looked over to Declan. "We have some phone calls to make."

CHAPTER 5

Given the fact the other paintings could be stolen, Kate and Declan got the name of the private collector who had the *Man in the Field* painting and headed directly to his home. Preventing that theft was more important than going over evidence at the National Gallery.

It turned out the owner wasn't in D.C. but in Chevy Chase, Maryland right outside the district borders. Mick Sutton lived in a five-thousand-square-foot grand Tudor home on East Lenox Street. The home was currently worth close to four million dollars and Mick had lived there for the last thirty years. A quick search on the man indicated he was nearing sixty and had been a lobbyist, although now retired. His three children lived on the west coast. He lived in the home with his wife.

Kate and Declan had called the driver Spade offered them. On the ride over, Kate asked Declan what he thought of the scene at the National Gallery.

"I think it was someone who knew the layout like the back of their hand," he said definitively. Before leaving, Marcy had shown them the basement studio where Gabriel had been shot and the door that was potentially used as the entrance of the killer. "It's possible we are dealing with one person working alone. He could have stolen the painting and carried it out of there. He would have had the technical knowledge to disable the door locks and the security system and have been in the gallery more than once to know the layout. All I know for sure is that there was heavy recon before this heist."

That was typically always the case with a heist like this, so Kate wasn't surprised by the assessment. They'd have more work to do at the National Gallery but wanted to get to Mick Sutton before he was targeted.

"What did you think of Marcy?" Kate asked, studying his profile as he looked out the window. She wondered what was on his mind because she had to ask the question twice before he heard her.

"What?" Declan asked, turning to her. He saw the look on her face and chuckled. "Sorry, I was thinking about the scene in the restoration room. The way the chair was thrown in the middle of the room. It looked like he was in the middle of restoring a painting but the room was a mess. He was shot in the chest but there was a brush in his hand and paint tipped over on the scaffolding. It doesn't make a lot of sense. He climbed down for a reason."

Kate didn't disagree with any of that. "What did you think of Marcy?"

Declan ran a hand down his face. "I don't know what to think of her finding the Curators' card. Why would she pick it up? She knew two guards had been shot and a painting had been stolen."

"People react differently to shock," was all Kate could say. She wasn't sure how she was feeling about it after having spent time with Marcy. "What did you think about the card though? It's different from every other card the Curators have left."

"That struck me as odd too. Has the original card ever been made public?"

Kate shook her head. "I don't think so. It's been discussed but the card hasn't been shown."

"Maybe they are changing their branding." Declan had a smile on his face as he teased her. "It's possible Leo is getting fancier in his old age."

Kate didn't take the bait. "Does it feel like a heist the Curators would have pulled off?"

"I don't know."

The driver pulled the black SUV into the driveway and let them out. He said he'd wait for them. They walked the short distance to the house and Declan knocked on the wooden slated door that curved at the top and had an iron door handle and knocker. They had not called ahead and were hoping someone was at home.

A moment later, a woman with a halo of short blonde hair opened the door. "Hello," she said with a tiny voice that matched her height. She looked to Kate to be in her sixties. "Can I help you?"

Declan flashed his badge and introduced them. "We are working on a case of art theft at the National Gallery of Art and need to speak with Mick Sutton."

"Yes, I saw that on the news this morning. It's a terrible thing what happened." She stepped out of the way and let them enter the home. "I'm Mick's wife, Olivia. He's down in his office working on a puzzle. Let me take you there. His hearing isn't that great these days." She smiled up at Declan the way most women did. "Not that he'll listen to me and get a hearing aid. Men can be as vain as women sometimes."

Olivia put her hand on Declan's arm as she guided him through the foyer and into a formal living room that exited on the other side of the house to a short hallway. Kate trailed behind them like she wasn't even there. Declan had this power over women that she couldn't say she was immune to. Thankfully, he had started using his charms for good.

He chatted with Olivia about her home and praised her for her choice of décor. She fawned over him in response, offering him coffee or tea and cookies. Declan thanked her and realized as quickly as Kate did that saying no wasn't an option. She left the two of them at a closed office door and promised to return in a moment with refreshments. Kate thought it odd she didn't open the door and introduce them to her husband. Declan seemed to be caught off guard by it too.

"Who don't you charm?" Kate teased and bumped her hip into his leg, smiling up at him.

It caused the right kind of response. "Do you have any idea how much I want to kiss you right now?" he whispered.

Kate laughed. "Focus on the task at hand. There will be time for that later."

Declan knocked on the door. "Mick Sutton," he called and was told to enter. Declan opened the door and introduced himself and Kate to the man who sat in the far corner of the office hunched over what looked like a thousand-piece puzzle.

Mick raised his eyes but didn't put down the puzzle piece in hand. "Let me just figure out where this goes and I'll be right with you. Take a seat."

Normally people dropped whatever they were doing when the FBI showed up at the door. The Suttons seemed unphased by the experience. Kate and Declan sat down on the brown leather sofa. She wondered if there was an unwritten rule between the couple that Mick wasn't to be disturbed while he was focused on a puzzle, which is why Olivia left them at the door to disturb him themselves.

After a moment, Mick cheered, "I got it! That piece has been bothering me for the last fifteen minutes." He looked up at them with a smile so big it crinkled the corners of his eyes. "We are going to call it a win for today." He got up from the chair, came around the table, and perched himself on the end of the leather armchair across from the couch. "How can I help you?"

Kate didn't see any reason not to get to the point. "We have concerns that you might be a target of a burglary. We were told that you own the *Man in the Field* by Henri Chevalier. *Lady in the Field* was stolen last night from the National Gallery of Art and we believe it's possible whoever stole it might be looking to steal all three. Is that painting in your possession?"

Mick's good mood quickly turned sour. "I had some threats a few months back and I shared them with your colleagues but nothing ever happened. The painting is still in our library." He pushed himself up from the chair and gestured for them to follow him. "I have a few paintings that I've had for decades and this is one of them. It was passed down to me by my mother."

Kate wanted to ask about the threats but she wanted to know the painting's history more. "How is it that your mother came in possession of the painting? We only just learned that Henri Chevalier died under mysterious circumstances and there are only three of his works left."

Mick nodded as he made his way down the hall. "It was her side of the family, Bellerose was their last name, that Henri had entrusted with the paintings. I'm sure you also heard that if all three paintings are seen together, it might explain how Chevalier died." He turned back to them before entering the library. "I saw a photograph of the backs of all three together when I was a boy. If there is a mystery in them, I didn't see it."

"There is a painting on the back?" Kate asked, surprised that someone had seen the whole thing.

Mick shrugged. "It looked like a shop. I don't know what it was supposed to tell us."

"Do you still have the photo?"

Mick shook his head. "Lost to history, like most things."

"The paintings are worth more together. Is that correct?" Declan asked as they entered the room that sat in the back of the home. The room had high ceilings and bookshelves that went from there to the floor. They were stacked with books, some looking more than a century old. The floor had a plush rug and the same leather furniture found in the office was replicated in this room. Both were masculine spaces missing any feminine touches. It was a stark contrast to the lighter décor in the foyer and living room.

In between each built-in bookcase was a framed painting. Mick walked them over to *Man in the Field* and stared at it in wonder. He looked over at them. "I suppose I should keep it under lock and key the way some do, but what's the point of owning it if I can't admire it?"

Kate agreed with him there. He still hadn't answered her question. "You said you were able to see all three paintings as a boy. How did that come to pass?"

Mick tapped the side of his head and smiled. "Right, you asked me that. Sorry, my memory isn't what it used to be." He gestured for them to sit and they followed his lead. Once he was comfortable, he said, "My mother's family is from the same village in France as Henri Chevalier. Her family goes back generations and it was my great-grandfather that Henri gave the paintings to for safekeeping. After his barn, which he used as a studio, was set ablaze, that's all there was left to his collective works – just those three paintings. *Man in the Field* was my great-grandfather's favorite and he sold the other two sometime later in life. He thought someone should still be able to enjoy Henri's magnificent artistry."

"This painting was then passed down to you?" Declan asked the obvious and Mick confirmed. "We were told *Lady in the Field* was from the Andrew W. Mellon Collection and it was donated when the funding for the museum was donated. The other in the series is at the Metropolitan Museum of New York. Is that all correct information?"

"I'd have to dig through the old family records to see exactly how the paintings ended up where they did. I remember my mother telling me the stories as a child but I can't recall all the details now."

Kate didn't want to get too consumed with Henri's murder but her curiosity was sparked. "How did he die?"

"Probably today we'd say poisoned, but it was never confirmed," Mick said matter-of-factly. "Everyone at the time believed it was either suicide or an accident."

"No one thought murder?"

Mick shrugged. "There were rumors but my family didn't seem to think so. Henri never expressed any concerns to them."

Declan's interest was piqued too. "When was the studio burned?"

"Same day. Henri died with food still on his plate at supper. It was the barn burning that drew everyone's attention and then they found Henri's body. There were signs of poisoning."

"No one questioned that?"

"Of course but nobody could prove anything. They weren't even sure how the fire started." Mick pinched the bridge of his nose. "Fires were all too common back then, so were people dying of things that couldn't be explained. He wasn't shot or stabbed or anything obvious that it was murder."

Kate didn't want to get caught up in an old case that would never be solved. "You said you had threats, Mick. Can you tell us more about that?"

Mick got up from the couch and walked across the library. He went to an ornate antique box on one of the bookshelves and came back with a small white unlined index card. He handed it to Declan. "I found that on my doorstep. It clearly says that someone was after *Man in the Field* and that it was going to be stolen. The FBI got involved but found no credible evidence and no one ever tried. My wife wanted me to lock the painting away but I don't see the point. I received two more index cards like that in the weeks that followed. Then they stopped. As you can see, the painting is still here."

"Mick, if they can steal a painting from the National Gallery then they can break in here and steal yours too," Kate said, not sure why he was being so stubborn about it. "Just because they haven't tried to break in yet doesn't mean they aren't going to. Three people are dead at the National Gallery. I don't want to see anything happen to you or your wife."

Mick sighed and glanced up at the painting. "Let me look into some options and I'll store it for now." When Kate looked at him skeptically, he reassured her, "I would never put my wife's life at risk. I'll have it done this afternoon."

"Until then, we are going to get some extra patrols in the neighborhood and a uniformed officer to sit out front," Declan said in a way that didn't allow Mick to argue.

"I think that's an excellent decision, Mick. You'll have it back before you know it." Kate reached for the index card still in Declan's hand. She wanted to snap a photo of it for evidence later if they needed it. The message on the card was more like a warning than a threat. As Declan put the card in her hand, Kate's eyes zeroed in on the handwriting. It looked oddly familiar to her, but she couldn't place it.

Olivia arrived at the door with coffee and snacks, which pleased Mick to no end. He waved his wife in and pecked her on the cheek. "It's going into storage. They convinced me." She seemed pleased with that.

Mick looked between Kate and Declan. "Now that we have that unpleasantness out of the way, please have some refreshments before you go. I'm sure you're both working too hard and haven't had much to eat today."

Declan stomach growled in response and Kate rolled her eyes. "I think that's a yes, thank you," she said while her mind was still focused on the handwriting.

"Do you think Mick is going to follow through and find a storage place for the painting?" Declan asked as they got back into the SUV. "I offered to help him but he declined." When he realized Kate wasn't focused on him, he pinched her side.

Kate swatted his hand away. She was still staring at the photo of the index card, not sure she should voice what she was seeing. After a moment, when Declan pressed her, she gave in. "Does the handwriting on this card look familiar to you?"

Declan glanced down at it and shook his head. "Does it look familiar to you?"

"I think it's Leo's," she said slowly. "Do you remember the replica painting he sent me?"

"How could I forget? I have to see it every time I walk into the living room." His jealous tone gave him away. Declan hadn't been happy Leo knew her home address or that he had sent her a gift. The initial reprieve Declan had been giving him for saving Kate's life had been erased with that one act. He groaned even louder when she hung the painting in the living room of her brownstone. It was her house though and he hadn't said another word about it until now.

Kate didn't want to get into it but the handwriting was more important. "Leo sent a card with the painting, remember. I didn't know if it was his handwriting or the handwriting of the artist who did the replica of *Café Terrance at Night*. I've never been able to prove it either way. This handwriting looks the same. Do you think it's possible Leo was warning Mick that someone was after his painting?"

"Warning?" Declan asked, confused.

"I see this message more as a warning than a threat. There have been no instances of Leo or the Curators sending a threat before stealing art. I think this was a warning that someone was after the painting."

Declan was quiet for several moments. "Maybe moving the painting isn't a good idea."

"What do you mean?"

"Before we left, I did a walkthrough of the house with Mick," he reminded her.

Declan had insisted on it, so Kate kept Olivia company while they did. She was glad Declan was talking security with Mick before they left. She didn't question what happened on the tour. "Was the security not up to standard?"

"It was better than the industry standard. I'd say it was probably one of the most secure homes I've ever been in. With a touch of a button, he can lock the entire house down. There is even a panic room built into his office. There are motion sensors on every window and door and around the perimeter of the house. They knew we were there before we stepped foot on the property."

That was not at all what Kate thought Declan was going to say.

"He's also armed, Kate. He showed me the guns he has stored in his office. Mick is prepared and that's why he didn't bring the painting to storage because he felt he could protect it better at home. He said he doesn't like to discuss things in front of Olivia because she gets panicky, but he has the place secured."

That was good to hear. "Then why are you concerned about them moving the painting to an even more secure location?"

"What if the warning was sent because the thief couldn't break into the house without being caught? The warning was sent so Mick would move the painting."

"Wouldn't the art storage facility be safer than his house?"

"Not in this case. It would also be at risk during transit. Any change in the status quo might give the thief a chance to strike." Declan grew quiet. "Maybe Leo didn't mean to kill those people at the National Gallery. Maybe he was trying to get Mick to move the painting weeks ago so they wouldn't have to break into the house. That's his style, Kate. From what we know about him, he's never harmed a private collector. He's never hurt anyone before. This fits with trying to get the painting somewhere else, so there'd be no chance of hurting Mick or Olivia in the process."

Kate couldn't argue with that. The one thing she knew was that the thefts from private homes occurred while the homeowner traveled. As Olivia said, they were homebodies at this point in their lives. Their home was so comfortable they rarely left except to go out to dinner here and there. If they weren't going to leave, maybe Leo wanted them to do the next best thing and move the painting. It still didn't account for the three dead at the National Gallery.

"What about the murders at the National Gallery? It still doesn't fit with the Curators."

"It could have been one of his crew," Declan suggested.

"What do you think we should do?"

"I don't know. If Mick moves the painting and it's stolen, we are in trouble. If he keeps it there based on our recommendation and it's stolen and they are hurt in the process, there's blood on our hands."

There was no good answer. "Mick struck me as an intelligent man. He had to be to have worked as a lobbyist for as long as he did. If security is as tight as you say then he must be working with a security expert. I say you call Mick and explain what we discussed and leave it up to him to make the decision. You can tell him the risk either way."

"That's about the only responsible thing we can do." Declan pulled out his phone and made the call while Kate focused back on the photo of the card.

She was angry with herself for ever trusting Leo. She had fooled herself into thinking they had formed a bond. She had hoped that he'd give up his life of crime.

Declan hung up, his energy lighter than before. "Mick said he already called his security expert and they are planning the move. He assured me the painting would be fine." Declan saw the worried look on her face and put his hand on top of hers. "I know it's hard to think of Leo as a criminal now. You never really could trust him."

Kate knew that down deep in her gut. Even for as long as she had done this job, she still hoped to see the best in people. She didn't have anything to say, so they rode in silence back to FBI Headquarters.

When they arrived back in the conference room, Kate called the Metropolitan Museum of Art, or MET as it was known, and warned them about the potential threat. It took a while for her to get the director on the phone but once she did, Kate gave Dr. Jeffrey Cain a stern warning.

"Agent Walsh, I assure you *Summer Sunday* is safe. We are all aware of what happened at the National Gallery. That will not happen here. No one can steal *Summer Sunday*."

While Kate had him on the phone she wanted to know more about that particular piece – the third in the series. "Do you have the provenance on that painting in front of you by chance?"

"I do but there's not much to tell. The painting came directly from the Bellerose family in Cassis. They were Henri Chevalier's neighbors. They sold the painting to us in the 1920s when the other was sold to Andrew Mellon. It has been with us ever since."

"We just met with Mick Sutton. He owns *Man in the Field*. He told us it was his family who were given the painting after Henri's death.

Is that your understanding?"

"Yes. I've met Mick Sutton a few times. He's a nice man and his wife is lovely. They have visited the MET a few times. It was his mother's family who knew Chevalier."

"What do you think about the theory that if all three of the paintings are together, it will show the true death of the artist?"

Dr. Cain chuckled. "I wouldn't put much stock into it. While there is another painting on the backs when shown together, it doesn't give any hints to murder."

Kate asked, "Have you received any threats the painting might be stolen?"

"No. If we did, the FBI would be our first call." Dr. Cain sighed and grumbled something Kate didn't understand. When she asked him to repeat himself, he said, "The lore surrounding Henri Chevalier is much more impressive than the man's artwork itself. There are only three of his works in existence. I'm not even sure how the man rose to such prominence after his death. He sold nothing that we can trace while he was alive and the rest of his artwork was destroyed."

"Other than the paintings being destroyed in a fire, can't that be said of a lot of famous artists?"

"It can," he conceded and then told Kate he had to go.

She was sure he was busy but she didn't like being rushed off the phone. As it was though, Kate didn't need any more of his time. "Please call us should you need anything."

Declan had his head bent over one of the files. He glanced over when the call ended. "That seemed hurried."

"Dr. Jeffrey Cain had no concerns. I got the impression he doesn't think much of Henri Chevalier. He thought the lore about him was more impressive than his art."

Declan shrugged. "Everyone's a critic."

Kate knew that to be true. She opened one of the boxes. "Did we get the list of the stolen artwork from Tom yet?"

Declan shoved two pages stapled together down the table to her. "He has what was stolen, the date of the theft, where it was stolen from, and the valued amount. Take a look at that total at the bottom."

Kate flipped to the second page and looked down. It took her a moment to process what she was seeing. "Is that three trillion dollars?" She wasn't sure she had ever seen the number written out like that.

"That's exactly what it says. Leo and the Curators have stolen more than three trillion in artwork over the last decade or more. He's taken everything from paintings and sculptures to Egyptian antiquities and artifacts." Declan turned his body to face her. "None of it has ever been recovered. No source on the black market or art dealer around the globe has even seen any of the missing pieces after they have been stolen. No one knows what he does with it, Kate."

That fact alone is what gave credence to Leo's story about returning the art and antiquities to the rightful owners. It still didn't account for how Leo made his money. She assumed people might pay him for what he returned. There was still so much unknown.

Countries across the globe had tried and failed to stop him.

Kate didn't think she was any better. She had failed too – twice now.

As Kate reached for the first file, a knock on the conference room door drew her attention. Tom stood with his body half in the room. "How was the walkthrough at the National Gallery?"

Kate waved him in. She had planned to find him after doing some research. This would save her some time. "What did you think of Marcy?"

Tom pulled out a chair and joined them at the table. "Honestly," he said with his eyebrows raised, "I didn't find her all that credible. I didn't want to say that to you before you left and bias you. She asked me a lot of questions and I shared information that I thought I could and held back other information I didn't think appropriate to share.

She was pushy with me."

Kate wanted to tell him about the Curators' card. Like him, she wanted to know his thoughts before explaining what Marcy admitted. "Was there something she did or said that caused you concern?"

"It was more the vibe I got from her. She first admitted that she knew Gabriel was coming in after hours to work on his project. Then later in the conversation, she said she had no idea why he'd be there so late. If that were the only thing, I might have chalked it up to shock." Tom looked past Kate as if he were trying to remember something. "It was a general vibe I got from her. I thought she was holding back a lot."

Declan slid the evidence bag down the table to him. "She gave us this and said she forgot to give it to you. It's a card from the Curators, except it's not like one we have ever seen before."

Tom furrowed his brow and strained to make sense of it. He reached for the bag. "Marcy hid this from us?"

"She said she didn't remember while you were there," Kate said evenly. "She explained to us that she found it right after she found the security guard's body. She said she started to search to see if anything was missing and discovered it on the floor. She picked it up and slipped it in her pocket and forgot to give it to you."

Tom dropped the bag back to the table and zeroed in on Kate. "Don't you find it strange that Marcy shows up to the National Gallery for work and finds two dead security guards but she still takes the time to search for what's missing? She had no idea if they were still in there. Her life, as far as she knew, was at risk. I find it odd that she said she went directly to the hall with the *Lady in the Field*. Now, she's picking up evidence and not turning it over. I don't know…" Tom trailed off not finishing his thought.

Kate didn't need him to finish because she knew exactly what he was saying – the National Gallery director had lied to them more than a few times. "We are going to have to go back and interview her again – this time as a person of interest."

Declan and Tom agreed with that.

CHAPTER 7

Kate wanted Marcy to think she was safe, so they didn't return to the National Gallery that afternoon. They had evidence to go over while they waited for the autopsy reports from the medical examiner and the lab reports back from the crime scene techs. Kate hoped to get some research done on the previous artwork the Curators had stolen but she never got the chance. The day had flown by. As if the weather mimicked her mood, there had been a fierce rainstorm that went late into the evening.

Kate and Declan sat in the District Chophouse on 7th Avenue not far from the Capital One Arena where the Washington Capitals hockey team played. The restaurant was one she had eaten at more than a handful of times with her father when he was called to D.C.

Joseph Walsh had been an ambassador who had been killed with Kate's mother, Madeline, during a terrorist bombing in Kenya. Kate had only recently started venturing back to places she had gone with her parents. The memories didn't sting quite as much as they once did. She wasn't sure if she was in a better place emotionally or if the evolution of her relationship with Declan had provided a safety net that made her feel less alone than she did after the devastating loss right before her college graduation.

"What's on your mind, Katie?" Declan asked as he sipped his whiskey. He had given up drinking for the most part but still indulged from time to time. When she didn't respond, he asked her again. "Your mind seems a million miles away. Thinking about the case?"

Kate looked up from her salad and smiled sadly. "I was thinking about all the trips to D.C. with my father when I was young. My mother didn't always travel with us. He was a huge hockey fan, loyal to the Boston Bruins, but we'd take in a Washington Capitals game too. He wasn't too happy when Adam Oates left the Bruins but was happy he landed with the Capitals. We saw him play more than a few times here. He was my father's favorite, but I was more partial to goalie Olaf Kolzig."

Declan had his glass suspended in the air as he listened to her talk about hockey. When she was done, he whistled lightly. "If it's even possible, you're even hotter than I thought you were this morning."

Kate's cheeks reddened as she laughed. "Why? Because I know hockey?"

Declan toasted her. "I learn something new about you all the time. I had no idea you even liked the sport, let alone could name a player. You keep your secrets well-hidden."

"It wasn't a secret I was keeping intentionally." Declan had played hockey for Boston College. She was sure they must have had some conversation about hockey, but she couldn't recall even one. "Did you ever think about going pro?"

Declan knocked back the rest of his whiskey. "Not even once. I knew from the time I was a kid that I was headed to the FBI. There was never any question about it. When did you know?"

Kate liked to tell herself she didn't know. She had toyed with the idea of becoming an American history professor like her father. She knew she was going to attend Harvard where he'd taught. But if she were being honest with herself, the first time she saw the FBI Headquarters in D.C. when she was ten, she knew she wanted to work there. "I didn't know if I'd be an agent or a criminologist consulting with law enforcement. I knew I'd be doing something in law enforcement."

"However it happened, I'm glad we met and were in the same training class."

She liked the darkness of the restaurant and the way the flicker of the candle accentuated his seafoam green eyes. It was probably his best feature – on his face anyway. Kate blushed at the thought of the last time they were in bed together and she glanced away. He was about to ask what she was thinking again, but the server chose that moment to deliver their food. Each of them got a steak medium and a healthy side of vegetables and baked potato. Kate wasn't sure she was going to finish it all, given she was halfway to full and hadn't eaten all of her salad.

They ate in a comfortable silence only chatting occasionally about the weather, renovations Kate was hoping to get done on her house, and the plans for the case the next day. They stayed away from any heavy conversation about the case since they were in public.

They had talked about her late afternoon call from Spade. He called to let her know that he had spoken with Senator Stephen Willis and told him they had been assigned to the case. Spade made no promises of arresting the Phantom. If the evidence didn't lead in that direction, then that's what the case showed. At no point would Kate be taking investigative direction from a bunch of bully senators. When Senator Willis attempted to threaten Spade, he told him he should rethink it because it wouldn't end well for him.

Spade assured Kate that he'd do all he could to protect her and her job. Kate believed that was true, but she also saw during her testimony that not everything was in his control. All she could do was her best and follow the evidence. The rest would take care of itself. If she was fired, Kate knew she could easily be paid more than she made at the FBI for lecturing or consulting. Not that she needed the money, her parents left her a small fortune and her brownstone was worth millions.

They finished their dinner and declined dessert. Kate stared out the window at the rain as they waited for the check and Declan went to the bathroom. She closed her eyes tight at the flash of lightning and roar of thunder that followed. The storm was right on top of them now.

The hotel was several blocks away and they'd be drenched by the time they got back. It was too much wind and rain for an umbrella. The lightning flashed again followed by another roar of thunder.

Kate thought she spotted someone standing under the streetlight across the street. She blinked and he was gone. She wasn't even sure it was real. It was so fleeting.

Kate inched closer to the window and scanned in both directions. He was down the road now near another light pole. He had a rain slicker buttoned high at his neck and the hood pulled low over his forehead. The build of the man was familiar to her even if she couldn't see his face.

The lightning flashed again, illuminating him. She inched back from the window and slid across the booth, knocking into her server as her feet hit the floor. "Declan will pay you," she yelled too loudly for the restaurant as she moved past the server to the front door. She nearly collided with another who was carrying a full tray of food.

"I'm sorry. Sorry," Kate said as she put her hands on his shoulders to slip past him toward the door. She hit the sidewalk in a run as the rain soaked her hair and clothes. She had to wipe her eyes to see as the rain pelted her. She ran up the sidewalk to where she thought she saw the man across the street but he was gone.

Kate cursed the sky and darted into the road having to stop as a car came toward her. She paused to let it pass and then crossed, running up and down the sidewalk looking into the short alleyways for any sign of him. She ducked her head low like that would help, as the sky lit up with a lightning strike. She was going to get herself killed out there, if not from the lightning then falling on the slick pavement.

Kate stood still for a moment and resisted the urge to scream.

"Kate!" Declan called from the restaurant doorway. "What are you doing?"

She whipped her body around to look at him. "I thought I saw..." Kate didn't know how to finish the sentence. She thought she saw Leo but now she couldn't help but wonder if it was a figment of her imagination. The image of the man was so fleeting and distant in the rain. She could have imagined it was him, standing there staring at her in the restaurant window. If Kate was going to be honest with herself, the man might not have been looking at her at all. He might simply have been caught in the rain and looking for a place to shelter until the storm cleared.

Even so, Kate couldn't shake the feeling she was being watched. Declan called her again and she waved him off. "I'll be right there," she called as she glanced up and down the road one more time. There was no one there.

Kate looked both ways before crossing the street back to Declan. Her hair hung wet and heavy against her shoulders and she was sure all the makeup had been washed from her face. Her clothes felt ten pounds heavier on her body. "Did you pay the bill?" she asked as she stepped under the awning with him.

"It's paid," he assured her as he reached for her shoulders and pulled her close.

"I'll get you all wet." Kate tried to pull back from him but he didn't let go.

"I'm going to get wet as soon as we start walking back. What happened, Kate? Why are you out here in this rain?"

"I thought I saw..." Kate still wasn't sure. "Leo, I guess. There was a man across the street and I was sure it was him. I couldn't see his face though."

Declan glanced up the road. "Did he do something to make you think it was him?"

Kate shook her head. "He was just standing there kind of staring across the street. It was probably all in my imagination."

"I don't think you were imagining it, Kate. If he's here in D.C. and knows that you are too, I'd think he might come looking for you."

Kate pulled her head back to look up into his eyes. "Even after robbing the National Gallery?"

"You have a connection with him, Kate. As much as I'd like to deny that fact, you do." Declan pulled her close again and she wrapped her arms around him, resting her head against his chest. "I don't like admitting it but there's a bond between you. You connected with him immediately and he doesn't strike me as someone who gets close to people."

Kate knew what Declan said was correct. It didn't make it any easier. The man was potentially costing her the only career she'd ever known. "Bond or not, I need to bring him in. If there's any chance of catching him, I wasn't going to let a little rain and lightning stop me."

Declan's chest rose and fell as he laughed. "I applaud your dedication but let's get you back and dried off."

They ran through the wet D.C. streets as the rain pelted down. For some reason, once Kate started running with Declan, she forgot about the rain and about seeing Leo. She ran faster trying to get ahead of him and then he caught up to her, running faster. It pushed her to run even harder. They both laughed at the unintended foot race back to the hotel. The sidewalks were empty giving them a wide path to compete.

It was Declan who reached the hotel door first. When she caught up to him, he wrapped one hand around the door handle and his other arm around her body, pulling her close and up to him. He kissed her passionately, telling her how much he wanted her.

It wasn't anything he needed to say. Kate felt the way his body moved against her and words weren't needed. Still, even in the heat of the moment, she worried who might be watching them. She stepped out of his embrace. "Not here on the street. Not after the hearing this morning. There are too many prying eyes in D.C. to let down our guard."

"I forgot," Declan said and tucked a wet strand of her hair behind her ear. He pulled open the door and they walked into the hotel side by side not touching. He didn't touch her on the walk to the elevator or up to their two-bedroom suite. After she unlocked the door and they stepped into the room out of sight from people in the hall and the cameras, Declan had her in his arms again.

As he walked her back toward the bathroom he peeled her wet shirt over her head and threw it to the floor. He traced a finger over her collarbone and kissed her deeply as he unsnapped her bra. He stopped kissing her long enough to undo the button of her pants as he kicked off his shoes.

Kate made quick work of helping him shed his clothes. Declan only stopped long enough to turn on the bathroom light and the hot water tap in the large walk-in shower. He pulled her in with him and wrapped his arms around her as the hot water poured down over them.

Kate left all the stress of the day and all thoughts of Leo behind.

CHAPTER 8

The next morning Kate sat in the conference room at FBI Headquarters alone. Declan had gone off with Tom to speak to the crime scene techs and left Kate to start her background research. She hoped that in one of the boxes there'd be evidence about where she could find the Phantom. Leo Lamiere was the name he had given her. A family friend had called him Leo, but Kate had no proof that's who he was now. She knew he used aliases. He had told her as much without telling her his other names.

Kate planned to spend the day researching each of his thefts to see if his story of returning Nazi-looted stolen art checked out. It was about his only saving grace if the story was true. First, though, Kate needed to know more about Nazi art theft. It wasn't a subject she had been well versed in.

She had read history books and was familiar with the Nazi practice of stealing art from Jewish families. But that was about as far as her knowledge went. She had never been interested in art theft crimes while at the FBI.

Kate knew the stories that had made the news of descendants suing to get their art back – one of the more famous cases told in the movie *Woman in Gold*. Attorney E. Randol Schoenberg was able to recover Gustav Klimt's famous *Portrait of Adele Bloch-Bauer I* or what was known as the *Golden Lady* painting. He had to sue the Austrian government which had possession of the painting. His client, Maria Altmann, the niece of the woman in the painting, was trying to recover six Klimt paintings stolen from her family home in Austria in 1938. Schoenberg was successful after taking his case to the United States Supreme Court and late arbitration. The painting was eventually returned to her in Los Angeles.

Kate knew it wasn't just governments paying the price. Museums had been harshly criticized through the years for having Nazi-stolen art. While the Louvre had been a target for art theft by both Napolean and Hitler, after the war the museum still had a vast collection of more than seventeen hundred Nazi-looted artworks. It wasn't until 2018 that they started displaying some, around one hundred of these pieces, in a dedicated section. An older news article reported that since 1951, the Louvre had only returned around fifty of the Nazi-looted paintings in its possession. The Louvre wasn't the only museum to have questionable practices in this regard.

Several databases provided the history of art. There was the Lost Art Database which documented cultural property stolen during Nazi persecution, especially from Jewish owners, between 1933 and 1945. Getty Provenance Index also had information for more than 8,700 German sales that took place from 1900 to 1945. More than 830,000 individual auction sales records for paintings, sculptures, and drawings had been extracted from these catalogs.

It took Kate a few more searches until she finally found the information she had been hoping to find. As she started reading, she quickly became overwhelmed by the scale of it all. The Nazis started in Germany in the early 1930s and continued across Europe throughout the war, looting art and objects from homes, galleries, and museums. One report said that Nazis stole more than twenty percent of all the art in Europe during the war and more than one-hundred thousand pieces have never been returned to their rightful owner.

Between 1940 and 1945, Nazis looted around one-hundred thousand works of art in France alone, mostly from Jewish victims of Nazi persecution, whose homes were pillaged during Nazi Germany's occupation of France. For others, they were forced to sell their art to escape or survive. In Poland, the total cost of German Nazi theft and destruction of Polish art is estimated at twenty billion dollars, or an estimated forty-three percent of Polish cultural heritage. More than five hundred individual art pieces were looted and twenty-five museums were destroyed.

The pieces not kept for Hitler's planned museum, including artworks declared to be "degenerate," were sold at auction. The most notorious was organized by Theodor Fischer in 1939 at the Grand Hotel National in Lucerne, Switzerland. That didn't even account for all the private sales of the art and for all of the art that was destroyed – burned like books and Jewish writings. By the end of the war, the Third Reich amassed hundreds of thousands of cultural objects.

The Nazis were notorious record keepers though and the catalogs from these auctions and sales provided critical evidence for prewar ownership as well as clues to their trajectories and even possible current whereabouts. The catalogs included detailed descriptions of the art as well as handwritten notes about sale prices and buyers' names. The information has been a primary source for art historians and investigators.

Kate was overwhelmed by the sheer scale of the looting and by the efforts made after the war to return the art. The Allies created special commissions, such as the Monuments, Fine Arts, and Archives program to help protect famous European monuments from destruction. After the war, these Monuments Men, as they were known, traveled to formerly Nazi-occupied territories to find Nazi art repositories. They were able to recover thousands of pieces.

There was also the Art Looting Investigation Unit, a special intelligence unit during World War II whose mission was to gather information and write reports about Nazi art looting networks. The investigations started in 1944 and were focused in Germany, France, the Netherlands, Switzerland, Italy, Spain and Portugal. From their work, there are known art traders who specialized in Nazi art. These investigation reports were only declassified close to twenty years ago. A final report included roughly a thousand names of art dealers who were red-flagged for their illegal activity. Kate looked up the list and downloaded it. She assumed it might come in handy when researching Leo's thefts.

All in all, Kate realized that it was a global effort to trace and track down Nazi-looted art and it wasn't work that stopped right after the war. It continued well beyond the World War II era.

Even as late as 1998, the Department of State held a conference with the U.S. Holocaust Memorial Museum to come to a federal consensus on how to handle Nazi-Era looted art. The conference was attended by close to fifty countries and thirteen entities. One of the main reasons for the conference was that this art was still being found in U.S. museums from Chicago and Los Angeles to New York. Even the National Gallery of Art in D.C. identified more than four hundred European paintings with gaps in provenance during the World War II era.

After the conference, the Association of Art Museum Directors developed guidelines that required museums to review the provenance or history of their collections, focusing especially on art looted by the Nazis.

Kate sat back and reached for her phone to check the time. More than two hours had passed since she started the research. She resisted the urge to call Declan and check in on him. He was focused on the crime scene evidence and she didn't want to throw him off track.

Kate wanted to dive right into the files and start looking at the history of the artwork Leo had stolen, but she had been considering a phone call she could make to track him down or at the very least leave him a message. Kate hadn't spoken to the young woman since she was in Scotland.

She pulled up the contact for Tara DeBecker, whose sister Amelia was killed by a serial killer in Paris. It was the same killer who brought Kate and Declan to Scotland. Tara called Leo her uncle, even though they were not related by blood. As a child, Leo had befriended Tara's father, Jordan, and they became lifelong friends. Leo was raised by Jordan's family after escaping an abusive step-father. At least that's the story he told Kate and the DeBeckers. She had never been able to verify the details.

The phone rang a few times before the young woman answered. "Tara, this is FBI Agent Kate Walsh. I'm not sure if you remember speaking to me," Kate said, hoping she remembered.

"You solved my sister's murder. I don't think I'll ever forget you. I can't thank you enough for what you did."

Kate smiled with relief. "There's no need to thank me and it's your Uncle Leo you should be thanking. He was an integral part in helping us solve the case." Kate had not told Tara that Leo was an international art thief wanted by countries around the globe. It wasn't her place unless it was necessary to the investigation and right now, she figured she'd get further with a lie.

"Uncle Leo called me when the case ended. He's the one who told me of its resolution. Of course, he was devastated by the outcome."

"He saved my life," Kate said with fondness in her voice that she was surprised wasn't fake. "It's why I'm calling. I'm wondering if you know how to reach him. I can't seem to find his phone number."

Tara didn't even hesitate. "Sure," she said and gave Kate the phone number.

"Do you happen to know where he is? He told me he travels for work. I remember him telling me he had a home there in London, but now I can't recall the address. I want to send him something. With so much on my mind, I can't recall it either." Kate was lying with too much ease. Leo had not told her of any home he owned in London and it was a swing she hoped wasn't a miss.

"It's a hard address to remember." Tara provided that too without questioning Kate. She assumed since she was FBI and Leo had mentioned her name, there was no reason to suspect something was amiss. "Leo hasn't been back in London for a few months, so I'm not sure I'd send it there."

"Is there a better address for him?" Kate asked casually, rather than asking where he was currently. She'd get to that if she had to.

"He has a few homes around the globe he's acquired over the years. I don't have all the addresses."

Kate tsked as if she was disappointed. "Do you know when he'll be back in London?"

"I wish I knew," Tara said with a laugh. "One of the bakery ovens isn't working and I could use his skills to fix it. I texted him last night but haven't heard back yet. I can ask him to call you when he has the time. His schedule is so sporadic, sometimes he shows up here unannounced and other times I have to wait months before he's back."

The timing was suspicious. "You don't know where he was going when he left there last?"

"He never said. I learned a long time ago not to ask. It's not that he wouldn't tell me. There's just no point. Uncle Leo is constantly on the go. I don't think I could keep up with him if I tried." Tara shouted to one of her employees that she'd be right there. To Kate, she said, "We are in the process of closing up for the night."

"I didn't mean to keep you. I hope you're doing well." Kate didn't want to press her for any more information about Leo and raise her suspicions. Tara had provided enough for the time being. Kate didn't want to burn the source unless she had to.

"Thanks, Kate. If I hear from Uncle Leo, I'll mention you are looking for him, but I won't mention you're going to send him something. He does so much for everyone else, it's lovely that you want to surprise him." Tara ended the call and told Kate she'd stay in touch.

Kate looked over at the boxes of evidence of Leo's crimes. She was sure it would devastate Tara to know who Leo was and the things he'd been doing for all these years. There was one other contact she could try.

"Kate Walsh," Sam Harris said with a lightness to his voice. He was an inspector with the National Crime Agency in London, which was similar to the FBI. Kate had spoken to him a few times after their return from London. They had developed a friendly professional rapport and he was one of only a handful of people who knew the name Leo Lamiere.

Kate briefly explained the case. "I spoke to Tara DeBecker. She gave me Leo's cellphone number and an address in London. I was hoping you could check it out for me."

"She gave it over willingly?" Sam seemed surprised Kate would be able to access it so easily.

"She thinks Leo and I are friendly since the case in Scotland. I think he's mentioned me to her a few times. I told her I wanted to send him something for saving my life."

Sam chuckled. "I can see you being friends with an international art thief. That tracks."

Kate knew he was teasing her but there was a truth to it. "I was hoping you could go alone and snoop around. For all I know, Leo might not live there anymore."

"I'll go this evening and get back to you with anything I can find out. Do you think we should watch the bakery to see if we can pick him up?"

Kate had been wondering that herself. "It doesn't sound like he's there all that frequently. I'd say sporadic stop-ins at best. I'd hate to run through your resources like that."

"I probably wouldn't get approval anyway. Let me see what I can find out." Sam grew quiet for a moment and then said, "I know it's going to be hard to bring him in. It's hard arresting someone who saved your life. Just remember one good act doesn't erase all the bad ones."

Kate thanked him for the reminder as they ended the call.

CHAPTER 9

Kate took a quick break to walk down the street from FBI Headquarters to grab a cup of coffee and snack at a local bakery. She had been stuck in the conference room for so long that she needed to stretch her legs.

The rain that had been torrential the night before had turned into a light mist by morning. Now the sun was trying to peak through the clouds and the weather had warmed slightly. As Kate entered the shop, her phone chimed with a text. She waited until she was in line to read it. Kate assumed it was going to be an update from Declan. When she saw the number Tara provided, Kate steadied herself.

She clicked the text to read the full message. *I heard you're looking for me. Is everything okay?*

It was a simple message but the fact that he reached out so quickly meant Tara had called and told him as she said she would. It also meant Leo was willing to communicate with her. Kate couldn't deny that there seemed to be genuine concern for her in the message.

Kate got out of line and went to a table in the back of the shop away from other customers. She needed a quiet place to think through her response and fight the immediate desire to ask him if he committed the theft at the National Gallery.

Kate typed one message then deleted it. She tried again.

I'm in Washington D.C. There's been a theft at the National Gallery of

Art. Declan and I were assigned to the case. I need to know if... Kate left it at that. She didn't want to outright accuse him and left it open for him to decide himself what he'd tell her.

His response was quick. *I saw that on the news. It wasn't me, Kate. The Curators are no more.*

What does that mean, Leo? You disbanded? Kate had no idea what he meant. She knew there had been a faction of his crew that had grown tired of him trying to track down the serial killer who had killed Amelia.

Leo responded after a few minutes. The text was longer than the rest. *After I returned from Scotland, I had a mess to clean up, as you know. Those whose loyalty I no longer had were dealt with. The few remaining with me are my age and we knew our time had come to put our mission to rest. This kind of theft is not an old man's game, Kate. I'll be forty-nine soon. I can't do what I did in my twenties or even thirties.*

Kate wanted to press him on that statement. The FBI only had information on crimes going back a decade. That would put him in his late thirties and here he was saying he did this in his twenties. They had no record of it. Of course, the only crimes attributed to them were the ones the Curators had indicated by leaving a calling card. *The man who tried to shoot me in Paris and I spoke to in Edinburgh...is he dead?*

Yes. He cannot hurt you. I told you I'd protect you and wouldn't let him hurt anyone else.

Kate felt immediate relief at that. She knew the FBI agent in her should have cared that Leo or someone close to him had committed a murder but she was hard-pressed to care. *Where are you?*

You know I cannot tell you.

Kate hadn't thought he'd tell her. She still had to try. *Whoever stole the painting at the National Gallery of Art killed three people and left a calling card indicating it was done by the Curators. Is it possible any of the men on your crew committed this crime?*

NO! Leo's response was immediate and definitive. He didn't bother to explain the card.

Kate reiterated the point. *There was a card saying it was the Curators. Was it blue with white lettering and also included The Phantom under The Curators?*

This was information that had not been released to the news and had not been made public in any way. There were only a handful of people at the FBI who knew, other than the thief. *Yes. How did you know that?*

Leo had a question of his own. *Did you find a King of Diamonds at the National Gallery?*

Do you mean a King of Diamonds from a card deck?

Yes.

No. Why? Kate went into her recent texts and pulled up Declan's contact. She sent him a text asking him if a King of Diamonds had been found.

It's a lot to explain, Leo responded, leaving Kate feeling like he was dismissing her.

Explain, Leo.

Kate waited for several minutes for Leo to explain. Declan's text came in first, confirming that no King of Diamonds had been found among the evidence. He asked why, but Kate didn't have a response for him.

She sat staring at her phone, growing frustrated with Leo's lack of response. She cursed and texted Leo again. *I confirmed no King of Diamonds has been found.*

Leo finally texted. *Go back to the National Gallery and search. If you find it, I'll explain.*

It was a massive space. Kate wouldn't even know where to start if she wanted to. *Where do we start?*

Look where Gabriel Baptiste was murdered.

His name had not been on the news, so Kate was surprised Leo knew the name. *Did you know him?*

We knew each other. His work was like none other.

There was a subtext there that Leo wasn't saying. *Why did they kill him?*

Find the card, Kate. Then we'll talk more.

Kate cursed loudly, drawing the ire from a young mother with her child at the nearby table. Kate mouthed an apology and the mother went back to tending her child. *I thought I saw you last night. Are you in Washington D.C.?*

No. Do what you do best and get back to me.

Did you warn Mick Sutton?

No more questions, Kate.

Kate cursed again, under her breath this time. She forgot all about the coffee and snack as she raced out of the bakery and headed back toward the National Gallery. She called Declan on her way and told him to meet her with whoever he could round up from Tom's team. She'd explain when they arrived. He didn't question her and assured Kate he'd be there.

She arrived at the front security desk of the National Gallery out of breath and panting. The gallery had remained closed but the cops still stationed at the door provided her access. Marcy had questioned the need for it to remain closed another day. Kate was glad now they had insisted. The gallery was so large and the crime scene so vast they had wanted to make sure they wouldn't have to return for any reason after it re-opened. The last thing they needed was visitors trampling over potential evidence.

After Kate caught her breath, she went directly to Marcy's office. This time she wouldn't allow the woman to be with them during the search. She wanted to let Marcy know they were there and tell her to remain in her office.

When Kate arrived at the office, Marcy was nowhere to be found. While the FBI had asked that no other staff come to the National Gallery, they had not banned Marcy from coming in. Kate hoped that hadn't been a mistake. She went back to the lobby to wait.

Declan and Tom arrived together moments later. They looked equally rushed and out of breath.

Kate was quick to provide the information, even to Tom. "I was able to get a number for Leo Lamiere, otherwise known as the Phantom, but before I could reach out he texted me."

Declan seemed nonplussed by the admission, but Tom's face contorted wildly in excitement. "You have his name?"

Kate shook her head. "I assume it's an alias. It's what he told us to call him, but he uses aliases frequently."

Tom understood that. "We can trace his cellphone. Did you try to set up a meeting with him?"

Kate held her hand up to slow him down. "You're certainly welcome to try. My guess is it's untraceable. I did not try to set up a meeting with him. Catching him is not going to be that easy. He gives information slowly and at his pace. I gave a London address to my contact in the city who is going to check it out tonight."

"Sam Harris?" Declan asked.

Kate confirmed. "He said he's going to go by the address and see what he can find. That said, Leo told me that the Curators have disbanded and—"

"You don't believe him, do you?" Tom asked, his voice raising an octave and speaking over Kate.

She sighed. "I need you to calm down. I know this is the best lead we've ever had. I have a line of communication open with him and he's given us a potential clue in this investigation. Let's see what pans out here and go from there." She saw the skeptical look on Tom's face.

"My future with the FBI depends on bringing the Phantom in, so trust me when I say I'm going to do that."

Declan slapped Tom on the back in a sign of encouragement. "We can do that, Kate. What's with the King of Diamonds?"

"Leo asked me if we found the card here at the crime scene. I told him we hadn't and he told me to go search. He didn't tell me what it meant. I don't think he will unless we find the card."

Tom didn't seem to understand. "You trust him so much you're going to let him jerk you around like this?"

"He saved my life," Kate said her tone strong and clear. "If Leo said to look for the King of Diamonds that's what I'm going to do. He also described the Curators' card that was left. Those details have not been on the news at all. There's no way he would have known it."

"Unless he's the one who left it." Tom looked between them like they'd both lost their minds. "Declan, you're buying this?"

"Let's wait and see where this goes," Declan said cautiously. "While we were in Edinburgh, Kate developed a good rapport with Leo. If there's no King of Diamonds, we can dismiss it and refocus on the Curators. If there is one, then we need to pivot."

Kate appreciated Declan's cooler head about the situation. "Did you bring anyone else with you to search?" She didn't need an answer to the question because a moment later, a swath of FBI agents and local uniformed cops arrived at the door and Declan let them in. As all twenty of them gathered in the lobby, Kate explained what they needed to find. She also explained that Marcy wasn't in her office and should they find her somewhere in the gallery, they needed to direct her back to her office. They were not to tell Marcy about the playing card.

"Will you search with me?" Kate asked Declan as the rest of them dispersed.

"I assumed I would." They waited there until everyone was gone.

Then Declan lowered his voice. "What's going on, Kate? I backed you up with Tom but what do you mean you were in contact with Leo? I didn't know that you had given him your phone number."

Kate explained her call to Tara in detail. "She's a good source for us. Sam is headed to the address in London. When she asked me if she should tell Leo I was trying to get in contact with him, I said yes. He texted me right away, Declan. Not more than ten minutes had passed. He still trusts me. We can use that to bring him in."

"Do you believe what he said about the Curators?"

Kate shrugged because she didn't have a better response. "I know that his crew was unhappy and it created a great divide among his men. It stands to reason some splintered off and there were ones who were disloyal."

"That he killed or had killed," Declan said, leveling a look at her.

Kate didn't know what to say. She was walking a fine line even with Declan. "I don't know the details and I didn't ask. He said the man who wanted to kill me in Paris is dead. As for the rest of them, I don't know. Leo said his age and the age of some of his other men were a factor."

Declan scoffed in disbelief. "The man was more jacked than I am and he has ten years on me."

Kate sighed. "Do we have to argue about this now? Leo gave me a tip and I'm going to follow it. If we find the King of Diamonds, then he said he'd give me more information. I assume he knows something we don't."

"That's usually how it is." Declan ran a hand through his hair and looked across the lobby. "Did he give you any idea where to search?"

"Gabriel Baptiste's studio." Kate had intentionally held that information back.

"Does Leo know him?"

"I guess so," Kate said not standing around any longer. She crossed the lobby to the door to the basement knowing Declan would catch up.

CHAPTER 10

Gabriel's basement space looked like a typical artist's studio. There were blank canvasses, wooden easels, and paints of various shades and brands. A wooden table pushed up against a wide wall contained a myriad of brushes, more than Kate had ever seen in one place.

In the back was scaffolding and a covered painting hung on the wall. Marcy had told them it was one of the larger and oldest paintings in the museum and needed considerable restoration work. Gabriel had been working on it for the past five months.

While there was one other art restorationist and several others involved in preservation, Gabriel was the one who handled the most demanding and difficult jobs. Marcy had described him as a bit temperamental and persnickety. It didn't surprise Kate given the job. He was an artist in his own right and had gallery showings nationally and abroad. Marcy said Gabriel didn't need the job but that he had such a love for the art that his passion was restoration – a job that took precision, talent, and a level of artistry few had.

"I still don't understand why someone killed him, Kate." Declan stood in the middle of the room with his hands on his hips staring at the scaffolding and covered painting. "I spoke to the medical examiner this morning and Gabriel had one shot to the back and the kill shot to the chest. It appeared he might have been trying to run."

She agreed with Declan. "The chair has me thrown off. Why would this random chair be tipped over in the middle of the room?"

Declan didn't know. "Did Leo tell you where in this studio you'd find the card?"

"He wasn't that specific," Kate said, taking one side of the room while Declan went to the other. There were cabinets and shelves and more than a few places where the card could have been placed. She assumed if the thief had wanted the card found he'd have placed it somewhere easily seen. The fact that he was leaving a card like that was telling. He wanted to mark his crime like the Curators had. But the Curators never hid the card.

Kate searched from the tops of the shelves to the floor. She had to pull over a step ladder to see the highest shelves that were filled with painting supplies all organized and labeled. Gabriel had been meticulous with the care and organization of his instruments.

"Did you find anything?" Declan called over to her as they both made their way toward the back of the room.

"Nothing." Kate had a feeling the card might be near the painting Gabriel had been working on, but it was going to be hard to access. She wanted to rule everything else out first before climbing up there. They searched in silence in every corner of the studio but found nothing.

Declan groaned as he stood from a crouched position and looked over at Kate. "Is there any chance Leo is lying to you?"

"I can't rule out Leo is lying to me," Kate responded evenly. "But he has no reason to waste our time. Whoever killed those guards and Gabriel got out of here easily. If it was Leo, he could be halfway around the globe by now. I don't see why he'd send us on a wild goose chase."

"For fun?" Declan asked but he didn't even sound convinced. When he saw the frustrated look on Kate's face, he let the subject drop. He hitched his chin toward the massive, covered painting. "That's all we have left to search. The killer would have had to climb up there. Do you think he'd take the time to do that after killing Gabriel?"

"It depends how important it was to leave the card." Kate was having trouble processing the hidden nature of it. Most killers who leave a mark want it known. They don't hide it away unless it is some kind of compulsion. As Kate started to climb the scaffolding beside Declan, she had another thought. "What if he is leaving the card not for the cops to find but someone else?"

Declan didn't respond until he was up on the landing. He stepped around the dried paint from a can that had tipped over and pulled Kate up with him. "Are you suggesting he left a secret code to someone else?"

"I don't know that I'd call it a secret code." If Leo hadn't told her about it, even if they had found a playing card at the crime scene, she didn't think they would have paid much attention to it. "Maybe he's leaving it to alert someone to something."

Declan smiled. "So, a secret code."

Kate ignored him and turned to the painting. "This looks intimidating. The last thing I want to do is knock it down and destroy it."

Declan sat down on the landing and let his legs dangle below. He carefully pulled up the white canvas from one side and told Kate to look at the other. They were working at the bottom of the painting, which would have been the only thing the killer would have been able to reach.

Kate slowly pulled back the corner of the canvas and inched her way toward Declan as he did the same. They pulled up the whole bottom of the canvas until Kate yelled for Declan to stop.

"Right here," she said and reached toward the painting. Tucked into the bottom of the frame was the King of Diamonds. Kate pulled out her cellphone and took a photo of it before catching the corner of it with her gloved finger. Pulling it off was another story. The backing of it was stuck to the painting. The killer must have put the card in wet paint. She turned her head to look at Declan. "What do I do? If I rip this off, it's going to damage the painting. I don't want to tell Marcy until we know more."

Declan shrugged and didn't know any better than Kate what to do. "Pull it gently. I'm sure that this painting will need continued restoration."

Kate didn't think potentially destroying artwork was the answer. Then again, she didn't know what else to do. Kate slipped her finger under the edge of the card and tugged it gently back, pulling the card and a little paint with it. She got it free of the painting and the frame firmly in her hand as she surveyed the damage to the painting. Other than a little tiny smudge there wasn't any damage. She assumed it could easily be fixed when the next person worked on the painting.

"Got it?" Declan asked, slowly lowering the canvas back in place.

"I have it." Kate studied the card. Other than the smudge mixed into the red of the card, it looked like any other King of Diamonds. There was no additional message on it except for the card itself. Kate got herself into a squat and stood. The scaffolding swayed a bit under their weight and she resisted the urge to lean forward for support. "Let's get down from here. I don't know how Gabriel or anyone else works like this all day. I don't feel stable on my feet."

Declan climbed down first then held his hands out to steady Kate as she climbed down. Not that she needed the help but Kate noticed that since they had started sleeping together, he'd paid extra attention to the ways she might need help.

At first, it annoyed her, but once she settled into the feeling, Kate realized how kind the gestures truly were. Kate got her feet to the floor and handed Declan the card. "We can call off the rest of the search and get this back to the lab."

Declan examined the card and then slipped it into the evidence bag. "While I'm here, I want to check out a few things."

They had only explored this room with Marcy, and Declan hadn't had time to explore the angles of the room and see in his mind's eye how the killer had approached Gabriel. After looking at the photos of the crime scene and now being in the room, she was sure Declan might have a perspective on it.

There was a thick spot of dried blood on the floor in front of the scaffolding where Gabriel's body was found. He had a paint brush still clutched in his fist. The theory was that either he had been forced down from the scaffolding or he'd come down on his own and then confronted the killer. The chair was tipped over not far from where his body had been found. The back had blood and chipped wood from the bullet. Gabriel had been sitting when he was shot.

Kate stood out of the way while Declan walked the scene. Declan walked to the door, disappeared from view, then came back a few moments later. She stood in the doorway staring toward the scaffolding.

Declan stood with his hands on his hips. "I don't think he was shot immediately. If Gabriel was up on the scaffolding, the killer could have easily walked by this room without Gabriel even knowing."

"He might have been off the scaffolding though and facing the door."

"That's possible," Declan said absently as he continued his search. He went to a workstation not far from the door. There was a fine layer of dust over it. Declan stared down at it. "Come over here, Kate, and tell me what you see."

She crossed the room and looked down at the table. Kate didn't see it at first but as she focused her eyes it became apparent. "There's an outline of a frame in the dust. This bench doesn't look like it's used all that frequently, but I'm surprised there's any dust at all. Don't most of these rooms have to remain clean given the work they are doing?"

"I would think so, which begs the question of where did the dust come from, why wasn't it cleaned, and what was on this table." Declan took out his phone and snapped several photos of the area. "I saw a tape measure over on the shelf up there. Can you grab it for me?"

Kate crossed the room and grabbed the tape measure. "Isn't it possible that the crime scene techs got some dust on the table while they were looking for evidence?"

"Possible." Declan didn't sound convinced. "This could mean nothing at all. It just strikes me as odd and I want to get the evidence while we can." He measured the dimensions of the frame that had been imprinted in the borders of the dust. "What was the measurement of the painting?"

Kate recalled the details as best she could. "We'll have to refer to the report, but I believe it's two feet in height and one foot across. Marcy said it was in a heavy gold frame."

"Gold frame?" Declan asked, shifting his eyes back to the side of the room that he had searched.

"That's right. Why?"

Declan didn't tell her. He finished the measurement and left the tape measure. He went to where he had searched before and dug through a thick canvas on the floor. Kate thought it had just been a pile of cloth. She had no idea anything was under there until Declan pulled out a broken gold frame. It was heavy and ornate. "Like this?" he asked, holding it up.

Kate had a photo of the original *Lady in the Field* painting from when it was hanging on the wall of the gallery. She carried her phone over to show Declan while she looked at the details on the frame. "This looks like it could be it, Declan. I don't understand though. The crime scene techs went through this room and didn't find anything. Are you suggesting they missed it?"

"Maybe they didn't know what they were looking for at the time.

There's enough art supplies in here and other frames, this might not have jumped out at them." Declan glanced around the space again. "There's something not adding up for me and I can't quite put my finger on it." He went to the table and held it above the area he had measured. "It fits."

"Do you think someone hid the frame after the fact?"

Declan wasn't sure. "No one has been here other than Marcy." He handed the frame to Kate and walked toward the door. "There's still something about all of this that doesn't add up for me."

Kate wasn't sure of the explanation. "Let's get this evidence taken care of and we can come back and figure it out."

CHAPTER 11

By the time they made it back to the lobby, most of the uniformed cops had searched their assigned areas and left the National Gallery. Marcy stood with Tom in the middle of the lobby, demanding to know what was going on.

"We had a tip about some additional evidence," Kate said as she joined them. She followed Marcy's eyes to the frame in Declan's hands. "Is this the frame for *Lady in the Field*?"

"It looks like it." Marcy took a few steps toward Declan and examined the frame. "Where did you find it?"

"In Gabriel's studio," Declan said. "Do you have any idea why this frame would be hidden under a pile of canvas in the studio?"

"I have no idea. I thought the FBI searched everywhere for it."

"We did," Tom said, chiming in. He looked down at the frame and couldn't seem to make sense of it. "Once we had details about the missing painting, we scoured the National Gallery with a full team of people. No stone was unturned, so to speak."

Declan understood how they might have missed it. "There were other frames nearby. It could have gotten mixed in with the others and no one noticed since they were looking for a painting rather than an empty frame."

Tom didn't have an explanation. "It's possible," he conceded. "Did you find anything else?"

Kate knew what he was referencing. "There were some anomalies in the studio that we need to explore further," was all she'd say before turning her attention to Marcy. "I assume the studio would need to be kept clean. Is it fair to say that?"

Marcy nodded. "Gabriel was fastidious about it. Anyone in that position would be. Is there a reason you're asking?"

"There was a fine layer of dust on one of the worktables. The one closest to the door. It looked like the frame had been set down and the thief took out the painting and tossed the frame there."

"It would be easier to carry that way," Marcy explained. "Does it matter when we know the painting is still stolen and three people are dead?"

"The sequence of events matters greatly. The biggest question I have right now is if Gabriel was killed before or after the painting was stolen. If it was after, did he participate in the theft and his partner shot him before leaving?"

Marcy put her hand up to her neck and swallowed hard. "I can't imagine Gabriel would ever be involved in something like that."

"There was no forced entry," Declan reminded her. "The door in the basement goes to the outside and you don't need a key to leave but you need a key to enter. Unless Gabriel left that door open or he let him in, I'm not sure how the thief accessed the building. But it's a straight shot up the stairs to the security desk. All they had to do was open that door a crack and shoot whoever was at that desk. They didn't even need to show themselves."

"I don't know what to say," she said finally. "It's hard to fathom Gabriel would be involved in anything like this. I don't have any explanation."

Kate wasn't expecting her to. "We'll be in touch."

"Can we reopen tomorrow?" Marcy asked as they headed toward the front door.

"No," Kate and Declan said at the same time and then shared a look. Kate turned back. "Given what we found today, I think we need another day or two. Give us a week and then you can reopen."

Marcy's face contorted in shock. "An entire week? That's not possible. Agent Coburn said—"

"You don't have a choice," Declan reminded her, leveling her a look. "I think given the new dynamics of the investigation, even Agent Coburn would agree more time is warranted."

"It certainly is," he said, joining Kate and Declan at the front door. None of them were going to give an inch.

It wasn't until they were on the sidewalk in front of the National Gallery that Kate revealed they had found the King of Diamonds. She held the evidence bag up for him to see. "I don't know what it means. I'm going to text Leo and see what he can tell me. You're welcome to be there when I do."

They arrived back at FBI Headquarters and Declan left with Tom to process the new evidence. They wanted to be there for Kate's conversation with Leo and told her to give them twenty minutes.

Kate thought she could give them the time, but her patience was razor thin. She held out for ten minutes before she sat down and texted Leo. *I found the King of Diamonds. What does it mean?*

Then she waited sixteen minutes for a response. Kate knew exactly how long because she barely moved her eyes from her phone as she waited for the response.

There was a private collector in Paris who had two paintings stolen worth close to eight million and then a collector in Berlin who had a painting stolen worth three million. With each theft, the King of Diamonds was left.

Kate wished she could sit down and have a conversation with Leo rather than do this over text. *When here those thefts and how did you become aware of them?*

Four months ago, Kate. The private collector in Paris is one of my clients.

He called me instead of the cops and told me about the King of Diamonds. I thought it was a fluke at first. Then I heard through the rumor mill about the theft in Berlin and again the King of Diamonds was left. On that robbery, he also left the Curators' card. That's how word got back to me. It wasn't us though. I swear that to you, Kate. But I think they are trying to get my attention.

Kate had a rush of questions come to mind but she resisted the urge to ask everything at once. She had to slow down or she'd scare him off. *Client in Paris? Had you stolen for him before?*

No. My other work.

What other work? You told me about the Nazi-looted art, but I never fully understood how it worked or how you made money.

Someday we will talk about it all.

Not someday, Leo. Now. The FBI believes you are responsible for the theft and murders at the National Gallery of Art. I've been tasked to bring you in. My job is on the line if I fail.

It would be easier for us if you were not a cop.

Kate could see where he might think that. She was surprised he didn't say anything about her having to bring him in. *Do you know who is committing these thefts?*

No.

Do you know someone who might be the King of Diamonds?

Leo responded quickly. *Years ago I knew a man who called himself the Diamond King. He traded blood diamonds and stolen antiquities. He's been dead for twenty years.*

Leo had so many more connections in that world that Kate knew she needed his help. *Are you going to try to find out who is doing this?*

You are one of only a handful of people who even know my identity. There is no reputation to protect. I have never killed anyone during a robbery and I never would. My stealing days are over. Someone else can carry on my work – it should have been governments, museums, and galleries doing the right thing all along. If they had, I never would have had a mission to complete.

Do you think your mission is complete now?

There are other things that take my focus now.

It sounded to Kate like he was giving up. *I'm sitting in a conference room with boxes of evidence from your thefts, Leo. They only go back a decade. When was your first theft?*

Kate, you know I cannot admit such things to you, especially after you said you must arrest me. I will not spend the rest of my life behind bars for doing the right thing. That I can assure you.

At least tell me you've been doing this for more than a decade.

That is true.

Why suddenly start leaving a card behind? You got away with it long before anyone had ever heard of the Curators.

Protection. If anyone ever needed to connect my thefts then they'd all be connected and law enforcement would know what I was really stealing – Nazi-looted art. I was doing the right thing, Kate. I also wanted those who I had stolen from to know they weren't getting away with their war crimes. It was time for them to pay.

How did you first get started? Kate had to admit to herself she was more interested in his past than was professionally advisable.

As you know my mother's husband was Lucien Lamiere. His chateau had Nazi-looted art. He was proud of it and would brag often about how his family had come into possession of it. His father was a Nazi sympathizer and helped them with passage to South America after the war. The family was a recipient of much artwork from their Nazi friends. It was a source of pride for him to show it off. I was sickened by it. I hated him more.

Kate was riveted by the story and kept having to remind herself that it could be just a story. None of these facts she had confirmed yet. Kate also knew Leo had fled to London on his own when he was young. It sounded to her that stealing Nazi-looted art was a direct rebellion against his new family. *Did you ever steal anything from him?*

He was my first, Kate. I went back to the chateau and broke in while he was on a trip. I stole Lucien's three most prized paintings and gave them back to their rightful owners. Much to my surprise, they paid me. I refused the money at first but they insisted and promised to keep my secret. I never told them my name or anything about me and they didn't ask. They put me in touch with others who wanted me to do the same thing for them. It paid exceptionally well. I was highly motivated by the mission and I was an exceptional thief. When it became too much to do on my own, I found others who were like-minded. That's how the Curators was born. Later, when I grew more confident, I wanted the world to know that someone was still keeping score of their war crimes and misdeeds.

She had wanted the backstory and he provided it. *No one knew the real reason for your thefts, Leo. I never heard about it until you told me directly.*

Yes, Kate, but the right people knew. The people who were getting their family treasures back knew. Most importantly, those who I retrieved the artwork from knew the meaning of the Curators. That's all that was important to me.

Kate resisted the urge to dig open one of the boxes and get down and dirty in the details of a particular theft. Instead, she had an important question. *I asked you once before and you didn't respond. Did you warn Mick Sutton?*

Yes. There have been rumors for months that there was a new thief on the scene looking to target the Chevalier paintings. It seems the rumors were true. I've met Mick Sutton once or twice – he does not know me as the Phantom. He was a good man who showed me kindness once. I returned the favor.

At least that was answered. Kate still needed his help but she was more focused on what he was going to do now. *Aren't you going to be bored in retirement? I'm sure finding your clients, investigating the artwork, planning and committing the theft then making the delivery had to consume all of your time. What will you do now?*

I'm old and my body feels it. I'm taking time off and I have enough to keep me busy for the rest of my life.

Don't you want to stop this King of Diamonds, particularly if they are blaming you?

I don't think he's trying to blame me. I think he's trying to get my attention. I don't care if he's caught or not. That's your job. Not mine.

He's killed people, Leo. How can you not care?

I care the way people care about things they see on the news that don't impact them directly. There's a blip of interest and empathy and then I go make a cup of coffee and the details leave me minutes later. It's how the world works.

He had Kate there. He had helped her in Edinburgh because it had been personal to him. She had hoped he'd help her again. *Do you know anything about him that can help me catch him?*

I don't think you'll catch him.

Why?

He's better than me. There is no way possible to steal from my client's house. He has staff and security cameras and guards all over the place. Yet, this King of Diamonds managed to slip in, steal two paintings, leave the playing card, and slip back out unnoticed. The same with the private collector in Germany. The man is a master and I don't think you'll be able to stop him. We'll talk again later. I must go now.

Kate tried to text him again but there was no response. There was still so much more she needed to know. She had not even had the chance to find out how Gabriel might have played into the whole situation.

By the time Tom and Declan got back, Kate was sitting staring at her phone, unsure of their next move.

CHAPTER 12

"Sorry we took so long," Declan said as he sat down at the conference table. "We were having the techs dust the card and the frame for fingerprints but both were wiped clean." He looked down at Kate's phone. "Did you already text Leo?"

"I tried to wait but I wanted to see what he knew." Kate recounted what Leo told her about the thefts in Paris and Berlin. "They were private collectors. No one was killed, thankfully. Leo's client called him before he called the cops. I assume there could be a record of it with law enforcement in Paris and Berlin." She turned to Tom. "Do you have contacts in their art theft units?"

"I have contacts and I can make the calls." His expression said he wasn't buying Leo's story. "I appreciate you have a bond with him. Don't you think though that he might just be changing what he's doing to throw people off?"

That didn't make any sense to Kate. Even if she wanted to believe it had been Leo, the evidence didn't match up. "He's not going to leave a Curators' card that looks nothing like the cards he's been leaving for the past ten years and then slip a King of Diamonds in another painting near a murder victim. That doesn't make a whole lot of sense to me. He's not going to hide that card and then tell me about it."

"Maybe he's a narcissist and into mind games."

Kate had a master's in forensic psychology. She was not easily fooled and could spot a narcissist a mile away. Leo wasn't that. "You're going to have to trust me on this but that's not Leo's personality." She raised her eyes to Declan, but he couldn't read her mind. She looked back at Tom. "There's also the fact that *Lady in the Field* is not Nazi-looted art."

Tom pulled back in a question. "What do you mean?"

Over the next twenty minutes, Kate laid out Leo's history as she knew it. She told Tom about his background with Lucien, the Lamiere family history she just learned, and Leo fleeing France to live on the streets in London. She even told Tom about Leo being taken in by Jordan DeBecker.

"Leo admitted to me his first crime was long before the records you have. He stole from his step-father Lucien. I assume he researched the history of the artwork he stole to figure out who the rightful owners were and he returned it. From there, they connected him with others who paid him to steal other works of art. Leo told me everything he's ever stolen was Nazi-looted art that he returned to its rightful owners."

Tom furrowed his brow as if he didn't understand. "What about all the museums?"

Kate gestured toward her laptop. "Look it up for yourself. All of them are filled with Nazi-looted art. We have ten years' worth of Leo's crimes. Let's dig in and start confirming his story."

"What will that change?" Tom asked, looking across the table at Declan and then back at Kate.

"I don't know what it will change. It will make Leo a different kind of criminal and not one who'd go into the National Gallery of Art and kill two guards and Gabriel Baptiste, who Leo said was a friend." Kate didn't wait for either of them to confirm it was a good idea. She got up from the table and walked around the other side to the first box. She flipped off the lid, pulled out a file, and looked over at Tom. "Has the

FBI ever compared all the art the Curators were accused of stealing?"

Tom looked embarrassed to admit that they hadn't. "Our cases were a matter of finding the man rather than exploring the crimes, which seemed fairly cut and dry to us. As you know he never left physical evidence behind. There were no witnesses. He was never seen on camera and there were no sales of the stolen art on the black market. To this day, we haven't been able to figure out how the Curators made any money. If they can't move what they steal, we didn't know what they were doing with it and that's been a global effort, Kate."

Kate knew all of that. She felt like she had been studying Leo more than she had studied any other criminal they had encountered. The biggest challenge for all law enforcement across the globe was not only what the Curators did with the art and how they made money, but figuring out who the Phantom was and how he had remained so elusive.

She shook the file in her hand. "Let's figure out if Leo is telling us the truth. If he is, then we can safely assume he didn't commit the theft at the National Gallery of Art and we can turn in another direction."

Tom gestured toward the boxes. "Even if we confirm everything Leo said, we can't rule him out from this case, Kate."

Declan had heard enough. He stood to his full height, stretched his arms overhead, and yawned loudly. "We don't know what we don't know. The only way to find out is to dig in and do what Kate said. We can argue about the National Gallery later. Let's see which side of the law Leo has been on."

"He's still a thief and needs to be held accountable," Tom countered as he reached across the table and grabbed one of the boxes.

"Maybe," Declan said, surprising Kate. "It might also mean all Leo was doing was finishing what we, and I mean the collective global community, should have finished all those years ago. At the end of the day, we might just figure out that the Phantom and his mighty

Curators were heroes."

If they had been alone in their hotel, Kate might have stopped work and kissed him. She wasn't sure he had ever looked more attractive to her. Declan had a way of holding back, assessing, and then saying the right thing at the right time. Kate knew she was looking at Declan with a mix of lust and admiration and she didn't even care if Tom noticed.

As they sat down at the table, Declan sat next to her and rested one hand on her thigh. He gave it an affectionate squeeze but didn't lift his eyes from the file. They worked like that for a long time. Declan would only lift his hand long enough to turn a page in the file then return it to her leg. At one point, Kate put her hand on top of his and Declan turned his head slightly and smiled at her. It was a simple exchange but the meaning was clear – no matter what she was going to do in this case or with Leo, he had her back.

Tom seemed oblivious to it all. With each case they explored, they confirmed that the painting's provenance was either fuzzy during the World War II years or it had a direct tie to the Nazis. While Kate felt relief that Leo had not been lying to her, Tom seemed to grow more agitated.

It wasn't easy work by any stretch and they had only made it through a handful of the cases by early evening. When Kate didn't think she could sit still anymore, she closed the file. "I think we can probably call it for the night."

If the file Tom had been holding had been a door, when he slammed the cover closed the whole room might have shaken. Instead, there was a swift rush of air.

"What's wrong with you?" Declan asked as he slipped the file he'd been reviewing back into the box. When Tom looked over at him but didn't say a word, Declan didn't let it go. "I don't understand what your problem is. Let's clear the air now before we leave for tonight."

Tom sat back in the chair and folded his arms over his chest. "How could we have missed this all these years? Then Kate has a handful of conversations and he spills his guts. It doesn't add up."

"We miss things all the time, Tom." Declan eased himself back into the chair. "This doesn't reflect badly on you if that's what you're worried about. The whole world missed this."

Kate understood it was more than what the art theft unit had missed. She lowered her voice. "Tom, listen, I understand what it's like when you want someone to be the bad guy. I hated the Phantom for what he did to me in Paris. He tricked me in a café and then took me hostage. I was angry at myself that I could have missed it. I chatted with the man like he was any other guy. I had no idea he was the infamous Phantom. I had him right in my hands on that rooftop and he escaped. I was disgusted with myself, and then him for getting away. When I saw him in Edinburgh, I chased him through the city streets. Had we been in the United States and I could have used my gun, I would have either had him on the ground in handcuffs or I might have shot him."

Tom brushed her off. "You don't need to say all that."

Kate raised her voice. "I'm not saying it to make you feel better. I would have shot him. I was in that cemetery and all I wanted to do was shoot him. The anger bubbled up inside me but then curiosity got the better of me. I don't know how exactly it started happening but he started confiding in me. We needed each other and I had to let down my guard. It caused him to let down his guard. When I heard that he robbed the National Gallery of Art, rage burned in me again. There's still a part of me that doesn't trust what he told me. It's why I needed to sit here and go through these files. I understand how you're feeling to have wanted this man captured for so long and the frustration of not being able to find him. It's hard to learn he might not be as bad as you once thought. It's a tough mental transition to make. It can play mind games with you. Just give it time and let it settle in."

"I still hate him," Tom said with disgust in his voice. "Even if he thought he was doing something noble, there were better ways to go about it. His behavior is still criminal and he deserves to spend the rest of his life in prison. No excuses and no exceptions."

Kate knew exactly what he was feeling. She was still coming to terms with the fact that Leo might not have lied to her. "If everything he told me is true, then this is a personal issue for Leo. He hated his abusive step-father and was repulsed by his repugnant ways. He had to look at that Nazi-looted art and hear Lucien speak of it with pride. Kids that grow up in that kind of environment only go one of two ways – they either become Nazi sympathizers like the rest of the family or they are adamantly opposed. There's not a lot a gray area to the issue."

Declan cleared his throat. "Not to mention, governments only did so much to help. Look at museums like the Louvre. They still have a massive amount of Nazi-looted art and are doing very little to return it to the rightful owners. You might not like Leo's tactics but you can't fault him for trying."

"Are they the rightful owners though?" Tom asked and then backtracked. "That's not what I mean. Of course, those descendants are the rightful owners. I just think there are better ways to handle such matters."

Kate wanted to tell him they could agree to disagree on that. "All I can say is Leo and the Curators never killed anyone in their pursuit of taking the art back. Not one incidence of violence occurred. Even in the cases where they tied up guards, the reports I read said the thieves were polite and went out of their way not to harm them. Did you read anything to the contrary?"

Tom sighed loudly. "No. That's all the accounts we have as well. When they stole from private homes, most never even knew they were there until someone noticed the artwork was gone. In museums, not one person was ever injured, not even while being tied up. We even have guards who said they were the nicest criminals they had ever met."

All of it only confirmed what Kate thought about Leo. "I know this is hard for you. It was hard for Declan too until Leo saved my life. The only reason I'm standing here is because he protected me. I don't have a problem bringing him in, but if he can help us catch whoever this King of Diamonds is, I'm going to use him to help us. Then we will go after him."

Tom pushed himself up from the chair. "It's going to take some time to accept all of this. I'll get there. Let me know how I can help."

"Can you start digging into the background of Gabriel Baptiste? I think he might have known the thief," Declan said, speaking before Kate had the chance. "I want to know everything there is to know about him. And call those contacts in Paris and Berlin. Maybe we can learn something from those earlier crimes."

"I agree that would be helpful," Kate echoed. If Tom was focused on something other than Leo it would give them some breathing room too. "There was a lot about the scene in the studio that doesn't add up. I also need to interview Marcy again. Tom, you were right not to trust her."

Tom thanked her and agreed to look into Gabriel. He gathered up his things to go but turned back when he got to the door. "I'm sorry I'm pushing back on Leo. I don't mean to give you a hard time."

"No need to apologize," Kate assured him as he left. With them alone in the room together, she raised her eyes to Declan. "Let's get dinner and go over the full list of art Leo stole. I want to text him tomorrow and get more information from him."

Declan made a sweeping gesture toward the door. "Lead the way."

As she made her way out of the room, Kate grazed her hand against his. "I appreciate you always having my back."

CHAPTER 13

That night the rain came again, harder than the night before. They ordered dinner in their hotel room from a restaurant down the road. Declan paid for it while Kate showered and then the two sat side by side on the small couch eating dinner and watching a rerun of a sitcom that had been on television years ago. Kate had never been much of a TV watcher, so she had missed a lot.

When they were finished eating, Declan leaned back on the couch and rubbed his stomach. "I think I ate enough for three people."

Kate glanced over at his extended belly, which wasn't much of a belly at all. "You were hungry and we had a busy day." She wiped her mouth with her napkin and turned to rest her back against the arm of the couch. She crossed her legs and rested her hands in her lap. "I forgot to tell you. It was Leo who warned Mick Sutton. He said they had met some time ago and Mick had been helpful to Leo. He returned the favor."

"You think he knows more than he's telling us?"

"I do," Kate said and wished Leo was more willing to help. "There's not much we can do unless he's willing to talk. I want to see the list of the rest of the paintings that Leo stole. I want to see if we can confirm more of their origins."

Declan reached to the floor to the files they had brought with them from FBI Headquarters. Kate used her phone to research while Declan read off the name of the artwork, where it was stolen from and the basic details. They sat like that with the television on softly in the background while they worked through several more of the stolen artworks. All of them had dubious pasts, either directly tied to Nazi-looted art or had missing historical details during the World War II years. There was no denying it now – Leo's crimes had that one common denominator.

She wondered if Leo kept records. He must have kept some kind of list of his clients and the art he'd stolen. Given the information had checked out, Kate wasn't sure what kind of case a prosecutor would have against him. Sure, he stole it but returned it to its rightful owners. Tom was right that there were better ways to go about it. There might have even been a time early in her career when she agreed with him. Since Scotland, Kate had been operating in more of a gray area and she'd come to appreciate the perspective change – even if she wasn't always comfortable with it.

When they were done, Kate rested her phone in her lap. "What do you think about what Leo told me?"

Declan arched an eyebrow and looked over at her. "What thing specifically?"

"That he isn't the one who robbed the National Gallery of Art." Before he could answer, Kate told him to wait. "I know I can't trust everything he told me. But many things have checked out. Every theft confirmed Leo is stealing back Nazi-looted art. I spoke to Tara and she confirmed at least part of the life story Leo told me, so if he's lying then he's lying to someone close to him as well. We know there was a Lucien Lamiere and that he lived on the outskirts of Paris. All of that has been confirmed. The only thing not confirmed is that the Curators are done and the chateau Lucien owned in the south of France. We can probably easily find that information. I'm only trying to figure out our next course of action. Do we keep pursuing Leo or do we assume this is being committed by someone else?"

Declan sat for a few moments in silence. "You're looking at it all wrong. I think you're being too quick to judge. We have to follow the evidence, Kate. If the evidence shows us it's Leo, that's the direction we go. If it shows us someone else, that's the direction we go. I know you want to rule him out because you have a connection to him."

"No, it's not about that," Kate argued, leaning forward to make her point. "I was never the one who brought Leo into this. It was Senator Stephen Willis who said it was the Phantom and I had to hunt him down to keep my job. He's asking me to disregard the evidence and bring in Leo. You said it yourself, I don't know that I would have even thought it was Leo when we arrived on the scene because it doesn't look like any of his other thefts."

"What about the King of Diamonds? Is there some significance in that card?"

"It's just a playing card, Declan. I'm not sure we know what it means." Kate readjusted herself on the couch to get more comfortable. She was stalling for time, but Declan was still looking at her for an answer. "I stand by the fact that I don't know what it means. That said, I have a feeling the card was left because whoever this is wanted to make a name for themselves. Leo thinks they are trying to get his attention by leaving the fake Curators' card. There's been rumors milling around for years that the Curators leave a calling card. As far as I know, no one outside of law enforcement and a few staff of museums and private collectors have seen it. As Leo told me, he left it because he wanted them to know someone knew of their misdeeds procuring and keeping Nazi-looted art. It was a bit like Leo telling them they were on notice. He doesn't care about this though. He seems so out of the game. Depressed, maybe."

Declan looked at her in surprise. "Katie, are you worried about him?"

"I don't…" Kate's voice trailed off because she had started to say she didn't know. That wasn't the truth. She was worried. While she couldn't hear the tone of Leo's voice, there seemed to be a spark that had gone out of him. "He didn't seem himself when we were texting. He said he's taken himself out of the game because of his age. It's not like he's in his late sixties or seventies and you saw him, he was still in excellent shape."

"I'm fairly certain he could have taken me in a fight," Declan echoed and meant it. Kate didn't know if that was true because Declan was stronger and younger than Leo. But it would have been a match at least. Declan's features grew soft. "Do you think whatever is wrong with him is because of guilt over the murder of his niece?"

Kate thought that could be part of it. "Going after that killer took a year of his life. During the process, he came to realize he'd been betrayed by some of his men, those closest to him and who he thought were loyal to him. It sounds to me like he had a challenging childhood and he ran from it. My guess is he never dealt with it and now he doesn't have a choice. He might be tired of life as he knew it and is trying to reset, knowing he's a wanted man. That has to weigh heavily on him."

Declan shifted his eyes to the side to look at her. "It sounds like there might be something else too. I can hear the words unspoken in your voice."

He knew her too well. There was something else. "While we were in Edinburgh, Leo told me that if I had a chance at love not to turn my back on it. That was the biggest regret he had in life. He encouraged me not to sidestep it for my career or fear or anything else that might be holding me back."

Declan sat up a little straighter. "Are you telling me that not only did Leo save your life but I have him to thank for you finally sleeping with me?"

Kate wouldn't have put it like that and it wasn't until this moment that she even connected the two herself. While they had continued their relationship back in Boston, they had not discussed the why or more importantly the *why then*. Kate could see Declan was ramping up to have that conversation. To be fair, she had opened the door. She just wasn't sure she wanted to walk through it.

"Well?" he asked, his tone more serious now. "Don't get me wrong, I'm not angry about it. But we have been dancing around this for years. I want to know what finally got you to say yes." He held a hand up to stop himself. "Let me be clearer. You didn't say yes. You walked into the apartment and you started it. I said yes."

Kate's cheeks reddened because that's exactly how it had happened. She didn't regret her decision at all but it was unlike herself after holding back her feelings for Declan for so long. Kate was worried she might say the wrong thing. "Since the cult case in California, I knew I had stronger feelings for you than I was acknowledging, not just to you but to myself as well. Being undercover as a married couple and then being drugged, the truth slipped out. Then we did this dance for a while and I was tired of dancing. Yes, Leo encouraged me that if there was someone special in my life to stop holding back. When I thought I was going to die, the only person I thought about was you. I didn't want to leave you." Kate could feel her eyes growing wet and the last thing she wanted to do was cry. She wiped them and turned away from him.

Declan reached for her and pulled her into him, resting her head back on his chest. "Why are you crying?"

"I'm not," she said, trying now not to nervously laugh. "You know I'm not great with emotional things."

"You're a psychologist. You should be better than all of us," Declan teased her.

"Forensic psychologist. Criminals are the only people I understand."

Declan laughed and her head rose and fell on his chest. He knew she was telling the truth. "I'd ask you why you finally gave in, but I already know the answer."

He didn't need to say it but he did. "I wanted you from the first moment I saw you in the academy. I chose to be your partner and friend, which is still more important than anything else we could be doing. I never thought the day would come. I'm happy as long as you're happy." He switched gears on her too quickly. "What do you want to do about Leo?"

Kate snuggled into him. "I don't know that I have the brain power to think about that tonight. I could try to get him to see me and then we can bring him in. I'm hoping through conversation I might be able to figure out where he is."

"Do you have any idea?"

"None. He didn't give me any clue." Kate yawned and closed her eyes. It had been a long day and tomorrow would be even longer. She hoped that by late in the day Tom would have some information about Gabriel. That seemed to be the only solid potential lead they had. She had scheduled an early morning meeting with Marcy to interview her again. Kate knew it would be an antagonistic conversation at best.

Declan brushed the hair off her forehead. "You'll figure it out. You always do."

Kate felt herself close her eyes and tried to will herself to get up to go to bed. Declan changed the channel on the television and seemed content to sit there holding her while she drifted off to sleep. When the cellphone rang, Kate didn't know if she'd been asleep for ten minutes or two hours.

Declan gently pushed her aside so he could answer the phone. Kate heard the professional tone in his voice take over with sharp answers and promises to be there as soon as they could. By the time he finished, Kate sat upright, rubbing the sleep from her eyes.

"What's happened?" she asked, even though she had a sense of it before he could tell her.

"The Smithsonian American Art Museum has been robbed. Two guards have been shot. One of them is dead and the other is being rushed to the hospital for emergency surgery. You need to get dressed. I promised Tom we'd be there in twenty minutes. It's at the corner of G Street and 8th Street. It's about a fifteen-minute walk for us. We can call a cab if you'd rather."

Kate glanced toward the window and noted the rain had stopped. "Walking will be faster," she said as she pushed herself off the couch and headed to the bedroom to change.

CHAPTER 14

They made it down to the Smithsonian American Art Museum in less than fifteen minutes. Declan didn't have much more information than he'd already told her. Kate wasn't surprised to see the media had already been informed. The lights from the police cars cut through the dark streets providing a kaleidoscope of blue and red. The medical examiner's van was already parked outside.

It seemed Kate and Declan were late to the show. They cut through the crowd to the barrier that had been set up. They flashed their badges and were let through. When they entered the lobby of the museum, a frantic man rushed to them. His bald head had beads of sweat as did his upper lip, even though it was cold as an ice box inside.

He extended a sweaty hand to Kate. "I'm Dr. Don Flicker, the director here. He stole the *Major Benjamin Tallmadge* portrait by John Trumbull. It's like they ripped a piece of history right off the wall. You must find it at once."

"Who is…" Declan didn't even get out his question because Dr. Flicker scoffed at him and walked away.

"I'll explain," Kate said and followed the frustrated museum director toward the scene of the crime.

Dr. Don Flicker was shorter than Kate and round in the belly. His shoulders slumped forward and he walked like a duck with his toes pointed out. It was more of a waddle but he moved swiftly for a man of his size. He mumbled to himself as he guided them through the gallery to where the portrait had once hung.

When they got to the space on the wall, he turned to Kate. "Please tell me you know the historical meaning of this theft. I can't even imagine they have any appreciation for what they have stolen."

"How much was it worth?" Declan asked. He was met with a groan but he pressed on. "Most art theft is for the money. We need to understand the value of the painting."

"The historical significance is more important," Dr. Flicker countered and raised his eyes to Kate. "Is money all that's important to you? I know who your father was, Agent Walsh. I heard him speak several times about the American Revolution. He'd care far more about the historical significance than the money."

Kate wasn't surprised that the man had known her father. Joseph Walsh had been well known across the nation for his research and lectures. That Dr. Flicker had made the connection between Kate and her father is what caught her off guard. She did not know nor ever remember meeting the man.

She turned to Declan to explain. "John Trumbull was an American artist during the American Revolution. He was a veteran of the war and notable for his historical paintings of people at the time and important moments in our history's founding. The signing of the Declaration of Independence for one. He painted George Washington and Alexander Hamilton. The Battle of Bunker Hill."

Declan seemed to quickly understand the significance. "Who is Major Benjamin Tallmadge?"

"How could you not know?" Dr. Flicker growled in response.

If Kate hadn't been raised by an expert on the subject, she might not have had the knowledge she had. "He was an Army officer and later served in the House of Representatives. Most famously, he's known for being the head of the Culper Spy Ring, which was pivotal in our success in winning the war. They were tasked to provide George Washington with information on British Army operations in New York City, which was home to the British headquarters."

"Caught up to speed now?" Dr. Flicker barked and then pointed to the space on the wall. "You tell me how one person got that off the wall and walked it out of this museum."

The space was far larger than the one at the National Gallery of Art. The size of the painting of Major Benjamin Tallmadge was at least six feet tall and three feet wide.

"How heavy would you say the painting was?"

"The painting itself not much but with the frame at least a hundred pounds." Dr. Flicker tapped his foot on the concrete floor. "What are you going to do about this? We need to get this back immediately."

Kate needed the man to calm down because she had questions that he probably wasn't going to like. "As Declan initially asked, we need to know its monetary value."

"Two million. Far less than its historical importance."

· Kate understood why the painting was so important to him but there was more he wasn't saying. "The Culper Ring was known to hide clues into everyday things, like hanging wash on the line. Is there something about this painting we need to know?"

"Clues to a treasure map, perhaps?" Dr. Flicker asked with his eyes widely mocking her. "Don't be ridiculous. This isn't the stuff of movies."

He might have mocked Kate but the question wasn't as far off as he might have believed. "We are going to do everything we can to find the painting and the person responsible."

"We know who is responsible. It's the Phantom and the Curators." Dr. Flicker turned to her and propped his fists on his hips. "I blame you for this, Agent Walsh. My understanding is that you've had quite a love affair with the man and it's impacted your work."

"I'm not sure where you get your information but no such thing has occurred." Kate might have said the words but her voice cracked as she said it. She was tired of the accusations.

"Don't argue with me, young lady. Do your job!" he shouted back, his voice echoing in the museum's wide hall.

Declan stepped around Kate to put a barrier between them. "Don't ever speak to Agent Walsh like that again. You can think I'm an idiot, but you're not going to disrespect her again. Got it?"

Dr. Flicker turned on his heels and walked back out the way they came in, leaving Kate and Declan alone in the hall.

"At least you got rid of him," Kate said with a nervous laugh after he was out of sight. When she saw the concerned look on Declan's face, she shook her head. "Men are ridiculous sometimes."

"Not all of us."

"No. Not all of you." All Kate wanted to do was look for the King of Diamonds. "Help me search the other Turnbull paintings, will you?"

Not all of the paintings were lined up together. They were spread out down the hall mixed in with other artists of the same period and style. They had no choice but to touch the frames of the artwork to see if anything was behind them. On the second Turnbull painting, one from a battle, Kate found the card tucked neatly into the back of the frame.

"It's right here," she called, holding up a gloved hand with the card so Declan could see it.

Declan came down the hall to join her. He took the card from her and slipped it into the evidence bag he had pulled from his back pocket. "I don't see any blood on the floor around here. I don't think the guards were shot in this area."

Kate realized then that they had been so consumed by the marching orders of Dr. Flicker that they had bypassed the deaths that had occurred. "Let's head back to the lobby and Tom can give us an overview of what he's found so far. The murders are far more important than the missing painting."

"Don't let Flicker hear you say that. He might have you banned." Declan said it with a good-natured smile on his face but there was truth in his voice. "I hate guys like that, thinking they are smarter than everyone. He shouldn't be talking down to anyone."

Kate raised her eyes to him, knowing that being talked down to was a sore spot for Declan. Some people saw his handsome face and decided on the spot that he must not be as smart as Kate. It had been a long-standing source of annoyance for him to the point where he had started to dumb it down on purpose. He had decided there was no point trying when he'd never convince them.

"Declan, you graduated top of your class at Boston College and you were one of the top recruits at the FBI Academy. Don't let some stuffy know-it-all get to you."

He nodded but kept walking and didn't respond until they were back in the lobby. "I'm just tired."

Kate's eyes were heavy with sleep too, but it didn't look like they were going to get much. They waited for Tom to finish speaking to one of the uniformed cops and then joined him.

Declan held up the King of Diamonds in the evidence bag. "Kate found it behind another painting from the same artist."

Tom looked it over. "I hadn't even had time to search for it. As you can see the crime scene team is just getting started."

Declan looked around the area. "What have you found out so far? Flicker was less than helpful."

Tom shook his head in disgust. "Did he talk down to you like you're a total moron?" When Declan confirmed he had, Tom added, "It was like that as soon as we arrived. I could barely get information out of him as he was lecturing me about the importance of the stolen painting. It wasn't even the most valuable piece of art in that hallway."

Kate wondered why it had been stolen when others were easier to steal and were valued more. If Flicker hadn't mocked her about her question about its other value, she might have discovered the reason it was stolen.

"Can you walk us through what happened?" Declan asked as he stepped off to the side away from the crime scene techs and uniformed cops. "How did this get called in?"

Tom gestured toward the other end of the lobby where it was quieter. When they reached an area far away from everyone, he explained, "Scott Morris was shot. It should have hit him in the chest but he turned in time and it hit his arm and side. He was able to crawl away once the killer left the hall he was in. Scott called 911 and alerted the police. He believes the killer thought he was dead. We are working to keep his identity out of the media for as long as we can. We don't want this sicko coming back and finishing the job. They were gone by the time we got here though."

"They?" Kate asked, knowing that there had to be more than one of them.

Tom nodded. "There were three of them. One is obviously in charge and then two others helping. They were dressed all in black from head to toe and wore black ski masks. The only thing showing was their eyes. Scott said even those looked like they were wearing some kind of colored contacts. Their eyes were a blue he'd never seen in real life before, kind of glowing sea blue. We don't have much on them but at least someone has seen them."

"What about their build?" Kate asked, thinking about Leo and his frame as he huddled near her in the cemetery.

"The main guy is about five-eight and wiry, Scott said. The other two were massive muscular men. Tall too." He leveled a look at Kate. "Since you're the only one who has seen the Phantom, does it sound like him?"

Kate didn't even have to think about it. "No. Leo is about Declan's height, well over six feet, and has a bigger build but not massive. There's also nothing small or wiry about him. He does not take orders from anyone. That much was clear to me. He was the one in charge of the Curators."

Tom didn't have much to say to that. "We haven't found a Curators' card here like we did at the National Gallery of Art."

Kate wanted to remind him that they hadn't found the card there because Marcy had taken it and kept it in her office until she and Declan arrived. She didn't want to antagonize him though. Instead, she asked, "Who alerted Dr. Flicker?"

"I did. He arrived shortly before you did. We needed to ask him questions about security and to see if anything was missing. We did a quick walkthrough and found one painting was missing, but for all I knew they had removed it themselves for restoration. We needed someone in the know." Tom turned to look at Dr. Flicker across the lobby standing with two uniformed cops and shook his head. He turned back to them with an expression of disgust. "He was worried about what was stolen. He didn't even seem to care that a guard had been killed and another wounded. I didn't let him go anywhere unaccompanied though, not even to his office."

Kate told him she appreciated that. She still wanted to get a lay of the land. "Do we know where they entered?"

"That's the thing," Tom said dragging it out, "we don't know how they got in. There doesn't seem to be any sign of forced entry anywhere. The alarm system and the video surveillance system are shut down. Scott said he was shot while doing his rounds. He never heard a gunshot, so we can safely assume a suppressor was used. The sound would echo through this whole place otherwise. He said he saw a shadow and was headed down the hall when three men appeared. One took a shot and Scott slumped on the floor. He half-closed his eyes like he was already dead and got a good look at them as they walked by. When they passed, he called 911. It took the police less than ten minutes to respond but they had no idea how to get into the building. The doors all seemed to be locked."

"How did they get in?" Kate looked toward the front and didn't see any windows smashed.

"There's a side door they found unlocked. If the thieves went in that way, there was no forced entry. It had either been left open or they had a key."

The similarities between the two robberies were uncanny. "Are we sure there's no one else dead?" Kate asked.

Tom nodded. "I swept the whole place."

"Even the restoration area?"

"I…" Tom's voice trailed off and then he shook his head. "I had Dr. Flicker walk me through the whole place or what I thought was the whole place."

Kate couldn't blame him. "Let's head there now." She started to walk off and then turned back. "Let's walk through the whole building together and double-check everything."

CHAPTER 15

By the time Kate made it to the National Gallery of Art in the morning to meet with Marcy Reinhold, she had downed three cups of coffee and had the shakes from the rush of caffeine. She didn't know any other way she was going to make it through the day.

They had stayed at the Smithsonian until the wee hours of the morning. She had been surprised and relieved to find there were no other bodies. No one had been shot in the restoration studio and there seemed to have been nothing else stolen or disturbed.

Declan was sure the thieves entered from the unlocked door then shot and killed the first guard who was doing rounds not far from there. Then they went to the area of the gallery that had the John Trumbull painting and shot Scott Morris. He was recovering and they'd interview him soon. They had guards outside his hospital room to make sure he remained safe. Tom told them it probably wouldn't do any good to rush to the hospital and they'd be better off waiting until later in the day to interview him once he was awake and his condition improved.

That was fine by Kate because she needed to get to the National Gallery of Art.

"Dr. Reinhold," Kate said as she knocked twice on the door and nudged it open when she was told to enter.

"I told you to call me Marcy." She waved Kate in and gestured toward the chair in front of her desk. "I was surprised you still wanted to meet this morning given the theft at the Smithsonian. I hope Dr. Flicker didn't give you too much of a hard time. He's a hard man to deal with on most days."

"Difficult is a good word for him. Has he been in contact with you since last night?"

Marcy raised her perfectly arched eyebrows. "No. Should he have been?"

"I didn't know if he'd reach out about the ongoing investigation." Kate glanced down at the chair and thought better of it. If she sat, she was afraid she'd doze off. "Let's walk and talk if we can."

"Certainly." Marcy got up from the chair and came around the front of the desk. Gone was the pantsuit she had worn when Kate saw her last. She was wearing designer jeans and a blouse. She had flat loafers on instead of heels. When Marcy noticed Kate looking at her jeans, she said, "There's no point dressing up when no one else is here. I hope today will be the last you need this kind of access because our staff is ready to reopen and so is the community."

Kate gave a noncommittal nod. "We want you to be able to open as soon as possible. Unfortunately, this isn't just the site of a theft. There were three murders and that complicates the investigation."

"Of course." Marcy led Kate out of the office. She didn't ask Kate which way she wanted to go, she just started giving a basic tour of the place, something she had probably done countless times in the past. "I can't remember if you said you've been here before this case."

"Years ago. Not anytime recently." Kate knew her voice sounded tired and she tried to shake it off. As Marcy gave the tour and pointed out the different artworks, Kate's mind was on Gabriel Baptiste. She stopped Marcy mid-sentence. "Can you help me understand your relationship with Gabriel?"

"Relationship?" Marcy asked, a hitch in her tone. "What do you mean by that?"

Kate hadn't been suspicious that there had been anything more between the two until just then. "I meant your professional relationship, but it sounds like it might have been more than that."

"No," Marcy started to say with a shake of her head. Then she must have thought better than lying to an FBI agent. She sighed and wrapped her arms around herself. "We were involved for lack of a better word. I knew Gabriel for years, long before he ever came to the National Gallery of Art. We met in Paris about twenty years ago and had a brief affair. I was going through a divorce and he had a myriad of lovers. It didn't even occur to me that I might have meant anything to him."

"When did the relationship pick back up?"

"Before I took this job. Gabriel kept in contact over the years and I came to learn he was here working in D.C. We saw each other a few times for lunch or dinner." Marcy saw the way Kate was looking at her. "It was after I took this job the affair resumed. He was my employee at that point. There was no way we could be public with it."

"You're two consenting adults and neither are married," Kate said but even as she said it she knew it wasn't that simple. "I know D.C. can be a rough place on your reputation."

"It's all about reputation here." Marcy stepped toward the *Madame Camus* painting by Edgar Degas. Madame Camus is shown sitting in an armchair in her apartment wearing a red dress and holding a fan. "She was a lifelong friend of Degas. I've often wondered what she was looking at. It's hard for me to decipher the look on her face. Sometimes I see amusement or boredom, depending on my mood." She turned and smiled at Kate. "That's the nice thing about art. The meaning is a little different for each person who views it."

Kate wasn't sure if she was stalling or simply commenting on the artwork in front of them. She didn't want to push too hard but needed the information. "Were you still involved with Gabriel at the time of his death?"

Marcy turned back to look at her. "We were arguing over going public. Gabriel was tired of living in the shadows and I was concerned I'd lose my job. He told me he'd go to the board himself and let them know that the affair had started long before he was my employee and if they were that concerned, he'd resign." She chuckled softly at that. "They'd sooner fire me than lose Gabriel. He was one of a kind. Every museum across the globe would have hired Gabriel in a heartbeat. We were lucky to have him."

"Do you think you would have eventually gone public?"

"I don't know. It's different for women." Marcy raised her eyebrows to Kate. "I'm sure you know what it's like trying to have any kind of relationship in your position."

Kate knew all too well. She wasn't sure why she felt the need to admit anything to Marcy but she felt compelled to tell her about the recent hearing. "I had a chance meeting with the man they call the Phantom on another case. I was accused of sleeping with him."

Marcy's eyes softened. "The rumor is already going around. The same with your partner." She shrugged and stared back up at the painting. "Any time a woman is attractive and interacting with an attractive man, there will be rumors. It's how it goes. I went out of my way to not interact with Gabriel around the other staff. It drove him mad most days."

Kate felt no need to defend herself. She skipped over the suggestion of rumors and went right to the heart of what was most important. "Marcy, do you think there's any chance Gabriel knew the man who robbed the museum?"

Marcy turned to her sharply and with anger in her tone asked, "Why would you suggest something like that?" It was clear by her expression she couldn't conceive of it. "Gabriel was a good man and the best restoration artist in the world. I can't believe he'd be involved in art theft."

"The scene in the studio." Kate didn't want to stand still. She wanted to keep walking, so she began to stroll again and waited until Marcy caught up with her. "There are things that don't add up. The studio was a mess. You said he never kept it like that. What was he doing there after hours?"

Marcy folded her arms across her chest. "He was supposed to be meeting me but I was running late. I had gotten caught up with something at home and I was late meeting him. If you look at his cellphone records you'll find the phone number I used to communicate with him. It's not my normal cellphone."

Kate didn't understand why they were going to such lengths to keep their relationship a secret. "I understand not wanting to come forward with the relationship but why another cellphone?"

"I was paranoid," Marcy admitted. "The board is always watching and I didn't want to lose my job. I thought if I had one of those prepaid phones, it might never be traced back to me. I was always careful not to text anything that might give away my identity."

"Then why meet here late at night?" Kate asked, not understanding.

"It wasn't romantic," Marcy assured her quickly. "Gabriel wanted to show me something that he had discovered late that afternoon. I hadn't had time to come down to the studio before I left. I had dinner with a board member and I couldn't be late. I promised I'd come back. While he was working on the current piece, he found there had been additional layers of paint added over the original. It happens sometimes but Gabriel was surprised to find new meaning in the painting. The woman was shown holding a dagger and not a book. It changes the whole meaning of the piece. It's significant."

"Did he leave the back door unlocked for you?"

Marcy sighed again, this time deep and heavy. "He must have unlocked it for me right around the time I was planning to be there. He probably didn't want to climb back down the scaffolding to lock the door again when I said I'd be late."

"Was this something he'd done before – unlock the door for you after hours?"

Marcy shook her head. "We never met after hours like that. It was a coincidence that it happened on the same night of the robbery." She turned to Kate with fear in her eyes. "I'm the reason they were able to steal *Lady in the Field*. I'm the reason they are all dead."

Things were starting to make sense in a way they hadn't before. "Is that why you picked up the Curators' card from the ground?"

Marcy took a deep breath. "I was wracked with guilt and distraught. I wasn't thinking. I was in shock about what had happened. I never made it there that night. You can find the text on Gabriel's phone. I canceled on him when I realized how late I'd be. He didn't respond and I thought he might be angry with me. He could be moody sometimes." She raised her eyes to Kate. "I wasn't even thinking when I picked up that card. I saw something on the floor and put it in my pocket. I didn't even realize until later."

Kate finally believed she was telling the truth. "What about the dust and debris on the workstation?"

Marcy looked away. "I'm not sure. Gabriel never kept the room as messy as it was found."

"Did Gabriel ever tell you he knew a man named Leo Lamiere?"

It took Marcy a moment but she shook her head. "He had many friends in the art world. I don't know that name though."

Kate asked a few more questions about Gabriel but none that Marcy could answer. They continued their walk through the rest of the West Building and back to the lobby. Before leaving, Kate stressed, "It's important that if you think of anything else, you let me know."

"I will. I'm sorry I didn't tell you about the relationship sooner." Marcy stared off down the hall toward her office. "I understand if you need to tell the board about my actions."

Kate saw no reason to put her in that position. Not now anyway. "I don't need to tell the board anything. I'm not looking to get you fired, but I also can't control where this investigation is going. Any secrets you have might come out eventually. I'll let you decide how to handle that."

Kate left Marcy standing there with an expression of concern on her face. It was true though. While Kate wasn't going to out the relationship to the board, she didn't know what other secrets Gabriel had. If he knew Leo, there was something amiss in his life. The King of Diamonds had also been left in his studio rather than near the missing painting. He wasn't in the clear yet.

CHAPTER 16

Kate made it back in time to go with Declan to the hospital to interview Scott Morris. They had received word that he was awake and alert, although in considerable pain. He wasn't out of the woods yet and Declan wanted to get there as soon as possible.

There was only one witness and his life still hung in the balance.

"You look tired," Declan said as they walked the few blocks from the Metro to the hospital.

Kate tightened her ponytail. "I had enough coffee to keep me awake for days. Did you have a productive morning?"

Declan sidestepped a woman coming at them with a stroller and smiled down at the chubby baby. "I went over the crime scene evidence to see if we missed anything. I found out what the dust was on the workbench."

Kate looked up at him. "What do you mean – *what it was*?" She had assumed it was garden-variety dust or like Marcy had mentioned the remnants from cutting the frame.

"It wasn't dust." Declan paused dramatically as if he were holding in a bombshell of a story. His smile broadened. "It was cocaine."

Kate stopped dead in the middle of the sidewalk nearly bumping into a man in a suit who cursed at her as he passed. She ignored him, too focused on what Declan said. "It must have been a lot of cocaine.

That bench was covered."

Declan agreed with that assessment. "I assumed it was dust and debris from the studio. The crime scene techs had already taken a sample of it because one of them suspected it was cocaine. That message never made it down to Tom or us."

"What do you think was going on?" Thinking back to the fine dust Kate assumed the bag of coke must have exploded or tipped over and then someone tried to clean it up or Gabriel was selling drugs. There were too many scenarios to consider and none of them were adding up. "Do you think it was Gabriel's?"

Declan didn't know any more than Kate did. "We'll know when the toxicology comes back. There were no other drugs found in that room. I find it hard to believe it was the thieves."

Kate thought back to her conversation with Marcy. She hadn't mentioned that Gabriel did drugs, but then again, she had held a lot back. "Gabriel and Marcy were romantically involved. She admitted they had plans to meet at the National Gallery that night. Gabriel wanted to show her something he found while working on the current painting."

Declan absorbed the information better than Kate had. It didn't seem to surprise him at all. "They were about the same age and she expressed such respect and fondness for him, it's not surprising. Would he have done drugs there that night if she was on her way to see him?"

"I don't know," Kate said and then considered it. "He was a great artist and maybe Marcy accepted that doing coke was a part of his process. Seems strange to me but if that's how he was always known to work – that's how he worked."

Declan peered down at her amused. "Sounds like you're giving him a pass."

Kate shook her head. "I'm looking at it from Marcy's perspective.

She was keeping the relationship a secret far longer than she needed to and he was pushing for it to be public. She said it was because she was his boss. That didn't feel like the whole story to me. What if she was keeping it a secret because she knew about his drug use? That could be reason alone not to be public about the relationship." Kate looked up at Declan and he agreed with her assessment. "Marcy believes the door near his studio was unlocked that night because Gabriel had left it open for her. She was running late and ended up canceling. Marcy has a lot of guilt thinking if she had just shown up when she'd planned, the whole thing might not have happened."

"Did Gabriel leave that door unlocked often?"

"Marcy didn't seem to think so. Then again, she didn't give me the full story. The thieves could have tried a few doors and got lucky. Maybe Gabriel left it unlocked and someone had been watching him."

Declan chewed on his bottom lip as he considered the evidence. "Tom said he's going to explore Gabriel's background today."

"I can ask Leo as well. I can tell him about this most recent theft and ask him more questions about Gabriel's background. He said he knew him, but I don't know how recently they spoke."

"It's an avenue," Declan said but didn't say more.

She let the subject drop. "Has Scott given any statement yet?"

"Nothing other than to the responding officer before he was brought to the hospital. Tom has been keeping watch on his condition and said he'd rather us interview him. I think he didn't want to step on your toes."

Kate knew it must be a challenge for Tom to step back from what otherwise would have been his investigation. The only reason they were there was to catch Leo and it was looking more and more like he wasn't involved. She half expected to be called off the case.

They got to the hospital just as the doctor was leaving Scott's room. He warned them not to stay too long or cause the young man any stress. His condition was improving but still delicate. The doctor also told them Scott was on some strong painkillers so his memory might not be the best and his words might be slurred. His last warning was stern. "If he falls asleep, don't you dare wake him up. He needs all the rest he can get." Then he looked at Kate's face and probably wanted to offer her the same advice but he left without saying anything else.

"We have our orders," Declan said as he pushed open the hospital room door. The lights were low and the television was replaying the news coverage of the burglaries. The head of Scott's bed was raised slightly and he had more tubes and wires connected to him than Kate could count.

"Scott," Declan said quietly and the young man turned his head toward the door. When Declan had his attention, he introduced them.

Scott tried to push himself up in the bed but Declan assured him he was fine. "They said you'd be here sometime today. I was trying to keep myself awake to speak to you."

"We won't take up too much of your time," Kate assured him and came around to the far side of the bed. Declan stood next to her, so Scott could communicate with them both. "We are trying to find the men who did this to you. Can you tell us what happened?"

Scott took a shallow breath and winced. "I work the overnight shift at the Smithsonian American Art Museum. It's a shift I've been working for the past five years. Ned Baker and I have been working together for the past three years. I heard he's dead."

Kate nodded her head. "We believe he was on rounds when he was shot."

Scott shook his head. "He was supposed to be at the front desk but he radioed to me that he heard something and was going to check it out. I told him to wait for me but he went anyway."

"Did he say what he heard?"

"He said he thought he heard people talking." Scott reached for the water cup on the tray. Kate handed it to him. He took a slow sip. "He radioed and told me that he didn't want to wait. That he was going and then told me where to meet him."

"Which was where?"

"There's a side entrance in the lobby that connects to a ramp for people with disabilities. We also sometimes get school groups that come in that way. No one should have been out there that late at night. We've never had an issue like that before." Scott took another sip and rested the cup in his lap. "Before I could make it down there, Ned radioed again and said he was heading back and that all was clear. He joked the Smithsonian ghosts must have been getting to him."

Kate imagined working that late there must be all kinds of bumps in the night. "Did he go outside?"

"I believe so."

"What happened next?"

"I continued my rounds. Maybe ten or fifteen minutes pass and three people rounded the corner at the end of the hall." Scott paused and collected his thoughts. He apologized that reliving it was difficult. "They were dressed all in black from head to toe, including gloves. I saw immediately that all three had guns in their hands. I told them to stop and I aimed my gun but I never got a shot off. One of them shot me." His voice caught and emotion swelled in him.

"It's okay. Take your time," Kate reassured him.

Scott put his hand above where he was shot. "I thought for sure I was dead. I closed my eyes and tried to breathe as shallowly as I could as they passed. The one who shot me bent over me and that's when I saw the glowing neon blue eyes. I knew they had to have been contacts. The rest of their faces were covered by the mask. I only had my eyes open a sliver, but I guess I faked dead good enough or they assumed I'd bleed out right there because they left me alone after that."

"Did they say anything to you?" Declan asked.

Scott shook his head. "Not to me but to each other." He raised his eyes to Declan. "The smaller one gave the orders. They weren't American. The smaller one sounded…" He didn't finish his sentence and seemed unsure if he should say it at all.

"Whatever you heard, Scott, you can tell us." Declan put a hand on the man's arm. "I know in the middle of the situation things might not make a lot of sense. I've been shot and your mind can play tricks on you. You can tell us anything and we can sort it out from there."

Scott licked his cracked lips. "I think the smaller of the three was a woman and British, like fancy British."

"Fancy British?" Kate asked trying not to hide her shock that one of the robbers and the main one at that could be a woman. "I'm not sure what you mean."

Scott crinkled up his nose. "You know how some British people can sound very proper? Like they went to boarding school or something. That's what she sounded like. It wasn't just the accent either. It was the way she spoke, the words she used."

"You're sure it was a woman?" Declan asked, his tone giving away the same shock Kate felt.

"I told you I'm worried I might be wrong," Scott reminded him, shifting in his hospital bed to get comfortable. "If it wasn't a woman, then it was a man who sounded very much like a woman. Her build was much different than the other two. Smaller shoulders and head and slimmer. Shorter. I'd put her at probably five-eight, but the more I think about it, she could be shorter. She sounded young too – like in her late twenties."

Kate needed to clarify something. "The person you believed to be the woman was the one who stood over you to make sure you were dead?"

"Yes. She barked 'we must hurry' and 'the painting is this way'. She was leading them and was the one in charge. I think the other two were her muscle. They were big enough for it."

Declan thanked him and told him he was doing a good job. "Did you see them again?"

"No, thankfully," Scott said, his tone full of relief. "They must have gotten out of the museum a different way. They didn't pass by me again. I crawled down the hall away from them as soon as I thought they were gone and called 911. I was on the floor until the cops and paramedics arrived. I tried to tell them what I saw and heard but I was in too much pain."

Kate reminded him how well he did on the scene. "You might not remember but you did give the cops a fairly detailed accounting of what happened, Scott. You've been a great help."

Scott's eyes grew wide hearing that. "I don't remember any of that. But I know what I saw."

"You've done great." Declan stood back from the bed and looked over at Kate. "Is there anything else for now?"

Kate looked down at Scott and only had one last general question she used at the end of each interview. "Is there anything else you think we should know?"

Scott shook his head. "I know it's hard to believe but I'm sure the smaller one was a woman. British too. I'm sure of it."

She thanked him for all the information and wished him well. When they were outside the room, Kate asked, "What do you think?"

"I think we need to change how we've been thinking about this case."

CHAPTER 17

As they were leaving the hospital and still processing what Scott told them, Declan paused outside by the doors. "There's something I've been thinking about related to the drugs that we found. We don't deal with drugs enough and it didn't even occur to me at the scene. I'm annoyed the crime scene techs didn't let us know right away." Declan looked across the parking lot. "I've been thinking about this for a while but haven't said anything because I wasn't sure it was my place."

Kate wasn't sure what he had on his mind but she knew it was serious when the worry line creased his forehead. "Declan, whatever it is we can figure it out."

He looked down at Kate. "I want to ask Spade for a crime scene tech. Someone who works directly with us, so we aren't having to rely solely on locals. That way things like this don't escape our attention. We should have heard it from the techs sooner before you went to speak to Marcy today."

"The results weren't even back yet. I couldn't have gone to her with speculation." That said, Kate didn't think it was the worst idea she'd ever heard. They had specialized agents for nearly everything else on Spade's team. "Did you have someone in mind?"

"Sharon Esposito from the Boston FBI field office. I talked to her about it a few months ago and she'd be willing to travel with us."

Kate couldn't help but laugh. "You only want Sharon because she's secretly in love with you and gives you a hard time every time she sees you."

Declan shrugged. "She's sassy and I like it. But seriously, Kate, she's one of the best we have ever worked with in the field."

"I don't disagree. As long as Sharon knows what she's getting herself into."

"I want her to supervise the locals and be a liaison for us. We are still going to need to use the local labs. She knows that and these are her people. Sharon knows how to play the game."

Kate had only met Sharon a handful of times, but the cases they had worked together had run smoothly and nothing was ever missed. "If you pitch it to Spade, I'll back you up. It would be good to have a better ally with the crime scene evidence."

Declan traced his fingers along her jawline and lingered for a moment. Kate thought he might lean in and kiss her, but he knew better out on the street. The gesture was enough to express his gratitude. "Where to next?"

"Back to regroup. I'll need to speak to Marcy eventually but she said she was leaving for the day."

The Metro ride back was uneventful. Declan texted Tom to see if he had any news about Gabriel and then told Kate he was still working on it. When they reached their stop, neither of them felt like going back into the conference room at FBI Headquarters.

"I need to walk," was all Kate said when they left the Metro station. The rain had let up although the sky overhead had a slew of grayish clouds with peeks of sunlight trying to burst through. She figured the rain would hold off for a little while.

As they walked the D.C. streets heading nowhere in particular, Declan asked, "What do you think about what Scott said? Seems too brutal to be a woman."

Kate had thought that initially too. Then she remembered all the women who killed patients in nursing homes, killed their husbands, or abused their children. "Women are capable of violence, Declan. We haven't seen many women involved in art theft of this kind, especially not when people are killed, but I wouldn't discount it so quickly."

"I didn't mean to imply I thought Scott was lying," Declan amended. They waited at the stoplight for the all-clear to walk and crossed with a handful of other people. When they got across the street, Declan stopped walking. "He's on a lot of medication. I believe he thinks he heard a woman's voice. He had just been shot and now he's all doped up. Do you think it could be?"

Kate wasn't sure based on the evidence. "The King of Diamonds is a male card. I'm curious why she'd choose to leave that. I'd think she'd leave the Queen of Diamonds."

"Unless she's going out of her way to conceal herself while also leaving a marker or the card means something else."

Kate just didn't know. "This is the first time I don't understand the reasoning behind leaving a marker at the scene," she admitted much to Declan's surprise. "Thieves and killers leave their mark in a certain way. Killers leave signatures because it's a compulsion and part of their rituals. This is something different – hidden but taunting almost. There's also no reason to kill the guards. They cut the surveillance and alarms before they even go in and are dressed in black from head to toe including shielding their true eye color. They could have overpowered the guards and tied them up. I hate to say it like this but killing the guards is overkill in the situation. It seems to me they want to instill fear."

Declan pulled Kate out of a line of walkers coming at them. They weren't far from the Capitol Reflecting Pool. There were benches and other places to sit near the water far away from other people. Declan suggested the location. "Let's sit and talk. If you need to pace, there's more room on the sidewalk than here."

As Kate sidestepped another person, she accepted the plan. Once they were over by the Capitol Building, she stared up at its grand architecture feeling a mix of wonder and defeat. "I wonder if that smug…" Kate didn't call him the name in her head aloud. She stopped herself and then said softly, "I wonder if he's keeping track of the investigation."

"Senator Stephen Willis? I doubt it, Kate. He probably forgot all about it as soon as he left. He has many other people to terrorize." Declan knew the hearing was still bothering her even though Kate had assured him it wasn't. There were few things Kate liked less than having her character called into question. "What will make you feel better?"

"Solving this case and shoving the evidence in his face." Kate stood with her hands on her hips looking up at the building. Her shoulders were raised and her back tight.

"You need to relax," Declan said, reaching for her hand and pulling her down to the bench.

Kate took a breath and stared off at the traffic going by. Then she turned her face up to the little bit of sun coming through the clouds. "Do we know how they are cutting the alarm and surveillance?"

Declan had asked Kevin Detrick, who went by Ditch on their team, for help. He was a master hacker who knew everything tech. "We got word back from Ditch who said it's a virus in the system. They are overriding it before they even enter the building. He said they are probably sitting a few blocks away and doing it. He is still in the process of chasing it down to see if anything is identifying about it. It's sophisticated though. Ditch said whoever is doing this isn't an amateur."

Given Ditch's skills that was a compliment from him. "That's at least one thing settled."

"We know a lot more than you think, Kate." Declan looked over at her and didn't hesitate to take her hand in his. He stroked the back of her hand with his thumb. "We know there are three of them and potentially one is a woman. We know what they are wearing and they are accessing doors that have been left unlocked. Gabriel left the door unlocked at the National Gallery of Art and I suspect they followed the guard at the Smithsonian when he went outside to check the noise he had heard. He was shot near the door. They drew him outside and then attacked him on the way back in. We are further along than you think."

There were still big missing pieces she didn't understand. "Why are they choosing the paintings they are taking? They aren't the most valuable or the most prominent. I thought they might go after *Man in the Field* next. Why break into two museums right near each other? Most thieves have better sense than that. There are too many lingering questions."

"Have you considered that each of the paintings has a mystery surrounding them?" Declan asked and Kate shook her head. "*Lady in the Field* is part of a series that could potentially solve the artist's murder. The *Major Benjamin Tallmadge* portrait is of the man who started and ran the Culper Spy Ring. Both of the paintings represent something mysterious."

Kate was momentarily speechless. "I was so focused on the who, I missed that completely."

"Do you know what it means?" Declan asked, his tone serious. "I noted the pattern but I don't know that it means anything."

"I'm not sure I know." Kate expelled a frustrated breath. "We figure out one thing and it brings more questions."

He caught the undercurrent in her tone. "Do you want to reach out to Leo again?" He didn't wait for her to answer. "Kate, if you think Leo has answers to those questions, reach out to him. I'm going to head back to FBI Headquarters and speak to Tom. Sit here and text him. Maybe you'll feel better once you either figure out what he knows or realize he isn't going to help you. Either way, you need to stop thinking about Leo and get your head back in the game."

Kate's head snapped up. "You think my head's not in the game?"

"I think you got knocked down at the hearing and you lost some mojo," Declan said, standing. "You got your character called into question and your ego is bruised. These thefts happening here, it's a slap in the face, Kate. I get it but—"

Kate held her hand up for him to stop. She had been listening to him and her anger had started to rise but then she was struck by something he said. "It's not a coincidence, Declan. When was the last art theft in D.C.?"

"More than a decade ago," Declan said with a shrug. "It might have even been longer."

The pieces were starting to fall into place for Kate. She pushed herself up from the bench. "This thief tried to get Leo's attention twice already. Once in Paris and once in Berlin. Leo never responded to any of it. Senator Willis announced weeks ago that they were holding a hearing about the FBI letting the Phantom go in Edinburgh. He said he was going to get to the bottom of it and was calling us to Washington. He provided the dates of the hearing on air. Now that we're here in D.C., there are two thefts. One painting represents a spy ring and the other a mystery or riddle to be solved. They knew by leaving the Curators' card the Phantom would be blamed. They wanted us involved because we have a connection."

"Are you saying this is about getting Leo's attention or to blame him for the crimes?"

Kate didn't think it was about blame. "This is about getting Leo's attention. I don't know why though. Maybe to draw him out – force him out of hiding and learn his real identity."

It was too much mental gymnastics for Declan. "I don't see how you can come to that conclusion. No evidence points to that other than leaving the Curators' card. Even that was a half-hearted attempt because it didn't look like a real Curators' card."

"It was enough to make Tom question it." Kate didn't have all the pieces together to have it fully make sense. She stepped toward him and put her hands on his arms. "My head is in the game. I promise you that. There's just something huge we are missing and I have a strong feeling it's connected to Leo."

"Then talk to Leo." Declan smiled down at her but there was a frustration in his eyes not echoed in his words.

Kate watched him walk off before she sat down, pulled out her phone, and called a familiar number instead of texting. This required a real conversation.

Leo didn't answer as Kate had expected he wouldn't. She sent him a quick text telling him she needed to speak with him and texting was too hard for the conversation she needed to have. She snapped a photo of herself alone outside and included that with the text.

She assured him she couldn't trace the call even if she wanted to.

A few moments later the phone rang. "Pretty ballsy to call me while sitting in front of the Capitol Building, Kate." Leo's voice reminded Kate of bourbon – warm, smooth, and with a hint of danger. She liked the way his accent was a blend of several places and how he sometimes sounded more French than Bulgarian.

"I need to speak to you. I'm alone." Kate paused to see if he'd hang up or tell her he didn't want to speak to her. When all she was met with was silence, she went on. "There's been another theft. This time at the Smithsonian. We have a witness."

Leo admitted to having seen it on the news. "It's a global story, Kate. It wasn't me. I'm far away from Washington D.C. and I told you, I'm out of the game."

"I believe you, Leo. That doesn't mean I don't think this case has something to do with you."

Leo didn't argue or debate her. "How do you think it's connected to me? I've checked with all of my men who remain and none of them are involved. They'd tell me." He had a confidence in his voice that reassured her.

Kate hesitated for a moment unsure of what she wanted to share first. "We have reason to believe that the thief might be a woman – a young British woman with a fancy-sounding accent is what the witness said."

"Fancy?"

"It was the same reaction I had when he said it. I think he means posh, probably from some society family in London is my best guess."

"Was there another King of Diamonds card?" Leo asked, his voice suddenly tight.

"Yes. Why?" He knew more than he was saying. The rigidity in the way he asked the question was enough for Kate. She was coming to learn his speech patterns in much the same way as she knew Declan's. "He heard her speak after he'd been shot. They thought he was dead but he lived and called for help. Declan and I interviewed him at the hospital." That was met with silence, so Kate gave him a few more seconds and then asked, "Are you having trouble believing a woman could carry out these crimes?"

"No, it's not that. I've seen women do much worse." Leo grew quiet again.

"Do you have a suspect in mind?"

"No," Leo said a little too quickly. "I told you I don't have any information about these crimes. This isn't what the Curators was all about, Kate. We certainly never killed guards in the process. I made sure that no one was harmed. The only thing we ever did was take back property that didn't belong to the person or organization that was holding it."

Kate watched two birds fight over crumbs in the grass. The smaller of the two was surprisingly strong and winning against the other. She loved a good underdog and it made her smile. She turned her attention back to the call. "I believe you, Leo. The FBI has analyzed your thefts and each one was Nazi-looted art. You told me the truth about that."

"I told you the truth about everything, Kate." Leo chuckled softly and cursed himself. "I'm not sure why I'm trusting you but I am. Had we met years ago, I would have never told you a thing. You know more about me than most and I fear if we keep speaking you'll come to learn too much."

"We did meet years ago, Leo. When you took me hostage, remember? You said I was a pushy American woman and you didn't like my kind. The only piece of information I walked away with was that you had a Bulgarian accent mixed with something else. I've come to learn since that it's French." Kate had never told him she had picked that up in his voice, not even when they were in Edinburgh. She could feel him smile through the phone.

"I didn't realize you were that perceptive. I don't think I could ever forget holding you on the rooftop like that." As soon as the words were out of Leo's mouth, he changed the subject. "What else have you found out about the thefts?"

Even though Leo seemed to dismiss what he said, it didn't stop the warmth that spread through Kate's stomach, which triggered immediate guilt. Kate pushed the thoughts of being in Leo's arms aside. "I was curious if the stolen paintings have any meaning for you. I told you about *Lady in the Field* and the one stolen last night was the *Major Benjamin Tallmadge* portrait by John Trumbull. Do either of those hold any significant meaning for you?"

It took Leo a few beats too long for him to respond. "No," he said, his tone curt.

Kate didn't push him. "I was also curious why the card was hidden with Gabriel's body in his studio and the other was hidden near the theft. Any ideas about that?"

"I can't possibly know what's in this person's mind. I thought that was your job."

"It's my job to get to the truth." Kate felt she was doing far from that on this call. She knew Leo was holding back on her. "I'm going to be straight with you, Leo. I think you know who this is or at least might be able to figure it out. I believe the person who is doing this is trying to get your attention but I'm not sure why. I was hoping you'd be able to help me figure that out, so I can make sure no one else is killed."

"I don't know what you want me to say."

"I want you to say that you're going to help me like in Edinburgh." In some ways, Kate hated to admit it but she added, "We were a good team then."

"I can't help you."

"That's not true," she argued. "You don't want to help me because it would mean shaking yourself out of whatever depression or funk you're in. It might also risk you being arrested. You already told me you won't spend the rest of your life behind bars."

"I won't, Kate. I couldn't stomach that, not for doing something I feel was right." Leo launched into a long-winded diatribe about how if governments had honored their promises and commitments after World War II what he did wouldn't have ever been necessary and he might have been able to live a normal life. "I did what I had to do and I'll apologize to no one for it. I only wish I had the time in this life to steal back all of it."

Kate wasn't sure she had ever heard anyone have such strength of conviction. Leo had initially said it was his hatred for his step-father that had motivated him but his passion for it ran much deeper. Kate finally admitted something she hadn't admitted, not even to Declan. "I started this case feeling betrayed and ready to take you dead or alive. Speaking to you again now, I don't want to arrest you, Leo. I've become completely compromised in this situation."

"I'm glad that you don't want to arrest me."

Kate laughed lightly. "You have to help me." She didn't give him time to say no again. "Declan noticed something about the paintings that were stolen. As you know, *Lady in the Field* is connected to a series that when together is said to reveal a mystery and the portrait is of a man who ran a spy ring that was critical to the United States winning the American Revolution. I didn't see it at first but when he pointed it out, I couldn't help thinking how that might be representative of you. A mystery and the leader of a ring. They called you the Phantom after all."

"I see what you're saying." Leo didn't elaborate more than that and it was starting to grate on Kate's last nerve. He was a harder nut to crack than most. "I'm not sure why this would be about me. People don't even know who I am."

"To draw you out. You've disappeared off the scene. Maybe this thief is trying to draw you out in some way."

"If anything, Kate, I think they are trying to show me up. Most people don't know my mission. They saw a master thief who slipped in and out of places with no one being the wiser. We took art and it was days and months sometimes before a private collector even noticed. It's not what you're dealing with here. These are bold and brazen thefts, Kate. They are killing people when murder is unnecessary. If anything, I think they are trying to show me up and tell me to stay in retirement because they are on the scene now. If they wanted to draw me out, it might only be to kill me and put me out of commission forever."

Kate had thought along the same lines but hadn't gone as far as Leo had stated. "You left a vacuum and it's now being filled. Would they *really* want you dead?"

"More people than I can count want me dead, Kate. I'm only surprised law enforcement didn't figure out what I was doing sooner."

"Law enforcement is disjointed, especially when trying to connect things happening across the globe. It doesn't surprise me no one in law enforcement noticed. I didn't even notice. To be fair, unless someone looked into the history of the art, they still might have missed it."

"I guess that's true," Leo said. "I wish I could sit down and have a cup of coffee with you and talk."

"We can, Leo. Tell me where you are."

"That can't happen and we both know that. As much as you don't want to arrest me, you'll have to." Bells chimed somewhere in the distance and the phone went silent. Kate wasn't sure if he had hung up or was drowning out the sound.

She pretended she hadn't heard. "There's some static on the line. Are you still there?"

"I'm still here," he said after a moment. "I need to go."

Kate didn't want the call to end, mostly because she hadn't made any progress at all. "If you can't help me with the thief, can you at least tell me more about Gabriel?"

"What do you want to know?"

"There was cocaine found in his studio all over the top of a workbench. Did he do drugs?"

Leo sighed loudly as if expelling a breath into the phone. "Yes. It was a point of contention between us. Gabriel started as a forger a long time ago, Kate. He was one of the best around and then someone at the Louvre found out about him and offered him a job doing restoration work. They paid him a lot of money and it was more honest work than forgery. He took the job but that didn't mean the rest of his life fell in line. He was still an artist – moody, manic, disturbed sometimes, and careless with women. The drugs were a part of that. There was no one better at his craft though. Just because he was getting honest work didn't mean he stopped his forgeries either. He still carried on when he found the time."

"His girlfriend didn't know you two knew each other."

"She wouldn't, Kate. Gabriel didn't know me by my name. He knew me as an alias I used while I was the Phantom. None of them knew my real identity."

Kate wanted to ask the name he went by but figured he wouldn't say. She kept her focus on Gabriel. "It was a lot of drugs. Do you think he was selling it too?"

"No. That he wouldn't do. He bought a lot at a time back when I saw him regularly. He never slowed down it seems."

"Was he an addict?"

"That's a tough question to answer. Gabriel could go without it but he said his work suffered. In a sense, sure, he was. But it was not something he was going to stop. He wasn't going to go into treatment or get help for it because he had convinced himself the cocaine is what made him paint so well."

Kate knew the clinical impact of the drug. It wasn't something she had ever tried. "Have you ever tried it?" She was hoping for someone's perspective because she didn't think Declan had either.

"No, Kate," Leo assured her. "I don't like the loss of control that alcohol and drugs bring. That was one of the rules I had with the Curators. None of my men did drugs or they were kicked out. I couldn't stand for that. We couldn't take any chances."

His tone was so adamant that Kate had no choice but to believe him. "Given Gabriel's background, is there any chance he knew the thieves? Could he have been double-crossed?"

"Absolutely not. Gabriel didn't run in that world. He never knew what I did, Kate. I used his services as a forger on occasion." Leo paused and let Kate wonder what he was about to say. "There were a few times when a painting was so high profile and worth so much that I didn't want the current owner to know it had been stolen. More than a few forgeries are hanging in museums while the originals were returned to their rightful owners."

Kate's eyes grew wide with the thought of what that meant. She wanted to ask what paintings but knew he wouldn't tell her. "Is there anything in Gabriel's life or background we should know? An FBI agent on the case is looking into him because his actions that night are questionable, particularly with the drugs we found."

Leo's tone was firm. "I can't imagine any scenario where Gabriel would have been involved with the theft. As I said, he lived an artist's life but he wasn't always on what you'd consider the right side of the law. He was no thief though and he certainly wouldn't have helped anyone steal a painting from the National Gallery of Art. He loved his work and his life there in D.C."

Kate made one last plea. "Please think about who could be doing this. It's only going to continue and more lives are at risk."

"I'll think about it." Leo drew in an audible breath. "I meant what I said that if life were different, I'd love to spend some time with you. I think you'd be surprised how much you'd like me."

Kate felt herself smiling and bit down on her lip. She already liked Leo a little too much. "Maybe one day," she said and the call ended.

CHAPTER 19

Kate thought back over the call as she crossed the street and headed back toward FBI Headquarters. She replayed everything Leo had told her and claimed he didn't know. Kate suspected he might know the thief or at least could have helped her figure it out. Most importantly, he wasn't surprised it was a woman.

As Kate walked down Constitution Avenue, she had the overwhelming sensation that she was being watched. She slowed her pace and looked to the front of her and both sides and no one caught her eye. She knew then if she was being watched, they were most likely behind her. Kate stepped toward the building and out of the flow of traffic on the sidewalk. She pulled out her phone and pretended she was going to make a call while she glanced to the left. Stopped in the middle of the sidewalk was the man similar in build to the one she had seen on the street in the rain. Kate was sure it was him, even though she hadn't been able to see his face. It wasn't Leo.

Kate held the phone up as if she was texting and snapped as good a photo as she was able to get. The man wasn't staring directly at her, but she'd be able to enlarge the photo later. She had two choices now – keep walking and let him follow her or go and confront him. Kate shifted her eyes to the left and noticed he was still standing there, not looking at her but not looking away either.

Kate put her phone back in her pocket as if she were done texting and started to walk back toward the FBI building. She made it about twenty feet then pivoted quickly. He was about ten feet behind her and with her swift movement was taken off guard.

"Why are you following me?" Kate yelled as she moved toward him. She worked to memorize his face – dark, deep-set eyes a little too close together, his nose looked like it had been broken at least twice, he had a scar on his left cheek and his jawline was strong but his lips thin. He had a high forehead and closely cut dark hair. He stood a few inches taller than Kate and had a thick muscular build.

He froze for a moment as she advanced then turned on his heels and took off down the street with Kate closing in behind him. She shouted her question again while she still had enough breath to do so.

They made it halfway back toward the Capitol Building, covering a few tenths of a mile. She had no idea where he was headed or if she'd be able to catch him. He was faster than her by a considerable amount. Kate understood now why he'd been able to get away so fast the other night. She shouted again but he kept running, pumping his legs faster and faster while hers were starting to feel like Jell-o.

They shoved by startled people as they went. Kate wasn't sure if anyone noticed her FBI badge slapping against her chest. She wasn't going to stop until she physically had nothing left. The man had other plans though. He made a quick right at the corner. Kate ran faster and was now only a few seconds behind him. He ran two more blocks then turned back to see Kate gaining on him.

Then, without warning, he ran right out into traffic. He made it to the center and looked back at Kate one more time before stepping into oncoming traffic. His body slammed into a taxi, shot up over the windshield, and crashed back down to the ground.

Kate screamed in horror when he was struck again by another passing car. With her eyes wide and breath caught in her throat, Kate held out her hands to stop the traffic and moved across the road as cars came to a screeching halt. She pulled her phone from her pocket and called 911 as she ran to his broken crumpled body in the middle of the road.

As a driver from a nearby car approached her, Kate flashed her badge. "FBI."

"I'm a medic," he shouted to her above the din of the cars and chatter of people.

She waved him over and the two of them went directly to the man who was on his side facing away. Kate walked around his body and stared down at his face. She knew immediately that he was dead. His mouth was twisted in a silent scream and his eyes were open, a blank death stare.

The medic crouched beside him and turned him as gently as he could on his back. He leaned down over his chest to see if his heart was beating. He checked the man's pulse and felt for breath. Then he looked up at Kate. "He's gone."

As the sirens started to wail, she said, "I don't know if he meant to kill himself or if he thought he'd be able to get across. He turned back to see if I was following him when he was hit by the taxi and then the other car. I don't know what he was thinking." Kate's words spilled out. She felt responsible for the man's death, even if he had made the ultimate decision to dart into heavy traffic.

"What did he do?" the medic asked as he stood up.

Kate shook her head, not able to quite articulate herself any longer. "He was following me," she said, knowing how silly that sounded. "We're in the middle of the art theft case and I thought it might be connected."

"That's serious then." The medic asked Kate if she needed anything else and she shook her head. "You're shaking," he said as he reached out and touched her arm.

"Adrenaline. I chased him for probably half a mile, maybe more. I nearly caught him which I think is why he tried to cross the road." Kate stared down at the man's face. She was having trouble forming thoughts now. "I think he did this on purpose."

"I'll wait with you," the medic said but Kate brushed him off.

"You need to move your truck out of traffic. Pull off to the side of the road and make sure you give a statement to the D.C. cops."

Two cops were already in the middle of the road redirecting traffic and clearing the area.

"I'll move my truck and be right back."

Kate stayed with the dead man, all the while second-guessing her decision to chase him. She wasn't sure what else she was supposed to do though. Kate raised her phone to make another call and noted the medic was right, she was shaking.

As her finger fumbled on the screen, Kate took some deep slow breaths, trying to regain her composure. As she calmed herself down enough to find Declan's contact, she hit call. It rang a few times and went to voicemail. She left him a detailed message about what happened. She realized halfway through the message that her voice was cracking and she was having trouble speaking.

With nothing else she could do, Kate ended the call, bent down, and checked the man's pockets for a wallet or any identification. There was none in the front and she couldn't roll him over to check the back pockets of his jeans. She didn't have gloves on, but she desperately wanted to know his identity.

After what felt like an hour but was probably less than ten minutes, an officer arrived and Kate flashed her badge. She explained she had been in pursuit of the man who had been following her when he darted into traffic.

The officer pointed up to two street cameras. "We should have the whole thing recorded. Do you think it was an accident or did he do it on purpose?"

"I have no idea." Kate glanced up in the direction the cop had pointed. She was glad it had all been captured because for as horrific as it was, she wanted to see it to determine the answer to that very question – had he killed himself or was it a tragic accident? The officer asked Kate a few questions and she gave the overview of what would later be her formal statement.

As Kate finished, the ambulance arrived and the medics officially pronounced him dead at the scene. She explained to the cop that the man had been hit twice, once by the taxi and then by another car.

"We have both drivers giving statements right now," the cop confirmed. "The taxi driver said he saw him in the middle of the road but thought he was just trying to cross. The man stepped in front of him before he could do anything. Is that your recollection?"

Kate nodded and tried to swallow but her mouth felt like cotton. "He got out to the middle and stood as the cars went by on each side of him. He looked back at me once before he was struck." The more Kate thought about it, the more she knew the answer. "It had to be intentional. There was too much heavy traffic for this not to have been intentional."

"He got across two lanes of traffic."

"Nothing was coming then. The road was clear on that side. It was once he got to the middle there was traffic on each side." Kate tried to recall what she was looking at during that time but her mind was blank other than the look on the man's face for a split second. She hadn't seen the cars or anything else, it was only the slim memory of his face looking back at her.

Even now, Kate couldn't read the expression – resignation, maybe.

"Agent Walsh," the cop said and touched her arm. "You spaced out on me for a moment. Are you okay?"

Kate blinked rapidly and stuttered over her words. The smell of car fumes and the man's blood made her recoil. She instinctively rubbed her nose to rid herself of the smell, not that it helped. "I'm okay. I was trying to recall the look he gave me before he was hit."

Kate figured she was experiencing shock. The therapist the FBI made her speak to after they got back from Edinburgh had warned her that any trauma she experienced after might feel compounded, bigger than it normally might. Kate knew that in theory but had brushed it off, thinking she was fine. She had only gone to the two forced sessions. When the therapist asked Kate if she wanted to continue, she declined. Declan hadn't said a word to her but his raised eyebrow when she said she had quit therapy said it all.

Now, Kate was wondering if she was experiencing what the therapist had warned. It was akin to being inside someone else's body. Her movements and emotions felt foreign to her. Kate's mind wasn't as sharp and with each wave of dizziness that washed over her, she felt like she might fall.

Kate looked around. "I need to get out of the middle of the road."

The D.C. cop waved over one of the paramedics and said something to him Kate didn't process. The next thing Kate knew there was a paramedic practically holding her up as he walked her to the sidewalk and gently helped her sit on the curb. He flashed the light in her eyes and took her blood pressure.

"It's low. Does your blood pressure always run low?"

Kate raised her head to look at him – she wasn't sure. "I don't know. Sometimes. Maybe." She needed to snap out of it. Only she wasn't sure what was happening. "I'll be okay," Kate assured him even though she didn't know if that was true.

"Kate!" Declan screamed her name through the crowd as he jogged to her. He spotted her with the paramedic. Declan spoke to him and was warned Kate was dizzy and weak and her blood pressure was low.

Declan told him he had it from here and then sat down on the curb with her. "Kate," he said gently, putting his finger under her chin and turning her face to his. "I got here as soon as I could. Do you want to go to the hospital?" He looked her over but she had no physical injuries.

Kate was glad he didn't ask her what happened. She didn't want to relive the details right now. "I don't know what's wrong with me. I don't think the hospital will help." She held her hands out so he could see that she was still shaking. "It's a mix of adrenaline and fear," Kate said quietly, barely admitting it to herself. "I was scared and I never get scared."

Declan took her hand in his. "It's okay, Katie. You're going to be okay. You were alone on the street and he was following you. I'd be freaked out too. I would have chased him. He didn't leave you much of an option."

Kate didn't care who was watching them, she rested her head on his shoulder. "I didn't mean for him to die. He was following me, Declan. I turned to him and asked why he was following me and he ran and I chased. I nearly had him but he ran out into traffic. He's the man I saw the other night at the restaurant."

"You'd think with all of that your blood pressure would be high."

"Training, maybe." Kate didn't know and she didn't care what her blood pressure was doing. "Let's wait here for the medical examiner. I want to see if he had identification on him. I need to know his name."

They talked and processed what happened for a few more minutes and when the medical examiner arrived, Declan made Kate stay on the curb while he took care of it. Kate watched him as he worked with the medical examiner to turn the man over and check his pockets. Declan didn't come back with a wallet but he came back with a photo of his identification card.

"Neil Clark," Declan said as he handed Kate the phone. "He was a British citizen from London. I think it's too much of a coincidence for it to not be connected to the art theft."

Kate stared down at the man's photo. She couldn't say anything for sure but she suspected Declan was right.

CHAPTER 20

Kate and Declan got back to the FBI office after she gave a formal statement to the D.C. police. Knowing the man's name and country of origin gave them the lead they needed to begin some research. Kate didn't want his death to be in vain.

Whatever had come over her out on the street had started to dissipate as they walked back to the office. Declan kept watching her, looking for signs of trouble. By the time they reached the office, Kate had gotten tired of being watched. She was not used to weakness and she didn't want to talk about it anymore.

When Tom asked if she was okay, Kate responded, "I'm great. I hate that the poor guy died but if it means we get a lead on the thefts, then we did our job." It was a harsh and callous response and she knew she was overcompensating. But even Declan wasn't going to question her at that point. "Let's get down to work. Tom, what have you found out about Gabriel?"

Tom handed her the file as they sat down at the conference table. "He has no criminal record here or in Paris where he was working before coming to the National Gallery of Art. He lives in the Adams Morgan neighborhood in D.C. and has lived there for the past five years. There are no anomalies in his banking or credit. He has some charges on his credit cards but it looks like he pays them off every month. He has sizable savings and no debt. This guy is as clean as you get."

Kate had a feeling after what Leo said that would be the case. "I confirmed the cocaine found in the studio was his. He was a regular user."

"A drug addict?" Tom asked with skepticism in his voice.

"I don't know if addict is the right word. He was a long-time cocaine user and had convinced himself that he needed it to paint. I was told that he was one of the globe's best forgers, which is what drew the attention of the Louvre where he worked before the National Gallery. I'm assuming the National Gallery offered him some serious money for him to make the change from the Louvre and come to the United States. He was also having an affair with Marcy."

"Declan told me about Marcy," Tom said and then tapped his fingers on the table as if waiting for the rest of Kate's information.

"You're wondering where I got the information about the drugs?" Kate asked, rhetorically. "Leo told me. I called him and he called me back. We had a conversation about Gabriel and I questioned him about any possible connection he might have to these thieves. He denied knowing them but I'm not so sure. He also speculated that they might be working to draw him out so they can kill him."

Declan sat back in the chair and considered. "That's an interesting theory."

Tom shoved himself back from the table, rocking the whole thing. He didn't get up though. "You're taking advice from an international criminal. What is wrong with the pair of you?"

Kate was over Tom's inability to see the bigger picture and she wasn't going to give in to his outburst. She ignored him and kept her focus on Declan. "I thought they might be trying to one-up him now that Leo is out of the game and retired. I hadn't considered that they'd be trying to draw him out to kill him. It's clear they want to be the big player in the game but they haven't figured out Leo's mission had far less to do with art theft for monetary gain and far more to do with righting a wrong."

"Do you think there are more?" Declan asked, peering across the table at her. By his expression, that's what he was thinking.

Kate had been thinking along those lines but hadn't voiced it yet. "I think we are safe to assume so. We know of at least two in Europe and there are probably more. These are brazen burglaries. They didn't just come out of the gate swinging like this."

Tom agreed with that as well. "How do you see Leo fitting into this?"

Kate wasn't sure exactly how to articulate it. It was a theory she was still rolling around in her mind, but she'd give it her best shot. "The art theft world is smaller than we know. They at least heard the rumors that the Phantom either retired or is just missing in action. I assume they think they can take over where Leo left off. Maybe they get it in their head that they want to be top dog but can only do that if he's truly gone. Remember, the Phantom is legendary and he's larger than life to most, even other thieves. I assume they think they can draw him out. Now whether the end goal is to kill him, I can't be sure. It's what Leo suspects and I have to respect he might have more knowledge on these things than I do. Either way, we have a dual threat here that isn't going to stop until they reach their goal."

Tom had settled back into his seat and was watching Kate. "Is there even an end goal? If the Curators were committing these crimes over a decade, then—"

"Two decades," Kate reminded him. "Leo said they started long before they ever called themselves the Curators or left any calling card behind." She pointed to the end of the table with the boxes. "Those are only a drop in the bucket."

Tom held his hand up in defeat. "I'll say more than two decades. Given that we have to assume these thieves will continue for as long as they can, killing Leo or not."

Confusion fell over Declan's face. "Was there ever any doubt?"

"I had been hoping they'd be after the three paintings in the Chevalier collection and be done with it. I was hoping they were after the mystery of whoever killed the artist."

Kate had been hoping the same. "I think that might have been all of our assumptions at first. Given the recent theft, I think we can safely say it's also about something else."

Tom gestured with his hand. "That goes back to my question about their end goal."

"To keep on stealing for as long as they can," Declan said evenly.

Tom shook his head. "I meant with Leo."

Kate reasoned as best she could. "I think at a minimum, they want him to acknowledge they have one-upped him. As I said, the Phantom has become this mythical figure for law enforcement, governments, and the museums, galleries, and private collectors he's taken from over the last two decades. Very few people know the man. Those who do know the man have no idea that he's the Phantom. I'm among a handful of people who know both."

"You think they want to find out the man behind the myth?" Tom asked.

That was one way to put it. Kate turned her body so she was looking right at him. "I suspect one of their goals is to uncover the Phantom and identify the man and possibly rid the world of him while stepping into his role as one of the greatest art thieves to ever live. It's why they have left their signature and the Curators' card. It's why they have stolen the artworks they have taken. All of the theatrics aim to bring Leo out into the open. They have wrongly determined Leo is going to care that they are trashing his reputation. They are trying to pin the violence on him to bait him."

Tom shifted his eyes between Declan and Kate. "Does he care?"

That was the question of the hour it seemed. Even after the call with him, Kate hadn't been able to figure out if he was depressed, resigned with his fate, or just over everything. She had to admit that as bad as the last case had been for her, it had been deeply personal for Leo.

"I think Leo is traumatized by the murder of his niece." Kate raised her eyes to Declan and was not even sure what was compelling her to say what she was thinking, but it was on the tip of her tongue and she didn't want to hold back. "I'm a little traumatized by the last case and everything that has happened since then."

Declan let his head fall to the side and he looked at her with his eyes soft. "Everything?" he said and Kate knew exactly what he meant.

Kate shook her head realizing what she had said. She wanted to reach her hand across the table and take Declan's hand to reassure him, but she couldn't with Tom there. "No. Not everything." Kate expelled a breath. "You know it was a hard case and traumatic for me at the end. I nearly died and..."

"You don't have to say more," Declan said, understanding finally, or at least Kate hoped he did. "If these thieves aren't going to stop until they draw Leo out and he's refusing to take the bait, what do we do?"

"I'm not sure what we can do. If Leo identifies himself, he'll be arrested."

"At least that will keep him safe," Tom said and then thought better of it. "Maybe not but they can't target him in custody."

"He'll spend the rest of his life bouncing from prison to prison subject to more than a lifetime of sentences. They can still target him in prison." Kate had told Leo the truth, she didn't want to arrest him and she didn't want to see him in prison. "I don't know that we can do anything other than stopping these thieves ourselves. This is like any other case. Let's start with Neil Clark. If we believe he was watching us related to these art thefts, then there's a connection there."

Tom cleared his throat and had a tentative look on his face. "Do you think he was watching you because of the case or your connection to

Leo?"

While Kate remained quiet, Declan added, "Our connection to the Phantom was all over the news. We have to assume so."

Kate couldn't argue that point. "Tom, do you think they might have been watching me in the hopes I'd lead them to Leo?"

"It's possible. Don't you think?"

"If what Leo said is true, then I'd say it's probable. Senator Willis announced the hearing more than two months ago. They had a long lead time."

Declan watched Kate carefully and then turned to Tom. "Let's figure out what we can about Neil and go from there. I know the crime scene techs mentioned they'd have a report for us soon. Do you want me to run upstairs and check?"

"I'll get it." Tom stood from the table and passed by Kate but stopped at the door. "For what it's worth, Kate, I would have chased him too. I don't think you had much of a choice about that."

She appreciated his words and didn't mind admitting her struggle. "It's going to take me some time to be okay with how it ended."

"He made choices, Kate. That's not on you." He left without saying more.

When he was gone, Declan got up from his chair, grabbed Kate's laptop at the end of the table, and sat next to her. She thought he was ready to get down to work but he had something else on his mind. He slipped her hand into his. "Would you tell me if you regretted what happened between us?"

"You have nothing to worry about. It's the one nice memory I have from that case." Kate shrank back feeling momentarily self-conscious. "Do you have regrets?"

"Not at all." Declan ducked his head low and dropped his voice. "I just saw your reaction outside and I'm worried about you. Hearing you talk about how traumatized you were in Scotland made me think you weren't making clear decisions."

Kate smiled at his sweetness. He was truly concerned about her. "I'm not telling you that you shouldn't be worried about me because I'm a little worried by the physical symptoms I had out there in response, but this…us…was the most clear-headed decision I made in years."

"Okay," Declan said and flashed his winning smile that made most women swoon. "I'm not going to stress it. Did Leo say anything else?"

Kate thought back to what he said about holding her and hoped she didn't blush. "He sounds lonely and dismissive. The fire in him has gone out." Kate couldn't shake the feeling that Leo knew who was committing these thefts. He had to have some idea but just didn't seem to care. "I wish I knew where he was. I'd go and talk to him and convince him to help us." She glanced over at Declan who seemed to be anything but interested in that.

"Let's get down to work finding Neil Clark," was all Declan said in response. He fired up her laptop and plugged the man's name into the FBI database.

CHAPTER 21

Late that evening Kate and Declan sat in the same booth at District Chophouse as they had the previous night. Spade had called around six to check their progress and wanted to ensure that Kate was doing okay after what happened with Neil Clark. He'd seen the street surveillance video the D.C. Metro Police had sent him and it showed Kate was nowhere near the man when he darted out into traffic. By his estimation, Spade agreed that it looked like a suicide.

Neil had a criminal record back in London for hacking into banks and the electrical grid. He'd already spent a few years in prison and traveled to the United States on a fake passport. The address he'd listed for his whereabouts in New York City was bogus. After checking with the New York Police Department, there was only one apartment over the deli and it was occupied by an elderly woman who had lived there for the last fifty years. There was no known connection between her and Neil. It was a dead end.

There was a stack of pages Kate and Declan still had to go through of known associates of Neil, but Declan's growling stomach had proven stronger than their need for information. He had looked up at Kate across the conference room table and pleaded with his eyes. She took pity on his pathetic look and they left for dinner.

Before leaving, Tom had stopped back in the conference room and delivered some lucky news. There had been a partial fingerprint found on the edge of the King of Diamonds left at the Smithsonian. He ran it through the FBI database but didn't get a hit. He wasn't sure if the partial fingerprint wasn't enough to match or if there wasn't a match in the database. An unknown partial was better than nothing.

Late that afternoon, Kate had also received a call from Sam Harris with the National Crime Agency in London. He assured Kate he'd been by the address listed for Leo several times but never saw the man. He spoke to the building owner and found out that no one named Leo Lamiere had ever lived there. When Sam went through the previous rental files, he found one for Declan Walsh and knew Leo had been there. He had called Kate and she rolled her eyes at the news, not planning on telling Declan.

In Scotland, Leo had used their combined names as an alias and it seemed he had been doing that long before that case. He had told her he started using it after their encounter in Paris but Kate hadn't believed him. Now, she knew it to be true.

Unfortunately, the address in London was a dead end. Sam promised to check that alias against other records in the city and get back to her. Kate was fairly certain he wasn't going to find anything. She assumed Leo used aliases for credit cards, passports, and an array of other documentation and probably changed frequently. She promised Sam she'd be in touch with any other promising leads. There was no point wasting resources for a fool's errand.

Once at the restaurant, Kate felt her whole body start to decompress. She'd barely slept the night before and she was running on empty.

Halfway through his dinner, Declan glanced up at her. "You're not eating," he said, pointing to her plate with his fork. "You need to eat, Kate. Look at how weak you were earlier today. I don't think you've been eating nearly enough. That's probably a part of your problem."

Kate stared down at the steak, mashed potatoes, and asparagus she had ordered. She'd had an appetite when she sat down but it had waned while they were waiting for their food. Kate had taken a few bites of each and was working up the energy to eat the rest. Her mind had been elsewhere during dinner.

She was thinking about the bells that had chimed when she was on the phone with Leo. "He's not far from a church."

Declan pointed to her plate again. "I'll listen to anything you say about Leo after you eat."

Kate was about to make a joke about keeping her figure trim for him but knew he didn't care. When they were in the FBI Academy, Kate had a front-row seat to the women Declan had dated and they had come in all shapes, sizes, hair colors, and backgrounds. He was a man without a type. He told her once that if he felt a spark, he felt a spark. There wasn't always a good explanation for how or why it happened, he just went with it when it did.

"Why are you smiling?" Declan asked, taking a bite of his steak. He was looking at her with a bemused expression on his face. "Are you going to tell me to stop being bossy or were you thinking about throwing potatoes at me?"

"Neither. I was thinking about all the different women you dated while we were at the FBI Academy."

Declan scrunched up his face. "That makes you smile? I thought thinking about that time might make you jealous. I wasn't the respectable man I am today."

Kate shook her head. "It doesn't make me jealous. It's too much to explain. I'll eat and make you happy." She heeded his advice and dug into her dinner. After a few bites, her appetite returned and Kate finished her dinner.

When they were both done, she asked, "Can we talk about the bells now?"

Declan sat back and rested his hands over his full stomach. "What about them?"

"I feel like I've heard them before."

"They are bells, Kate. Don't most church bells sound the same?"

That could be true. Kate had no idea. "There was something distinctive about these. I can't quite put my finger on it. I'm sure if I heard them again or for longer, it might come to me."

"Even if you figured it out, what would it mean?"

It would mean Kate would know where to find Leo. She told Declan as much and he laughed. "I could go there. We'd know where he was at least. I don't know if he stays in one place for very long."

"What are you going to do, show up and have a chat with him?" He leaned his arms on the table. "Be straight with me. Could you arrest him if you had the chance?"

Kate shifted her eyes away from Declan's. There's no way she could look him in the eye and lie. "Of course, I could. It's my job and no matter what he's done, there has to be some justice." She didn't sound convincing. Kate looked directly at him now. "I'm unsure whether I believe he deserves jail time for what he's done. He's nearly convinced me that if governments and others did the right thing, his mission wouldn't have been needed."

Declan wasn't even trying to hide his smile. "I believe the last part. I don't believe you'd arrest him and that's okay, Kate. The man saved your life and you've built a rapport with him. You're only human, even if you like to pretend you're not. I'm not sure I could arrest him and half the time I'm jealous of him."

"Jealous?" Kate asked not sure she had heard him right.

"International man of intrigue. Handsome. So charming he compromised you. The Robin Hood of the art world. Come on, Kate. Most men would be jealous of him." Declan was laughing now and Kate couldn't help but join him. He might have been laughing but there was a truth in Declan's words. It seeped into his tone and Kate could see in his eyes that he was serious. She didn't want to press the subject.

Kate reached for the file on the table while Declan ordered dessert. He had a bigger sweet tooth than anyone she'd ever met. She flipped open the file and took out the first page and then the second. The database had brought back known associates of Neil Clark from public records, places he had lived in the past, and those with criminal records he'd been arrested with or served jail time at the same facility.

That's what interested Kate the most – the prison records.

"He wasn't in prison that long ago," Kate said absently doing the mental math. "He was arrested five years ago and served three and a half years. I would assume these burglaries started soon after."

Declan reached his hand out for a stack of the pages. "If you're going to work, I'm going to work. I can't sit here and watch you. It makes me feel like a slacker."

Kate smiled up at him and gladly handed over the pages. "The sooner we solve this case, the faster we can get back to Boston."

"You don't like D.C.?"

"I'll always feel a fondness for it, especially having been here so much with my father. I love Boston though and it's been nice having some time at home."

"I like having the freedom we have in Boston without so many eyes on us." Declan lowered his eyes to the pages and started to go through the stack. He skimmed the pages as Kate did hers but it wasn't long before he got her attention. "Look at these, Kate. These two are brothers who served at the same time as Neil. They were in for burglary and assault. Duncan and Bertie Munson."

Kate took the pages and stared down at them. There was biographical data next to mugshots. The Munson brothers were hulking men with thick biceps, broad shoulders, and mean-looking expressions, even for a mugshot. Duncan had a shaved head and neck tattoo while Bertie had a thick wave of dark hair and a bulging vein on the right side of his neck. They were from Essex, England and were roughly the same age as Neil, all in their early thirties. The date of their incarceration was a match. The Munsons were two years into a five-year stint when Neil showed up. They were let out of prison within two months of each other.

Kate rested the pages on the table, her mind reeling with the possibility. "These look like they could be the hired guns of the operation. It certainly fits if Neil was their tech guy and these two went inside with the woman. They are all English too, which backs up what the witness said about the woman with the fancy accent."

Declan stacked up the pages and handed them back to her to put in the file. "It's nearing nine and you've had very little sleep all week. I suggest we go back, take a hot shower, and settle in for the night. No more talk about work and international criminals. I want to see how the Red Sox are doing in the pre-season and I want some quality time with you." He gave her a look that showed exactly what he meant.

Kate appreciated that he was taking care of her, as much as she would allow. "You'll get no argument from me."

Declan flagged down the server and paid the bill while Kate gathered up their things to leave. She glanced outside before sliding out of the booth. Earlier today, after the rain stopped it had turned into a fairly warm spring day. Even at close to nine, it was still in the high sixties and the perfect night for a walk. "Let's take the long way back to the hotel."

"It's a nice enough night for it." Declan held the door for her as she stepped outside to the sidewalk. She waited for him and even though Kate was the one who had warned about not being too touchy in public, especially in D.C. with all its prying eyes, she laced her fingers through his. Kate turned to look up at him to make sure it was okay. He leaned down and kissed her sweetly. "You never have to ask to hold my hand."

The road was fairly empty and they hadn't passed anyone on the sidewalk. Kate was surprised given the weather. They were in a part of D.C. that had a lot of business traffic but if there wasn't anything happening at the arena, there weren't a lot of other businesses open at that time of night.

Kate held tightly to Declan's hand, letting herself process the wave of emotions that came over her. She had to admit it was a strange feeling walking with him like that. Outside of a short relationship in college, if she could even call it that, she hadn't had what could even amount to a short-term adult relationship. She hadn't lived a celibate life. She'd given in to attractions and urges over the years. Kate wasn't a saint by any stretch, but she lacked time and opportunity for anything long-term.

She had mostly been involved with men she met along the way through work. There had been a CIA operative in Marrakesh while she was working a case. There had been a local detective in Seattle when a case had taken her there shortly after she had started her career. They had felt the heat and tension throughout the investigation and when the missing girl had been found safe, they gave in to a night of passion in her hotel room. There had also been an art dealer, with whom she had what amounted to two weekend flings and Kate ended it not that long ago.

In her pathetically short history with men, there had been nothing with the potential to be *something*. With Declan, it was already *something*, even if the two of them had never spoken it aloud.

Declan's dating history had more depth and breadth to it. There had been short-term flings, women he dated for months and he'd even been married for several years. Kate's chest constricted when she thought about it. She didn't know how to be someone's girlfriend. She knew how to be his partner and for a lot of years the one who harped on him for drinking too much.

Kate didn't know how to settle into the relationship and relax.

"Your hand is tensing. What's on your mind, Katie?" Declan bumped his body into hers playfully and squeezed her hand. "There must be something. I'll tell you what I'm thinking." He bobbed his eyebrows up and down, making her laugh. "I want to pull you into that alleyway—"

The first shot silenced Declan. The second shot sent them to the ground.

CHAPTER 22

Kate threw herself to the ground taking Declan with her. She rolled over onto her back and reached for her gun. The parked car beside them acted as their only shield.

"Are you okay?" she asked through a hushed breath.

Declan patted himself down. "I'm good. You?"

Kate didn't feel like she'd been shot but then again the adrenaline that coursed through her could be deceptive. She realized then they were still holding hands. Kate let go and checked herself over. "I think I'm okay." Two more shots ricocheted off the building behind them.

They were pinned down behind the car, unsure of where the shots originated. There had been no car driving by at the time and Kate didn't recall seeing anyone on the street with them. The buildings around them had been dark.

Declan got to his knees and crawled toward the back end of the car while Kate crawled to the front. "I don't see anyone," he said as another shot sailed over his head.

Kate leaned low to the ground and took her time scanning the area. She caught the glint of movement through one of the first floor windows in the building across the street.

"Two o'clock from your position. First floor," Kate directed him. She had no idea if they'd get a shot off from where they both were on the ground. The only way would be to risk exposure. She couldn't even be one hundred percent sure that the movement she saw was the person shooting.

"What do you want to do, Kate?"

Kate kept her eyes on the building while she reached for her phone. She fumbled it until she got it on the ground in front of her and called 911. They needed backup and to close off the area as soon as possible. Kate was worried for Declan and herself but she was more worried about the other diners still in the restaurant or who might round the corner and walk into gunfire.

As they remained there trying to decide the best course of action, three more shots hit the car, triggering the car alarm and flashing lights.

Then the shots stopped as quickly as they started.

Kate and Declan still didn't have enough information to confidently get up off the ground or to take a shot in the direction of the building.

The wailing sirens from the D.C. Metro Police joined the grating sound of the car alarm. Kate and Declan shared a look and then slowly inched off the ground. With no further shots, Declan darted off across the road to the building with Kate right behind him.

They checked the front door of the building but found it locked. "I'm going around back," he shouted and then took off in a sprint.

A man shouted from behind Kate and she turned sharply with her gun aimed at him. He dropped his keys on the ground as his hands shot up in the air. "I'm trying to shut off my car alarm," he said with his eyes wide with fear.

Kate told him to keep his hands up. She trusted no one at that moment. He looked like he was in his late twenties and had on sweatpants and a Washington Capitals tee-shirt. He yelled to Kate his name and address as she approached him.

Kate identified herself and asked if he minded a pat down. He told her to do whatever she needed to do. She patted him down and then cleared him. "We had someone shooting at us from across the street. Do you know what's on that first floor?" she asked, pointing at the window where she thought she'd seen the shooter.

The man lowered his hands and picked his keys up from the ground. He clicked off the car alarm before answering. Kate could still hear the sound reverberating in her ears.

"It's an empty apartment. I don't think it's been rented out yet." He glanced to the side of Kate and looked across the street. "I take that back. I don't see the sign in the window that was there yesterday. Maybe it's been rented."

"Do you know the landlord?"

The man shook his head. "I think he owns the whole building." He looked away from Kate and got a good look at his car. He ran a hand over the three bullet holes in his driver's side door. "What do I do about these?" he asked, looking up at Kate.

"Call your insurance company," Kate said dismissively. She didn't mean to sound so cold but his car was the least of her worries. Someone had been watching them closely enough to get a jump on them on the street. When the first D.C. Metro cop arrived on the scene, Kate crossed the road and gave him the overview of what happened.

He looked at her quizzically. "This is the second incident of the day for you, Agent Walsh. I was at the scene with the guy who ran into traffic earlier today. I'm working a double."

Kate thought he had looked familiar. "Bad day, I guess." She had no other explanation and she wasn't going to get into the totality of their case right there on the street. "My partner went down the alleyway and around the back of the building. I'm going after him. Tell the other cops when they arrive that we'll be back. Whoever shot at us is still on the loose."

Kate headed off in the direction Declan went and met him in the alleyway.

"I can't find an access point into the building and I didn't see anyone leave," he said, frustrated and annoyed. "I don't know where they went, Kate. I don't think he could have gotten out of the building that fast."

"We were on the ground long enough that they could have escaped." Kate walked down the alleyway to see for herself. She tried one door, tugging on it to no avail. She followed the alley to the other side of the building and tried what appeared to be the front door. It too was locked but there was a keypad on the front door that Kate assumed tenants used to open the door. There were no signs indicating who owned the building or a phone number to call for access.

"We are going to have to get property records if one of the local cops doesn't know." Kate wanted to search the building as quickly as possible. She left Declan standing at the front door and jogged down the street at the front of the building, instead of the alley, back toward the cop who had been first on the scene. At this point, other cops had started to arrive.

When Kate reached him, she asked, "Do you know who owns this building? I need to access it."

The cop rattled off the name of a well-known D.C. developer. "He doesn't even live in D.C. anymore. Last I heard he was in Miami. I think there's a building manager." He radioed someone and asked for the information. Whoever he spoke to told him to hold on and then they radioed back with a name and phone number. "Devin Katz. If someone broke in, the alarm should have been triggered. I wouldn't be surprised if he's on his way here now. I was told he lives up in Silver Spring so it might take him some time." The cop gave Kate the phone number.

Kate thanked him and then walked away to make the call. The phone rang three times before a man answered. She confirmed it was Devin Katz, the building's manager, then introduced herself. "We believe someone broke into your building and was shooting at us from a window on the first floor. Are you able to get here to let us in?"

"I'm on my way there now. The silent alarm was tripped about an hour ago. I assumed it was a mistake when the alarm company called me. It's been tripped a few times in the past three weeks. Each time, I've come down and found nothing amiss. I believe there is some faulty wiring. An alarm company representative is coming out tomorrow to take a look at it."

"Can you confirm who lives in the front corner apartment?"

"I only rented it earlier today. No one has the key. No one should have been in there." He yelled at a car in front of him. "You'd think this late there wouldn't be idiot drivers," Devin said and cussed loudly. The sound of screeching brakes and a horn came through the phone.

Kate asked for the code to get into the building. She didn't want to wait until he arrived. "We need to move quickly on this. If they have been going in and out of that apartment, I need to get a crime scene tech team down here now. The sooner they can sweep the place, the sooner we can get it back to you."

Devin gave her the code. "I should be there in about twenty minutes," he said and then laid on the horn again. "I don't know that you'll be able to access the apartment. If the door isn't open, I have the key and you'll have to wait."

Kate thanked him for the information and ended the call. She headed back to the front of the building as she slipped her phone back in her pocket. As she rounded the corner, Declan stood at the front door with one of the FBI crime scene techs.

"I called them while you were hunting down the building's owner," Declan explained. "Turns out, he lives around the corner."

Kate introduced herself and explained, "It's not the building's owner who is coming but the manager. In the meantime, I have the code to get in. It sounds like this isn't the first time the silent alarm has been tripped. He thought it was faulty wiring. I assume it was whoever was shooting at us. I don't know what we are going to find when we get in there."

"Do you think there's something to be found?" Declan asked, handing her a pair of gloves the tech had given him.

"If they have been in and out of this apartment for a few days than anything is possible. I don't think it's going to be anything too glaring as the apartment was just rented and Devin said he'd been down the last few evenings when the alarm tripped. He didn't indicate that he noticed anything amiss." Kate snapped on the gloves and asked the tech if he wanted to dust the keypad for prints right now or wait until they were inside. The reality was there were so many people in and out of the building that the keypad was probably the least reliable surface to get a good print.

"Let's get inside and then we can take it from there," the young tech said, indicating that another person from his team was on their way.

Kate punched in the four-digit code and the door beeped and she was able to pull it open. They assessed the small lobby that had a bench and a row of metal mailboxes. There was no doorman or other seating area. Kate thought it was fairly sparse for a downtown D.C. building where the rents ran in the thousands.

There were two halls off the main foyer and two elevators that would take them to the top floors. Kate decided the left was probably the hall rather than the one on the right, which seemed to go in the opposite direction they needed. She was a bit surprised that with all of the shooting no one was out of their apartments talking to their neighbors and asking what was happening. In her neighborhood in Boston, gunshots would have surely brought her neighbors to the street.

Kate counted off the apartments as she went and then found the one Devin indicated. The number one in the 112 was slightly askew and Kate resisted the urge to straighten it.

Declan tried the door handle and turned it without resistance. "It's unlocked," he said as he pushed it open. He had his gun drawn at his side and the crime scene tech stood down the hall as they breached the entrance.

Kate went in after Declan and surveyed the living room of the apartment. It wasn't furnished and there was nothing in the space except the smell of fresh paint and a newly shampooed tan carpet. The lines from the steamer still creased the rug. She moved from the living room to the small square dining space that attached to the galley kitchen. Kate could stand in the center, reach out her arms, and touch both sides. She opened the cabinets but there was nothing but ugly yellow shelving paper.

Declan had headed down the hall toward what she assumed was the bedroom. "In here, Kate," he yelled not even a moment later. "They were here and they left a note."

Kate stopped looking through the cabinets and rushed down the hall to the bedroom. She entered the empty bedroom and went to the window where Declan stood. His body blocked what was in his hand. "What do you mean a note?"

He flicked the paper toward her. "It's not so much a note as it is an address. Do you know it?"

Kate took the paper from him and glanced down at it. She didn't know the address but knew the neighborhood on River Road in Potomac. It was one of the wealthiest areas in the D.C. Metro.

Kate pulled out her phone, plugged the address into the search engine, and read aloud. "The thirty-thousand square foot French Baroque-style mansion sits on ten acres of land. It has a four-car detached garage, a guest house in the back of the property, a pool house, and a large pool. There are seven bedrooms, nine bathrooms, and a media room." Kate raised her eyes to Declan. "What do you want to guess that someone right now is dead inside of that house and a painting was stolen?"

Declan cursed loudly, grabbed his phone and made a call to get all units available to that address. He looked down at Kate. "Who owns it?"

"A tech billionaire," Kate said, feeling her throat constrict as she completed the search.

CHAPTER 23

By the time Kate and Declan showed up on River Road with Tom behind the wheel of his SUV, the place had been surrounded by cops. Kate had tried several times to reach the owner of the home but each call went straight to voicemail.

The house was the fifth one on the street but stood far away from the others. There was a wrought iron gate across the entrance that had been left open and a steep climb to the house. Kate was sure if someone was alive inside the home, they would have come out by now given the flashing lights. As the SUV approached, Kate surveyed the land and then zeroed in on the one light downstairs that was on. The rest of the mansion remained dark.

Kate got out of the SUV and tightened her vest. She unholstered her gun and waited for Declan to ready himself. There was a swath of other FBI agents and local police in the large rectangle path of concrete that was carved into the well-manicured lawn in the front of the home.

Declan and Tom went first with Kate right behind. They reached the door and Declan called, "Alexander Branston, this is the FBI." He shouted other instructions should the man be in his home. The door had been left ajar and Declan nudged it open further. It swung inward and he stepped into the home. He swung to the left and then to the right with his gun leading the way.

"I don't see anyone," he shouted and then continued his search with Tom and Kate joining him. They went from room to room and found nothing. There was no person, piece of furniture, or object in the house out of place.

Tom and other FBI agents broke off from Kate and Declan and went upstairs to search. Kate continued to go through the sprawling rooms on the first floor. There had been a map of the house on the real estate website she had saved to her phone.

Alexander had bought the home only six months prior, for thirty-four million dollars. By all accounts, he was in his late forties, hailed originally from Seattle, and was unmarried with no children. She wondered if he was even there. Kate assumed men like him probably traveled extensively more than they were ever in one place.

Kate couldn't help but notice the ostentatious display of art on the walls in every room. If someone had told her Alexander was planning to turn the home into a gallery she wouldn't have been surprised. She clocked a Renoir in the sitting room and a Degas in the dining room. The man's taste spanned centuries, countries, and styles.

Declan got to a door in the far back corner of the home and paused. He tipped his head toward the door, nearly resting his ear against it. "There's music playing inside."

Kate glanced down at the map on the phone. "It's the media room."

Declan turned the handle slowly and pushed it open. He stepped into the room with plush gold and red carpeting and matching fabric on the walls. There were six rows of seats that went six across in a sloping fashion toward the large screen at the front of the room. *The French Connection* with Gene Hackman and Roy Schneider played on the screen.

At first, it didn't appear that anyone was in the room until the lights from the movie brightened and Kate saw the back of a man's head in the second row. It took a moment for her eyes to adjust to see that he was sitting perfectly still, not moving at all.

"We need the lights," she said to Declan who was already a step ahead of her.

As he flicked on the overhead lights, Kate squinted at the brightness. She and Declan walked toward the unmoving man. It only took her a few steps to realize the red mixed in with his blond locks was sticky blood and brain matter. There was no question that he was dead.

Kate approached the row and looked down the length of it to the man's body. She noted that there was something crumpled up in his hand. What was left of his head rested back on the seat and his vacant eyes stared forward. There was a hole in the center of his forehead where the bullet had entered. Kate had seen a few photos of Alexander online.

"It's him, Declan," Kate said and took a few tentative steps toward the man's body. She had no idea if anyone was still in the home, so the threat wasn't technically over. But Kate assumed they were long gone and that shooting at them in the street had merely been used to get their attention rather than injure or kill them. She holstered her gun and tugged on gloves she carried in her back pocket.

While Declan called the medical examiner and a crime scene team, Kate looked over the man. She snapped a few photos. Then she uncurled his fingers and took out the crumpled piece of paper that looked like it had been shoved into his hand after he was already dead. His nails were perfectly manicured and nothing about them or the rest of his body indicated that he had put up a fight.

Kate assumed he was sitting watching a movie when they walked to the front of the screen and shot him before he even had a chance to react. She smoothed out the note and read the few words scrawled on the page.

The Death of Marat. *Bring us The Phantom and we'll stop. Don't and more will die.*

The Death of Marat was an oil painting created in 1793 by French artist Jacques-Louis David depicting the assassination of Jean-Paul Marat, a radical activist during the French Revolution. Kate only knew the highlights about Marat. He had been a physician and publisher and at the start of the French Revolution in 1789, used his newspaper to voice his support for radical and democratic measures. Later, he joined the National Convention, the assembly that governed France after the overthrow of the monarchy. Kate needed to do a quick search to see where she had seen the painting long ago. It was supposed to be in the Royal Museums of Fine Arts in Belgium.

Kate scrolled through links until she found an article that explained the painting had been stolen from the museum three years ago. It seemed it ended up in Alexander's hands and was now stolen again. Kate tucked her phone back in her pocket and searched the surrounding seats and floor for a King of Diamonds but found none.

Kate waited until Declan came back into the media room with Tom in tow. She walked the distance back up toward the door. "The victim is Alexander Branston, the tech billionaire."

Tom cursed softly under his breath. "He sold his artificial intelligence software and one of his companies last year. He said he was leaving New York City for a quieter life here in Maryland. He opened new offices in D.C. just a month ago."

Kate glanced back at him, thinking about the wasted life and then turned back to Tom. "What do you know about *The Death of Marat*?"

"It was stolen from Belgium a few years ago. It was one of nine paintings stolen that night. The thief was arrested four months later on another heist. They never recovered what was stolen though. Why?"

Kate thrust the note toward Tom and he took it. "It appears Alexander had the painting and it was stolen again by whomever killed him. I want to search the house to see if I can find where he had it and if there is a King of Diamonds card."

Tom pointed toward the ceiling. "There's a painting missing from his office upstairs. I didn't search for the card though. We were just sweeping the house making sure all was clear."

"I'm going to head up there and search. If you need me, just call." Before she left, she said to Declan, "We need to figure out how they got in. I don't know that Alexander would have left his front door unlocked while he was here in his media room." She texted him a map of the house which also indicated all the windows and exits. Kate knew Declan would want to get a jump going over the scene before the techs arrived.

She went back out the way they had come into the front of the house, through the foyer, and then climbed the stairs to the second floor. She peeked her head into several of the rooms until she came to the office. The whole house had a staged feel to it almost as if Alexander didn't live there. While he could more than afford the home, she had no idea why anyone would need or want that much space. The home also had a cold feel to it. Her brownstone was much too big for her, which is why she had invited Declan to move in after his divorce. Her house was cozy and well-lived – especially with him there.

Kate stood on the threshold of the office. There was cold marble flooring and a rug only under the desk and chair. The room was three times the size of her office but held about half of the furniture, books, and knickknacks. If anyone looked in Kate's office, they'd have a roadmap of her career and travels. This room gave no real sense of a person – other than compulsively tidy, sparse, and cold. It could have been Alexander's personality for all she knew.

The one thing the man liked more than anything else was expensive art. There were four paintings on one side of the room and three on the other. Tom was right that the space where *The Death of Marat* had been hung was now empty.

Kate searched the area around the painting but there wasn't anywhere to tuck in a card. There was no rug or space between the floor molding. She carefully went to the painting next to it, lifted it forward, and looked behind it. There was nothing there. Kate repeated this on all the other paintings in the room and found nothing at all. She stood in the middle of the room with her hands on her hips, wondering if there was someplace else in the office where she could search. There were two shelves of books, mostly biographies of military generals and titans of industry. She had no idea why the thieves would tuck a card into those, but Kate did not doubt that one would be found eventually.

She assumed they left the handwritten note because they had grown tired of the FBI not understanding their clues. If Senator Stephen Willis hadn't gone public with the fact that Kate had been in contact with the Phantom, the world might never know of their connection. If there was anyone besides the thieves to blame for this debacle and the deaths it was him. Not that Kate would state that publicly. If given the chance, she might say it to his face. Kate imagined telling Senator Willis how complicit he'd been in the things happening in D.C. and it brought a smile to her face.

"Are you thinking about what we should be doing back at the hotel right now?" Declan joked as he entered the office.

Kate glanced over at him. "Don't mean to disappoint, but no. I was thinking about telling off Senator Willis."

Declan chuckled. "That will do it." He handed her an evidence bag with the King of Diamonds. "I found it taped under one of the seats in the front row. I figured while I was waiting for the crime scene techs, I'd do a thorough search of the media room. I didn't want you to waste any more time up here." Declan made a full turn as he took in the surroundings of the office. "This is sterile and boring. All this money this guy had, you'd think he'd get an interior designer in here."

"I think he probably liked it like this. His whole house is this way.

Like it was staged for sale and he walked in and said he'd take it as is." Kate didn't want to disparage a dead man, but he was also the owner of stolen art. "Has Tom started taking inventory of all the art? We are going to want a list and alert the estate that nothing can be sold or transferred. If he had one stolen painting, the likelihood is he had more."

Declan nodded. "There's an entire basement full of art that Tom needs to go through. They are still in shipping containers. It wouldn't surprise me if this guy made some of his money by means other than his tech business."

It was probably one of the reasons he'd been targeted. The painting that had been stolen went right to the heart of what Leo told her. "Leo was right. They want him dead and they want me to draw him out so they can kill him. I'm not going to do that, Declan, even if it costs me my job."

Declan could see the conviction on her face. "I don't think anyone can expect that of you." He said the words but his tone implied something else Kate couldn't quite decipher. She wasn't going to dwell on it now.

"I want to look around this office a bit more and then I'll meet you back in the media room."

Declan asked her if she was okay and when she assured him she was fine, he left her there alone. Kate wasn't sure why she wanted to search the office but Alexander had his secrets. She wanted to know more.

Kate went to the bookcase and thumbed through the books, opened the desk drawers, and looked through them. When she got to the bottom drawer there was a stack of postcards. She flipped through them taking in the landscapes, monuments, and historic buildings. She looked at the back but not one of them had been filled out.

Kate flipped through them one more time and stopped at a familiar stone chapel. The name said St. Michael's Chapel, Cassis, France. Kate knew the chapel. She had been inside on a trip with her parents, sitting in the front pew while her parents spoke to the pastor. She had loved that little chapel.

She looked up from the postcard and stared at the doorway, trying to recall more of that memory from her childhood.

It hit her all at once. The bells. The seaside fishing village.

Leo.

CHAPTER 24

Kate's mouth felt like she had eaten cotton balls but her palms were sweating so badly she kept wiping them down her pant legs. Over the next two hours, Kate tried to contain herself as they went through the mansion looking for other evidence. She still had a job to do.

Declan had glanced in her direction more than once. He had noticed her strange behavior but thankfully didn't raise any questions while they worked with the crime scene techs, spoke to the medical examiner, and checked in on Tom.

He was busy creating a plan on how to categorize all of the art found at Alexander's because the collection was vast. Tom would need a team to help him. Given they had already found one stolen painting, the FBI had probable cause to go through all of it. While Tom was focused on other potential stolen art, Declan speculated about Alexander's possible involvement in the current crimes.

It meant his estate would be tied up for a while. Not that they even knew who to identify for next of kin. Tom mentioned a sister in Seattle but they'd yet to track down her information. Surely, there were business partners or staff or someone, but in the wee hours of the morning, they'd yet to find anyone.

Alexander's phone was locked and even though they had tried, they couldn't crack the code to get in. The same with the laptop on

Alexander's desk. It was work that would be carried over to the next day. Kate hoped she could keep the whole thing out of the newspapers until next of kin could be notified. She couldn't imagine having to hear over morning coffee that someone in their family had been murdered.

The fact that Alexander had a stolen painting, the front door of his home was unlocked and slightly ajar, and after Declan's speculation, Kate had one important question that needed an answer – what were the chances Alexander knew his killers? She couldn't be sure but Kate thought they were high.

As the crime scene techs were finishing in the media room, Kate took one last walk through the house. She went through all of the rooms on the first floor and then climbed the stairs to the second. She started in one spare bedroom and went through four more, each with a neatly made bed, dresser, and large armoire. They were replicate rooms of each other. The only thing different was the color paint on the walls and the style of the accessories.

Kate left Alexander's bedroom for last. It was the largest by far and had an attached sitting room, walk-in-closet, and bathroom. There was also a small office off the sitting room. Nothing like the size of the other office. It was more like an alcove with a desk with a laptop on it and a small lamp. There was a small chair with an ottoman to the side of the desk. It looked to Kate like a cozy reading nook. She assumed this laptop would require a passcode but she tried it anyway. Kate hit the start button and pulled back in surprise when the laptop went through its starting process and directly to the home screen. There was no passcode.

Kate pulled out the chair and sat down, eager to see what she could find. She clicked on the file icon and was disappointed to see there were only two saved files – one said taxes and the other was just labeled legacy. Kate clicked the legacy file first and her eyes scanned over all the documents that came up. She couldn't make sense of what she was seeing – there were contracts, signed memorandums of understanding between different companies, and docs full of tech speak Kate didn't understand.

Not that she cared about the man's taxes, but Kate clicked that file next. Instead of the PDF documents she assumed she'd find similar to her tax file on her laptop, Kate found photos – lots and lots of photos. She clicked the first and then went through them one by one. They were all of Alexander and an unknown woman. She looked to be late twenties with short dark hair cut in a severe bob with straight thick bangs that came over her forehead. She had a squarish face, a thin pointed nose, and deep-set blue eyes. Her lips were painted in a stiff, red smile in every photo. What was most haunting was how she looked almost expressionless. She seemed to stare past the camera as if she were indifferent to being photographed and the entire situation. She looked like a woman at a party who was over the whole scene and waiting patiently to make her exit. Alexander beamed happy and content in every photo. It was a stark contrast.

Kate snapped a few photos of the images with her cellphone. They would have to see if they could find this woman. There was nothing though to indicate her name. Each photo file was named with an event and the date. A few of the photos were at the current mansion so Kate knew the relationship between them was recent. The date of the last photo was only three weeks ago at a society dinner in D.C.

Kate pushed her chair back from the desk and went to the bathroom and searched the medicine cabinet and under the sink, looking for women's toiletries but found none. She flipped on the light in the walk-in closet but there was only men's clothing and shoes. Whoever this woman was, she didn't live here with Alexander. There was nothing in the rest of the house to indicate a woman's touch.

"Kate!" Declan called her name as she was backing out of the closet and turning off the light. "I'm ready to go if you are." He found her standing in the short hallway between the walk-in closet and the master bathroom.

As Declan caught up to her, she pointed toward the sitting room. "I found a laptop that doesn't have a passcode. There are some photos of Alexander with a woman and some work documents in another file. I didn't go through everything but the techs will probably want to take the laptop and analyze it. I didn't find anything related to next of kin."

Declan held out his cellphone. "I have the sister's information. Ava Branston. She also works in tech and lives in Seattle. Get this, Kate. They are twins."

"Twins?" Kate asked, even though she had heard him just fine. That wasn't the woman in the photo. "I wonder why there's barely a mention of her in the articles about him. There's also nothing around this house to indicate a family."

Declan didn't know the answer to that. "Maybe there was some falling out."

"How did you find her?"

"One of the local D.C. cops said he thought he heard on a tech podcast Alexander say he had a twin sister and her name is Ava. We know he's originally from the Seattle area so I searched and found Ava. There are a handful of articles about her medical tech company and in one of them, there's mention of Alexander. I have a phone number for her. Should we wait until morning to call her?"

Kate checked her phone. It was nearing four in the morning, which meant that it was only one in Seattle. "Let's call her now. By the time she wakes, his death could be all over the news. All it takes is a leak and the press will have the story."

Declan backtracked out of the small alcove office with Kate right behind him. He leaned against the wall across from the bed and called the number. A woman answered after the first ring surprising them both. "Ava Branston?" Declan asked and then identified himself and

Kate.

"Yes," she said with a sigh.

"We are calling about your brother, Alexander Branston."

She groaned. "What has he done now?"

Kate shared a look with Declan and leaned toward the phone. "We are sorry to tell you but your brother has been shot and killed. He was murdered in his home earlier tonight."

There was a long pause where they could only hear her breathing. Ava took a loud breath in and thanked them for calling her. "I'm surprised you found me so quickly. My brother and I haven't spoken in a long time. We had a falling out several years ago."

"I don't mean to pry especially at this delicate time," Kate started and waited to see if she heard any resistance. When she didn't, she proceeded, "You didn't seem to be surprised that the FBI would be calling."

"No," Ava said, stiffly. "Alexander has been doing illegal things in business and his personal life for a long time. Back when we were in our twenties and starting together, he had a serious drug problem. I urged him to go to rehab but he refused. He eventually got clean and sober, but he was taking other risks, dealing with unsavory people. I was worried that would spill over to our business. When I found out that he was committing tax fraud that was the last straw for me. I demanded he buy me out and I went a different direction. In a way, I've been expecting this call my whole life."

There was a lot to unpack there. "Was Alexander ever married?"

"No. I don't know much about his dating life either. Honestly, we haven't spoken in years. We've had some email communication related to our mother's health and we saw each other at our father's funeral three years ago. If we can go without speaking, we do."

"Was it just the business falling out that caused the separation?" Declan asked.

"Alexander was reckless with his life and it spilled over to the rest of the family. Early on, he had some gambling debts and someone broke into my parents' home and stole my mother's jewelry. I was threatened in the office one night when I was working late over other money Alexander owed someone. After we split the business, he started to make it big, so money was no longer the issue. He lived in New York City for a while and dated socialites, but there were always rumors about the people he was spending time with. There were some Russians who had invested in his business and had questionable backgrounds. There's been a lot over the years. I couldn't take it anymore, especially after I had children. I didn't want Alexander around. The contact between us became further and further apart and neither of us seemed bothered by it."

Declan raised his eyes to Kate in a question. She jutted her chin forward, indicating for him to go on with his question. "Your brother's murder is connected to a series of art heists happening here in the D.C. Metro area. There was a painting stolen from your brother's home, which was initially stolen in Belgium. He has quite a collection of art. Do you know anything about your brother's art dealings?"

"It doesn't surprise me. I don't know anything though. Alexander was never someone who appreciated art other than for its monetary value. He did most things for the money," Ava said with a sarcastic undertone. "If he had art it was for that. It would be like a prize on his wall to show people what he can afford."

Kate could see that given how the rest of the home looked. "Do you know of any connections he might have in the art world?"

"No. My father was a corporate attorney and our mother never worked. Our father was quite successful and he gave us part of our inheritance to start our businesses after college. It worked for a while until it didn't. Then we went our separate ways. Now, on paper, Alexander has eclipsed my net worth five times over, but I question how he made all of that money."

They talked for a few minutes more but it didn't yield much. Ava had no idea who her brother could have been involved with that wanted him dead. She told them he certainly had enemies and probably more than she knew. Ava also had no idea what passcodes he'd use for his phone or laptop, so they'd need Ditch to work his magic later.

At the end of the call, Kate asked one final question. "I know you said you don't know much about Alexander's dating life. I found recent photos of him with a woman on a laptop. Do you have any idea who she could be?"

"I don't know anything about his dating life," Ava reiterated and then asked Kate to text her one of the photos. Kate sent it and Ava confirmed she received it. "I have no idea who this is. She doesn't look happy whoever she is. Do you think she's a suspect in his death?"

"I don't know," Kate said, honestly not wanting to get into the specifics of the art thefts. "Until we can identify her, it's hard to say either way. We know for sure his death is connected to the art thefts and the other burglaries. Are you aware of the Curators? They are international art thieves."

Ava said she wasn't. "Are they the ones responsible for this?"

"No. We believe these people are after the head of the Curators. I was just curious if that was a name you ever heard your brother mention."

Ava sighed either from growing weary of Kate's questions or possibly the late hour. "I don't know much of anything about my brother's life. I'm sorry, I wish I was more of a help to you."

Before ending the call, they arranged for Ava to meet with the medical examiner when she arrived later that day. Kate told her she'd be happy to meet with her at her brother's house if she liked. It would still be considered an active crime scene and she wouldn't be able to access it without law enforcement with her. Ava assured Kate she'd call her when she arrived.

With that call out of the way, Declan glanced down at Kate. "We need some sleep."

Kate let herself be led out of the house and to the car. The whole ride back her mind wasn't on Ava or Alexander.

All she could think about was the chapel in a small fishing village in the south of France.

CHAPTER 25

That night, Kate dreamed of Cassis and the small chapel with the distinct bells. She sat inside staring at the small stone altar, waiting for Leo to arrive. Kate waited and waited, the feeling of desperation washing over her. She wanted to scream out in frustration and anger but knew she needed to be still in the chapel. It was a paralyzing feeling and she woke with a start.

Kate rolled to her side but found herself alone. She curled her body into itself and closed her eyes. Kate knew she would find Leo no matter what it took.

"Kate, I have coffee for you," Declan said from the doorway. "You were restless all night and you've been grumbling for the past fifteen minutes."

Kate rolled over to her back and pushed herself upright. She reached for the coffee and took a sip, savoring the warmth and taste. "I don't remember the dream," she lied with too much ease.

"Are you sure about that?" Declan pinched the bridge of his nose. "You called out Leo's name…twice."

"I don't remember it," she said, lying again. "He's been a focus of the investigation and I spoke to him yesterday. Things seep into your subconscious. Has the murder made the news yet?"

Declan sat down on the edge of the bed. He looked like he wanted to say more about Leo but changed his mind. "First thing this morning.

It was good we spoke to Ava last night."

Kate fixed the covers on her lap. "I thought it was important she didn't find out her brother was dead on the news. I'm not sure Ava would have cared."

"She cares," Declan said with his voice tight. "It might be hard for her to show it or to come to terms with the fact that her brother is dead. There's no chance of repairing the relationship. People always think they have time. I'm not that close to any of my brothers and they are always in trouble. I wouldn't have wanted to hear about their death from the news."

Kate took a sip of her coffee. She knew Declan's brothers and their misdeeds were a sore spot for him. It was something Kate was aware of but never discussed much. She had no problem changing the subject because she didn't want to hurt his feelings. "What else do we have this morning?"

Declan looked relieved. "Spade wants to see us as soon as we can get there. He told me to make sure we were well-rested. He knows how little sleep we've had. Not that either of us got much last night. Tom is headed back to Alexander's today with a team, so we are on our own for most of the day. Was there something specific you wanted to do?"

Kate didn't want to bring up Leo again. "There's some research I want to do on Neil Clark and the Munson brothers. I'd still like to figure out if Alexander is connected to them. If the goal was to steal *Death of Marat* specifically, they had to have known Alexander had it. There isn't going to be the same paper trail as paintings bought legally. I'd also like to figure out who the woman is in the photos with Alexander."

Declan yawned loudly. "Are you still as tired as I am?"

The tiredness was like a heavy coat over her. She had no idea when she'd catch up on sleep, but that's how it went sometimes. "We are going to have to power through. Fingers crossed we get one calm day."

When Declan didn't say anything and didn't make a move to get up from the bed, Kate asked, "Are you okay?"

Declan took a loud audible breath and turned to look at her. He locked his gaze on hers. "You need to stop lying to me, Kate. If you don't want to do this with me anymore, tell me. If you want me to move out, tell me. None of it will impact our work partnership. The one thing I can't handle though and will kill all of it, is lies. I know you well enough to know you're lying. You might be the forensic psychologist who can read people better than I can, but I can read you. We have been doing this far too long for me not to know you."

Kate lowered her eyes to the coffee cup and took a sip. She should have known she couldn't hide anything from him. When she looked at him again, his gaze was softer but still steadfast.

It was time for Kate to admit the truth. "When I was in Alexander's office last night, I found a stack of postcards. They weren't written on or addressed. It looked like he might have picked them up in his travels. One of them was a small chapel in Cassis, France. I was there with my parents on a trip when they were visiting villages in the south of France. I remember that chapel and it had distinct bells. I think those were the bells I heard on the call with Leo. I was dreaming about him last night." Kate held her hand up and corrected herself. "He wasn't in the dream but I was in the chapel waiting for him."

"It's the same village Henri Chevalier lived and died."

"That's right," she said.

Declan absorbed the information and didn't say anything for a few moments. "Is there a reason you felt like you needed to lie about that or keep it from me?"

"We were so busy last night I didn't want to bring it up, especially not in front of Tom. When we got back last night, I was too tired."

"Stop making excuses," Declan said gently.

Kate turned her head from him and felt an urge to argue her point.

She sat with her anger and didn't snap back at him. It took time but she settled into knowing he was right. There had been time to tell him. She met his eyes. "I feel a weird bond with him I can't explain. It's like a chemistry or attraction or something and it makes me feel guilty."

Declan's features softened fully until he was nearly smiling. It was not what Kate had been expecting. She had assumed he'd be jealous or angry with her. "Are you planning to do something about that?"

"No. Of course not." Kate didn't even need to think about that answer. "It's just such a weird feeling to have and I feel such guilt about it."

Declan patted her leg through the blanket. "Katie, it's fine to feel that way. You have a bond with him. I don't love it but he saved your life. I owe the man. The fact that he's willing to take your call and help you now is a testament to the bond that you have. You're human. I don't expect you to never be attracted to anyone ever again. That's ridiculous."

Declan had a way of surprising her sometimes that cut right through the armor she wore around herself. "I thought you'd be angry with me."

Declan shook his head and reached for her hand. He pulled her into a hug and she rested her head against his shoulder. "If you told me you were leaving me for him, I'd be hurt. I wouldn't understand it because it would seem so unlike you. But I'm never not going to want you in my life. This, our partnership, friendship, and relationship, only works with trust. You can't lie to me because I don't know if it's personal or work. I can't have my investigative partner holding back on me. We've never done that before and we can't start that now."

"I promise, I won't again." Kate felt safe in his arms and comforted by the fact she had confusing emotions. Saying it aloud had helped to alleviate the guilt of it all. When she pulled back from the hug, Declan surprised her again.

"Do you want to go to Cassis and see if he's there?"

Kate would be lying if she said she hadn't considered it. "It's not that small of a village and I need to show up right where he is or he might hear that an American is there and get spooked. He's not going to agree to see me."

Declan agreed with that. "What were the other postcards? Could they also be related to Leo?"

"What do you mean related to Leo?"

"We know Alexander was involved in some shady business. Is it possible the postcards were from places they knew the Phantom to be? We don't know how Alexander communicated with these thieves. He could be the money behind the operation or he could be more involved."

Kate hadn't considered it at all. The chapel had hit her out of the blue and she was so taken with the idea that Leo might be there in Cassis she didn't pay too much attention to the others. "When I meet his sister today, I'll take a look at the others."

Declan raked his fingers through his wet locks. "Do you have any way to narrow down finding him?"

"I don't think so…" Kate's voice trailed off as she thought back to her conversation with Leo and it hit her all at once. "He told me that he got his start stealing Nazi-looted art when his step-father showed off his art collection at his chateau in the south of France. Leo said he spent time there as a child. He never said the name of a town or village. I wonder what happened to his estate."

"It would have gone to his son probably. He was living in the main house in Paris, right?"

Kate nodded, recalling their last case. "Now that he's dead…"

"Could Leo be the only heir?"

The question surged an excitement in her. Kate put down her coffee mug on the nightstand and threw off the covers. She leaned into Declan and kissed him firmly on the lips. "You're an absolute genius."

"Well, I know," Declan said with a laugh as he blushed. He called to her back as she moved across the room to the bathroom. "Why, specifically?"

Kate didn't hear the question as she was already ripping off her pajamas and turning on the water in the shower. She got in and closed the door. As she finished rinsing the shampoo out of her hair, she noticed Declan leaning against the counter.

He was smiling at her. "I like that I can do this now."

"What?" Kate asked, rinsing her hair clean.

"Be in here while you shower. I don't think you know how many times I wanted to follow you and keep our conversation going."

Kate applied the conditioner knowing full well that wasn't the reason he wanted to be in there with her. She tipped her head back under the water. "You just want to see me naked."

"Always," Declan said emphatically. "But I wanted to know why you sprinted in here. We have time before meeting with Spade. You called me a genius too, which is the first time in our history."

Kate shut off the water and he handed her the towel as she stepped out. "We should be able to pull a property record search from the estate information. Even if Leo changed the name of ownership to something we wouldn't know, the records will be available to us under Lucien or his son, Markus Lamiere. We can find that property in the south of France as well as any other they owned."

"You can find Leo that way and surprise him."

Kate nodded. "I'm convinced after *The Death of Marat* that these thieves intend to kill him and they aren't going to stop until we bring him in. I have to arrest him to protect him."

Declan opened his eyes wide. "Do you think you'll be able to do that? He said he's not going to prison."

That was the hurdle Kate couldn't get past. "I'll have to figure it out. I'm going to do a property records search before we leave. If I can confirm the Lamieres had property in Cassis, then I'm going to tell Spade I need to go to France."

"Will you go alone?" Declan asked, his tone indicating he didn't think it was a good idea.

Kate reached for him and pulled him down to kiss him. "I'm not going to France without you. I couldn't arrest Leo in Edinburgh. I'm going to need the help. He won't come in willingly and we have to bring him in." As much as Kate didn't want to arrest him, she knew she'd have to.

"Then I guess we are both going to see Leo."

Kate shooed him out of the bathroom feeling a renewed sense of excitement for the case and the potential that it might be solved. She hoped she could do that before anyone else had to die.

With the frequency of the art thefts so far – she was under a ticking clock.

CHAPTER 26

"You're going to France alone," Spade said after he heard Kate's proposal that she and Declan make a quick trip to Cassis to arrest Leo.

The property records search showed that Lucien Lamiere had owned a chateau in Cassis, France, and that it was still owned by the family up until a few months ago. Now, it was owned by a corporation but there was no holding information about the company. Kate assumed it was one of Leo's many aliases. There was no way this was a coincidence.

The meeting with Spade had been going well right up to that point. They had updated him about the case and even suggested Alexander might have had some connection to the thieves. Spade noted that it would be better for public perception for the FBI if he did. Right now, there was an outcry that a tech billionaire could be murdered in his home. The FBI was getting raked over the coals in the media. They had not mentioned publicly yet that he had a stolen painting. The FBI statement indicated that a painting had been stolen but that they weren't releasing the name of it to the public yet. Some reporters were suspicious but Tom wanted the information locked down until he could complete the inventory and see if there were others.

Spade had let them know that so far, Tom had found three other stolen paintings. When they went public with the information, they wanted to have a strong case.

A connection to the thieves could only bolster it.

Spade had listened intently while Kate detailed her conversations with Leo, the bells she heard through the phone, and then about the postcards at Alexander's. Kate explained the trip with her parents and how she had connected all of it. She told him how when Declan mentioned the Lamiere estate, she was able to put the whole thing together. She was convinced Leo was there, especially since France had been as much his home as London had been in his later years.

Kate had been expecting some resistance about traveling to France in the middle of the investigation. It was important given the note in Alexander's hand that they try to bring Leo in for the good of the case, if not for his safety. She was visibly shaken when Spade came back with full support for her to go to Cassis, but she'd go alone.

Declan was the first to argue. "It's not safe for Kate to go alone, Spade. He is an internationally wanted criminal. He's been helpful in the past, but if Kate tries to bring him in who knows how he'll react."

Spade pointed a finger at Kate across the desk. "Are you afraid of Leo?"

"Well, no—" Kate started to say when Spade cut her off.

"Then there is no reason for you not to go alone."

Kate looked at Declan and didn't know what to say. "I don't know if I can get him to come in with me alone, Spade. I wasn't able to do it in Scotland."

"You didn't have a rapport then."

Kate didn't think that was the only caveat. She focused her attention back on her boss. "Leo said that under no circumstance will he come in willingly. He told me there is no way he's going to spend a minute in prison for something he felt justified in doing."

Spade arched an eyebrow. "Did you confirm all the art he stole was Nazi-looted art?"

Kate nodded. "Every file the FBI has on him was Nazi-looted art. Leo even admitted to me that his crimes go back a decade before we had any idea the Curators were stealing art. He told me they left the calling card to connect all of their thefts. He also left the card to send a message to those he stole from, to put them on notice. He was brazen about it. He wasn't in it for the fame, glory, or even the money. He felt compelled and just in his cause. It's why he's so adamant that he shouldn't go to prison. Leo said that if governments did their jobs, he wouldn't have been needed."

"He's right," Spade said matter-of-factly, surprising them both. He jutted his chin toward Declan. "What do you think should happen to him? I assume you're more impartial than Kate."

Spade's words stung but he was right. Kate couldn't even argue the point. She turned and looked at Declan too. He ran his hands up and down his thighs the way he did when he got nervous. Kate knew he had to be weighing what he really thought with what he thought Kate might want to hear, and more importantly, what Spade wanted to hear.

"Well, I..." Declan started and then stopped.

Spade wasn't going to stand for any wishy-washy nonsense. "Speak your mind, Declan. I've never known you to hold back. You wouldn't be in this unit if you were the kind of agent who held back."

"It's not an easy answer, Spade. I'm not sure that I know." Declan looked over at Kate with a sympathetic smile then back at his boss. "What Leo did was illegal. He is by every definition the best international art thief ever known. But if he had not helped Kate on the last case, no one would even know his name or the connection he has back to the Lamieres. He could have drifted off into his retirement and no one would ever be the wiser. I can't downplay the assistance he provided on the last case and I won't ever forget that he's the man who saved Kate's life."

She had never heard Declan go on so long to answer a simple question.

"Are you sure you want my opinion?" Declan asked again.

"I wouldn't have asked for it," Spade said, his expression patient and calm.

"I think we should make Leo an asset to this unit," Declan said with a strength of conviction Kate had never heard. If he had turned to her and punched her in the face she would have been less shocked than she was by his words.

Spade didn't flinch. "Go on."

Declan licked his lips nervously. "No one knows who he is. Leo Lamiere has never been connected to the Phantom by anyone other than Kate. There are six of us who know. You, me, Kate, Tom, Sam Harris in London, and Chief Inspector Cameron Fraser with Police Scotland. After Leo's help with the last case, Harris and Fraser aren't a problem. They haven't disclosed his identity and I don't think they will. Tom might take some convincing but you outrank him. We let the Phantom disappear never to be seen or heard from again and we bring Leo Lamiere into this unit. We'll give him a credible backstory. He has contacts and good investigative skills and instincts. We offer him the chance to continue to do good. It's that or prison. If you can get Ditch into the FBI, there's no reason why you couldn't make it happen for Leo. At least Leo did some good in the world and righted some wrongs."

Spade did not react. He simply shifted his body toward Kate and pointed a finger at her. "Your thoughts?"

Kate had so many swirling thoughts she wasn't sure what to make of Declan's declaration, Spade's reaction, or even how she felt about working with Leo long-term. It felt a bit like getting too close to a burning candle that was about to erupt into a full-blown fire. "I don't know if he'd be interested."

Declan turned to her, arguing the point. "You said he sounded bored and depressed, Kate. He's only in his late forties. It's much too young to be retired."

Kate knew Leo had considerable wealth, especially if he was the only heir to the Lamiere fortune. He could do any number of things he wanted to do. "I don't know."

Spade knew. "It would legitimize him and take off any speculation that he might be the Phantom. I think Declan has an excellent idea."

"Can you push it through?" Kate asked, still not sure Leo would ever go for it. "Senator Willis wanted me to bring in the Phantom, not give him a job."

That was no problem for Spade. "There's no connection between the two. Besides, we can fake the Phantom's death if need be and tell the international community the Phantom is no more. The FBI gets the win, Leo remains out of prison, and the threat of the Curators is over."

Kate knew what Spade had done with Ditch. They had used special effects and a faked death certificate. There was even a burial plot to convince the Russians and the Chinese that Ditch was dead, killed by the FBI. His crimes stopped after that point so there was no reason to suspect that the FBI had lied. Kate assumed it could work just as well for Leo.

There was still the matter of working closely with him – that's the part that worried her the most. Kate chewed on her lip as she considered all the implications. "What would he do? He's not a trained investigator. He's not like Ditch in that regard where he has a specific skill that could help us."

"I don't think that's true, Kate," Declan said, drawing her attention. "He could help on art theft cases or other burglary cases. He knows how to breach security, which is a factor in nearly every murder case we have. He knows how the criminal mind works because he is a criminal. I'm sure there are a host of other skills we will discover. We know he's good with a gun, isn't afraid to get his hands dirty, and has no problem ending a life if the situation calls for it. We know he'll protect you even if it means risking his life."

Declan was pushing hard for this and Kate didn't know why. Her suspicion of him was growing. She caught his gaze. "Are you sure you'd be okay with this?" What Kate wanted to ask was if he was okay given she had just admitted she had chemistry and an attraction for Leo. She couldn't ask that because Spade would know they were involved. Kate didn't know what Declan was trying to prove or if this was some huge test of their new relationship.

With sincerity on his face, Declan nodded once. "I think this is best for everyone. Besides, if he goes back to a life of crime, we are right there ready to catch him."

Kate almost believed him. She took her gaze off him and looked to Spade. "If you can make this happen, then I'm in. I don't know if Leo will agree."

Spade sat back and appraised them both. "That's what you're going to go to France and convince him of. He either comes back willingly or in handcuffs. It's his decision."

Kate still didn't like the idea that she was being sent alone. "Why do I need to go without Declan? Don't you think having backup would be beneficial?"

Spade shook his head. He wasn't going to budge on this. "I need Declan here working with Tom. If you have the connection you think you have, I think Leo would be more receptive to you going alone. He might trust it more."

For as onboard Declan was with bringing Leo onto the team, he didn't look like he was okay with her going to France alone. He wasn't going to argue with Spade any more than Kate was. They had their orders and Kate promised she'd head back to the hotel and be at the airport for her flight.

"I'll have a private plane ready for you, Kate. I want this entire operation as quiet as possible and we don't need a paper trail. I'll figure out the closest airport and you can get a car from there. I'll handle Tom when the time comes and Declan can speak to your London and Edinburgh counterparts when we know of Leo's decision. I want you in and out of Europe as quickly as possible. You'll have no clearance for your weapon so leave it here in D.C."

Kate's mouth opened but no words came out. She reconciled the demand and then stood. "You know you're asking the impossible of me."

"I'm sure you'll get it done," was all Spade said as he dismissed them.

They left the office without saying another word.

Kate walked in front of Declan down the hall, past Spade's assistant, and out into the sterile hallway. She knew there were probably eyes on them and this wasn't the place to say what she wanted to say. Declan knew better than to say anything either.

She wrapped her arms around herself and held her tongue while they were in the elevator, through the front lobby and outside. Once in the fresh air, she turned to him in anger. "What do you think you're doing? I just said I had chemistry with Leo. Do you *really* want him around me all the time? What kind of game are you playing?" Kate spit out each staccato sentence, trying to form thoughts and speak at the same time.

Declan reached for her but she pulled back out of his grasp. "Katie, you weren't going to be able to arrest him. You and I both know that. You'd be miserable if Leo was sitting in prison or worse he killed himself because of the arrest. I thought this was better for all of us including Leo."

Kate stared up at him breathing short breaths out of her nose while her mouth remained in a firm line.

Declan walked down the block raking a hand through his hair. He turned around and came back to her, hot and angry now. He jabbed a finger at her. "I don't ever want you to be around him. The thought of you near him makes me jealous. It makes me feel crazy and out of control. I was doing what I thought was best for you." He lowered his voice and leaned down close to her face. "I only want you to be happy even if I'm miserable. Spade put me on the spot—"

"Just stop," Kate said, lowering her voice.

"I—" Declan started but Kate cut him off.

"Let's go." She didn't wait for him to say anything else. Kate took him by the hand and marched back toward the hotel.

CHAPTER 27

Kate slipped the key in the lock, pushed open the door, and took three steps into the room as Declan closed the door behind them. He leaned against the door and looked at her with a mixture of sadness and confusion on his face. "Please don't—"

Kate didn't let him finish his thought. She grabbed the front of his shirt and pulled him into her for a kiss. Her hands dropped to his belt undoing it with a natural ease. When she went for the button of his pants, he pushed her hand aside and moved her against the door.

Declan dug his hands into her hair, taking control of the situation. He leaned low so they were eye to eye. "I don't understand. I thought you were furious with me. I thought you were dragging me back here to tell me it was over."

Kate licked her lips, tasting him on her tongue. "We aren't that fragile, Declan." Looking him right in the eyes, punctuating each word, she added seductively, "I'm not that fragile."

Declan sucked in a sharp breath, understanding her double meaning. This time when he kissed her, he possessed her mouth, digging his hands into her hair and grinding his body against hers. There was no doubt he wanted her in a way he hadn't before. In a way he didn't know he could have her – totally, completely, and wantonly.

Their lovemaking over the last couple of months had been timid, shy almost as if they tested out what each other liked. Kate knew

Declan was being reserved with her. He was gentle when he could have been rougher. He was laid back and unpossessed. There had been passion but it was as if they were still a little uncertain about the other. That wall was down now.

When he kissed her now, there was no doubt in Kate's mind she was his. He was hungry for her and unreserved. His kiss and the way his body moved against hers said it all. Declan never broke the kiss as he pawed at her clothing and she undressed him.

They stumbled over themselves to the bed. Declan laid her down and followed. He parted her legs with his, kissed her once on the lips, and left a wet trail of kisses down her body. Kate closed her eyes and gave herself over to the sensations and when she reached the peak, she groaned his name in a way she had never allowed herself to do before. Before she could reach for him or respond, he was inside of her moving their bodies at a frantic pace.

Suddenly and too quickly Declan stopped, leaned down, and kissed her. "Open your eyes, Kate. You always close your eyes. Look at me."

Kate flicked her eyes open as he moved inside of her again and again, building to the crescendo. She had never watched his face in that moment. She did now. Never taking her eyes off him.

When it was over, she was glad now she knew him so intimately. As they caught their breath, Kate touched his cheek and nipped him on the ear.

Declan moaned against her ear and then started to softly laugh as he disengaged their bodies and pulled her onto his chest. He stroked her naked back with his fingertips. "What was that? I feel like something shifted between us. Am I wrong?"

"You're not wrong. We stopped worrying about what the other was going to think. I stopped worrying about what you'd think." Kate propped herself up on her elbow so she could look in his face. "You've been dancing around me since we started this thing. You go between being polite and reserved to dopey and sweet. I've known you for more than a decade and have never seen you act this way with other women. Just now, you seemed like yourself."

Declan responded with a slight nod of his head.

"Are you afraid you're going to hurt me or upset me?"

Declan shook his head.

"What is it?"

Declan pulled her closer but didn't respond.

Kate wasn't going to let it go. He had done this incredible thing for her recommending they let Leo work with them instead of going to prison, even though the man's presence would make Declan jealous. She had never had someone do something so utterly stupid and selfless for her before and she had no words to express it.

She nudged his side. "You said we had to be honest with each other."

Declan rolled to his side, taking her with him until they were face to face. "Are you sure you can handle it?"

Kate wanted to be vulnerable with someone for the first time in her life. "Please tell me."

Declan searched her face, took several deep breaths, and then exhaled. "I'm in love with you, Katie. I've been in love with you for as long as I can remember and now that we are together, I'm terrified of screwing this up. It makes me unsure of myself."

She felt every ounce of that. "I've never even been in a real relationship before now." Kate paused and looked at him. "Is that what we are doing? Is this real?"

Declan cracked a wide smile. "I just told you that I'm in love with you. This is as real as it gets for me. I think this is the first time I've truly been in love." He wasn't even looking at her expecting a response, which is what made Kate want to tell him.

"I'm in love with you too." She ducked her head low and broke eye contact. He lifted her chin, forcing her to look at him. "I'm not good at this."

"I'm not complaining." Declan caressed the curve of her face with his fingertip. "You look like you want to say something else."

Kate looked at him and then rushed her admission. "I've been in love with you for so long I wanted to stop you from getting married."

"You did not." Declan's voice raised about three octaves and he practically shouted it.

Kate put her head down and couldn't meet his surprised expression. "You know I told you she wasn't right for you. As my friend, I could see that Lauren wasn't going to be a good fit for the lifestyle the FBI forced us into. But it was much more than that. The night before the wedding, I went to your apartment and stood outside. I wanted to go inside and tell you not to marry her because I was in love with you. Saying it to myself on the sidewalk shook me out of the craziness. I couldn't do that to you the night before you got married. You seemed so sure of the decision and in love with her. I wanted you to be happy even if it broke my heart."

Declan breathed heavily. "I had no idea, Kate. You never acted like you even liked me. You seemed to barely tolerate me the first year after Spade partnered us up. You turned down every advance I ever made."

Neither of them could count how many times Declan had asked her out during their time at the FBI Academy. He zeroed in on her the first day they met. But Kate had watched him flirt with other women in bars and he seemed to have a string of love interests. "I didn't want to be just another fling for you. I chose to be your friend instead. Then when I realized you were capable of being serious about a woman—" Kate looked up at him. "I wanted to be that woman."

It took Declan a moment to process her confession. It was probably the biggest one between them. "I don't even know what to say. You wouldn't have been another conquest, but I wasn't ready for someone like you when I was younger. If you had come to me before the wedding, I don't know what I would have done. I can't even imagine how hard that was for you."

Kate kissed him gently, letting her lips linger against his. "It was as hard as it is for you to tell Spade you're okay with Leo being on our team. You did something selfless for me even though ultimately it's not what you want. You seemed to love Lauren and I thought getting married would make you happy. Once you made the decision, I tucked those feelings away and chalked it up to a crush I'd have to get over. I never got over it though. It all bubbled up again when you got divorced and moved into my house."

"Why did you act like you hated me so much sometimes?"

"I thought if I didn't I might slip and you'd figure it out."

Declan wrapped his arms around her and pulled her closer. "Do you know why I'm okay with Leo working with us?"

"I have no idea."

"I don't want to upset you," Declan said to start. She urged him to go on. "You don't have many people in your life. I have an entire family, even if I'm not particularly close to them. This job doesn't lend itself to a lot of friends. If anything ever happened to me, I don't want to leave you alone. You have a connection with Leo and at least you'd have him if I was gone."

Kate snuggled into him closer and rested her head on his chest. "You are the best thing I have in my life." She wanted to close her eyes and stay like that forever. They didn't have much time though. "I need to pack and get to the airport and you need to get back to the office."

"We will. Give us a few more minutes. I don't want to let you go just yet."

Kate couldn't argue with that.

A little more than an hour later, Kate stood in the doorway of the hotel room with her luggage. She stood up on tiptoes and kissed

Declan goodbye. "I'll text you as soon as I land. I'll keep you updated as soon as I find him."

Declan wasn't satisfied with her leaving him at the door. He walked Kate down the hall to the elevator and said goodbye at the front door of the hotel. They had to be careful that Kate wasn't followed to the airport. The only good thing was that it was a private government flight and the information wasn't going to be easily accessed.

Kate stepped out of the hotel to the waiting car. She checked her watch as she slipped into the back seat. She would be wheels up in an hour, just about nine hours to Marseille Provence airport, and then another hour's drive to Cassis. She would need to fight against her instinct to be awake and alert on a flight and instead get some sleep.

As the driver got into the car, he put down the divider glass between the front and back seats. "There's a file tucked into the pocket on the door. Spade said it would give you all the information you need." He didn't wait for a response from Kate. He put the window back up and she was left alone again.

Kate reached for the file and tugged it out of its hiding place. She set it on her lap and opened it. Inside was a formal employment letter with a generous salary and benefits offer. There was a description of Leo's role within Spade's unit. He'd be primarily assigned to work with Declan and her, but he'd also be pulled into other cases as Spade saw fit. There was a working term of ten years and after that was fulfilled, Leo was free of the FBI and could go live out his retirement with a clean slate. Spade noted he was only offering this once.

There was a small handwritten note for Kate. She recognized Spade's chicken scratch handwriting. *Go to Cassis and work out whatever attraction is between you. Then leave it permanently in France.*

That's why Spade was sending her alone – he knew there was something between Leo and her.

Kate rested her head back on the seat. She had gotten herself in some mess.

CHAPTER 28

The next day Kate let the wind blow through her hair as she drove to Cassis from Marseille, where she had spent the night after landing in France. Kate had spoken to Declan, who had interviewed Ava Branston when she arrived at her brother's house. Declan was sure she had no knowledge of Alexander's current life and she did not recognize the woman in the photographs with her brother. Declan told Kate that she had been forthcoming with all the information she knew and was giving the FBI a wide berth in the house to do whatever they needed to do. He didn't think they'd get anything else out of her even after building rapport with her over their sibling difficulties.

Kate appreciated Declan's efforts and his candor. They had ended the call and Kate had collapsed into bed. She had been asleep for about two hours when he called her back, excited about what they had found in Alexander's house. Kate had been expecting to hear about more stolen paintings…they were up to five now. But it wasn't that.

Declan had found a notebook in a locked safe with information about the Curators and the Phantom. It seemed Alexander was obsessed with the Phantom and was going to do everything he could to hunt him down, including paying close to ten million dollars to hire a team to do that. There was no information about the people he had hired. There were, however, details about the two paintings that had been stolen from the National Gallery of Art and the Smithsonian. It was all part of the same elaborate plot.

Alexander had photos of Kate and Declan around D.C. during the time of the hearing. Neil had been following them for some time. As Declan said, something had gone wrong because Alexander was dead, the stolen paintings hadn't been found in his collection, and the team stole *The Death of Marat*. They had taken Alexander's money and run but eliminated him in the process.

The whole scheme seemed predicated on identifying the Phantom. They were using Kate and Declan to do that. Nothing had gone as planned though. Whoever Alexander had hired had a plan of their own and wanted the glory for themselves. Kate realized then that was why they were leaving their calling card. They wanted to be the best and to be the best they had to take out the reigning king – the Phantom. And they were willing to do that by any means necessary including manipulating the FBI.

Alexander's notes didn't indicate they knew Leo's focus on Nazi-looted art. That much had remained a mystery for everyone other than Kate's team and that was only because Leo had told her. There was also no mention of Leo's name or the Lamieres. Declan had been right that the postcards connected with places where Leo might have been, which made Kate's mission even more critical.

They had connected the Phantom to Cassis.

Kate had to get to Leo first and convince him to return with her. She stepped on the gas as the car bumped down the A7 and then the A507. She made good time and wanted to stop at St. Michael's Chapel before heading straight to Leo's. She thought better of it though as she pulled down a small alleyway near the chapel.

The fewer people who saw her the better. She wanted the element of surprise with Leo.

The whole trip Kate had been mindful to make sure she hadn't been followed. It was only now pulling into Cassis and sitting in her parked car that the worry had peeled away from her. There was no way anyone followed her given the secrecy of the private flight, her checking into a nondescript hotel in Marseille, and the drive to Cassis. She had watched on the road and there simply wasn't anyone tailing her.

Kate checked her reflection in the mirror and reached for her makeup bag. She hadn't seen Leo since Edinburgh when she had been covered in mud and barely alive. The least she could do now was present herself well, especially given the conversation she was about to have.

While Spade didn't seem to know about her and Declan and had encouraged her to get whatever she had with Leo out of her system, no way was that going to happen. She would not disrespect Declan, not after everything he had done for her. Kate was fully committed to their relationship. That didn't mean it was going to be easy.

After fixing her hair and applying a little makeup, Kate put the car in drive and followed the directions around the port to the other side of Cassis. The road she was supposed to turn down wasn't marked and she could only guess that it was correct. The paved road quickly turned to a dirt track and the whole area opened up to a vast field and countryside.

It was only ten minutes outside the main village of Cassis but it felt like it was a world away. There were vineyards in the deep inlets sheltered by the Massif de Calanques, the highest cliffs in France, stunningly dressed in white limestone. Kate felt like she had stepped into an Impressionist painting and the stress in her shoulders and neck melted away.

She could see why Leo retreated to this area and a little sadness crept its way in thinking that she'd have to steal him away from such loveliness. Kate's GPS alerted her that she had arrived. She hit the brake, screeching the car to a dead stop in the road and looked around.

Carved out between two tall trees on her right was a one-lane dirt road. The tree cover was thick and she wasn't able to see a house or anything from her vantage point. Kate turned into the lane and hit the gas, lurching the car up the slight incline.

As she came around a sharp bend, the magnificence of the chateau came into view. Kate had been expecting something modern and grand. While it was grand, it looked like something ripped out of a fairytale.

The chateau had two medieval round towers, a south-facing façade that looked like it had been designed in the Renaissance period, and mullioned windows. There was an entrance pavilion, outbuildings, and an Italian-style garden. Kate pulled to a stop near one of the outbuildings, cut the engine, and got out of the car, the loose gravel crunching under her shoes. She looked out over an orchard and what she believed was a walnut tree plantation. There was a man, who wasn't Leo, working on one of the trees in the orchard.

Kate considered speaking to him before venturing to the front door. It turned out she wasn't going to have to do that much work.

"What took you so long?" a deep familiar voice said from behind her, amused rather than angry.

Kate hesitated before turning around. When she did, she tucked her hair behind her ears as she came face-to-face with Leo. Kate swallowed hard as she took him in. He was as handsome as she remembered and he looked like he had even gained some muscle across his shoulders and arms, more than he'd had before. Leo was never a small man by any stretch. He stood about the same height as Declan but carried at least thirty pounds on him, most of it Kate assumed was muscle.

"You knew I'd come for you?" she asked.

He gestured toward the field. "You heard the bells of St. Michael's over the phone. I know you, Kate. You're relentless and you'd figure it out." He smiled slyly at her. "I thought you would have been here last night. I had supper waiting for you."

It was Kate's turn to be amused, although she tried poorly to hide her smile. "You were going to feed me?"

"Not me," he said with a chuckle. "I'm a dreadful cook most of the time. I have a handful of staples I can make, but otherwise, I'd starve. I had my cook prepare extra and she added another place setting." He took a few slow steps toward her. "You were delayed. Second thoughts?"

Kate shook her head. "After I got off the phone with you, I ended up chasing a man who had been watching us. I believe he purposefully ran into traffic. He died at the scene. Then we had another murder. Alexander Branston."

Leo's features narrowed. "The tech billionaire?"

Kate was surprised he hadn't seen it on the news. "He was killed in his home and *The Death of Marat* stolen from him."

He cocked his head to the side in a gesture of not understanding. "That painting doesn't belong to him. It was stolen from a Belgium museum. The thieves were so clumsy that they tripped the alarm. Had the guard been better they might have been caught. It was one of the few heists not blamed on me. Museum officials knew that we were never so careless."

"Curious, right?" Kate asked, amused by how offended Leo was that someone had stolen a painting and been careless in their methods. He took it as an affront to his profession. "It's Alexander we should thank for me being here. I knew the bells were familiar but I couldn't place them. He had a stack of postcards – one of them was the chapel and then I knew. There were others, Leo. Places you have been. I think he was involved with the thieves. I believe the man who died in the street was too. Neil Clark. Did you know him?"

Leo stepped back from her now and looked out over the orchard. "I knew Neil. He tried to become a part of the Curators. He came to me through my legitimate business channels and wanted to know if I had any inroads into the Curators. Part of what he was asking me felt like a test and I had wondered if he figured it out. Another part of me just thought since I was so well-connected he probably thought that I must know something. He was an erratic guy and I'd never trust him. It doesn't surprise me that he'd get caught up in something like this though. Still stings that he had to die for stupidity." He turned back to Kate. "He didn't hurt you, did he?"

Even in all of that Leo still seemed to be concerned about her safety. "He didn't hurt me. He was watching us and I didn't know why. The first night that I saw him, I thought it might have been you out in the rain watching Declan and me at the restaurant. I realized quickly it wasn't you."

"I told you I'm not involved in those burglaries."

"The FBI knows that," Kate said evenly then with more emotion added, "I know that too, Leo."

"You said Alexander had postcards from where I was known to be, including here. Do they know my name or any of my aliases? My connection to the Lamieres?"

Kate didn't know all of his aliases. The only one she knew for sure was the one he had pairing her and Declan's names. "There was no mention of you or any name for that matter. There was a note left in Alexander's hand for the FBI to bring you to them or they'd keep stealing and killing."

Leo raised his eyebrows. "Is that why you're here? You're going to bring me to them?"

The accusation stung as if she'd been slapped. "We'd never do that. I thought after all this time you'd know I wouldn't want anything bad to happen to you."

He turned around and stared back down the gravel driveway where Kate had entered. "Are there other law enforcement out there? Are you arresting me?" Leo turned to her. "Where's your partner?"

Kate went to him then and he didn't move away from her. "I came alone, Leo. Declan is back in D.C. The French authorities have no idea I'm here and there are no other law enforcement agencies involved. It's not a social call though."

Leo nodded his head in understanding and his features softened. He looked less ready to run. "Then let's table all talk of anything unpleasant and get you settled. I'm sure you're exhausted after your flight." He took her car keys out of her hand without asking and went to the car. He pulled out her suitcase and gestured toward the house. "I'll show you to your room, we can get something to eat if you're hungry and then we can take a walk. I'll show you the grounds."

"I'm rested," she told him as she caught up with him. "I spent the night in a hotel in Marseille before driving here. Some coffee would be nice though."

"You can't just have coffee. You need some meat on your bones. I have lovely kouign amanns and pain au chocolat about to come out of the oven." Leo moved toward the chateau faster now as if just remembering that something was baking.

"I thought you didn't cook," Kate said to his back as they entered. The smell of sweet baking wafted through the air.

"I don't cook but I'm a terrific baker," he said with a wink and disappeared down a hallway, leaving Kate to stand in the small living room with her suitcase. He was one surprise after another.

CHAPTER 29

As Leo brought Kate to her room, he explained the chateau had been created in the 15th Century and then updated over the years. Lucien Lamiere had invested millions to modernize it, shore up its foundation, and add modern amenities to it. They had not discussed how it had come into Leo's possession.

After she deposited her things, Kate found her way back down to the first floor and followed the path from the living room through the dining room to the kitchen in the back of the home. There were wood beams throughout the home and the ceilings were much smaller than her brownstone giving the entire home a cozy warmth even though the structure itself was probably twice the size. She found Leo bent over the oven with a dishtowel thrown over his shoulder and potholders on his hands as he brought out another pan of sweets.

Kate watched him for a few moments, wondering how life might be different if he wasn't an international art thief and she wasn't the FBI. If they had met on holiday in Paris and simply been attracted to each other and could explore like normal people. She was so lost in her daydream that she didn't notice Leo staring at her.

"Whatever you're thinking about must be lovely. Care to share?"

Kate felt her cheeks redden. "I was thinking about what life would be like had we met under different circumstances."

"Ahh. That's a dangerous game," he said with a smile. Leo jutted his chin toward the wooden kitchen table that had long benches on each side. There was a carafe of coffee with cups as well as milk and sugar in the center of the table. "I wasn't sure how you took your coffee."

Kate sat down at the table and poured two cups and then asked Leo how he liked his. When he told her just two sugars and a splash of milk, she fixed it for him and then put his cup across from her on the table.

He watched her curiously. "Other than ordering coffee in a shop, I'm not sure a woman has ever fixed my coffee for me. Thank you."

Kate raised her eyes to him as she took a sip. "The house is wonderful. Have you lived here long?"

Leo finished with his baking then joined her at the table. "I took ownership about two months ago. After Markus…died."

"I didn't realize you'd inherit anything."

"Neither did I," Leo said and reached for his coffee. "It came as a surprise to me. I was living in London and I was notified I would inherit the entirety of the Lamiere estate. I guess Lucien had set it up that way. Should anything happen to Markus whatever was left of it would come to me. This was the only property I had any interest in living in so I moved here. Markus never used this house. The staff were taking care of it."

Kate didn't know how he felt about the place. "Did you spend much time here as a child?"

Leo offered her a sad smile. "After my mother married Lucien, he'd bring us here often. This was my mother's favorite of all of his homes. I loved it here in the early years. I was free here in a way I wasn't in Paris. There were no rules. I could ride my bike into the village, run through the fields, and be a normal boy. I had friends here I didn't have in Paris."

"You said in the early years. Did it change?"

Leo took a sip of his coffee and stalled. Kate thought he might dismiss the question. After a few beats, he said, "The Lamiere line is about as old as the country itself. During World War II, they came to this home but not to hide from the Germans. They were Nazi sympathizers and opened this home up to them. They hid the stolen art here and acquired some themselves. I didn't know about this dark history early on. It wasn't until Lucien thought I was old enough to appreciate his way of thinking. He was proud of his heritage. That's when my entire relationship with him started to turn. As I told you, that was the first time I considered righting some wrongs. Still, though, this place was my mother's favorite and I had such fond memories from before that time. I was never more happy than when I stole the first paintings from Lucien. It funded my whole operation."

Kate could see why he had such an attachment to the place. "Given that relationship with Lucien, weren't you surprised he left it all to you?"

"I don't think he ever meant me to have it. I think he assumed Markus would squander all his money. Knowing the man the way I did, Lucien probably meant it as some cruel irony if his son died before me. Little did he know how Markus would turn out."

"What are you going to do with it all?"

"Sell most of it off and keep this house for myself. It's a good refuge and as I found out recently, there's still work to be done."

"Work?" Kate asked, not sure of what he meant.

Leo pushed the bench back from the table and stood. "Bring your coffee and come with me. I'll show you what I discovered."

He went out the back kitchen door with Kate right behind him. They followed a stone path to an outer building that looked like it might be set up as a guesthouse. Once inside, Kate realized it looked like an informal sitting room with couches and a large television affixed to one wall. There was a full bar on the other. The furniture looked new, as if no one ever used the space.

Leo locked the door behind them and pointed down to the throw rug. "I need you to step back over there."

Kate did as he asked and moved to the far side of the room while he bent over and pulled up the corner of the rug, pushing the entire side back and revealing a latch in the floorboards. He pulled the handle to reveal a wide set of stairs that went into a basement.

If Kate had any concern about going down there with Leo, she wasn't going to show it. "What's down here?" she asked as he took her hand and guided her down the steps.

Once at the bottom, Leo flicked on the overhead light to reveal its contents.

Kate's eyes adjusted and she blinked several times, not sure what she was seeing. She initially thought wrongly it was going to be an old dirty basement. Instead, she was met with a state-of-the-art facility that had lights and glass cases and went on for what seemed like miles. She couldn't see the end from left to right or judge its depth.

She turned her head up to look at Leo. "What is this place?" The rows of glass encasing reminded her of a library she once visited with her father in Egypt where all of the books dating back centuries were meticulously preserved.

"Impressive, right?" Leo reached for her hand again to guide her to a glass door. He punched a code into the keypad and the glass door unlocked, making a vacuum-sucking noise as it did. "It's sealed off from the outside air and has a ventilation system." Leo led her down four rows and then stopped. He released her hand and cranked a wheel-shaped device on the end and a mechanism above their head started to turn.

Kate was holding her breath waiting to see what would happen. Slowly, a painting encased in glass attached to a mechanism gripping the frame delivered the painting to them. It was of a woman sitting on a chair with her back turned toward the painter. She had long dark hair and her robe was halfway off her naked shoulder. Her face was in profile and she had striking red lips. It was a provocative image even though the woman was covered.

Leo turned to her. "Do you know the painting?"

Kate stared at it mesmerized. She wasn't sure she'd ever been this close to a work of art so beautiful. She could see the brush strokes. "I've never seen it before."

"It's from the 1700s by an artist known as Jean Siméon Chardin," Leo explained. "He painted a lot of scenes of fruit but also middle-class women and children. There are a few of his more risqué works like this that had gone undiscovered until the 1920s. This was stolen from a home in Paris in 1940 and presumably brought here." Leo held his hand up to stop himself. "Actually, I don't know that it was brought directly here but this is where it ended up."

Kate couldn't be sure but she thought Leo was implying it had been stolen during the Paris occupation by the Germans. "It was stolen by the Nazis?" she asked with her eyes wide.

Leo nodded and stepped back. He made a sweeping gesture to the rows and rows that stood before them. "Every painting I've found in here has come back as Nazi-looted or at least suspected to be. It made me sick when I found this place."

Kate's breath caught in her throat. "How many paintings are there?"

"I haven't gone through them all. I'd estimate close to five hundred. I've cataloged and done background research on only one-hundred-forty of them so far. There is still much work to be done." Leo locked his gaze on her. "That doesn't even account for the time to research and find the rightful owners and deliver them. I don't know how I'll ever manage this on my own."

The amount of work Leo had already put in impressed her. "You didn't know this was here?"

"Lucien never showed me this. When he told me about his family during World War II we were in his office and he only spoke about the paintings he had displayed there. I stupidly thought that was all he had. I had no idea his crimes were this…" Leo's voice trailed off because there wasn't anything to say.

Kate didn't need him to. She was stymied for words herself. It was so tragic and overwhelming to now be the owner of this. "What will you do?"

Leo stared at the vastness in front of them and sighed. "I decided while in Scotland I didn't want to continue with the Curators. I told you that, Kate. It was hard work and my abilities aren't what they once were. My temperament and interest in the danger of it all aren't there either. There are too many risks and too many people hunting me, even though I covered my tracks well. I decided that while the Phantom is still a legend, to simply get out. Let the stories carry. They can think I'm dead or old or maybe in prison for something else. Eventually, they will stop hunting me."

"What is your business? You never told me of anything legitimate. I thought the Curators were all you were doing."

"Art brokerage," he said, searching Kate's face to see if she believed he was telling the truth. "My business was only so much of a cover and it allowed me to meet enough people that I was able to access who had what art. It also allowed me to earn a significant income that helped fund what I do. On occasion, I'd move a black market item but not very frequently. I wanted to be completely above board."

That had been a missing piece for Kate. She had long wondered how Leo had been able to know who had the Nazi-looted art. Museums were easy enough if one researched the provenance. Private collectors were another matter. Being a legitimate art broker would give Leo all the access.

"What name did you use?" Kate asked, knowing the man had more aliases than she could track.

"Pierre Legrand. No one knows me as Leo Lamiere. Not even the men I worked with in the Curators. They knew me as Pierre. They have no idea why I did what I did, only that I was driven to do it."

Kate didn't understand. "No one knows you as Leo Lamiere? Why would you tell me?"

Leo brushed Kate's hair off her shoulder and looked her deeply in the eyes. "I've never been anything but real with you, Kate. You asked me my name and I told you my *real* name. The one I had as a boy after we came to live with the Lamieres. Before that, I had my mother's last name. I've never known my father. He left her when I was young and they didn't have other children."

Kate shivered against his touch and could still feel the coolness of his fingertips against her collarbone long after he pulled his hand back. "You have a lot of aliases including using Declan Walsh. That's how your house was listed in London."

He smirked and shrugged it off. "You have been looking for me. Declan is a strong name. I like it and the Walsh made me feel closer to you. You have to understand, Kate, in my line of work I have to take every precaution." He licked his lips but not in a nervous way. He was slow, deliberate, and methodical and Kate couldn't help but stare. "Choosing Declan Walsh was nothing more than a game I wondered if you'd figure out."

Kate had assumed he'd only used it that one time in Scotland. She had no idea he'd be so bold to keep on using it. "Did you hope I'd come looking for you?"

"I had hoped but then you didn't. I thought maybe..." He stopped himself and stared straight ahead and wouldn't meet her gaze.

"Maybe what?" Kate persisted not wanting to let it go.

Leo shook his head. "No point going down that road."

Kate didn't want to let the issue drop even though she knew she was heading into dangerous territory. "Please tell me."

Leo turned to her then and put his hands on her shoulders squaring her so they were face to face inches from each other. He smiled and searched her face. "I have those daydreams too. The ones where you and I meet under different circumstances. I thought you might have felt the spark between us I did. Maybe I was just imagining it, given the amped-up energy in Scotland. It was probably just the case, the fear."

"I felt it too," Kate admitted softly, barely audible even to herself. It would have been easy to lean in and kiss him. She was surprised he hadn't tried. An image of Declan flashed in her mind and she stepped back. "We can't…"

"I know." He touched her under her chin. "You and I live in two different worlds. There is a big age difference too and I've complicated your life enough." He stepped back from her, letting his hands fall to his sides. "Speaking of that, how did you sneak off in the middle of a case to see me? Not that I'm complaining. You are welcome here anytime."

Kate wanted to pull him close again. She didn't want the electric air that seemed right on the surface between them to be extinguished, but it slipped away as they separated. "You said you didn't want to talk yet."

"Let's go outside and get some fresh air. I can show you the grounds and you can tell me why you're here."

Kate agreed although her confidence in the plan was shaken.

Leo had more than enough to do here.

CHAPTER 30

Leo and Kate walked his property in relative quiet, except for the occasional description of the land and orchard and introduction to one of the staff. She loved learning the history of the land and meeting the people who worked there. She found their stories fascinating.

It wasn't until they were at the far back of the property sitting on a bench under one of the trees that Leo turned to her. "Why are you here, Kate?"

Kate had considered how she'd tell him. She had worked over several scenarios to convince him. In the end, none of the preamble she had rehearsed seemed to matter. "These people are planning to kill you and I'm concerned they will find you. I'm here to bring you back with me, to protect you and have you help us solve this case."

Leo's features were a mix of confusion and surprise. "The FBI needs my help? You'll arrest me once you bring me in."

"That's the thing, Leo. The FBI has an offer for you. A way to clear you once and for all. The Phantom will be no more and you will never have to worry about another law enforcement agency trying to capture you. You won't ever be arrested or spend even a day in prison."

Leo cocked his head to the side, not believing what she was saying. "There has to be a catch."

Kate took a deep breath and said it on the exhale. "You have to come work with me at the FBI. It's a specialized unit and we will use your skills to help us solve cases, much like we did together in Scotland. You'd be one of us. It would further legitimize Leo Lamiere and no one will be the wiser. Once you're working with Spade, no one will ever suspect that you are the Phantom. If it's needed, the FBI can say they killed the Phantom and create a whole fake identity for him, but that's a last resort." She turned to look at him. "I have an employment contract. It's for ten years with a salary package and benefits. Not that you need the money, but it's generous."

Leo stared at her, his mouth slightly open as if he were having trouble processing what she was saying.

Kate rubbed her hands down her pants and stood. "The FBI has a lot of resources, Leo. We have an entire art theft division. I'm sure they can help you catalog and go through all of the art in there and help you get it back to its rightful owners. I can tell Spade that you won't accept without that. It can be one of your assignments."

His lips turned up in a smile. "Would you be my boss?"

"No," Kate said, shaking her head. "Spade would be but he listens to what I recommend. You'd be on a team with only a handful of people. We aren't regular FBI field agents. We are a specialized unit for only the worst of the worst cases. You'd have a home base but would need to travel to where the case is like Declan and I do. No one but Spade, Declan, and I would know who you are. There's one other agent in the art theft division working on our current case who'd know but Spade is handling that."

Leo stood from the bench and put his hands in the pockets of his jeans. He turned his back to Kate and stared out over the open field. Kate let him work through whatever he was thinking and didn't push him for a response.

After some quiet reflection, Leo turned back to her. "What does

Declan think about all of this? He tolerated me before but he doesn't understand my situation the way that you do."

Kate had not been expecting the question. "Declan is the one who suggested it, Leo. I think it's partially because he knows that you saved my life twice. We spent time researching all of the thefts we know are yours and the Curators. They all came back to being Nazi-looted art. He knows you were on the right side of things, even if he doesn't necessarily agree with how you went about it."

Leo didn't have the reaction Kate had been expecting. He chuckled. "Keep your friends close and your enemies closer."

"What do you mean?"

Leo took a step toward her. "He's in love with you, my sweet Kate. It was obvious watching you two interact. I suspect if you let yourself, you're in love with him too. It's why you didn't kiss me earlier when you so obviously wanted to." The way he held his gaze on her, Kate couldn't argue with him. He reached out and gently placed his hands on her arms. "I should have said the way we wanted to. You weren't alone in the feeling."

Kate felt no need to lie or hide the relationship. "We have been together since Scotland, mostly because of your advice. You told me not to hold back if love was available to me. I suspected jealousy was the reason for Declan's decision. That's not what he told me privately."

Kate couldn't remember how much about her personal life she had shared with him. For all she knew, he had researched her. She was embarrassed to admit Declan's reasoning but felt it was only fair. "I believe I told you that my parents were killed when I was in college." He nodded, confirming and she went on. "I'm an only child and neither of my parents had much family. Friendship is hard in this line of work. Declan is the only person I have that I rely on consistently." Kate reached out and put a hand on Leo's chest. "Declan said that a connection like ours isn't found that often and he wanted you to be a part of my life, especially if anything ever happened to him. I was honest with him and told him there was chemistry between us."

Leo shook his head and cursed softly. "He's a better man than I am. If the woman I loved told me she had chemistry with another man, I'd not be encouraging the connection. He cares about you deeply, Kate, to allow it."

Kate didn't want to push him. She knew better than to prod or push a man like Leo. Still, she needed an answer. "What do you think? Are you willing to work with me?"

"Do you honestly believe the FBI is willing to help me go through all of that art and get it back to its rightful owners? It's the only thing I have planned for the next few years." He paused but before Kate had a chance to answer, he added, "Kate, I don't have any people either. I had the Curators but since we disbanded, it's too risky to see them. I've been on my own here and had planned for a solitary life. You can't have relationships with anyone when the threat of prison looms over your head. I chose this life and I was willing to live with the consequences of it. What you're offering me now changes everything."

"Is that why you seem depressed to me?" When she saw his expression, she amended, "Maybe that's not the right word. Sad, possibly. You have a melancholy about you. I picked it up in your voice when we spoke on the phone. You're young still, Leo, with the rest of your life in front of you. As magical as this place is, you don't have to make it your prison. Join me at the FBI and you'll have people. Declan and I will probably annoy you so much you'll want to be alone."

He laughed with her and took a deep breath. "I'm considering it. I never even considered something like this was possible."

"What about your art brokerage business? Are you still doing that?"

"I officially retired. I wanted to be as off the grid as possible. I was starting to worry people might connect the dots. I was away from that at the same time the Phantom was with the Curators. I figured someone savvy might put two and two together at some point. I stopped working with clients over a year ago to focus on finding Amelia's killer."

For the first time, Kate thought she might have a shot at bringing Leo in to work at the FBI. When Declan first suggested it, she imagined she'd have to convince Leo, beg and plead. Ultimately, probably threaten him with arrest. The conversation wasn't going anywhere near the way she had planned. It was far better than expected. "There are a lot of benefits to this plan. What do you say?"

"Do you honestly believe they intend to kill me?"

"I do and I think it's only a matter of time before they find you. If they do, they will connect the Phantom and Leo Lamiere for the world. We need to beat them in their own game and prevent that from happening. With your help, I think we can solve this case." Kate pulled out her phone and scrolled to a photo of Alexander with the unknown woman. Declan still hadn't been able to figure out her identity and no one had come to the house inquiring about Alexander as they hoped she might.

Kate flipped the phone around to show him. "Do you know this woman? We believe she was involved with Alexander. We know from a witness that a posh-sounding British woman might be the leader of this group."

Leo took the phone from her and looked down at the photo. He stared at it for several moments and then went to hand it back to her but stopped himself. "Tell me again about the accent."

"The security guard said fancy. I don't know how many British accents he's heard, so take that with a grain of salt. I don't know that the two women are the same but they might be. Do you know her?"

Leo raised his eyes to her. "Do you have any idea how old she is?"

Kate shook her head, wondering what was going through his mind. "I don't have any idea. The three men who might be involved are in their early thirties. We don't know if this woman is connected but I suspect."

Leo didn't respond to Kate. Instead, he handed the phone back to her and started walking toward the house. He called over his shoulder for her to follow. "The woman looks familiar to me but I cannot place her. There are documents I have inside that might help me."

Kate caught up with him, glad he was willing to help. "Is she someone you know? An old girlfriend, maybe?"

Leo shook his head and smiled in the same way he had been smiling at her when she said something silly. "I don't have girlfriends. Women are much too perceptive and I never let anyone get close. There'd be too many questions about my life."

"I'm sure the aliases would get confusing too," she teased. "One morning you're Leo. Another Pierre, Declan, or Matthew. She'd get confused as to what name to call out in bed."

"You're being playful with me, Kate." Leo wasn't the kind of man who blushed but he had a glint of mischief in his eyes. "The few women I have taken to my bed always knew what to call me and they never forgot even long after."

Kate swallowed hard trying not to think about him that way. She had never let her mind wander there. She had considered it akin to cheating on Declan. The guilt always diverted her thoughts if her mind went down that path. "I understand what you're saying about relationships. It's why I've never had more than a few flings myself. It's difficult to have someone come into my world and fully understand my work."

Leo guided Kate back into the house and had her follow him to the right down a long hallway. She'd yet to see this part of the house. He passed by a few doors then opened one into a sunny office. "I closed off Lucien's old office and don't use that room. I can barely stand to look at it. This was my mother's study and I use it now as my own. It makes me feel closer to her."

Kate knew the pain of losing her mother, so she understood what he was saying on a deep level.

Leo went to a filing cabinet and riffled through papers. "I kept meticulous notes on every one of the Curators' heists – from whom we took a painting or sculpture to where it went after it passed through our hands. I even made notes of the heists themselves with times, dates, addresses, and what we encountered. Most of them were clean and we were in and out before anyone was the wiser. There was one though early on that didn't go as planned."

"You know if law enforcement got their hands on this, it's evidence," Kate reminded him, wishing he hadn't told her. If he didn't say yes to joining the FBI, she knew exactly where to find all the evidence to put him in prison for life.

Leo grabbed a file and tugged it free of the cabinet. "That's not going to be necessary." He went to the desk and pulled out a small photo from the file. He stared down at it as he spoke. "When we hit a private collector's home or gallery, we always did it when no one was home. This one time, we were surprised by a young girl, no more than six years old. She was there with a nanny while the parents were skiing in Switzerland. The nanny never heard us but the young girl did." He raised his eyes to Kate. "She was terrified. I scooped her up and carried her back to bed, promising her we weren't there to hurt her. I tucked her back into bed and even told her a story while my men took what didn't belong to the family. When she asked me why I was there, I told her that her father had a few things that didn't belong to him and that I was returning them to the rightful owners."

Kate wasn't quite sure what to say. It was a touch of humanity on Leo's part during the commission of a crime. "What did the little girl say?"

"She was still scared. I was wearing a black balaclava over my face and all she could see were my eyes. I lifted it for only a moment to show her my face. She's seen me, Kate."

"What happened to the family?"

Leo took a breath as he held onto the photograph. "She must have told her father what I said about taking what didn't belong to him. He killed himself three months later, probably worried we were going to expose him for having Nazi-looted art. We stole all five paintings he had that night. The newspaper said the police found more in his finance office after his death. The scandal broke anyway." He pinned his gaze on her. "He was known as the Diamond King, Kate. That's him."

Kate knew they were on the right track. "What happened to the little girl?"

"I have no idea," Leo said with a touch of sadness in his voice. He walked around the desk and handed the photo to Kate. "Look at this photo and tell me if they are the same person."

Kate glanced down at the photo and realized right away that Leo was right. She had the same eyes and nose and pout to her mouth. The same short dark hair too. "What's her name?"

"Camilla Bancroft. She came from old money in London."

She was exactly the kind of woman Kate could see Alexander Branston being linked to romantically. Kate knew that he'd been used as nothing more than a pawn.

CHAPTER 31

Kate spent the rest of the afternoon holed up in Leo's office in front of her laptop and on the phone with Declan researching Camilla Bancroft. It took help from Sam Harris to track down even more information. The family still retained much of their wealth and Camilla was educated at the finest boarding school in Switzerland and then Cambridge for university. From there, she traveled extensively including regular trips to the United States – New York City, Seattle, and Washington D.C. It was no surprise to Kate that the timing of her trips often matched where Alexander was living at the time. Kate could only surmise that they had met several years ago.

Based on the records Kate found, Camilla Bancroft had just turned thirty. Her father had been dead for twenty-four years, which would have made her six the night Leo had broken into her home. While six-year-olds retained some memories, especially traumatic ones, Kate couldn't be sure how well young Camilla had been imprinted with Leo's face in the dark during a scary event.

She had no idea if Camilla came face-to-face with him now if she'd remember him.

While she didn't have any concrete evidence to connect Camilla to the current rash of thefts and deaths in D.C., Kate was fairly certain she was behind it – a long-awaited vendetta against the man she probably blamed for her father's death.

While highly intelligent, Sam Harris said that her boarding school records indicated Camilla was a troubled young woman with little impulse control, prone to bouts of anger and violence, and she had scored high on the narcissism scale when she'd been referred to psychiatric care. Kate didn't ask how Sam had obtained the records so quickly, but he assured her they were accurate.

There had been two incidents at Cambridge that nearly cost Camilla her education. She had attacked a professor for a poor grade and had broken into the apartment of a man she had been seeing and attacked him. The professor had walked away unscathed, but the boyfriend had a broken hand as he tried to protect himself. Neither had reported the incident to the authorities but it had been a part of her university record. The incidents were two months apart and she'd again been referred to therapy. It appeared to Kate that it was her family money that got her the pass at Cambridge. Her mother had made a sizable donation to the university shortly after the incidents.

Also absent in the record was confirmation that Camilla had graduated. There were only two years of school records and no record of her achieving a degree. She had taken a range of classes, none of which hinted at a possible career path.

Shortly after, the records on Camilla disappeared except for her travels which took her around the globe. She was last known to have entered New York City four months ago. She had stayed past the time allowed on her visa. Given she was a British citizen, she'd be low on the threat list at immigration and her family money would probably ultimately get her a pass. Her passport photo was a solid match to the woman in Alexander's photos.

On her third call of the day with Sam, he said, "Are you sure this is her, Kate?"

She wasn't sure of anything. "To be perfectly honest with you, I don't know. All I know is that she is connected to one of Leo's heists and she is the woman in all of the photos with Alexander."

On the subject of Leo, Sam told her he had spoken to Declan. "What do you think he'll do?" he asked, after promising never to reveal Leo's true identity.

"I think he'll work for the FBI," Kate said with confidence in her voice. "He's intelligent and motivated. I don't believe this is an offer he'll turn down."

Sam agreed with her. "I'm a little jealous I didn't come up with the idea. Not that the National Agency would agree to it. Leo is an asset who shouldn't waste away in a prison cell."

They talked for a few more minutes about the case. Kate assured Sam she'd be in touch if there was anything else she needed. She had just finished the call with Sam when Declan's face appeared on her cellphone. Before she could even say hello he started right in.

"When do you think you'll be on your way back?" he was out of breath.

"Is there something wrong?"

"Senator Willis has been kidnapped."

"Kidnapped?" Kate asked, her voice louder than she had intended. "What do you mean kidnapped?" She didn't know what this would have to do with her. Many other FBI agents could handle the case. If anything, after his tirade at her, Kate was the last one who should be taking the case.

Declan didn't waste any time laying out the situation. "They are willing to exchange him for Leo. That's what the note in his apartment said. They took him from his D.C. apartment and will exchange him in New York City at the Metropolitan Museum of Art. There's a charity gala and they said we should meet them there and the exchange will happen at the event. You need to get back here now with Leo."

"We aren't exchanging him for Senator Willis." Kate's tone was stern and she couldn't believe Declan was suggesting such a thing. "That's not happening."

"Of course not, Kate. We have to come up with a plan. We might be able to use him as bait and get the senator back." He paused for a moment and caught his breath. "We are scrambling here without you. Even Spade isn't sure of the best course of action. We need you."

"Okay." Kate said the word but she had doubts that anything would be okay. Declan was turning to her for a plan, only she had no idea how they'd ever pull off such a feat. "I'll speak to Leo and make a plan for returning. We'll be there as soon as we can."

"Did he say yes?" Declan asked.

"I don't know. I've been in his office working on finding out more about Camilla Bancroft. I believe she is the ringleader. I'm not able to find any real connections between her and the Munson brothers and Neil Clark but I'm about eighty percent sure it's her. She has also lived in Manhattan, so she might have a home address there that we can dig up. See if Alexander Branston still has any property there. We might want to check that location first. They are keeping Senator Willis someplace."

"We are running down every lead possible. We will add that to the list." Declan paused and took a breath. "This is a mess, Kate."

"It's his fault." Kate meant every word of that. It wasn't fair to blame a victim of a kidnapping, but Senator Willis had made himself a target. "He told the world we were connected to the Phantom. They must assume he knows something or that we'd be more motivated to track down the Phantom and hand him over. As far as I'm concerned, they can keep him."

"You don't mean that, Kate."

The sad reality was that Kate did mean it. There wasn't a cell in her body that cared what happened to Senator Willis. Congress would be better off without him. "I'll let you know after I speak to Leo."

Declan exhaled a breath. "I don't want to pressure you but you have to make this happen."

Kate sighed loudly into the phone. "I got it, Declan. I'm fully aware of what I need to do and have been working on it since the moment I arrived."

"I know," he said softly before hanging up.

Kate understood the pressure he was under being the face of the team back in D.C. It must be bad if Spade couldn't even come up with a workable plan. Kate logged off her laptop and left Leo's office, making her way back through the maze of hallways. She had thought for a moment she had forgotten her way when she heard Leo's voice echo upstairs. He was singing something Kate couldn't quite make out.

He didn't have a bad singing voice and she was surprised how light and happy he sounded.

Kate climbed the stairs to the second floor. "Leo," she called at the top of the stairs. The upstairs was a match of the first floor with confusing halls and many doors. She knew how to get back to the bedroom where she had left her suitcase but that was about it. "Leo," she said again, following his voice.

"I'm here, Kate," he called out when he heard her the second time. He poked his head out of the room. "Did you need something?" He stepped back to let her into the room, which turned out to be his bedroom. He had heavy navy blue drapes on both windows and a white and blue duvet on the bed. The dresser and armoire were a dark wood to match the headboard and nightstands. The room suited him.

What drew Kate's attention was the suitcases on the floor and the pile of clothes on the bed. Leo was packing. "Did you decide to take me up on my offer or are you running away?"

Leo laughed lightly as he folded a shirt. He shifted his eyes over to Kate with a meaningful expression on his face. "Would you think it strange if I said since you arrived, I've felt better than I have in a year?

Possibly years if I were admitting it to myself. I had a solid group of men with the Curators, but in that line of work, you can never fully trust someone. I don't know why but I trusted you from the moment I saw you."

"In Paris?" Kate asked, stepping closer to him.

"Not in Paris. In Edinburgh. As soon as I knew you were investigating the case, I knew there'd be justice for Amelia. When you didn't arrest me in the cemetery, I knew a day would come when we could stand together like this and talk. Seeing you here, the fog that's been over me for a while feels like it's been lifted. I have at least one other person I can trust with my life."

"You can count Declan among the ones you can trust."

"Eventually. Probably. It will take time."

"Does that mean you're coming? You haven't said it directly to me and I need a direct answer. There are things about the case I need to tell you. I need to know you're on the team first."

Leo jutted his chin toward his dresser. "I put the employment contract over there."

Kate walked over to the dresser and pulled it from a pile of other papers. She flipped to the second page and for the first time saw Leo's signature. He had dated it and initialed where it was required. Kate held the document in disbelief, wondering if there was a catch. She had been sure that Leo would have put up a fight. She had also been sure that Declan never would have volunteered to have Leo on their team.

It was all coming together too easily and she didn't trust it.

Before she could turn back to him, Leo read her mind. "I want to, Kate. It's as simple as that. I want to come out of the shadows and more than anything I want the FBI's help in returning all those great works of art. They can take full credit for all I care. I just want desperately to undo all the bad the Lamieres did before I die. I'm willing to give the FBI ten years of my life. It's more than a fair trade." He held her gaze. "Actually, getting to work with you, I feel like I'm the one who is getting the better end of the bargain."

Kate hoped he didn't change his mind when she told him the news about the case. "They kidnapped Senator Willis and want to exchange you for him. If not, they said they'd kill him."

"Sounds like we have a lot of work ahead of us." Leo didn't seem worried or distracted by the news. "I'm sure you are more than capable of coming up with a workable plan. I trust you with my life, Kate. All I hope is that we have one night here. I made dinner reservations at my favorite place in the village near the water and I'll show you Cassis. Tomorrow, we can leave first thing."

Kate thought that was more than fair. There wasn't anything she could do back in D.C. right now anyway. She needed time to plan. "Let me call Spade and tell him we are good to go." Before she left the room, she turned back to him. "I'm looking forward to tonight."

Leo met her smile. "I'm looking forward to the next ten years working with you."

Kate believed he meant every word.

CHAPTER 32

For the first half of the flight back to Washington D.C. Kate thought about the previous night with Leo. He had taken her to a seafood restaurant where he was known and loved by the staff. They had the best table near the water and had impeccable service. Leo had asked what she liked on the menu and then ordered a range of items for them to share. She felt entirely taken care of in Leo's hands.

After a delicious dinner, they strolled the village of Cassis. Leo pointed out his favorite shops and restaurants while also telling her tales of his childhood. He pointed to one small alleyway that dead-ended at the sea where he had his first kiss when he was eleven. The girl had been from the village and they used to play hide and seek. One time when he found her, she told him she wanted to kiss him. Leo admitted he had been terrified. The kiss had been awkward at best. Kate loved the way he laughed at the memory and how animated his face and gestures were while he was talking.

Kate had promised him a similar tour of Boston when they returned. She had asked him if he had any idea where he'd like to live in the United States in between cases. She hadn't been surprised when he informed her that he already had both an apartment in Manhattan and a brownstone not far from her own in Boston, not that he had spent much time in either. Leo admitted the brownstone would probably need a major renovation inside to get it up to his standard of living but he was looking forward to the project. He figured Boston would be a good location because he could easily fly back to France and work with the FBI on returning the art that was in his possession.

While Leo focused on many of the positives of living in Boston, the one thing he stressed the most was that he liked the idea of living in the same city with her and Declan.

When Kate informed Declan that Leo had agreed to join the FBI, he told her Spade had approved Sharon joining their team. It would mean all four of them would be in Boston. One of the hardest parts of their work was being at a distance from other team members. Others from the unit joined in cases when needed, but Kate and Declan never felt like they had that strong of a bond or working relationship with them. With the four of them all residing in the same city, Kate hoped the trust and the bonds would be strong and be a benefit to the casework.

Later, after they had settled into the flight and were halfway over the Atlantic, Kate still had no more of a workable plan for the gala at the MET. She had been wracking her brain for how to make an exchange without really making an exchange. The only thing she had come up with was using an FBI agent in Leo's place and then tracking them and taking them down.

Leo had outright vetoed the plan, not that he had veto power. Kate was glad to see that he was quickly asserting himself though. She didn't mind being challenged. When she asked him why, Leo said he didn't want to put anyone else's life on the line for him. Kate had spent at least a half hour arguing with him that she wasn't going to hand him over to the thieves.

When he continued to nix the plan, Kate said, "Leo, you're not trained. These people have already shown they are willing to kill. If this woman is Camilla Bancroft and I believe it is, then she killed Alexander, a man she had been involved with for some time. Maybe he wasn't proving useful to her anymore. It's possible he got cold feet and didn't want to move forward with the plan or maybe she got everything she needed from him and then disposed of him so he couldn't tell anyone. Either way, it's sociopathic behavior and she is a danger not only to you but to all of us. I can't let someone untrained go in there."

"I've been in dangerous situations before and she knows my face. It's not going to work with anyone else. She might know." He looked across the aisle at Kate. "Do you want her to kill Senator Willis? I can't imagine that would be good for your career."

Leo had touched on the one variable Kate didn't know and couldn't control. She had no idea if Camilla would remember what Leo looked like. The reality was even at six she might have been so traumatized by their interaction and then the death of her father following that she never forgot his face. It might be seared into her brain and she'd know immediately if it wasn't him.

Before they left Cassis, Kate had asked to see a photo of Leo in his twenties to compare how closely he resembled how he looked today. His features hadn't changed much. His body was heavier and his hair and the scruff on his face were a little gray in spots but there was no denying they were the same man.

If Camilla remembered him, no one other than Leo could be exchanged for Senator Willis. She might kill the senator in a fit of rage if the FBI tried to scam her. Then again, Senator Willis might already be dead and Leo would be next. She fell into silence as she mulled over her limited options.

"What are you thinking about, Kate?" Leo asked, pulling her out of her racing thoughts.

"You're right. We don't have the option of using one of our agents given Camilla saw you when she was a child. For all we know, she remembers you."

"I have a face that's hard to forget." He was teasing her, but Kate wasn't in a laughing mood. He reached over and touched her arm. "Relax, please. I've been in more danger than this before and it's always worked out for me."

"It will work out for you until it doesn't. I don't want it to be on my watch." Kate rested her head back on the plane seat. They had about an hour before they landed. "Do you have any idea what we should do?" She couldn't believe she was asking this of Leo before he even officially started with the FBI. It was his life on the line though, she might as well hear his plan.

"Put a tracker on me and have your agents follow us. If she wants me dead and she remembers my face, then I'm always going to be at risk of her trying something like this again. I'd rather face the threat head-on than be in Boston someday with my guard down and take a shot to the head. Now, I've got a fighting chance."

"What do you mean *if* she wants you dead? It's what she said and I assume she meant it."

Leo sat up straighter in his seat and angled his body toward her. "Camilla comes from money and Alexander has more money than most people across the globe. If they only wanted me dead and they had a list of postcards of where I might be, then I think by now they could have found me. I'm hidden but I'm not *that* hidden, Kate. Surely they could have found someone who knew someone and paid off a lot of people if killing me meant that much to her. Ultimately, will she try to kill me? Sure. But I don't think that's all she wants."

There was logic in what Leo said. Kate was stumped about what she might want. "What have you considered?"

"Tell me about the paintings they have stolen so far?"

"There were three of them. The most recent is *The Death of Marat*. The second was *Major Benjamin Tallmadge* by John Trumbull. He was the one who set up the Culper Spy Ring during the Revolutionary War.

The first painting was *Lady in the Fields* by Henri Chevalier. When we looked at all three we realized they were sending us a message about you. By the time they stole *Death of Marat*, they figured we weren't smart enough to figure it out and left us a message in Alexander's hand spelling out what they wanted. We didn't act fast enough because they kidnapped Senator Willis and demanded an exchange."

"You do know the mystery surrounding *Lady in the Field*?"

"We learned it after it was stolen," Kate explained, feeling out of her depth with Leo. While she knew fine art, she had nowhere near the knowledge Leo had. "As you know, we immediately contacted Mick Sutton who owns *Man in the Field* and we called the Metropolitan Museum of Art which has *Summer Sunday.* We thought wrongly that they were after the trio to solve the mystery of who killed Henri. There's been no attempt to go after *Man in the Field.*"

"That you know of. As I said, I heard rumblings that it was to be stolen. I had no idea where the threat was coming from at the time. I just had to warn him."

"I think Mick Sutton would have told us," Kate responded with an edge to her tone she hadn't intended. "Do you think that may still be their goal?"

"It's curious, Kate. The first painting they steal is from Henri Chevalier who was from Cassis. It was the Bellerose family who had those three paintings. Cassis," he said again with meaning.

Kate hated to admit it but once she had dismissed the idea they were after the three paintings in the series she hadn't given another thought to the mystery surrounding Henri Chevalier or where he had died. "Was that another clue we missed connected to you?"

"I don't think the coincidence had anything to do with me," Leo explained and then spotted the confused look on her face. "I think this is all about the fame of solving the mystery once and for all. Art brokers have been begging for years to get their hands on all three paintings and we have all been denied. The Metropolitan Museum of Art has it under lock and key. The real one isn't even on display. The one hanging in the museum is a forgery. Do you know who created that forgery?"

"Gabriel Baptiste." Slowly a picture was starting to emerge for Kate. That's why that scene looked so staged and Gabriel was killed. Kate had to assume they questioned him about the forgery and where the real painting would be stored. She didn't share these thoughts with Leo but asked, "Where is the real painting?"

"I assume at the museum. I don't think if they went to the trouble to create a forgery they would be keeping it at some offsite storage facility. Other thieves have tried to steal it and failed."

Kate had so many questions. "Why was the MET not concerned about the theft then?"

"They should have been," Leo said matter-of-factly. "I assume the thieves must have thought Gabriel knew where the real painting was or maybe they thought he knew what was on the back. If they couldn't get possession of the painting then talking to someone who might know its secrets would be the next best thing. Gabriel had seen *Lady in the Field*. Maybe they thought he knew the secret."

"Mick Sutton said there is a painting on the back. He saw a photograph of the three together. He said it didn't show anything though. Do you believe it reveals who killed Chevalier?"

"It doesn't matter what I believe. It's what they believe." Leo unbuckled his seat belt and stood from his seat and took the seat across the small table from her. "Kate, listen, art is all perceived value. Someone is willing to pay something astronomical, so it's worth that much. The mystery surrounding these three paintings has been going on for more than one hundred years. Perception is everything. That's what has made this so valuable. I don't know one art thief besides myself who hasn't at least toyed with the idea of stealing all three paintings. I don't know what's on the back of them. For all I know, there are clues on the back that could solve the mystery of Henri Chevalier's murder. Honestly, he could have painted clues right into the canvas that the whole world has missed. There is a legend in Cassis that someone had tried to kill him before. People say he knew his days were numbered and he knew who was trying to kill him. I wouldn't be surprised if he left clues behind. They are his only paintings to survive."

"Then you think the legend could be true?"

"Possibly."

It made sense to Kate. Chevalier knew his killer and knew it was only a matter of time. He put clues into those three paintings and then gave them to a neighbor. After he was murdered, his barn with the rest of his works of art was burned to the ground. "Why didn't he just go to the police?"

Leo shrugged. "They already thought he wasn't in his right mind half the time. He was a drunk and rowdy and like most artists a little bit mad. He might have assumed no one would believe him, so he chose to do the next best thing."

That only left one question for Kate. "Then how do you fit into all of this?"

Leo locked his gaze on her. "I'm the best art thief in the world. I assume they want me to help them steal *Summer Sunday*. They want to use me to steal it before they kill me. She can take credit for the greatest art heist in the history of the world – effectively topping the Phantom once and for all. They can solve the mystery, sell off the paintings to the highest black market bidder without telling them the mystery is solved, and then post the solved mystery online for the world to see once they have their money. It's why they are leaving a signature – the King of Diamonds. They want to be known. It's a sign to me too that it's about her father. I should have connected it sooner.

It didn't occur to me though that the sweet little girl I saw that night could turn into a monstrous killer."

For the first time, the whole thing made sense. "We have our work cut out for us."

Leo nodded along with her. "That's why you have to swap me, Kate. You have to let them take me."

Kate couldn't even argue. She knew she was going to have to let them, even if it meant leaving Leo's life hanging in the balance.

CHAPTER 33

Kate had not expected to see Declan standing next to the black Town Car as the pilot pulled the plane into the hanger. She had assumed the same driver who had brought her to the airport would be there to take her and Leo back to FBI Headquarters. Kate knew Spade wanted to see them both when they arrived.

"It seems he's here to welcome us, Kate," Leo said with his lips turning up into a smirk. "I'll try to behave myself with you when we are around him. I can't help if he picks up what I'm thinking."

He was teasing her and by the look on Declan's face, he wasn't going to be in the mood. "While I appreciate that, this isn't a welcome meeting. Something has happened."

"More than a senator being kidnapped?"

"I'm afraid so." Kate waited until the plane stopped and the pilot told them they could take off their seatbelts. The only flight attendant, also employed through the government, opened the door, extended the stairs, and ushered them out. Kate made it down to the ground as Declan walked over to her. "I assume you're not just here because you miss me."

Declan cast his eyes up to Leo and gave a slight nod of his head. "Does he know?"

Kate knew exactly what he meant. "He knows and he's not going to say anything. If we are going to be working this closely, we aren't going to be able to hide our relationship. It was better to tell him than not." Kate wanted to ask if Sharon knew too but she assumed she did. "What's happened?"

"Mick Sutton is in the hospital," Declan said and shook his head in disgust. "They broke into his house, looking for *Man in the Field*. He took our advice and moved the painting but they beat him nearly to death. His wife is the one who stepped in and told them where they could find it and gave them the key. They were faster than Mick's home security."

"Is Olivia okay?"

Declan nodded. "I don't know why they didn't kill her. She's fine. They didn't touch her. The doctor thinks Mick will pull through but with his age…"

"I know," Kate said and put her hand on his arm. "Leo and I talked on the way back and he has an interesting perspective on the case, which fits with them stealing *Man in the Field*. We can tell you about it on the way back. I know Spade wanted to see Leo before we head into the field. Is Tom okay with this?"

"Spade didn't give him the choice."

Leo had been standing near the plane while the two of them spoke. Kate realized then that the two had never actually met. Kate turned her body to look back at Leo. "This is my partner, Agent Declan James. Declan, this is Leo Lamiere."

Kate wasn't surprised that Leo hung back and waited for Declan to take the lead. She was happy when Declan extended his hand and welcomed him to the team. Leo stepped forward and shook his hand without hesitation. Kate exhaled a breath she hadn't realized she'd been holding.

As Declan helped them put their luggage in the trunk, he said to Leo, "Kate was just telling me you have a perspective on the case. I'm looking forward to hearing about it because we are in the weeds right now. I was just telling Kate that *Man in the Field* was stolen."

Leo looked over at Kate who was getting into the passenger side of the car. "I believe that's their ultimate aim to steal all three in the series."

"What about the other paintings that were stolen?" Declan asked as he headed around to the driver's side.

"All to get the Phantom here." Leo got in the back passenger side of the car and gave Declan the full overview of his perspective as he had shared it with Kate. "Ultimately, they want two things – to steal all three of the paintings and they believe they need my help to do that. Then Camilla, if she is the woman involved, wants to kill me for what I did to her father."

Kate asked, "Have you gotten any further hits on Camilla's location or any more information about the background research?"

"No. The last known place was a Manhattan residence and there is no one there. The penthouse apartment was owned by Alexander Branston, which now that we know of their connection isn't a surprise. We checked other real estate we know he owns and there's been no sign of her. Alexander's sister has given us access to whatever we need. We haven't even had to get a warrant. She made calls for us and informed people of his passing and told them to give the FBI full access too. None of it has paid off in finding Camilla though." Declan glanced in the rearview mirror at Leo. "How well do you know her?"

"I don't," Leo said with a shake of his head. "I met her one night when she was a small child. She was scared when we broke into the house and I put her back to bed and read her a story. That's why she saw my face."

"Big risk." Declan's tone was as much a mix of curiosity as it was surprise.

"It was a risk but what kind of man would I be if I was okay terrifying a small child. We never wanted to harm people or scare them, even if they had done wrong."

They were quiet for a few miles.

Kate broke the silence. "Has there been any word on Senator Willis?"

"No. We had the one ransom note and that was it. We have no way to contact them either." Declan glanced over at Kate. "It's an assumption he's even still alive. For all we know he was killed and his body dumped someplace. They could be faking the ransom to get what they want."

Kate had thought about that. "Leo doesn't think they would do that given how much they want to make the exchange. He assumed we'd force them to show some proof of life and if we don't receive it, we wouldn't turn him over."

While Leo had spelled out the backstory for Declan about Camilla and the mystery behind Chevalier's paintings, no one had told him the plan for the MET gala. Not that a full plan had been established.

It didn't surprise Kate when Declan asked, "What do you mean turn him over?"

Leo moved between the two front seats. "You are going to give me to Camilla and the Munson boys. I'm not sure what I'm going to do after that, given I don't know where the real painting is or how I would steal it."

Declan didn't look happy with the plan. "Why wouldn't they suspect he's working with the FBI?"

"We have to think that through," Kate said because it was a real worry and a hiccup in their plan. Then again, they had asked for the FBI to make the exchange. Maybe they hadn't thought it through. She could see Declan wasn't on board. He was white-knuckling the steering wheel and his jaw was tense. The last thing she wanted was for her and Leo to steamroll him. "What do you think of the plan? I know it's not fleshed out, but we didn't have much to work with while we were flying."

"I don't know about handing Leo over," Declan said, his voice calm and steady. "What if they just want him dead and it has nothing to do with stealing the other painting?"

It wasn't Kate who answered. It was Leo. "If they only wanted me dead, they wouldn't have chosen such a busy event to kill me. They would have wanted to meet in a field, which would be much easier to escape. They also wouldn't have stolen *Man in the Field*. Now all they need is the third in the series, which is at the MET."

"Why the weekend of a gala?" Kate asked what she hadn't on the plane. She turned to look at him. "I meant to ask that before. If they want to steal this painting why not do it on some random Tuesday night?"

"How much do the both of you know about art theft?"

"Not enough," Declan admitted, not seeming to care that they were out of their depth on the case. "We normally handle serial homicide cases. Give us your garden variety serial killer and there's no one better than us. This kind of case isn't our specialty and we probably wouldn't have even been assigned to it if we hadn't been in D.C. being questioned by a senator for letting you go in Scotland. He challenged her to either bring you in or lose her job. Kate's whole career is on the line."

Leo's head turned sharply toward her. "Is that true, Kate?"

Declan was now looking at her too. "You didn't tell him."

She had mentioned it when she had called him but had glossed over it quickly. She wasn't surprised that he didn't remember. She hadn't brought it up again in Cassis because she didn't want him to be suspicious that she was luring him to the United States under false pretenses to arrest him. She also didn't want him to work with the FBI out of guilt to save her job.

"Kate," Declan and Leo said at the same time.

She turned her body so she was fully looking at Leo and explained she had mentioned it on the call.

"I didn't think you were being serious. You didn't sound serious."

Kate explained, "Senator Willis can make my life difficult but he can't fire me. I had a feeling that if you knew my job was on the line you'd make decisions based on that."

"I wouldn't have let you arrest me," Leo said softly. "I'm still a criminal, Kate, in the eyes of the world. It doesn't matter what I stole or my reasoning for doing it. I'm still an international criminal who most people will never trust. I'm not always as nice to others as I am to you."

It was a good reminder to Kate that she was still dealing with someone she didn't know that well. They had created an early intimacy that had lulled her into a certain complacency.

"No one is arresting you," Declan assured him. "I know it's going to take you some time to trust us. I don't know if I was in your shoes I'd trust us at all. The offer was serious and you've already proven beneficial. I'm not second-guessing the decision. Spade is eager to meet you too. I think during our meeting with him we can come up with a workable plan."

Leo said he appreciated Declan's words. "It will take some time to trust." He glanced over at Kate. "I trust Kate completely. It's why I'm here. I'll come to trust you as well. What is Spade like?"

Declan and Kate shared a look and both chuckled at the same time. Declan pulled into a parking spot and put the car in park. "Let's just say, Spade always gets his way and there are few people even in the highest government offices who'd dare question him. He was military intelligence. He's worked with all the big three-letter agencies and people know him about as well as they know the Phantom."

"Well," Leo said with a laugh, "I think we are either going to get along very well or we might kill each other."

"My money is on Spade," Declan responded as he got out of the car.

Kate was glad there was some easy early banter between the two of them. She had been expecting tension but there wasn't any. Kate only hoped that they didn't become such good friends she became the third wheel. Her partnership worked so well with Declan because she had a way of talking him into things. She didn't need Leo interfering in that.

After the long walk through the parking garage and down to Spade's office, Kate wondered if despite their reassurance Leo felt any fear that he'd been duped into coming to the United States and to FBI Headquarters only to be arrested. If there was any fear or concern he wasn't showing it.

Leo seemed loose, content, and ready to meet Spade. He said hello to Spade's assistant and Kate watched as the young woman, who had been stone-faced with them, blushed and batted her long eyelashes at him.

Declan leaned into Kate and whispered, "I barely got a hello. She's tripping over herself to talk to him."

"Hush." Kate bumped her hip into his. "He might be able to charm a few people you can't."

Declan groaned. "You're killing me."

As they approached the door, the young woman let Leo enter and closed the door right behind him, turning back to Kate and Declan, blocking the doorway. "You need to wait here until Spade comes for you. He wants to speak to Leo privately."

"Are you serious?" Declan asked, annoyance tinging his voice.

She flicked her eyes up and down and pursed her lips together. "I don't waste my breath saying things I don't mean. Wait here." She left them there and disappeared down the hall.

Declan had his hands on his hips. "Well, what do you think of that?"

Kate wasn't sure what to make of it. "It's Spade, Declan. Don't take it personally. Who knows what he wants to say without us present?

Maybe it's a test. I was a little surprised Spade agreed to this plan so readily."

"He let Ditch on the team."

"Ditch is easier to hide. He spent his whole time behind a computer screen. He was wanted by countries not friendly to the United States. Leo is wanted by most of our allies. I'm sure the politics of it are different. How did Tom take it?"

Declan raised his eyebrows. "He was angrier than you can imagine. He said he was going to his supervisor and was going to cause a big stink over it. Spade took him to his office and an hour later he was singing a different tune. I don't think he'll make trouble."

"It's going to work out, Declan," Kate said, hoping it was true.

After a few minutes of silence, Declan nudged her. "I like him. I didn't think I would. How was France?"

Kate thought back to the previous night. "I'm happy to be home."

CHAPTER 34

About a half hour later, long after Kate had grown tired of standing in the hallway, the door opened and Leo invited them in. He saw the concerned look on her face.

"It was a good talk," he assured her as they walked by him into the office.

Spade sat behind his desk, with an expression that was difficult to read. He gestured toward the chairs in front of his desk. There were three now instead of the usual two. "It all worked out, Kate. I commend you for convincing Leo to make the right decision. I think he's going to make an excellent asset to the team. He filled me in on his thoughts about the case. Do you agree with him?"

Kate took the middle chair with Declan and Leo on each side of her. She was directly across from Spade. "Based on what I know so far, it's as good a theory as any. Given *Man in the Field* was stolen and Leo's history with Camilla and her connection to Alexander, it's certainly connecting to the evidence that we have so far. It also explains the strange crime scene in Gabriel's studio."

"Declan said there were a fair amount of drugs found too," Spade said evenly and then glanced over at Leo. "You said he had a known drug habit. Is it possible that he was high at the time and told Camilla any information about how to steal the final painting in the series?"

"From what I know, Gabriel painted high all the time. It was more his natural state than anything else." He paused for only a moment as if to consider the question. "I don't believe Gabriel knew how to steal *Summer Sunday* or where the MET was keeping the painting. While he would have needed to see the painting while he was creating the forgery, I don't believe the MET would have shared the real painting's location with him after he was done. It wouldn't make sense to me if they had. The whole goal was security. They wouldn't leak the information like that."

Spade tapped the end of a pen on his desk. "When I called, the MET's director Dr. Jeffey Cain denied the forgery."

Leo didn't waver. "Many museums have forgeries for viewing and won't admit it. That's the whole point. I'm sure the MET director assured you that it can't be stolen and wouldn't elaborate when you pressed him."

"That's true." Spade looked at Declan. "Do you believe this theory?"

Declan nodded. "It fits the evidence as Kate said. We need to figure out what to do now. They still have Senator Willis."

"We need proof of life, first. If we can confirm that then we need to plan for the event."

"You're on board with swapping Leo then," Declan said but didn't give Spade a chance to respond. "Are we sure this is the best course of action?"

Spade corrected him. "We won't be swapping him. Leo will contact Camilla, if this is her, ahead of the event and offer to help them. He'll say that he heard they were looking for him. That's what we discussed while you two were outside. He will go in alone, unwired, and work to free Senator Willis from the inside. Then during the gala, he will help them steal *Summer Sunday* but only if they release Senator Willis. Leo will say he's a liability and needs to be released."

Kate's eyes grew wide the more Spade went on with the plan. "This is a suicide mission, Spade. You can't be serious."

Declan was equally shocked. "He can't go in alone. We don't send anyone in alone. They have already shown us they are willing to kill."

Kate looked over at Leo. "How is this going to work? You don't even know the location of the painting."

"He does," Spade corrected her, drawing Kate's attention to him. "But he doesn't have to steal it. During the gala, they will attempt to steal the painting and the two of you will make sure they never leave the MET by any means necessary. The goal is to extract Leo before they can kill him."

There were holes in the plan. "What if Senator Willis isn't at the MET with them?"

"You'll have to improvise," Spade said not wavering.

It was clear to Kate that neither Spade nor Leo was going to budge on the plan. "How do we make sure Leo isn't suspected of working with the FBI?"

"That's why you don't swap me and I go in alone." Leo touched her arm and drew her attention to him. "When we leave here, I'm going my separate way. We won't be seen together again until the case is over. I'm sure I can get a message to them by working my contacts. If Neil wasn't dead, I could have reached out to him. I can use his death as a reason to make contact."

"If you can't find them?"

"I'll find them. This is what I do, so let me do it." Leo turned his gaze from her. Kate started to argue again but Leo asked her to stop. He wouldn't even look at her now. "It's the only way, Kate. There is no way they were serious about a trade unless they suspected I was in FBI custody. They'd have no reason to believe that given it would be international news the moment it happened. It was a distraction technique and a way to get a message to me. I'm sure they were counting on you going public with their demand, which you need to do now."

"That's not what you thought before," Kate argued, wondering why the sudden change.

"I thought about it more and there was one part that wasn't making sense. How would you exchange me when you have no idea where I am? I've evaded police custody for decades. I'm only sitting here now because I chose to be. You have to let me do this alone."

Declan let them bicker back and forth. He looked up at Spade. "We are going public with their demands for Senator Willis's safe return?"

"Yes," Spade said evenly as he gestured toward the phone. "I've set up a press conference in an hour. You are going to say that the FBI is working to get Senator Willis back but we need proof of life. You can also tell them we are working to find the Phantom but that the man remains elusive. Leave it at that. The FBI will have plausible deniability if anything goes wrong with Leo's plan."

Kate was stunned into silence, thinking initially this had been Spade's plan and Leo was just going along with it. "This was your idea, Leo?"

He turned to her then. "It's the only way. Let's consider this my last heist," he said with a nervous laugh. "It will work out how it works out, Kate."

She shook her head not understanding. "You can't possibly be this blasé about your life. They could kill you inside the MET. They could make a public spectacle of your death."

"Then they won't get away to carry out the rest of their plan."

Spade quieted them down. "We don't have much time left. Kate, is there anything you want to do before you head to New York?"

"I want to speak to Marcy Reinhold, the director at the National Gallery of Art. She was having a relationship with Gabriel and I want to see what else she might know about the forgery he painted of *Summer Sunday*. I've felt for a while she was holding back. I thought it was just about the drugs but now I'm not so sure. Leo might know where the MET's secret storage is but if there's any chance the painting isn't there, then we need to know a potential secondary location."

Spade agreed with that. He grabbed a phone from his desk and handed it to Leo. "This is how you'll communicate with Kate and Declan. If you need help, contact them. Keep them updated on your movements but do not be seen with them. We cannot wire you for sound or visual because we can't chance that they will check." Spade then reached into his desk and pulled out a Glock. "This is your FBI-issued weapon. We are sending you in the field without any formal training but you're smart enough to know when to pull the trigger and when not to. If you kill any of them, make sure it's a clean kill. I can't protect you if it's not."

Kate felt like they were rushing the whole thing. "What about after, Spade? Let's say we get Senator Willis back unharmed and we arrest them in the process of stealing *Summer Sunday*. What then? Senator Willis might see Leo and know he's the Phantom. Camilla will certainly know and can tell the world. I don't understand the plan here for the long term."

Spade looked to Leo to explain. "The goal is for Senator Willis not to see me. If he does, we can say that I work for the FBI and I was a plant and not the real Phantom but an expert in art theft. If Camilla lives through this and my guess is she won't, no one will believe her. She was a child when she saw the Phantom." When Kate still didn't look convinced, he said, "I'm here because I trusted you. It's time for you to trust me."

"You're not trained," Kate argued back, knowing this plan wasn't going to work. Swiss cheese had fewer holes. But she couldn't convince them.

Leo wasn't deterred. "I've trained for this my whole life. I know how to steal art, Kate. It's about the only thing I'm good at. I've gone up against tougher people than Camilla Bancroft. I'll be fine and you and Declan will be there to rescue me in the end." Leo stood from the chair and reached across the desk to shake Spade's hand.

Kate was still sitting, wanting to argue with both of them. She had been steamrolled, which had never happened before. She wasn't happy about it and Declan had remained annoyingly quiet. She pushed herself up from the chair. "Since I don't get a say in this, I'll head over to speak to Marcy. Are we telling the MET director and security about this ridiculous plan?"

Spade shook his head. "No. We have set a trap for Camilla and she's going to be led right into it."

"If you say so," she said with a sigh. "Declan, are you ready to go? We aren't needed here." Kate saw the look on Spade's face and he knew she wasn't happy. He didn't care about her happiness though. He didn't pay her to be happy. Kate walked to the door and waited for Declan who hadn't risen from the chair. "Declan," she said again with annoyance. When he didn't move, she opened the door and left the meeting alone. If they didn't want her input, Kate wasn't going to stick around. She knew Declan would catch up eventually.

Kate had made it down the hall, past Spade's assistant, and stepped out into the main hall to the elevator when she heard footsteps behind her. She turned to speak to Declan but came face-to-face with Leo.

He reached out his hands and pulled her close in a hug before she had a chance to resist. "Please forgive me. I didn't know until I was in there speaking to Spade that I would need to go this alone. He asked me questions and I responded and the plan came together. I meant it when I said I need you to trust me."

Kate felt herself soften but she pulled back. "I'm not a child, Leo. You don't need to pacify me. We are supposed to be a team and you don't shut out team members like that." Kate knew she wasn't being rational. She had done the same thing to Declan when speaking to Spade and he had done the same to her with other cases. The issue was that down deep she had to admit to herself she didn't trust Leo yet. "It's fine. It's your life to throw away."

"Kate, please," Leo said, his tone soft. "I can't go into this thinking that you're angry with me. I thought I was doing the right thing. We don't have many options. I need to know you and Declan have my back."

Kate realized then that Leo might not be saying it but there was fear in his eyes. She shook herself out of her annoyance. "Of course, we will be there for you. I understand how persuasive Spade can be. Declan and I don't work well with surprises. Please keep us updated as things develop."

Leo seemed to understand. "Spade put me on the spot. I felt like I had to prove myself."

"You probably did but this might be too much." She hugged him this time allowing herself to feel his body against hers. She rested her head against him, hoping this wouldn't be the last time she saw him alive. "We will do everything we can to make sure you're safe."

Leo kissed her lightly on the cheek. "I promise to tell you as soon as I know anything. The hardest part is going to be convincing Camilla to let Senator Willis go. Are you sure you want him released safely?" he asked, his tone teasing.

Kate laughed lightly and pulled back. "Yes, I'm sure."

"I'll do my best." Leo let go of her and told her that he would text her soon. "Declan said he'd meet you outside."

Kate nodded and left Leo standing there as she walked to the elevator. She looked over her shoulder once to see him watching her. He had an expression she couldn't read. It was possibly a mix of fear and concern and possibly hope. She wanted to assure him again that all would be okay, but she didn't know if that was true.

Kate stepped into the elevator and waved to him as the doors closed.

Once on the street, Kate sucked in a deep breath of fresh air, wondering if she had handled the situation as poorly as she felt she did. She found a bench down the block and waited for Declan. She didn't have to wait long. She had barely gotten settled when he walked toward her.

"That was the closest to a tantrum I've ever seen from you. Spade is worried. You okay?" He sat down next to her and angled his body to face her. He waited for a response and when he got none, he asked, "What's going on, Kate?"

"I thought I trusted Leo but when push came to shove, I didn't."

"Is that all?" he asked, no surprise in his voice.

"It's a big thing, Declan. We have to work with him."

Declan wasn't going to give her time to wallow in her feelings. He stood and grabbed her hand, pulling her up with him. "He's a criminal, Kate. I'd be surprised if you trusted him. It's going to take time. Give yourself a break for being human."

"We don't even know for sure that it is Camilla Bancroft." While Kate felt like it was, they had no evidence to back that up. Circumstantial, sure, but nothing solid.

Declan took her hand. "As Leo said, it will work out how it works out. Let's let him do his thing while we go talk to Marcy Reinhold and come up with our own plan for keeping Leo safe. Maybe we'll come up with something better."

Kate doubted it but she allowed herself to be led down the sidewalk toward the National Gallery of Art.

CHAPTER 35

They found Marcy Reinhold sitting at her desk with her phone pressed to her ear. With her brow furrowed and the line on her forehead creased, Marcy spoke sharply to the person on the other end of the line. "I'm not going to tell you again. I don't care how much he costs, we need him here at the National Gallery of Art. Make the deal and don't call me back until you're done." She slammed the phone back down into the receiver and only then realized Kate and Declan stood in the doorway of her office.

She shrunk back in the chair and apologized. "I didn't realize you were standing there. I'm desperate to find Gabriel's replacement and the headhunter I'm working with is complicating my life. Can I help you two with something? I was hoping we could get back to normal without the FBI coming and going. It reminds visitors about what happened and ruins their experience."

Kate had noticed as they entered the National Gallery and walked through the visitor sections that everything appeared to be back to normal as if the murder and theft hadn't happened days ago. Unless someone was looking closely at them, no one would have known they were FBI.

Kate approached the desk. "I understand you want things to get back to normal as quickly as possible but we have a case to solve. More information has come to light since I spoke to you last."

"Alexander's murder," Marcy said evenly and peered up at her.

Kate hadn't realized they were on a first name basis. "Did you know him?"

Marcy shrugged it off. "D.C. circles are small. He was a donor and visited the gallery frequently. He did so with a lot of the Smithsonian Museums. I last saw him at a fundraiser at the Smithsonian Air and Space Museum. He was a generous man."

Kate and Declan sat down across from her desk without being invited.

"Did you know him personally?" Declan asked.

"What do you mean *personally*? I didn't date him if that's what you mean."

Declan had meant that but persisted. "Did you socialize with him outside of these events and outside of him being a donor here? Did you have dinner at his home? Double date with him and his girlfriend?"

Marcy looked at Kate as if she couldn't believe what he was asking. Kate didn't say a word but stared at her waiting for a response. "Is this necessary? You've torn my work life apart. I already told you about Gabriel. Please don't involve me in yet another murder."

Kate didn't feel bad for her at all. "While I understand this can be difficult, it's imperative you answer the questions – no matter if I ask them or Declan."

Marcy turned her nose up to Kate. "Yes, fine, I knew Alexander socially. I've been to his home. It started as simply courting a big donor. I grew to like the man and his girlfriend was an interesting woman, more so than most women around here. She was cultured and had an interesting life, traveling all over the globe."

"What is her name?" Kate asked.

Marcy stared at Kate with a quizzical expression on her face. "I assumed you would have already spoken to her."

"We've not been able to locate her," Kate admitted. "We believe her name is Camilla Bancroft. She was not at home when Alexander was murdered and we've yet to be able to reach her. I assume she knows of his death at this point. It's been all over the news. Still, we'd like to speak to her. I need to confirm that she's safe. Do you know where she's living or have a phone number for her? Alexander's phone was locked and we've yet to be able to access it."

"Oh." Marcy looked genuinely worried. "I hope nothing has happened to her. Last I knew she was living in an apartment in Georgetown. Let me get you that information." Marcy grabbed her cellphone from the desk and scrolled through. When she found the right contact, she texted the information to Kate.

When the text came through, Kate glanced down at her phone and noted the information. She raised her eyes to Marcy. "Please don't contact Camilla and let her know you gave us her information. We'd rather speak to her directly. I know some people can be shy about speaking to the FBI and we don't know her immigration status."

"I'm sure she's here legally." There was indignation in her voice, but Marcy relented quickly. "I'll abide by what you ask. I didn't speak to Camilla directly other than setting up a dinner reservation once. Gabriel and I attended a dinner party at her apartment one night. They invited him and we went together but not as a couple. Neither of them knew we were involved."

"Why did they want Gabriel to go then?" Declan asked, shifting in his seat.

"I assume because he did such great work as an artist for us. He is quite well known and people loved meeting him. Even people visiting the gallery knew Gabriel's name. He was a genius and was able to restore works of art that no one else would touch." Marcy pointed to her phone. "That's why I must find his replacement, not that anyone will ever be able to take his place. Whoever takes the job next won't ever live up to Gabriel's talent and ability." She grew quiet as tears stung the corners of her eyes. "Of course, that doesn't even compare to what I'm missing personally. I know I might have a tough exterior but he meant a lot to me."

Kate tried to sympathize. "We are so sorry for your loss, Marcy. Gabriel is why we are here and what you just told us about Alexander brings up even more questions. Were you aware that Gabriel painted a forgery of *Summer Sunday* for the MET?"

"I had heard mention of that from him early on after I took the job," Marcy said casually. "The MET had contacted him and asked him to replicate the painting. This was well before he and I were involved. Gabriel felt like it was disloyal to freelance another assignment for the MET without speaking to me first. He wanted to make sure he was fine to take some time off and there wasn't a conflict of interest. He was in New York for about a month – which tells his level of talent to be able to accomplish the task so quickly."

"Were you okay with him taking the project?" Kate asked, thinking about the odd exchange that might have been between them.

"I did but only after their director called me, asking if we could spare Gabriel for the project. I didn't want to allow it but I gave in."

Kate could understand that. "Was it because of the time commitment?"

Marcy nodded. "I also didn't understand why it was important. Then the legend about the series of three paintings was described to me and I was told it would help to secure *Lady in the Field*. If no one could access *Summer Sunday,* then none of them would be at risk of theft."

Declan's brow furrowed. "I don't understand. Is it common knowledge that the *Summer Sunday* hanging in the MET is fake?"

Marcy shrugged and sat back in her chair. "I don't know how common it is to everyday visitors. I suspect word got through backchannels to the right people that there'd be no point stealing the paintings because the third in the series wasn't going to be accessible. No one was supposed to know Gabriel had painted it and no one would know where the real painting would be stored. I assume the casual visitor has no idea. The MET director does not even acknowledge it."

Kate knew from Leo that information traveled in his circles and the people who might be tempted to steal it would get the message. "Did you ever discuss this with Alexander or Camilla?"

"That Gabriel forged *Summer Sunday*?" Marcy asked and Kate nodded her head. "No, that never came up in conversation. It was never anything I heard them ask Gabriel either. I know they were interested in his restoration work here at the National Gallery. They had come into his studio a handful of times to see his work."

Kate and Declan sat forward in their chairs. It was Declan who spoke first. "Alexander and Camilla were here in Gabriel's studio? Downstairs?"

Marcy picked up on their concern. "Only a few times and it was after hours. I know I shouldn't have allowed it, but he was such a big donor after all. They wanted so badly to see his work. I didn't think it would hurt anything and they were in and out without anyone being the wiser." She must have misread how they were looking at her because she added, "I know it wasn't right, but it wasn't just me who allowed such things. I know Alexander and Camilla had private tours of other museums and galleries around D.C. and in New York too. He was such an art lover and devoted donor. As the saying goes, money provides access. It's just how it is."

It meant that the two of them knew their way around the museums, after-hours protocols, and possibly even the security staff. They knew where to find certain works of art and even potential security breaches they could capitalize on.

Kate asked the most pressing question on her mind. "Did they know about Gabriel's drug habit?"

Marcy looked uncomfortable answering the question. "They did but only because Alexander was known to partake socially once in a while. He suggested a dealer who catered to high-profile clients and that's who Gabriel used."

The follow up was key for Kate. "Is it fair to say that they might have known if Gabriel kept that back door near his studio unlocked while he worked?"

Marcy caught Kate's meaning and righted herself in her chair. "What exactly are you getting at, Agent Walsh? I don't understand this line of questioning." She had an air of defiance and indignation Declan couldn't stomach. Kate was used to dealing with people like this.

Declan wanted no part of it. With his voice tinged with anger, he said, "What Agent Walsh is saying is we believe Alexander had prior knowledge about the art thefts and was financially backing the operation." He didn't go as far as to say Camilla was the ringleader.

"That's not possible," Marcy retorted, keeping the same posturing. "It's simply not possible."

Declan leaned forward as he spoke. "Let me ask you this. Did you ever hear either of them mention the Curators or the Phantom?"

Marcy's mouth fell open but she didn't speak for several moments. "It came up in conversation."

"What was said?"

"Camilla said that her father had been robbed by the Phantom. She told us she had seen his face and that she would remember him for the rest of her life."

Kate cleared her throat. "Did she want revenge?"

Marcy shook her head but the response was weak. "The theft killed her father, Agent Walsh. He killed himself shortly after. She was a young girl at the time. Anyone would have considerable rage over the whole thing."

Kate didn't respond. She kept quiet in the hopes Marcy would fill the void.

She didn't disappoint when she tried to plead the case. "Camilla was surprised the Phantom was able to carry on as long as he had. She hated that he was known as the best art thief in the world. She was completely torn up that he had been venerated rather than arrested and punished for what he did. I agreed with her sentiments."

Kate started to speak but Declan interrupted her. He glanced over in apology to Kate and then focused on Marcy. "Would it surprise you to know that what the Curators stole was Nazi-looted art? They returned it to its rightful owners. It wasn't the most high-valued art or what could sell the best on the black market. They stole art that had been taken on the lead up to and during World War II."

Marcy shook her head in disbelief. "That can't be true."

"It's true," Declan said not leaving any room for argument.

Kate crossed her legs and kept her gaze focused on Marcy. "At the start of this case, we went through all of the Curators' thefts. We found that in each case it was Nazi-looted art that they stole." Kate let that sink in. Marcy sat there for a few beats and absorbed it. Kate went on. "As I'm sure you saw on the news, Senator Willis has been kidnapped. What's not been made public is that this King of Diamonds theft ring is demanding to have the Phantom brought to them in exchange. We believe they want to kill him. As you know, Alexander was murdered in his home. Camilla has been nowhere to be found. Up until your confirmation, we did not know for sure that Camilla was the woman in the photos with him. Thank you for that."

Marcy shook her head as if trying to dislodge something. "I don't understand what you're saying."

Declan slapped his closed fist into his other palm. He had grown frustrated with her. "What we are saying is we believe Camilla is the one who broke into the National Gallery and killed your guards and stole *Lady in the Field*. We believe she is behind all of this including killing Gabriel and Alexander. What we don't know is why she killed Alexander or where she is right now. We also cannot meet her demand of bringing her the Phantom. If we did, he'd be in FBI custody. Other than stopping her, finding Senator Willis is our only priority. If there is anything else you know, you need to tell us right now."

"Oh my God," Marcy said in a rush of breath. She repeated this several more times as she started to hyperventilate. She stood from her chair and started to pace behind her desk. "I don't know anything else I swear to you. It didn't even occur to me that Alexander or Camilla could be involved. That's why I never mentioned them before now. I had no idea it was relevant." She turned and faced them, leaving her palms on her desk. "You have to believe me." Tears rolled down her cheeks.

Kate believed the shock and raw emotion was genuine.

They asked her a few more questions and then left with two more addresses where Camilla might be found and a promise from Marcy not to release any of the information they shared. Kate told her to stay away from Camilla and not answer any calls or make contact.

They left the National Gallery of Art, where this had all started, feeling like they were one step closer to bringing Camilla Bancroft to justice.

CHAPTER 36

Kate stood back from the crowd of media that had gathered for the press conference. Declan was at the podium with Tom as they took turns giving updates about the case. Declan had become quite adept at being the spokesperson. It was a role Kate happily let him take.

She had been tempted to text Leo to tell him about their meeting with Marcy but decided to keep it between her and Declan for now. There was nothing Leo could do with the information until they confirmed Camilla's location. After the press conference was over, she and Declan were headed to check out the addresses.

They had already decided that they would go in alone without a SWAT team with them. The goal of the first conversation was not to arrest her but to see what she'd be willing to tell them. They had little evidence to connect her to the crimes and they didn't want to take a big swing and miss the chance at a confession or lose the time to gather solid evidence against her. They didn't even have enough to get a search warrant. Their case was still all speculation and circumstantial pieces tied together with loose string.

Declan adeptly made all the points Spade told him to make – the demand for proof of life for Senator Willis and the FBI search for the Phantom. When he was done, he backed away from the podium and went back into FBI Headquarters, leaving the journalists to disperse.

Kate met him and Tom in the lobby. "You both did great with the press conference." This was the first she had seen Tom after he found out about Leo. She wasn't sure what to say.

Tom spoke first though and let her off the hook. "Declan told me the plan with Leo. While I don't necessarily agree, I think it may be beneficial for the FBI in the long run. He'll have a lot of contacts we don't and he'll have some insight that none of us will have. It will be good to have him as a resource."

Kate assumed no one had told him about Leo's house. She had only briefly mentioned it to Spade during a phone call and he said if the art theft division wanted a crack at the art, then they could go for it. She told him now and watched as his eyes got wide and he appeared visibly excited by the prospect.

"How much are we talking about?" he asked when she was done.

"Hundreds," Kate said with emphasis and described the underground facility Leo had shown her. "It's all been well preserved. Part of Leo's willingness to accept the FBI offer was if they were willing to help him catalog, research, and return all of that art."

Tom was eager to help. "It would be a huge win for the FBI. We might even be able to secure some specific funding to help with that. Of course, we'd have to figure out the French authority's role in all of this."

"It's private property and Leo technically owns all the art. There's no current crime," Kate reminded him. "You can go work quietly and the French never even have to know."

"That's even better."

Kate was glad there was another positive for Tom in all of this. She had to admit he was taking it better than she thought. "We can set up some time for you to speak with Leo once this case is over. Did Declan brief you on the plan?"

"He did and I think it's reckless and stupid."

"We feel the same," Declan echoed. "I've already called the FBI office in Manhattan and they will provide us backup. Kate and I are on our way to see if we can find Camilla here in D.C. at one of the addresses we just obtained."

"Are you going alone?"

Kate noted the worry on Tom's face. "We're going to speak to her as a potential witness to see what happened to Alexander. We will figure out what we can while we are there."

"It could be an ambush," Tom warned them.

Kate had considered that, given Camilla might hold her responsible for Neil Clark's death. It was a chance she was willing to take. "We are prepared for that. We don't have evidence to hold her yet. I want to disarm her and let her think we don't suspect her. It will make her go into the whole thing in New York a lot more cocky, which can lead to mistakes."

"I can't argue with that." Tom stood as did Kate and Declan. "If you need anything, you know how to reach me." Tom wasn't going to be joining them there. He had other tasks to handle in the case related to the stolen artwork. They said goodbye and Kate and Declan headed for the door.

"I think that went as well as can be expected." Declan held the door open as they stepped out onto the sidewalk. They walked the few blocks to the first address Marcy had provided them for Camilla but were told by the doorman that the apartment had been vacant for at least three months. Declan was able to convince him to let them go up and check for themselves. It had been a waste of time though. No one was there.

The same pattern followed on the next two places they tried. They had worked the places closest to them and left the Georgetown house for last. It was the furthest in distance and required a short cab ride over.

Black shutters framed each window of the brick three story row house. The front downstairs windows featured blooming flowerboxes and manicured shrubs lined the brick walkway. The home had been well tended. Kate followed Declan up the three steps to the black front door and waited while he raised the brass knocker and hit the plate below it twice.

A moment later, much faster than Kate had expected, Camilla Bancroft, clad in tight dark jeans and a simple black scooped-neck tee-shirt, answered the door. Her feet were bare, toenails a dark burgundy, and she wore little makeup. Kate's first impression was that the photos of her with Alexander didn't do the woman justice. She had striking sharp features, big round eyes, and lips that almost looked like she had fillers but were probably natural.

Camilla raised her eyes to Kate, no recognition on her face. "Can I help you?"

They flashed their badges while Declan made the formal introductions. "I assume you're Camilla Bancroft," he said. "We've seen your photo at Alexander Branston's home."

"Yes, I am. He was my boyfriend." Camilla leaned against the doorframe as tears formed in her eyes. "I'm sorry for the emotion. I'm still dealing with the loss."

If Kate didn't truly believe this woman was responsible for Alexander's murder, she'd be hard-pressed not to believe the emotion was real. "We'd like to speak to you about Alexander. We have some routine questions as we are still trying to find the person responsible for his death."

Camilla stepped out of the way and let them into the home. "Unfortunately, Alexander and I had hit a rough patch a week ago and had a big falling out. Given that, we hadn't been in contact for a few days. I had no idea he'd been murdered until I saw it on the news. I assumed his sister would be there and she and I had never met. I figured it was best if I stay away."

Declan stepped aside as Camilla closed the door. They followed her into the family room off the main foyer. She clicked off the news and sat down on the edge of an ottoman. Declan took the couch across from her while Kate stood. "Did Alexander speak about his sister often?"

Camilla shook her head. "They weren't close. I knew his sister was his power of attorney and would be in charge of his estate. Alexander had mentioned that a while back. While they weren't close and might have even hated each other, he relied on her for that."

Kate assessed the room with its soft beige walls with white trim. The couches and two wide chairs were a shade darker than the walls with throw pillows in soft pink. The hardwoods were covered with a cream colored rug. All in all it was a soft feminine space that had a cozy vibe. It was the exact opposite to what Kate had imagined Camilla's living space would be like and she wondered who decorated it.

"How long were the two of you together?" Kate asked.

Camilla was forced to look up and over at Kate. "We've known each other for a few years. We met in New York and quickly became involved. He was a good man and he was good to me during our relationship. There was never anything I wanted for and he was kind to me."

"You're from London?"

"I grew up in London but have lived all over the globe." Camilla regaled them with a few stories about her life in London and about her mother. She left out any mention of her father, his suicide, or the stolen artwork. She didn't bring up the Curators or the Phantom. She was trying to cultivate her image as a shy, quiet girl who took a chance at coming to America and met a handsome billionaire. Even if Kate hadn't known the truth, the story would have been hard to buy.

Kate let her spin her tale for a few more minutes before redirecting. "Given the length of time you were together, were you surprised Alexander was murdered?"

Camilla blinked a few times. "I'm not sure what you mean?"

"Well, he was murdered in his home and a painting stolen. I'm sure you've seen the other cases in the news. It was interesting to us that this killer would target him. How did they know what art he had?" Kate let the information sit and watched to see if Camilla had any reaction. The one thing Kate noted was the muscle in her right bicep tensed and released. She might have been dressing to downplay her physique but as they walked into the house, the woman's jeans were tight enough that Kate saw her leg muscles, which were well-defined and strong.

Camilla was far from the meek woman she was currently playing.

Camilla clasped her hands together. "I didn't know much about art. He certainly had a lot of it and was a donor to several galleries and museums. Maybe he told the wrong people what he had."

Declan caught what she said faster than Kate. "You didn't know much about art?"

She smiled at him meekly. "It wasn't one of my interests."

"That's funny," Declan said with a hint of sarcasm. "We were told you and Alexander had been to the National Gallery of Art after hours and had met Gabriel Baptiste, their restoration specialist. We assumed you and Alexander were heavily involved in the arts scene."

Camilla knew they had caught her in a lie, but she recovered quickly. "It was one of Alexander's passions. Over the years, I had grown to enjoy it too. What I meant to say was that I don't know works of art in quite the same way he did. I didn't know the artists and backstories and deeper meaning in the paintings. I'm not able to read into art the way Alexander could. It was a hobby at best for me."

"You don't know why they would have targeted him," Kate said, pushing a little harder. "There are many private collectors all across the D.C. Metro. It doesn't seem like a coincidence that he had a good relationship with Gabriel and he was murdered as well."

"I don't know what to say." Camilla's eyes shifted between her and Declan. "Is there something you suspect about Alexander?"

"We suspect that Alexander might have known his killer," Declan said as they had planned. "If that's true, then you might be in danger or you might not realize that you know something that could help us."

Camilla stood and wrapped her arms around herself. "I don't think I'd be in any danger. I find it hard to believe Alexander would be involved in something so insidious. I've never known him to hurt anyone. I don't see how he could be involved with stealing art and killing people."

"We didn't say he was doing this himself. He might have been a financial backer." Declan waited and then added, "We believe he was manipulated into helping some very evil people."

Red flamed up Camilla's neck but she held her expression steady. "I don't think you should slander his name without any evidence."

"Who said we don't have evidence?" Kate asked, pushing harder. She was watching Camilla's anger grow and her personality shifted right in front of them. Kate could see this woman being a cold-blooded killer. There was a vacancy in her eyes she had masked as sadness earlier.

Camilla stared coldly at Kate and pointed toward the door. "You need to leave. I'm done with this conversation. I won't stand here and have you say such hateful things."

As Declan stood, a noise from another room echoed through the house. Kate went to her gun as Declan went for his. He barked, "Is there someone else here with you?"

Even Camilla looked startled by the noise. She had started to say no when Leo appeared from the foyer and took a step into the living room. Camilla turned to look at him and then quickly back at Declan. "I'm sorry, yes. I have a friend visiting from Paris."

Kate raised her eyes to meet Leo's. She didn't know what to think. "I'm FBI Agent Kate Walsh," she said to him. "That's Agent Declan James."

"Pierre Legrand," he said with a thicker French accent than she'd ever heard him use. "It's a pleasure to meet you both." He looked toward Kate's gun. "I didn't mean to startle you. I'll let you get back to your conversation."

"They were just leaving." Camilla brushed past Leo toward the door.

Kate had no idea how Leo had beaten them there. He looked her dead in the eyes one more time and nodded his head as if to say goodbye. She couldn't read the expression on his face. His whole posture was different too – much more the man she'd first met in Paris on the rooftop than the man she had visited at his chateau in Cassis. This man she needed to fear.

"We'll be in touch, Camilla," Declan said as he exited the house.

Kate followed quickly behind him, not sure what she was feeling. She didn't say a word to Camilla as she left. Kate had gone there to rattle Camilla but the tables had been turned on her.

CHAPTER 37

"What was that about, Declan?" Kate asked under her breath when they were blocks from Camilla's row house. She had to assume they were being watched, so she kept her head down and her voice low. "Why was Leo there already? How could he have possibly known where to find her? I didn't tell him the addresses Marcy provided us. We didn't tell anyone, not even Spade."

Declan looked as stumped as Kate felt. "He said he had connections and that he was going to seek her out. That's what he did. We can only assume he's deep into his assignment. Do you have concerns otherwise?" He reached out a hand to stop her. "I don't like being out here on the street."

They walked a few more blocks, flagged down a taxi, and went back into the heart of D.C. near FBI Headquarters. They walked a couple of blocks to make sure they weren't being followed and then went into a restaurant and grabbed a booth in the back. As they sat, Declan peered over at her with concern on his face. "What's got you so upset?"

Kate tried to shake off the feeling. "I wasn't expecting Leo to be there so soon. I thought it would take him a while to find her." She sat back and raised her gaze to the ceiling, trying to process what exactly she was feeling. Then she lowered her head and looked at Declan. "It makes me wonder if he knew Camilla all along and didn't tell us."

The server came over and asked for their drink order. Declan ordered food and drinks for both of them without asking Kate what she wanted. He knew she'd be too hyped up to even look at a menu. She appreciated the gesture.

When the server was gone, he sat back against the booth, looking too calm for Kate's liking. "He's a criminal and has been operating as that for the past two decades at least. Making him part of the FBI doesn't erase those years overnight. This won't work unless we trust him. He was tasked with contacting Camilla, gaining her trust, convincing her to let Senator Willis go, and steal *Summer Sunday*. You can't get this freaked out now that he's doing exactly what he told us he was going to do."

Kate knew Declan was right. Her feelings were irrational and she wasn't prone to irrational behavior. "It caught me off guard. I didn't think he'd contact her that soon. He also said he'd keep us in the loop and he didn't do that."

Declan raised his eyebrows. "Is there more?"

Kate stared off into the restaurant. "He seemed so different, scary almost."

"He was scary when he took you hostage, Kate. The man is a chameleon. It's what's going to make him good on our team." Declan didn't seem shaken by the situation. He casually rested against the booth and his arms were loose and relaxed on the table. "Maybe he heard Camilla was staying there and showed up like we did. He might not have had a chance to text you. He didn't seem to be in any danger and he let us know he was there. He also established that there was no connection between us. Neither of you even flinched when you saw each other. I don't think Camilla suspects. If anything, it was a good thing Leo came out when he did."

"He didn't need to come out at all," Kate said, thinking back on the situation. "If he had stayed in the back of house, we would have never known."

Declan nodded. "That's why I don't think he's doing anything wrong. Leo was trying to let us know he made contact. It was risky because Camilla could have picked up some familiarity between us, but she didn't."

"Maybe it was good then," Kate said softly, lost in her thoughts. She was filled with a mix of worry about Leo and concern that he was double-crossing them. "What did you think about her?"

"Steady. Calm. Collected," Declan said and then added, "She's a terrific actress. If she wasn't stealing art and killing people, she might have had a career on Broadway. She gave nothing away."

"She didn't even seem that broken up about Alexander. I was hoping to get some idea what they had fought about. Even the mere suggestion that he might have been behind this enraged her."

"Do you suspect why it upset her?" Declan asked and she knew what he was hinting at.

"I think when all of this goes down, she doesn't want to share credit." Kate hadn't considered that before she said it, but it felt right. "Ultimately, she got rid of him to prove she's more powerful and the one in charge. Camilla might have needed his money but that's all."

Declan didn't disagree with that. "She had dead eyes."

Kate had seen the same. They settled into relaxed silence as they waited for their lunch. The server dropped off their drinks and Declan read on his phone.

After their lunch was served, Kate said, "Did I tell you Leo has a brownstone in Boston?"

Declan's eyes flicked up from his burger. "What do you mean?"

"I asked him where he was planning to live. Spade never said he had to live anywhere specific. He told me he owns a brownstone in Boston and he intends to live there."

Declan's jaw tensed and he expelled air through his nose. "I didn't count on that proximity."

Kate knew he wasn't going to take the information well. "You have nothing to worry about. Besides, it might be good with the four of us in Boston together. Is Sharon excited about joining the team?"

Declan didn't relax as he processed that Leo was going to be in the same city as them. "She said she's happy as long as she gets access to the labs she needs. She's pretty set there in Boston and has everything she needs at her fingertips. Sharon said a lot of labs around the county aren't as high-tech as the one she has now."

Kate could understand that. "Sharon might be able to help the government recognize the gaps in access at different police departments and help us funnel money there for improvements. I'm certain we can make sure she has what she needs." They fell into silence again as they ate. Kate kept watching Declan to see if he was going to say anything else about Leo. After a while of quiet, she asked, "What plans do we have for New York City?"

Declan glanced up at her. "The train leaves tomorrow morning at ten and we have a hotel only a few blocks from the MET. We have a meeting with the FBI office to go over the plans for the gala. We've got a couple of days before the event. Spade said we can get a lay of the land and take a little down time to prepare. He also suggested we might set up a meeting with Dr. Jeffery Cain, the head of the MET. I know we aren't going to tell him the plan, but he might be able to tell us where the painting is."

"Do you think we should tell him we know the one on display is a forgery?"

Declan finished the rest of his burger and washed it down with his Coke. He wiped his mouth and sat back. "I don't think it matters if we tell him. He won't be suspecting what's coming. If he can confirm for us where the painting is and we can let Leo know for sure, then we'll go into this with better operational planning. Leo and Spade might have a plan but nobody said we couldn't investigate. I'm still convinced if we come up with a better plan, Spade will have no choice but to listen."

"That's true." Kate finished her lunch. She yawned as she pushed her plate away. "Is there anything else we need to do before we leave D.C.?"

"I don't think so," Declan said, giving her a smile. It was the first since he heard about Leo living in Boston.

It felt a bit unsettling for Kate to be leaving D.C. again with so much left unfinished. They had to go where the case was taking them and that was to New York. "I guess we can head back to the hotel and get ready for tomorrow."

"You need sleep." He reached for her hand across the table. "Between the lack of sleep on this case and the jet lag with your trip to France, I don't know how you're even still awake."

"I slept a little at the hotel in France after I landed." While that had been good, it hadn't been enough to catch her up. Kate had been running on pure adrenaline and she knew she'd crash at some point. While downtime in the middle of the case felt odd to her, she was grateful that they'd have a few days before the gala. "I'll get some sleep. As you said, there's not a lot we can do until we get to New York or Leo alerts us to what he finds."

Their hands were tied until then.

They walked back to the hotel and went directly to their room. Kate took a hot shower while Declan checked the news. She was towel drying her hair when her phone chimed on the bathroom counter. Kate reached for it and recognized the last four digits as the phone number from the phone Spade had given Leo.

The text was straight to the point: *He's not in D.C. They have moved him to New York already. Working on getting an exact location. Are you okay?*

Kate read the words a few times, stalling for a response. She didn't know if she should just tell him she was fine or be honest about how she was feeling. Kate chose a middle ground response.

It was jarring to see you there. I'm fine but curious how you found her faster than we did.

I broke into Gabriel's apartment. He used to keep contact information of everyone he ever met in a small notebook. I wondered if they had met previously. Her contact information was there.

That was as rational an explanation as any. Kate explained what she knew. *They had met several times. She was given insider access to the National Gallery.*

That's correct. She told me Gabriel wouldn't give her any information. Are you safe?

I promised her I'd help her steal Summer Sunday *and she promised not to kill me until then. She will not release Senator Willis though. He's alive but condition unknown. It's going to take some time to get the information.*

Kate thought he was doing better than she could have expected. *We are headed to New York tomorrow. When are you leaving?*

Tonight. I'll let you know where I'll be. She said she has an apartment there. I asked if Senator Willis was there and she said no. She won't tell me who else she's working with. She said I'd learn more in New York. But at least she's convinced I'm not working for the FBI. She laughed at how stupid you were to be standing feet from the Phantom and not know. She's convinced the FBI are idiots.

At least some good came out of the meeting. *Text us if you need anything.*

I'll see you soon.

Kate set the phone down on the counter and wiped the steam off the mirror so she could see her reflection. Her face was pale, cheeks hollow, and dark circles had formed under her eyes.

Declan knocked twice on the bathroom door and Kate called him in. "Leo texted me. He said Senator Willis is someplace in New York but he doesn't know the location." Kate gave him an overview of the rest of the texts. "He didn't mention anything about the stolen paintings. I assume they are in New York as well."

"Do you feel better about Leo?"

While Kate nodded, she added, "I'll feel better when this whole case is over and we all have some time to adjust to Leo being around. It would have been better had he not started in the middle of the case."

Declan leaned against the bathroom counter. "If it hadn't been for this case, I might not have suggested it."

"Fair enough." She untwisted the towel from her hair and let her wet hair fall on her shoulders.

Declan tugged the front of her bathrobe and pulled her in for a kiss. He let his lips linger and then rested his forehead on hers. "As much as I want you right now, you're going to sleep. I don't care if I have to read you bedtime stories or sing you lullabies."

Kate chuckled and leaned into him. "You can't sing. That would surely keep me awake."

"I can't be good at everything." Declan handed her the brush so she could untangle her wet hair. He had grown to know her routine. He stepped out of the bathroom so she could finish getting ready for bed.

When Kate was done, she went into the small bedroom area of the suite and found the bed turned down for her, two pillows arranged the way she liked them, and the small table lamp the only light on.

Declan came in behind her and had his hand out. "Give me your phone. I'll plug it in out there and I promise to wake you if they need anything. You don't need to worry about it right now though."

Kate wasn't going to argue with him. She knew if she kept the phone with her, she'd check it. While it was only close to five in the evening, Kate knew as soon as she closed her eyes she'd sleep uninterrupted until morning. She handed her phone over willingly. "You're good at taking care of me." She thanked him as she got under the covers.

Declan leaned down, kissed her, and then left her in darkness.

Kate was asleep before she even got comfortable.

CHAPTER 38

Kate and Declan walked the few blocks from the hotel to the Metropolitan Museum of Art. They had a three o'clock meeting with Dr. Jeffrey Cain. The sun was shining and it was the perfect New York City day. Kate felt more well-rested than she had in months and she was ready to tackle whatever came her way.

Nothing had happened overnight and she had been able to sleep well into the morning. She only woke once and found Declan turned on his side facing away from her. She snuggled into his back and fell back to sleep quickly. The train ride to the city had been uneventful and so had checking into their new hotel. Spade called once to check on them and assess Leo's progress.

Kate hadn't heard from Leo again since the texts after her shower. She didn't want to reach out to him because she assumed he was with Camilla. She wasn't going to risk blowing his cover, not when they were so close.

Declan had made the call to Dr. Jeffrey Cain and had been surprised that he was so willing to meet with them. He'd been so dismissive on the phone when Kate had expressed concern over *Summer Sunday* that she assumed he might give them a hard time about wanting to meet.

Their goal for the meeting was to get a layout of the MET, find out where he was keeping the real painting, and score an official invite to the gala. Kate had a plan for that as well. If they were there legitimately, than Dr. Cain might not suspect that something else was afoot.

They walked down 5th Avenue toward the MET, sidestepping young mothers pushing children in strollers and groups of students who were lining up outside after their visit. It was late in the day, nearing three, and the children looked to be tired and overstimulated.

"I remember trips to the museums in Boston when I was a kid," Declan said, hitching his jaw toward them. "I always managed to get in trouble for something. I remember one trip. Sister Elizabeth wouldn't let me go with my friends and I had to spend the whole day with her. It was pure torture."

"I'm sure it wasn't her best day either," Kate said with a laugh. While Kate and Declan had grown up nearly twenty minutes away from each other in Boston and they were the same age, their paths hadn't crossed until they were at the FBI Academy. Kate had grown up in the wealthier Back Bay area while Declan had grown up in South Boston. He'd gone to Catholic schools while her parents had sent her to public school. She saw photos of Declan as a child and he didn't look much different now – same messy wavy hair, broad mischievous grin, and eyes that made women look at him twice. Kate had been studious and even-tempered and couldn't remember a day in her childhood where she'd gotten in trouble for anything.

They walked up the steps to the MET and found Dr. Jeffrey Cain standing a few feet from the door. He had a badge attached to a blue string around his neck and he was speaking affably to a woman Kate assumed was a teacher. Kate recognized him from his photo on the website. He had a head full of dark hair, a handsome face, and round glasses perched on his nose. She knew from his bio on the website that he was in his late fifties.

They stood off to the side and waited for him to finish his conversation. When he was done, Kate walked over with her hand extended. She introduced them. "We appreciate you taking the time to meet with us today."

"No problem at all. Anything for the FBI," he said as he ushered them into the MET. He spoke briefly to security and another staff person who were standing near the front door and then directed Kate and Declan to follow him into a staff area. They walked a maze of hallways to a large sunny office. He told his assistant to hold his calls then opened one of a pair of doors to his office.

"Please take a seat," he said, gesturing toward the two chairs in front of his desk. He grabbed a file from the side of his desk, put it in a desk drawer, and sat down. "How can I help you?"

Kate and Declan had debated a few ways to address this. Ultimately, Declan decided to take the lead and be direct. He thanked Dr. Cain again for seeing them. "Through our investigation in D.C., we came to learn that *Summer Sunday* displayed here in the MET is a forgery."

"Why would you believe such a thing? I already told your boss it wasn't." Dr. Cain's voice dripped with indignation.

Declan sidestepped the tone. "As you are aware, Gabriel Baptiste was murdered at the National Gallery of Art during the theft of *Lady in the Field*. During the investigation, we discovered information that led us to know *Summer Sunday* was a forgery Gabriel painted."

Kate saw the uncertain look on the man's face. "You're free to do whatever you want in the MET. If you want to hang a forgery then by all means do that. As we told you before, we are concerned about a possible theft given both *Lady in the Field* and *Man in the Field* have been stolen. We are here to make sure *Summer Sunday* is someplace safe."

"I can assure you it's safe," Dr. Cain said without saying more.

"Where is the real painting?" Declan persisted. Even if he wasn't going to admit the one hanging on the walls of the MET was a forgery, they were going to press on like it was. They had no time to waste on the matter.

Dr. Cain looked between Kate and Declan and must have quickly realized that they weren't going to give up so easily. He stood from his desk. "If you insist on this matter, then you can follow me and I'll show you."

Declan looked over at Kate and she shrugged. If Dr. Cain was going to lead them to the painting, she wasn't going to complain about that. She sent a message to Declan with just a look. She needed his eagle eyes to watch for all layers of security to be able to report it back to Leo. The hope was that they wouldn't actually have to steal the painting as long as they had the others and Senator Willis back by then. Everything hinged on that.

They followed Dr. Cain back out to the main lobby of the MET and then through a door marked staff only and down another long corridor to a back elevator. Once inside, Dr. Cain typed in a code and the elevator doors closed. He tapped the button labeled G2 and they descended. "That's the first and second layer of security. They'd need to know where to access this elevator and then need the code to make it work." He had an air of confidence about him when he spoke as if he had thought of everything.

Once the elevator doors opened they were in a hall with white walls and blinding overhead florescent lights. Kate blinked a few times until her eyes adjusted. Dr. Cain stepped in front of Declan and navigated them down another hall, took a left when it dead ended, and then they came to another door that required another passcode. He looked back at them. "Third layer of security."

There were two more halls that followed and two more passcodes. Dr. Cain assured them that different passcodes were used each time. When they finally reached the end of a hall, Dr. Cain pressed his palm against a biometric security screen. It was only after the system recognized him that the door clicked and he was able to open it. He turned back to them and raised his eyebrows in satisfaction. "We were robbed years ago by the Curators and we installed all new layers of security since then. That was a previous director and it's not going to happen on my watch."

Once in the room, there were two guards with guns standing in front of another door. Dr. Cain flashed his badge even though Kate was sure the guards knew exactly who he was. This door had a biometric eye scanner. There was no way Leo was going to get past all of this.

Kate turned to Declan and read the same concern on his face. They kept quiet and followed him into a room that didn't look unlike what Leo had in Cassis. Only the art storage at Leo's was at least three times the size of this room.

"What else do you keep down here?" Kate asked, wondering what other works of art might be at risk if somehow Leo got access to the space. She trusted Leo wasn't going to be looking for anything else to steal. She couldn't trust that Camilla would stop at *Summer Sunday*.

"All of our most valuable pieces that we aren't showing to the public. Some are among special collections only taken out from time to time. Others are at risk of theft and kept down here for safe keeping." He went to a wall panel and typed in two codes – one to operate it and Kate assumed the second code was the number of the painting.

The overhead wires and pullies started to work and within minutes *Summer Sunday* encased in glass was delivered to them. Dr. Cain appraised it with smug satisfaction. "The key to open the glass case is around my neck. Unless someone is killing me to get it and can get past all of this security, the painting is safe."

The problem was it was a little too safe for the plan to ever work. Kate's mind spun at the complications. Leo's life was only good to Camilla if he could help her steal the painting. Even if they could stop them in the act, if Leo didn't have the location of Senator Willis, none of it would work. Leo would be exposed and Kate was sure with Camilla's money, she would go free.

"This isn't going to work, Kate," Declan said close to her ear. "None of this is going to work."

Kate nodded slowly, trying desperately to come up with something. "Dr. Cain, I need you to excuse us for a few minutes. We appreciate you showing us the painting is safe. I need to make a call back to FBI Headquarters and then we can resume our meeting. I have a few questions for you before we leave. I'll try not to take up too much of your time."

"Certainly," he said with a curt nod of his head. "I'll need to go with you though, you're not going to be able to get out. Security works both ways. Even if someone got down here, it doesn't mean they'd be able to get back out."

By the time they made it to the front door of the MET, sweat had pooled at Kate's back. She wiped clammy hands down the sides of her pants and gnawed on the inside of her cheek to the point it hurt.

"What are we going to do, Declan?" she said once Dr. Cain left them. "There is no way Leo is going to be able to get through that many layers of security. Not to mention those guards down there. Camilla will shoot them without thinking twice. We need a different plan."

"I know. I know." He said it twice more as he blew out a breath. "I'm happy we had this meeting. Otherwise, everything would have imploded on the night of the gala." Declan stared up at the building and listened to Kate as she talked through a few wild options. Nothing was going to work though.

Finally, Declan said, "We have to tell Dr. Cain."

"We can't tell him, Declan," Kate said even though she knew they were going to have to. "I'm most concerned that Leo still doesn't know where Senator Willis has been taken. If he comes here without knowing that, we are screwed."

Declan agreed with her. "The only way we can come up with a workable plan is if we tell him." He held the door open for her and made a dramatic sweeping motion for her to enter. "This is not going to go well."

Kate didn't need to hear him say that to know it was true. She was about to walk into the office of the director of the MET and tell him he was going to have to potentially allow the FBI to steal a painting as part of an operation. Even Kate was having trouble suspending that much belief. The secretary, who had the phone to her ear, gestured them through the double doors to his office.

"Dr. Cain," Kate said, trying to keep her voice steady. They sat down in the chairs across from his desk. He looked up at her. "Is there anything on the back of the *Summer Sunday* forgery?"

Dr. Cain peered over at her, a question on his lips that he didn't ask. "No. We saw no point in having Gabriel do that work. It would be nearly impossible to replicate what is on the back of the real painting. He wasn't even able to tell what it was, a scene of some sort. Nothing that made sense to either of us. Gabriel said it was pointless to replicate that. No one would be looking at the back when it's hanging on the wall."

Kate swallowed hard and summoned all the nerve she had. "The FBI needs you to swap the forgery for the real painting for the gala. There is a chance we have to allow it to be stolen by one of our operatives." Before Kate could say anything else, Dr. Cain looked like he had swallowed an apple whole.

"Are you out of your mind?" he said when he could finally speak. "There is no way that's happening."

Declan wasn't going to take no for an answer. He stood from the chair and crossed his arms, glaring down at Dr. Cain. "It has to happen for the plan to work." Declan outlined everything that had gone down so far – every complicated detail and everything that rode on the outcome. He did not tell him that Leo was the real Phantom. "The person we have posing as him is highly skilled. I believe he could get past all of your security. For the sake of your guards and the rest of your guests who might be killed in the process, we need the real painting hanging on the wall the night of the gala."

Dr. Cain digested everything and took a deep breath. "You'll recover it after it's taken?"

"We will track it and arrive before anything happens to it," Declan assured him.

As soon as Declan said the words, Kate felt in her gut this was probably a better plan. They could position a tracking chip in the back of the painting and know its location at all times. Stealing the painting from the main part of the MET would also allow Kate and Declan to better access the scene. "Where is it in the gallery?"

"I'll show you." Dr. Cain looked at Declan for several moments and then at Kate. "Is the painting going to be stolen no matter what we do?"

"There is a high likelihood that it's going to have to be for us to get Senator Willis back safely," Kate said with conviction in her tone. "Will you help us?"

"I don't think I have a choice," Dr. Cain said with resignation in his voice.

Kate didn't want to press her luck but there was one more thing they were going to need. "We also need four tickets to the gala. If our names are on the list, it won't raise suspicion. You are also going to have to tell your security to stand down."

Dr. Cain picked up his desk phone and went about setting the plan in motion.

For the first time, Kate had a glimmer of hope this whole thing might actually work.

CHAPTER 39

The three days between the initial meeting with Dr. Cain at the MET and the night of the gala went by in a crawl. Kate had informed Leo of the plan, assuring him that the real painting would be easy to steal. But not so easy that it would look like a setup. He still had no idea where Senator Willis or the stolen paintings were being kept. Camilla was keeping him in the dark, probably as she tested whether she could trust him or not. She told him all would be revealed once he stole *Summer Sunday* for her. No proof of life had been sent to the FBI either. Their hands were effectively tied. *Summer Sunday* would be stolen from the MET that night. Kate and Declan would track it and arrest Camilla wherever Camilla and Leo ended up. Kate was glad now they had told Dr. Cain and changed the plan.

She also let Leo know that there were two gala tickets available for Camilla and him. They were under the name Pierre Legrand. Everyone who knew Leo as an art dealer and as the Phantom knew him by that name – yet no one connected the two. His men with the Curators knew he worked as a legitimate art dealer in order to find and track the art they'd steal. No one on the legitimate side of his business knew Pierre was really the Phantom.

He'd never told anyone other than Kate his real identity. Even the DeBeckers in London couldn't trace Leo back to the Lamieres. Leo told her he was giving up his Pierre Legrand and every other alias now that he was committed to the FBI and never going back to his old life.

Kate and Declan had spent the three days meeting with Dr. Cain and interacting with his head of security who was the only other person at the museum who knew the real plan. That was only because someone needed to give security the order to stand down. The plan was to keep them focused on the areas of the gala and away from the hall where *Summer Sunday* would be hung. It was for their safety.

There had also been meetings at the Manhattan FBI office and time spent scouting all of the residences traced back to Alexander Branston. Neither Camilla nor Senator Willis were found at any of them. Leo was still at the hotel that the FBI had arranged for him and that is where Camilla would meet him. She would not tell him where she was living and he'd only seen one of the two Munson brothers. The information being shared with him was limited and intentional.

Camilla planned to get away and continue her life of crime.

Leo had tried and failed to talk her out of it, saying she still had time in her life to turn it around. Of course, she didn't. She had killed several people. But that didn't stop Leo from trying to reason with her and even apologize for what he had unintentionally done to her father.

When asked to describe her, Leo had said Camilla was ruthless and a cold-hearted killer. He said there was no reasoning with her. She was quick to anger but let it simmer until she methodically plotted her revenge. That's what scared him the most. It's not that she flew off the handle when her rage spilled over. Instead she became eerily quiet and withdrew into herself. It was rage that was fueling her actions and the need to best Leo in being the best art thief the world had ever known.

Leo asked her how that was going to rectify what happened with her father. For that, Camilla had no answer. He took full responsibility for the person she had become. Kate wasn't buying that though. She exhibited sociopathic tendencies and might have been a full-blown sociopath. Kate couldn't be sure without a true evaluation, but she knew that wasn't something born out of one tragic event in her childhood. Leo might have been her fixation and the fuel, but Camilla would have probably turned out just as criminally minded without what happened to her father.

Kate's guess was she had been coddled her whole life and told she could have whatever she wanted. She probably also never faced a consequence for her actions. That coupled with her biological makeup had pushed her into criminal behavior. What happened to her father was the match to a powder keg that would have blown regardless. If it wasn't that, it would have been something else. She might not have gone into art theft, but her true evil nature would have shown through in another way.

Convincing Leo of that was near impossible.

The only part of the last three days that Kate truly enjoyed was trying on gowns for the gala. Declan had been fitted for his tux that would fit over a bulletproof vest, but finding the right style of dress that would fit the occasion and accommodate the vest had proven slightly more daunting. As he tried on his tux, Declan made several James Bond jokes in front of the mirror.

Kate had rolled her eyes good-naturedly. Even as one of the top echelon of FBI agents, boys still wanted to be the most famous spy in the world. She praised him affectionately and even somehow convinced him he was hotter than James Bond and better at his job. Declan had left the shop with his chest puffed out and a slick smile plastered on his face.

Kate's dress shopping hadn't gone quite as easily. It was the seventh dress she tried on that worked the best for her. It was a simple sleeveless, scooped neckline, beaded bodice with a wispy chiffon bottom. She had her choice of blue or lavender. She had chosen the lavender and Declan sucked in a breath and his mouth dropped open when he saw her for the first time in the shop. She knew she had made the right selection.

Now that the hour was upon them and they were finishing dressing in their hotel room before their limousine arrived to pick them up. An FBI agent would follow behind them and wait outside the MET to follow Camilla and Leo when the time came. There'd also be additional agents outside, some driving and others on foot, ready to spring into action when Kate gave the signal.

They had planned for every contingency possible – at least they hoped so. Spade and Leo had acquiesced to their new plan. Kate was going into the night more secure than she had felt before and that's all that mattered.

She fixed the gun strapped to her thigh, adjusted her dress back in place, and took one last look in the mirror. Kate had worn her hair swept up into a chignon and had on dangling gold earrings that Declan had surprised her with that morning. She had put on just enough makeup to highlight her best features without overdoing it. Kate appraised her reflection and decided it was good enough. She hoped she wasn't going to have to chase anyone in the dress and shoes. It was made for a gala not running through the streets of Manhattan.

Kate flicked off the bathroom light and stepped out into the living room. Declan was standing near the couch fixing his cuff links. She watched him as he finished pulling himself together. She might have fleeting chemistry with Leo but Kate was sure she'd never seen a man more attractive than Declan. Her heart thumped twice in her chest.

"You look so handsome," Kate said as she moved slowly over to him. "We need to get dressed up more often." As Declan righted himself he put his hands on her arms, she rose on tiptoes and kissed him.

Declan smiled down at her with a hint of mischief in his eyes. "If you keep dressing like this, I'm never going to let you leave the house. We won't make it past the bed." He glanced back toward the bedroom. "If only we had more time."

"We definitely don't and I'm not sure I'd get into this dress again with the vest." Kate had her hands wide. "How does it look?"

"Perfect. I can't tell you're wearing a vest."

"Are we ready?"

"As we are ever going to get," he said as he reached for her hand.

Twenty minutes later, Declan still had a hold of her hand as the two ascended the red carpeted steps of the MET. Flashes from professional photographers flickered around them and Kate kept her eyes focused on the door. She and Declan were both wired for sound, which was being sent to the FBI van parked not far from them. They had covered all of their bases. She had only wished Leo could have been wired but Camilla had checked him repeatedly. The agent in charge of watching the tracking device on the painting had assured her that it was in working order and pinging at the location where *Summer Sunday* was hanging in the MET.

All they had to do now was enjoy the gala, mingle, and wait for Leo to give the signal.

The whole thing was out of Kate's control and she would have to steady her nerves to get through it. She allowed herself to be led by Declan as they entered the building. He gave their names to the woman seated at the table inside the door and were welcomed immediately.

"Dr. Cain said to be watching for you both. He was excited you could join us," she said as she gave them directions to find the main ballroom. They knew where it was located because they had been there earlier in the day.

Kate and Declan had traced and retraced the steps from the ballroom to where *Summer Sunday* was hanging in the hall on the second floor. Kate let go of Declan's hand and looped her arm over his as they entered the room. The lights were turned low and the space was illuminated by a cascade of small white lights on the tables, the chandelier, and light displays that had been tastefully arranged around the room.

Black tie waiters carried trays of hors d'oeuvres. The guests snacked and sipped their drinks from the bars that had been positioned in three corners of the room. There was a mix of high-top and low tables. The gala would not feature a full sit down dinner but the food passed would be plenty, Dr. Cain had assured them. Kate couldn't eat even if she were starving. They weren't drinking anything other than the water Declan would get for them eventually so they wouldn't look out of place.

The band had already started playing but the dance floor was empty other than people standing in small groups talking to one another. There was a sign in the back of the room pointing to a hallway where the tables were for the silent auction. It was beyond that and up a flight of stairs where *Summer Sunday* could be found. After it was stolen, Kate knew Leo would head down a back staircase to a street behind the building where he'd have a waiting car. From there, they could disappear into Central Park or around to the front of the building. Either way, the FBI would be there.

Kate put on her best game face and smiled and nodded to people they passed. To anyone else, they'd look like a normal Manhattan couple. Some were probably wondering their pedigree and where they went to school and resided in the city. That's what it was like at these galas. It was all about who you knew and your network.

"Not bad for a boy from Southie," Declan said as he smiled down at her but his face froze as he looked beyond. He got low to her ear as if he were kissing her cheek. "Camilla and Leo at two o'clock. She's talking to the mayor."

Kate couldn't turn her head so quickly it looked obvious. Instead,

Declan moved them around the room speaking briefly to each person they passed as if they were simply making the rounds. When Camilla and Leo came into view, Kate shouldn't have been surprised by how comfortable Leo and Camilla looked working the crowd but she was. Camilla was chatting amicably with the mayor, laying on the charm with a bright smile and touching his arm as she spoke. Leo smiled and nodded at all the right times giving each of them his undivided attention.

They were no more than twenty feet apart when Leo shifted and looked in her direction. For a moment, Kate stared into the eyes of a man she did not recognize. He had turned from being the Leo she had come to know back to the Phantom. The enigma who had taken her hostage in Paris. It was like looking into the eyes of two men at the same time. A chill ran down Kate's spine. But she couldn't help noticing how he was looking at her.

If Declan had an expression of appreciation of the way she looked that night, Leo's look could only be described as wonder. His gaze roamed over her and Kate felt naked under his look. When he brought his eyes to her, he gave the slightest nod of his head. While he didn't smile, his eyes said everything.

Kate breathed a heavy sigh, worried about him and his proximity to Camilla. Noticing him looking in their direction, Camilla took Leo's hand. Kate glanced away as if seeing someone she knew. They didn't make it far before Camilla and Leo were at their sides.

"I wouldn't think government employees could afford this kind of event," Camilla said, offering Kate a grin. "They must be paying you far more than I realize." She reached out and ran a hand down Declan's chest. "You clean up nicely, Agent James. Are you single? I'd love to meet you for dinner some night."

She was bold, brazen, and testing them.

Declan removed her hand from his chest. "I'm not single, Camilla.

But it's lovely to see you both." Declan extended his hand to Leo. "I'm sorry. I seem to have forgotten your name."

"Pierre Legrand," Leo said and shook Declan's hand.

The music changed and a few couples took to the dance floor. Camilla looked between Leo and Kate. "Pierre, why don't you ask Agent Walsh to dance while I chat with Agent James."

It was another test they couldn't fail. Leo looked to Declan. "Would you mind?"

"Please, go right ahead."

Kate offered her hand to Leo and he took it. She let him lead her to the dance floor and he took her in his arms. "She's testing us," Kate said as he moved her gracefully around the dance floor. "Are you doing okay?"

"All is going according to plan." Leo pulled her closer to him. "You look lovely, Kate. Declan is an incredibly lucky man but I think he probably knows that."

They danced without saying much more. Kate couldn't deny that she enjoyed being in his arms. He smelled woodsy and masculine. His hands were strong but soft in hers. He was an incredible dancer and she wasn't surprised by this.

As the music finished, Leo thanked her. "Ten, Kate. When everyone is slightly tired and a bit drunk, we will steal it."

Kate laughed as if he said something funny, tipping her head back and then wrapped her arms around him, whispering in his ear. "We'll be ready."

Kate let her hand linger on him as they broke apart.

After the dance, Camilla seemed satisfied with her test. She and Leo moved on to other conversations while Kate and Declan made the best of the time while they waited to spring into action.

CHAPTER 40

At a quarter to ten, Camilla was nowhere to be found. Kate had been trying to keep an inconspicuous eye on her for most of the night but had lost her in the crowd. While Kate searched the room, her earpiece crackled a message.

Two shots fired behind the MET. Going to check it out.

Kate kept her expression steady as she whispered the information to Declan. They had not heard the shots inside. She was not surprised given the din of conversation and the music. Leo stood at the far side of the room near the doorway that led to the silent auction. He was not the shooter and hadn't been shot. Kate had no idea what was going on.

A few moments later, Camilla returned to Leo as Kate's earpiece crackled again. *Munson brothers are down. One shot each to the head. Bodies dropped in the alley where they stood. Senator Willis not here.*

Kate cursed and turned to tell Declan the news when she realized that Camilla and Leo were gone from the room. "They're gone," she said loudly, getting Declan's attention over the music. They walked together quickly across the dance floor toward the door where she assumed they left. Kate turned the corner but was met with a crowd of people filling out last minute bids for the silent auction items. They had been hoping the hallway would have emptied out by then.

Kate and Declan moved through the crowd and got to the staircase at the end of the hallway. She glanced up but didn't see anything and couldn't hear anything above the crowd. All she could do was assume Leo and Camilla were in the process of stealing *Summer Sunday*. The head of security had shut down the security camera in that area so it wouldn't be broadcast to the guards watching the monitors, the trigger alarm on the painting had also been removed, and there were no guards in that area for tonight.

Kate saw a flash of movement overhead. It looked to have been Leo's arm as he moved down the hall toward the back staircase and doorway. "They are on the move," Kate said to Declan. That was their cue to head to the front of the building to their waiting car. They were fighting against the crowd to get to the front doors.

Kate's earpiece radioed again. *They are on the move. We have one car right behind them.*

They were faster than Kate had thought they'd be. "We need to hurry," she said to Declan as he used his body to part the sea of people and move them toward the front door. By the time they made it through the door and out into the cool night air, they were in a sprint. If anyone was paying attention to them, Kate didn't notice. All she was focused on was getting to the waiting car.

"Are you tracking them?" Declan asked as he slid into the front seat.

"We have them," the agent said and handed Declan his phone.

Kate inched up between the two front seats and looked at the red dot on the map which indicated the movement of the painting. They were behind the MET and making their way into Central Park.

"There are other eyes on them that are closer," the agent behind the wheel said. "Do you want to wait or go?"

Declan gestured toward the street. "Go. We don't want to get too far behind them."

"Wait," Kate said as she saw the dot stop and reverse course. "They are coming back toward us now." She assumed Camilla must have left another car someplace accessible knowing the car the Munson brothers had been near was no longer an option. She had clearly planned for everything. The main thing Kate wondered was if neither of the Munson brothers were with Senator Willis – where was he and who was watching him?

"They are right there!" Declan pointed to an older model Mercedes passing them on the left, heading south on 5th Avenue. The driver inched out behind them into traffic leaving two cars between them. They traveled a few blocks, then made a left on 79th Street and took that clear across Manhattan to FDR Drive.

Kate pulled out her phone and studied the map to see where they could be headed. She had no idea.

They made their way to lower Manhattan, passing the Manhattan Bridge and kept going. They were headed right for the financial district but there were no properties down there that came back to Alexander or Camilla. Kate kept looking between the road in front of them and the dot on the map. There were still a couple of cars between them. The agent at the wheel was far more adept at mobile surveillance on the streets of Manhattan than Kate and Declan.

"I think they are headed toward Brooklyn," the agent said after a moment. "Right over the Brooklyn Bridge are the piers and warehouses. It might be the perfect spot for them, especially this late in the evening. She has water access too for escape."

Kate had never been so happy to have someone else behind the wheel. She reached for the flat shoes she had kept in the car and switched them out for her heels. Part of her wished she had brought a change of clothes but she wasn't getting out of the dress without help.

She refocused her attention on the red dot as it moved through lower Manhattan, over the Brooklyn Bridge as the agent had guessed, and then looped back around toward the water. The traffic had thinned, and the agent held them back to keep the same distance between the cars. Kate could see it was Leo behind the wheel.

She took a breath to steady herself as her heart started to race. Her mind flashed back to her episode on the street and she willed herself not to fall apart again.

They followed Leo and Camilla off the main road to a side road and then through rows of warehouses. They had to stay back far enough not to be seen, so Kate lost sight of the car. When the dot stopped, Kate assumed they had parked. "You can let us out right here," she said. They were only a few buildings away. The agent would wait there in case they needed to leave quickly but there were others headed to them as backup. Kate could only assume they'd be along quickly.

They didn't have time to wait.

Declan and Kate got out of the car guns in hand and headed into the darkness between the buildings. The warehouses weren't well lit but the sky was full of stars and gave enough illumination to light the way. Declan had the phone showing the tracker they had put on the painting.

"They went inside a building, Kate. Second floor." Declan guided them as they ran in that direction. He stopped before getting to the building using the one next to it as a shield. He stuck his head around and looked before continuing. "There's light on the second floor."

Kate raised her head to see. "There is the shadow of a person but I can't make out who it is." The whole building was bathed in darkness except for the little bit of light coming from the second floor. What she didn't see was the car. "How far away are we from the tracker?"

"We are right there. This has to be them." Declan slipped the phone into his pocket and looked back at Kate. "Are we waiting for backup?"

She didn't even need to think about it. "If Senator Willis is up there with them, we don't have time. At the very least, we need to stall Camilla."

They readied themselves then took off in a run toward the door of the building. They had no idea what they were walking into. While the Munson brothers were dead, it didn't mean Camilla didn't have other muscle. They had no idea what they'd encounter inside.

Declan went in first while Kate covered his back. She took one last look behind them at the water and the night sky before entering the dark building.

As soon as they were inside, Kate heard Leo's voice echo through the old warehouse. He was discussing the paintings with Camilla and what they were seeing on the backs. His tone was steady and calm, even sounding in control of the situation. "It looks to me like Chevalier was telling us that it was his brother-in-law who tried to kill him," Leo said calmly. He pointed out different elements of the design on the backs of the paintings. "His brother-in-law, Nicolas, was notorious in the region for his shrewd business sense. He had argued endlessly with Chevalier about his art and how he should focus on the business end of selling his work. Chevalier didn't care about that. He cared about his art, not about making money. Nicolas thought art without sales was pointless. A waste of time when Chevalier could be doing something else. They clashed more than once. Nicolas was never accused of the murder. That has never been part of the legend. Most in Cassis think it was suicide or an accident."

Camilla wasn't buying that. "He wouldn't have painted anything on the back of this artwork and given it to his neighbor if he was going to kill himself. He was afraid for his life. That's what the stories have always said. That's why he took such action."

"Even if that were true, what can we do about this now?" Leo's voice was tinged with frustration. It seemed to Kate this was a conversation they'd had more than once. "You can go public and say that you solved the mystery and that Chevalier is indicating his brother-in-law killed him, but this hardly represents proof. How are you going to explain your access to see all three of them at once?"

Camilla chuckled and told Leo he was being paranoid. "When the news breaks that all three paintings are missing and the speculation why, I can come out and say that I've seen all three and know the answer to the riddle. I planned to use Marcy Reinhold as a source. She provided me with all the access I wanted. She's such a dumb woman to be in such a high position. She had no idea what Alexander and I were doing."

"What were you doing?" Leo asked and then added, "I don't understand why you killed him. You speak so fondly of him."

Declan started to move toward the stairs but Kate pulled him back. She shook her head and pointed to the ceiling. She wanted to hear what more Leo could get out of Camilla before disturbing the scene.

"It was never about Alexander. I seduced him for the money to help me fund this operation. He saw finding you as a great challenge and we had fun playing the game for a while. When I started going after the Chevaliers he backed out. He didn't want any part of it. Alexander wasn't a man who was ever going to get his hands dirty."

"I heard he had stolen artwork?"

Camilla sighed loudly. "It was status. He had money and people who did his dirty work for him. It's no more or less than that. Alexander did nothing himself."

"Why Gabriel? He was my friend and a good man. I should kill you now for having killed him." There was real emotion in Leo's tone. He wasn't faking that.

"He wouldn't tell me what we needed to know. Alexander talked to the dealer and knew when the cocaine would be delivered. We showed up at the same time. Gabriel had no idea what was going on. They cut the drugs right there on the table."

"Alexander was there that night?"

Camilla seemed tired and frustrated with his questions. "He got his drugs, tried to get information out of Gabriel, and then left before anything happened. I told you Alexander didn't get his hands dirty."

"What about the Munson brothers? They were loyal to you."

"There is no loyalty, Pierre. They were loyal for a time that was all. I needed to finish this on my own. This was always about you and drawing you out. Stealing the Chevalier series was a way for me to gain the fame you have. I stole the impossible, something the Phantom couldn't even do."

"But you needed me to steal the third."

"I would have been able to steal it without you," Camilla argued back with a haughty laugh. "I wanted to see how you worked and how well we worked together."

"Why? You said you're going to kill me when this is all over."

Footsteps creaked the floorboards above. "I don't have to kill you. I can make you work with me until I get bored of you and then kill you."

"I'm out of the game, Camilla. We discussed that." There were more footsteps, heavier this time and Kate assumed it was Leo walking. "This isn't what I do. I don't steal for the sake of stealing. I stole back what had been stolen. I righted wrongs. You've killed people, Camilla. In all my years, I never once caused physical harm to anyone. You of all people should know that. I can't do this with you."

"You're better than me then," she said with her tone dripping with angered sarcasm. "Is that what you're saying? Because you read a little girl a story and tucked her back into bed, you're some Robin Hood figure. Is that it? Is that really how you see yourself." Her statements were met with silence. "You're not the good guy, Pierre. You're a thief just like the rest of us. You can either come work for me or you can die right here. It's easier for me if I kill you. I can say you kidnapped me and brought me here after stealing this painting. I got away and killed you but not before you killed this idiot. Then I can have the fame of bringing down the Phantom."

Even then there was no panic in Leo's voice. "After what I did to your father, why do you want to work with me?"

"It might be fun for a while."

Kate had been so drawn into the conversation she nearly missed it. Camilla had said *this idiot.* It was the first indication Senator Willis might be up there with them. She wanted to race up the stairs but knew she needed to wait. Declan was still looking at her for the go-ahead.

"Even if you kill me, no one is going to believe your story, Camilla," Leo said a little too calmly for Kate's liking. "The FBI knows these thefts weren't the Phantom or the Curators. They suspect Alexander and, by extension, you."

Camilla howled with laughter. "Did you see the way Agent Walsh looked at you? She would have let you have her right on the dance floor and it was clear you felt the same. That puppy-eyed partner she's got. What's he going to solve? He can't even figure out she's in love with you."

Declan shifted his eyes ever so slightly toward Kate. He raised an eyebrow. Kate shook her head. The last thing she needed right now was him second-guessing himself.

Camilla was trying to get in Leo's head and now she was in Declan's.

Leo didn't defend himself or deny it. Kate had felt his desire when she was in his arms. There wasn't anything for him to say.

It was Camilla who spoke with annoyance in her tone. "I don't have time for this. You're either coming with me or you're dying here with him. You choose."

"You don't need to kill him, Camilla. You don't need to kill me. Take off and I'll clean up the mess."

"No," Camilla barked. "He's seen me. He knows what I've done. If you aren't going to do what I want, then you're of no use to me. You've got about ten seconds to decide if you live or die." The floorboards creaked again with two sets of footsteps. One ahead of the other.

Kate pointed to the ceiling and they ascended the stairs, not worrying about noise. It had escalated quickly and they needed to get there in time.

Kate's footsteps faltered when she heard the first shot. By the second, she was in a run.

CHAPTER 41

Declan cleared the doorway first and went directly to Senator Willis who sat with his face expressing a frozen scream. He had blood down one side of his face and his hands were tied behind his back. His dress slacks had been ripped and what had been a white shirt was covered in dirt. Declan worked to free him while Kate focused on another scene only feet from the senator.

Leo was on his back with his eyes closed as blood soaked the front of his shirt. Camilla lay on her side facing Kate. Her eyes were fixed in a death stare and a trickle of blood ran down the corner of her mouth. She had been shot in the center of her chest. The gun was near Leo's right hand.

Kate rushed to the floor near Leo. She reached for his shirt to try to stop the bleeding. She cursed over and over again, not believing he could be dead. There was so much blood.

"I can't believe we let you do this," she said in a rushed whispered breath. Leo was fine with giving his life to stop Camilla. Kate wasn't fine with it and she didn't know how to help him.

As she leaned over to get a closer look, she felt his breath against her ear.

"I'm alive, Kate," he said softly. "Is Camilla dead?"

Kate froze, unsure of what was happening. "Yes," she said in a swoosh of air.

"Help me up." Kate scooped her hand around his back, that's when she felt his vest. She got him into a sitting position. Once Leo was upright, he looked over at Camilla and without any emotion in his voice, said, "I killed her, Kate."

Kate didn't care about that right now. She pulled back and stared at the blood on his shirt. "Whose blood is that?"

Leo was only wearing a white tuxedo shirt with no tie or jacket. He pulled the shirt apart to reveal the vest and the remnants of a blood pack. "Spade thought it would be a good idea. She had shot the guards in the chest, so he assumed that's where she'd aim at me. If she got away or was arrested, he figured it was better if she thought I was dead."

Even after all of the planning, they had still kept something from her. "Leo, what happened? We were only right downstairs."

"He saved my life. That's what happened," Senator Willis said as Declan helped the man to his feet. "He jumped in front of that crazy woman as she tried to shoot me. She shot him instead. Even shot, he got the gun from her and shot her before she got a chance to try again." He thanked Declan and then took a few steps toward Kate and Leo on the floor. He extended his hand to Leo. "Who are you? She kept calling you the Phantom and Pierre but that can't be right."

Kate nervously licked her lips waiting to see what Leo would say.

Without missing a beat, he shook the senator's hand. "I'm Leo Lamiere and I work for the FBI. Spade brought me in for this case, but I'm thinking about staying in his unit for a while. I was posing as the Phantom to assess the situation from the inside. We had no idea where you were but knew she'd lead the Phantom to you eventually."

"I see," he said and turned to Kate. "You were tasked with bringing in the Phantom. What progress have you made so far? You know your job is riding on it." Even after they had saved his life, he was still giving Kate a hard time.

Before she could respond, Leo did. "Agent Walsh won't be able to find him, Senator Willis." He held onto Kate's hand as they stood. "I've been deep undercover for the past year. According to every reliable source close to the Phantom, he's dead. That's why they needed to bring me in on the case. I look enough like him that Camilla wasn't able to figure it out. She hadn't seen him since she was a little girl. With how I look and everything I know about him, I knew I could pass."

To Kate's surprise, Senator Willis looked convinced. "Were you tracking the Phantom for long?"

"A long, long time. I worked private security, sir. I was hoping to catch him and bring him in. I got close a few times over the last couple of months. Then I heard from reliable sources that he was dead. The FBI needed me and I'm here to help." Leo looked at Kate. "You'll have to give Agent Walsh a pass this time. She can't bring in a dead man."

"That's certainly true." Senator Willis put his hand on Leo's shoulder. "It's good that they had your help then. I'm glad you'll be sticking around. That accent I hear. Is it French?"

"It's French," Leo said. "I was raised there but have lived all over the globe. The accent has faded over the years. But like when speaking to Camilla, I can bring it back when needed."

"Well, I welcome you to the FBI and I can't thank you enough for saving my life. You certainly played the part well. I thought when we first met that you were the Phantom. You're a good undercover agent." Senator Willis turned to Declan. "You have a lot to clean up here. I know you need my statement. Do you want to do that now or back in D.C.?"

"Let's talk outside and then we can take a formal statement later. Are you feeling okay? Do you need to go to the hospital?" Declan was concerned he might have been injured.

"The only thing bruised is my pride," he said as he walked off, not acknowledging Kate in any way.

She hadn't been expecting an apology for the way she had been treated but something would have been nice. When he was gone, Kate turned back to Leo. "Are you sure you're okay?"

"Got the wind knocked out of me." Leo shrugged off the shirt and unclipped the vest. When he was standing in front of her with a bare chest, he touched an area near his heart where he'd been shot. "Why does it hurt so much?"

Kate was trying not to look directly at him, the intimacy of the moment was too much for her. "You'll have a good-sized bruise. I was shot once and it left a bruise for weeks. You should probably get checked out."

Leo shook his head. "I'm fine, Kate. I'm just glad you got here when you did."

Kate was glad too but it seemed Leo had it handled. "You did well with Senator Willis. He believed every word you said."

"It's no different than how I've lived. Telling one story or another, concealing my identity from everyone. There's a bit of relief now that I can be Leo Lamiere with the FBI."

It still sounded strange to her ears. "It's going to take me a while to adjust to that."

Kate stepped to the side and called for backup as well as the medical examiner. The local FBI field office would handle most of the logistical details. She and Declan would need to secure the art and make sure the pieces got back to their rightful owners. When she was done with the call, Kate walked over to the paintings that were hung side by side to show the scene on the backs. Put together it showed one lonely shop on an empty dirt road. Most striking in the painting was the shop window. Kate peered closer and noticed a shelf with three items next to each other – each item on the back of a painting. Together she was sure there was meaning. Kate just didn't know what it meant.

There was what looked like a glass jar marked poison, a book, and a raven. "Does this really indicate Chevalier's brother-in-law?"

"I can't be sure but he referred to his brother-in-law as a raven. When he saw him, like seeing a raven, it meant there was something bad to come. The book is a ledger, which Nicolas was known to carry everywhere. If you look more closely you'll see it written on the cover. The jar is obvious as it's believed Chevalier was poisoned. He foretold his death." Leo came to stand by her. "I can't be completely certain but that's what it says to me."

Kate would have to take his word for it. "What's the plan for you now?"

"I'm heading back to D.C. with you both. Spade said he wanted to meet with the three of us when this was all over." Kate told him about the train schedule and when they thought they'd be heading back. She turned and was headed for the stairs when Leo reached for her and pulled her back. They stood toe to toe. "Did Declan hear what Camilla said about us dancing?"

Kate had hoped they weren't going to talk about this. "He heard," she admitted.

Leo lowered his eyes to look at her face. "She wasn't wrong. I wanted you then and I want you now. I know I can't have you. Just tell me one last time you feel this between us so I know I'm not crazy."

"You're not crazy. There's something…but as I said in France, I'll never disrespect Declan." She sucked in a breath, realizing too late what she had said. She was still wired for sound. After a few beats, she added, "We have to find a way to work together."

"That's why I'm bringing this up, Kate. I won't disrespect Declan either. He's a good man and better for you than I am. But if he ever hurts you…"

"He won't."

"But if he did…" Leo breathed a sigh and let it stand between them.

Neither of them needed Leo to finish his sentence.

"Kate!" Declan called from below and the two of them stepped back from each other.

"I'll be right down." Kate moved back again from Leo and they shared a look that said everything that needed to be said. "When you're ready, I'll be downstairs and I can take your statement. Then we can clean up this mess and return *Summer Sunday* to the MET."

Leo didn't say anything but watched her leave.

Two weeks later, Kate and Declan were settled back into her brownstone in Boston. Spade had given them some time off after the meeting in D.C. The museums had their art returned and Declan had given a press conference naming Camilla Bancroft as the ringleader of the art theft gang and the one who kidnapped Senator Willis. He glossed over Alexander's involvement since it couldn't be confirmed but noted the man had stolen artwork in his possession.

Declan credited a new consultant working for his team who helped solve the case and bring Camilla to justice. They didn't need to name Leo but the people who knew were appreciative of his efforts. He was healing nicely and had told Kate the bruise was nearly gone. He was acquiring new ones from the training Spade put him through at Quantico.

Spade had requested Leo remain in the D.C. area for a couple of months of training before he'd be fully integrated into Kate's team. Everyone thought that was a good idea including Leo, who appreciated the training if not the beating his body was currently experiencing.

Kate got back to her routine of reviewing cases for local police departments and giving her insight remotely. Not all of them needed the FBI on the ground. She had even found a therapist in Boston she was seeing once a week. Her episode in D.C. had scared her into accepting the help. The therapist was private though. She wasn't going to give the FBI all her secrets.

Declan was spending time at the Boston FBI field office preparing Sharon for her transition. All was going smoothly for a change.

At night, Declan would cook or they'd order in. A few nights, they strolled the city hand in hand, seeing it together for the first time. Kate liked how love could put a little spin on things she'd passed by a million times and never noticed. She was in love. She was sure of that and she was sure of Declan's feelings too.

There was just one thing lingering between them. It crept in from time to time and Kate had to reassure him. Like tonight, he had gotten up from bed and walked to the window when he thought she was asleep. He parted the curtain and stared down the street at the brick brownstone with the stained glass windows on the third floor. Kate had loved the house as a child, but at some point, they had turned it into condos.

Last year, all the residents moved. There had never been a for sale sign but rumor was someone had purchased it in a private sale. There had been talk in the neighborhood that it was being turned back into a one-family home. It had sat empty and still all year.

Now construction crews went in and out all day hard at work.

Before leaving D.C., Leo had told her his new address and told her when he finished his training he'd be back in Boston. In response, Kate did not tell Leo that she lived across the street and three houses down. Then again, he already knew that. Kate wasn't sure how she felt about it all. Leo had wanted to be close to her long before he had a legitimate reason to be. Kate didn't know how she felt about that.

Telling Declan was something Kate had put off for a while. He had taken it outwardly well but she knew the proximity bothered him. He wouldn't talk about it. Ever since telling him though, he'd rise from bed when he thought she was asleep and stare at the house.

Tonight, Kate couldn't take it anymore. She sat up in bed and watched him, appreciating how his body clad only in black boxer briefs looked cast in moonlight. The muscles in his back and calves were well-defined. He had one arm thrown overhead holding the curtain back and he leaned slightly forward as he looked out of the window. He didn't realize it but it was seductive.

Kate threw back the covers and padded barefoot across the hardwood floors. She traced a finger down his back and wrapped her arm around him, snuggling into his side. "Stop looking at Leo's house. What's done is done, Declan. You have me here in your arms, in my bed. What more do you want?"

Declan wrapped an arm around her shoulders and pulled her closer to him. "I didn't realize when I said he could work with us that he'd end up our neighbor."

"It makes no difference where he lives," Kate said but she knew that wasn't true. She appealed to his kinder sense. "He doesn't have anyone, Declan. He's like me in a lot of ways. He's part of the team now and it will be an adjustment for all of us. You have to stop obsessing about it." Kate didn't admit that she had been obsessing about it, too. It was too weird for her, but she didn't want to worry him.

Declan sighed in resignation. "I complicate myself." He turned to face her. "I love you. Never doubt that."

"I love you too," she said in return, getting more comfortable with saying it. "Let's go back to bed."

Declan leaned down and kissed her. "I'm not tired. Since we're both awake..."

Kate led him by the hand back to her bed. She wasn't tired either.

About the Author

Stacy M. Jones was born and raised in Troy, New York, and currently lives in Little Rock, Arkansas. She is a full-time writer and holds masters' degrees in journalism and in forensic psychology. She currently has three series available for readers: the completed cozy paranormal Harper & Hattie Magical Mystery Series, the hard-boiled PI Riley Sullivan Mystery Series and the FBI Agent Kate Walsh Thriller Series. To access Stacy's Mystery Readers Club with three free novellas, one for each series, visit StacyMJones.com.

You can connect with me on:

- https://www.stacymjones.com
- https://www.facebook.com/StacyMJonesWriter
- https://www.bookbub.com/profile/stacy-m-jones
- https://www.goodreads.com/StacyMJonesWriter

Subscribe to my newsletter:

✉ https://www.stacymjones.com

Also by Stacy M. Jones

Watch for the next FBI Agent Kate Walsh Thriller in Fall 2024

Access the Free Mystery Readers' Club Starter Library
PI Riley Sullivan Mystery Series novella "The 1922 Club Murder"
FBI Agent Kate Walsh Thriller Series novella "The Curators"
Harper & Hattie Mystery Series novella "Harper's Folly"

Sign up for the starter library along with launch-day pricing and special behind-the-scenes access. Hit subscribe at http://www.stacy mjones.com/

Please leave a review for Diamond King. Reviews help more readers find my books. Thank you!

Other books by Stacy M. Jones by series and order to date

FBI Agent Kate Walsh Thriller Series
The Curators
The Founders
Miami Ripper
Mad Jack
The Fuse
Dead Senate
Close Killer

PI Riley Sullivan Mystery Series
The 1922 Club Murder
Deadly Sins

The Bone Harvest
Missing Time Murders
We Last Saw Jane
Boston Underground
The Night Game
Harbor Cove Murders
The Drowned Boys
What He Saw
Fear City

Harper & Hattie Magical Mystery Series
Harper's Folly
Saints & Sinners Ball
Secrets to Tell
Rule of Three
The Forever Curse
The Witches Code
The Sinister Sisters
Scandal Knocks Twice
A Treasure Most Deadly